duplicity

A Story of Deadly Intent

**a novel by
Renee Propes**

The Kimmer Group

The Kimmer Group
Publisher's Note: This is a work of fiction. Names, characters, places, and incidents are a product of the author's imagination. Locales and public names are sometimes used for atmospheric purposes. Any resemblance to actual people, living or dead, or to businesses, companies, events, institutions, or locales is completely coincidental.

Cover and design by 99designs-Aaniyah Ahmed

Author's Photograph - Simpson Custom Photography

duplicity-A Story of Deadly Intent/ Renee Propes. – First Edition
ISBN 978-1-7348219-0-1 (PB)
ISBN 978-1-7348219-1-8 (eBook)

Library of Congress Control Number: 2020906888

For Hardy, Zach, and Katie

I n late July of 2010, Theodore Alexander Williams III sat outside The Medical Center in Abington, Georgia, and wiped his sweaty hands with a handkerchief. The air was heavy under the scorching Georgia sun. Teddy needed to ask his parents for some money. Not a loan, mind you, but money from the estate his grandmother had left for him to fund a medical practice. He was a 34-year-old, formally educated man with a roman numeral behind his name, which suggested he should have out-grown any hesitation about asking his parents for something that was rightfully his. As sweat saturated the fabric of his blue oxford shirt, he chuckled as he felt his palpitating heart and thought, "the classic father-son relationship, it's either great, or it's not!"

Teddy walked into the V.I.P. Suite and saw his stylish mother stretched out on the sofa, reading a Southern Living Magazine. Claire Williams' dress implied she was going to a luncheon at the country club instead of spending the day in a hospital room with her sick husband.

Hearing the knock on the door, Claire looked up from the magazine, and Teddy noticed the joy in her eyes that was always there whenever she saw him. "Oh, look, dear," she said. "Teddy's here!"

The pollen from the vast arrangements of flowers and potted plants placed throughout the suite, tokens of good wishes from their many friends and business associates, caused Teddy's eyes to water and his throat to constrict.

Theodore Williams II slowly opened his eyes. "I heard the door open, but I thought it was the nurse. They won't let you sleep in this damn place!"

"Theo, please, I wish you wouldn't swear." Claire said.

Teddy was hoping his father would be in a better mood today. However, by his tone, he could tell he was his usual surly self. "Well, I thought I'd come by and check on y'all."

As Teddy reached for a throat lozenge from his coat pocket, he felt the envelope which contained a contract from the medical park clinic. His lifelong dream of practicing medicine in his hometown was about to become a reality.

Teddy approached his mother, leaned over, and kissed her cheek, "How are you guys? Any news on when Dad can go home?"

The bracelets on her wrist jingled as Claire lifted her crossed fingers and made air quotes. "Perhaps tomorrow."

"Well, you must be improving for them to let you go home so soon," Teddy walked toward his father's bed. "But, who wouldn't enjoy spending a few days in these plush surroundings; this is like a room down at the Ritz." He turned and winked at his mother, knowing that his comment would get a rise out of his father.

"At ten thousand dollars a day, we could've taken an exotic vacation. Your mother insisted on getting this suite. I would never indulge myself for this kind of luxury."

"Of course, you wouldn't, but perhaps this would be a good time for you guys to get away."

"Are you kidding? Unlike you, I have people depending on me. I have a business to run; this heart attack has set me back a few months."

Claire walked over to her husband's bedside and pulled up a chair and rubbed his arm. "Now, darlin', remember what the doctor said last night? You must take a sabbatical from work until you are strong enough to handle the daily pressures of your job. We must be realistic,

Theo; he said that it could be six months to a year before you're able to return to work."

Teddy listened to his parents and wondered how anyone could argue with a woman who spoke with a sweet southern drawl like his mother's. It was apparent his father was getting better; the curt tone had returned to his voice as he rolled his eyes at Teddy, and instead of challenging his wife, he dismissed her by closing his eyes.

His parent's conversation faded in the background; he was too excited about his news to pay attention. Teddy took a deep breath, removed the envelope from his pocket, and held it in the air. "Well, I have some good news for you guys. I've got a contract from the medical park clinic about the unit I plan to lease for my practice." Teddy watched his father for a reaction, something to show that he was impressed that Teddy had managed to negotiate a contract on his own.

Claire jumped up from her seat and ran over to Teddy and hugged his arm as she looked at the contract. "Congratulations, darlin'. After twelve years of training, you've finally done it. How soon can you move in?"

"The lease begins on the first day of next month, but there's a lot to do before I can open the doors. Now, I must deal with the State of Georgia to get a corporate status and apply for licenses to conduct business in the county and city municipalities. In the meantime, they will finish the interior offices and then, of course, I must furnish it and hire my staff. But, if all goes well, I should be ready to open for business within three months."

He noticed his father had turned on his side toward the window. Teddy knew he was no longer listening to him, so he motioned for his mother to move over to the sofa. He hadn't expected his father to show as much enthusiasm as his mother. As usual, his father wasn't interested in any conversation that wasn't about him.

"Now, son, if I can help you, please let me know. I've got plenty of time on my hands to pick out drapes, carpet and such as that." Claire said.

"Thanks, Mom. We are a way from making those decisions, but I'll let you know when I get to that part. Your interior design talents will come in handy."

Teddy and Claire left a note on Theo's bed and went out for lunch.

* * * * * * * *

Theo was sitting up in bed when they returned. His reading glasses had slipped to the tip of his nose as he scribbled on a notepad he had found in the bedside table.

"Hey, I must have dozed off. I'm glad both of you are here because I've got something I need to talk to y'all about."

"Let me put my pocketbook away in the closet and then we can sit down and have a nice chat, dear."

Theo reached for a Kleenex from the box next to his bed and deliberately cleaned his glasses.

Claire returned to the bedside and sat in the same chair she had occupied earlier, and she motioned for Teddy to sit down. Theodore cleared his throat and looked straight at Teddy as he pointed to the notepad.

"Son, I've got a dilemma on my hands, and you are the only person who can help me. Now that your brother and sister are gone, your responsibilities as an only child are greater, and I'm sorry about that. But, sometimes life deals us a specific hand of cards, and we must figure out a way to play them... and I need your help."

* * * * * * * *

Teddy recognized the sign of hesitation; it was his father's way of getting their full attention. Teddy shot a darting gaze towards his mother. But, her blank expression as she shrugged her shoulders told him she didn't have a clue about what was about to happen. "Sure, I'll help you out. What's the big dilemma?"

Reaching for Claire's hand, Theo cleared his voice, "Son, I need you to run my real estate business until I can return to work. As your mom explained earlier; the doctor won't release me to return to work for at least six months. We are on the cusp of purchasing the property to begin the industrial park, and you are the only person I trust to deal with the landowners. As you know, the Hawkins's property is the largest tract involved, and Tom Hawkins is our biggest challenge."

Teddy's facial muscles tightened, and he felt the color drain from his face as he held eye contact with his father. His father had never said that he trusted him before, and up until this moment, he would have welcomed it. But, trust usually comes with strings attached. Knowing his father was a self-made businessman and a successful salesman, Teddy knew it would never bother him to ask his son to postpone opening his medical practice for his own benefit. Teddy's smile was tight as he rubbed the back of his neck. He noticed his mother's eyes were gleaming with tears as she looked up at the ceiling. He could have cried, too.

(Two Years Later - October 2012)

Nora Hawkins peeked out the door at her husband, Tom, and watched him sitting on the front porch of their two-story farmhouse. He had already finished the last of his sweet tea. It was his second glass since lunch. Nora leaned against the wooden door frame and then tilted her head slightly and watched as her husband looked out over the land they both loved. She had lived on the farm her entire married life, and she wondered why he was hell-bent on making the biggest mistake of their lives.

She picked at her nubby nails as she considered their dilemma. Her lower lip was already sore from where she had picked at it, something she had never done before they started talking about selling the farm.

Nora wiped the kitchen counters again and looked around her modest-sized kitchen. It was as if she was seeing it for the very first time. She could almost hear the pitter-patter of her grandchildren's tiny feet scampering to the yellow Formica table and hopping into the chairs begging her for the stew she loved making for them on the old gas stove. The sweet memories of bathing her babies in the deep kitchen sink caused her eyes to sparkle. Her kitchen, with the stone fireplace that provided heat in the winter, was, in her opinion, the best room in the house. It was the center of a lifetime of family memories, and she was not about to let her husband sell this place to a bunch of developers who only wanted the land for an industrial park.

Nora mumbled as she walked through the foyer. "You'd think a realtor would be on time if he's serious about making an offer."

Tom Hawkins shifted in his chair and looked toward the door. "Mama, why are you staring at me through the door? If you have something to say, come on out here and let's talk."

Nora did not respond; she had already returned to the kitchen. Her granddaughter, Mary Katherine, followed her. "Nana, he just said something, should I ask what he wants."

"No. Tom's probably talking to that spark plug he's been tinkering with, dear."

"He's reading from that small notepad he carries around in his shirt pocket," said Mary Katherine.

"Yes. During lunch, your grandfather wrote down a few items to handle when he goes into town. He mentioned the bank, the lawyer, the seed store, and he needs more spark plugs for the lawnmower he's been rebuilding. As he finished the list, he said *being a farmer requires many skills these days*. Then he laughed at his joke."

"That's funny. He's the only person I know with a laugh as gruff as his voice. Gruff from a lifelong cigar habit, I presume."

Nora said, "That's true, and his voice can quickly reach a level that commands attention in a crowd."

"I'm going outside to find out what he said just now."

"Mary Katherine, will you take that pitcher of tea while you're going? Tom may want a refill."

"Papa, would you like a refill?" Tom turned toward the door when the screen door shut as she stepped onto the porch holding a pitcher of iced tea.

"Yes, sweetheart. Thank you." He continued to rock in his chair as he rubbed his chin.

"I know you're worried about Nana, and I can tell she's anxious too. She's cleaned every surface in that kitchen twice since I got here thirty minutes ago."

Tom shook his head, "It's that bad, huh?"

Mary Katherine raised her eyebrows and smiled.

As Tom reached for his glass, he looked out over the land.

"What are you thinking about as you gaze out across that field?"

Tom chuckled, "I was thinking the beautiful autumn sky is the same shade of blue as Mama's eyes."

Mary Katherine watched as his gaze settled on the field across from his house. "I see the boys have been working in the fields this morning."

Tom swallowed a sip of tea, and then he took a deep breath, and said, "Oh, the smell of the rich, pungent earth. I remember when I was able to work alongside them."

Mary Katherine reached over and grabbed his hand. "You miss working, don't you?"

Tom's eyes misted as he looked towards the driveway. "Sure do... But, if that damn realtor doesn't hurry and get here, your Grandmother's bottom lip will swell up from all of that picking she's been doing today."

"Don't think I can't hear you, old man!" said Nora.

Mary Katherine chuckled as she headed back to the kitchen.

"Why don't you and Mary Katherine come outside and wait with me?" Tom asked with a stern tone.

* * * * * * * *

In contrast to Tom's gruffness, Nora was a soft-spoken homemaker, who had spent her life nurturing the family. Their differences made them a more exciting and unique couple. But, she was no pushover!

As she watched their granddaughter return to the kitchen, she prayed Mary Katherine would continue to have the same passion for her home, that she had felt as a child. Nora needed an advocate since her husband was having serious thoughts about selling their farm.

Nora heard the back-door slam, and after a moment she glanced at the kitchen window where she saw Mary Katherine standing in front of the well drinking a cup of water. Then, she heard the Mercedes coming up the graveled drive, and she felt a sense of relief. She recalled a conversation she and Tom had with Teddy's father earlier in the week. 'Like your accomplished granddaughter in that picture, my son is a smart guy, too.' When Nora glanced back at the opened window, Mary Katherine was looking towards the driveway, and she couldn't resist thinking one Theodore Williams and her granddaughter would make a fine-looking couple.

* * * * * * * *

Mary Katherine finished the last of her water. She smoothed her hands over her professionally laundered jeans, a luxury she enjoyed because of the long hours she worked since moving to the city. She wondered why her grandfather had felt her presence was necessary to meet with Mr. Williams. She turned toward the window and said to her grandmother, "You know, he admitted that he has always obsessed over the decisions that affect his family, and business, and particularly you and me."

"My dear, that's an understatement. This land has been in Tom's family for over 125 years, and if he loves this farm as much as I do, then I don't believe he wants to sell it," said Nora.

"I don't understand. If Papa doesn't want to sell the farm, why did he arrange this meeting?" Her grandmother had moved away from the kitchen window and did not answer her. Maybe she didn't know the answer, and then it occurred to Mary Katherine that perhaps her grandfather was experiencing health problems since his retirement and was trying to get his affairs in order.

Mary Katherine's heart skipped a beat as she watched Mr. Williams approach the front of her grandparents' home dressed in khaki pants, a long-sleeved, white dress shirt, and a blue blazer. Although his hair looked as if he had ridden with the car windows down, he was also very polished. Even from afar, she noticed he had a 'little boy charm' about him, and that he was the most handsome man she had ever seen.

The realtor's son was a paradox in Mary Katherine's mind; her concern was so intense she had used her own money and paid an investigative firm to find some background information about Mr. Williams. Her sources confirmed that Mr. Williams had completed his internship and residency at Emory University Medical School and had also completed a fellowship in pediatric surgery at Children's Hospital in Atlanta. It worried her that someone they knew so little about had earned such a high level of respect from her grandparents. But, her more significant concern was the contradictions by her grandfather regarding the sale of the family farm.

As Mary Katherine walked around the side of the house, she mumbled a short prayer for patience. "Please let me have an open mind going into this meeting." Her gut told her that this meeting was about much more than a land deal for her grandparents' property. She completed her prayer, Mary Katherine smiled and said to herself as she walked towards the porch to meet their visitor, "*God knows my heart better than anyone.*"

CHAPTER THREE

Teddy Williams saw Mary Katherine walking towards the front steps and wondered if she was, indeed, the older gentleman's granddaughter. Somehow, he had expected someone much younger. Her long, brown hair fell just above her shoulders and provided a backdrop for her creamy complexion. She wasn't in any hurry as she stopped to smell the last of the summer roses remaining on the bush. The opened neckline of her white linen blouse revealed a silver necklace. The long-sleeved shirt, along with her faded jeans, gave her a casual, yet chic look. As she advanced across the front yard, he just stared. Aware that his feelings must be transparent, he became self-conscious, but, he could not force his eyes away from her. He was surprised by his thoughts because no one had ever stirred in him the same level of desire. He had met a lot of pretty women in his life, but their beauty differed from the graceful woman approaching him. Teddy wiped his damp hands on his handkerchief before walking up the steps. Waiting for the granddaughter to reach the porch, he noticed that Mrs. Hawkins had been watching his reaction. She was smiling at him.

"Mr. Williams, this is our little granddaughter, Mary Katherine." Tom paused. "Everyone calls her Katie except her grandmother and I. We prefer Mary Katherine." Another pause. "She's named after our daughter Katherine Noreen. Katherine died, along with her husband and infant son, in a car accident twenty-five years ago. Mama and I raised Mary Katherine from the age of four. Your father may have explained to you she handles our finances, and we thought it would be a good idea for the two of you to meet."

Teddy stepped back. "Wow, that's quite an introduction." He extended his hand. "The pleasure is mine," said Teddy, as he gazed into her green eyes. She appeared calm and unaffected by meeting him, and Teddy's features softened as he moved closer, closing the distance between them.

"Well, Mr. Williams," said Tom, "I think you can let go of her hand now if you don't mind."

Katie clung to his hand a little longer than necessary and, satisfied her grandparents could not see her flirty expression, she flashed him a sassy, wicked grin. "Come now, Mr. Williams, you must not try to hold my hand on our first meeting." She winked at him as she turned around to sit down on the porch swing next to her grandmother. As an afterthought, she looked back in his direction. "My friends and colleagues call me Katie."

Trying not to stutter, he responded, "Thanks, my friends call me Teddy."

Nora quickly got up from the swing and ushered everyone into the kitchen. "We will be much more comfortable inside. There is a nice breeze blowing in the kitchen, and the glare from the afternoon sun won't be as likely to hurt Tom's eyes in there."

No one would understand the jab unless they knew the couple well. Tom's face was blood red, and he puffed up while crossing his arms, like a young boy.

The ladies went ahead while Tom walked with Teddy. "Never underestimate the power of a woman, Mr. Williams. Nora may be small, but she packs a powerful punch with her sharp words. She knows damn well there isn't anything wrong with my eyes." He paused. "But, there's no need in me trying to change her after sixty years of marriage."

"Good point," Teddy chuckled, "my grandfather used to say, 'can't live with them, and can't live without them.' I'm sure there's an element of truth to that statement."

Tom held the door for Teddy, "I bet I would've liked your grandfather, son."

As they entered the kitchen, Teddy saw Nora wink at Katie as they watched Tom flop down in his recliner and continue to pout.

Katie's playful behavior and the brief walk inside to the kitchen allowed Teddy time to relax. He placed his briefcase on the empty chair next to him at the table, hoping to create a distance between him and Katie. He removed a legal-size manila envelope from the briefcase and placed it in front of him. Without hesitation, Mrs. Hawkins reached for a glass and poured him some iced tea.

"Thank you, Mrs. Hawkins. This drink looks delicious." As he took a long swallow of the cold drink, he could feel Katie's gaze, which he avoided. Instead, he focused on Tom Hawkins, who sat looking out the window, showing Teddy that he was uninterested in the meeting.

As the silence in the room became noticeable, Teddy's nervousness returned.

"Mr. Williams, my grandparents tell me that a group of speculators are interested in this property as a site for an industrial park. Perhaps you weren't aware, but, my grandparents have no interest in selling their farm. Please allow me to explain. My great-grandfather purchased this land with the funds he made from growing and selling cotton in the early 1900s. He worked hard to keep this farm. Grandfather was born the year the Depression started, and during those years, farmers almost starved to death. My grandparents inherited this farm after his parents' death. My grandfather struggled during those early years to pay off the farm. For many years, he could only pay the interest payments to the local bank. One thousand dollars was a tremendous debt, Mr. Williams. But, my grandparents were survivors, and they persevered as they worked from sunup to sundown to hold on to a piece of land which they inherited."

Katie went over to the kitchen counter and picked up the tea pitcher and walked back to the table to refill their glasses.

"Thank you. This iced-tea is great."

She suppressed a smile as she took another swallow of her drink and continued, "Please understand, Mr. Williams, my grandfather was an only child. Great-Grandma and Great-Grandpa Hawkins wanted a large family, but as it sometimes happens in life, things didn't turn out the way they had planned. I'm certain, Mr. Williams, you can understand their reasons for not wanting to sell their land."

As Katie walked over to her grandfather's chair and sat down on the ottoman, Teddy opened his notebook and saw the three rules his dad taught him regarding the power of negotiating: *Rule 1. Be prepared for the unexpected. Rule 2. Maintain control of the meeting. Rule 3. Never let the party with whom you are negotiating see you sweat.*

In a loving, unrehearsed gesture, she took her grandfather's old, wrinkled hands in her own. Then she turned her head toward Teddy and concluded. "Mr. Williams, my grandfather, was born on this farm. He and my grandmother married here. Together, they raised their family while working this land and it is here where they faced the tragedies and joys of life. After my parents' accident, they brought me here, and although we have a large family, they raised me like an only child. This farm, Mr. Williams, is where this precious man's life began 83 years ago, and this is also where he intends to draw his last breath."

The intensity in Katie's eyes revealed her fear of selling the family farm. But, it was the adoration that appeared on the faces of Mr. and Mrs. Hawkins as they looked at their granddaughter, which caused Teddy to hesitate. Selling the farm, along with losing her grandparents, would strip Katie of her security.

"The prospects of selling the family farm must be difficult for you to entertain right now. Please understand I heard the passion in your voice as you told the history of this place. I came prepared to offer you an attractive price… an offer that may not be available in the future."

Katie turned toward Teddy and said, "You don't understand, do you?"

"I think I do. But, please consider our offer before closing the door to any negotiation."

As Teddy felt the cool autumn breeze blowing through the kitchen window, he understood how one would enjoy the solitude of farm life. He shivered at Katie's mention of death. He reflected on his father. A 68-year-old, with a heart condition he had lived with for over two years.

When Katie walked from the ottoman to the sink, she looked at Teddy and with furrowed eyebrows said in a firm tone, "We're not selling."

Teddy looked out the kitchen window and saw the beautiful team of horses grazing in the schooling ring. Katie moved with the grace of a prized thoroughbred. Oh yes, she was beautiful, but she was also articulate and eloquent - and very strong-willed. He rubbed his hands together, and only then did he realize he had not worn his wedding ring.

It was time to end the meeting and leave. Teddy placed the manila folder back into his briefcase and walked over to the kitchen sink to deposit the empty glass. He paused at the window as he noticed a few dogs roaming among the horses. "You have a beautiful place here."

Apparently, sensing the awkwardness in the room and realizing there was nothing more to discuss, Tom turned to Teddy. "Thank you, son. As my granddaughter mentioned, we're not ready to sell our property right now. Your father and I thought it would be a good idea for you to meet Mary Katherine since she handles our finances. We appreciate you dropping by. Nora and Mary Katherine will show you out."

When Teddy and Katie made their way down the front steps and into the yard, their nervousness had disappeared. Katie dropped the formality she had used inside the house. "Teddy, I hate you've wasted your time coming out here today. But, I suppose rejection is an occupational hazard in your field, right?"

Teddy grinned and decided against debating the hazards of his father's business. "Yes, I suppose that's true. But, I must admit, the iced tea was worth the effort. Am I safe to drive an automobile after drinking two glasses of your grandmother's sweet tea?"

Recognizing the boyish charm, "Yeah, but prepare yourself for a rush from the cane sugar."

"I've already felt the sugar rush," he laughed.

She nodded in the window's direction, "If I were a betting girl, I would bet a steak dinner that my grandmother is watching from the window in the parlor."

He cocked his head to the side, "And, why is that?"

"She is making sure I extend southern hospitality to our guest."

"I'm sure your grandmother has good intentions."

"I agree. She's a sweetheart."

Teddy reached in his coat pocket and handed her a card. "Here's my business card. Please don't hesitate to call me if they change their minds."

Katie looked at the card and said, "Honestly, I don't think they will ever sell."

"Well, you never know. I've learned it just takes one event to change one's mind about moving from home." He flashed that charming smile and continued, "Anyway, I'm not going anywhere, so if you need me for anything, just give me a call."

She placed her hand on her chest and took a deep breath, "Listen, thanks again for taking the time to meet with us today."

"No problem, Katie," he said with a wink as he touched her arm. "It sounds like he just wanted us to meet. And, besides, this is their home, and if they want to die here, it's okay with me!"

CHAPTER FOUR

Teddy dreaded telling his father that the Hawkins couple would not sell. *"I'm not a realtor,"* He said to no one in particular as he rolled back the sunroof and lowered the windows to allow the fresh air and sunshine in as he drove toward the office. Teddy's thoughts returned to the Hawkins' kitchen. Life was much simpler in the country. He wondered how different his life would have been with a woman like Katie. Nancy Leigh, his wife of six years, was also a beauty with her curvy, petite body and long blonde hair. She had caused his blood to boil during their college days. But, the years of going to school and working eighteen-hour days had caused cracks in their marriage. He couldn't remember the last time he looked at Nancy Leigh with any level of desire. As he pulled into the parking lot at the Williams Real Estate Office, Teddy realized that he had spent the last 30 minutes comparing his wife to Katie O'Neill. As he cut off the engine to the E-Class Mercedes-Benz, he looked ahead at the clear autumn sky before him and wondered if he had ever felt as loved as Katie O'Neill.

Growing up, Teddy never seemed to please his father. Something as simple as cutting the grass provided an opportunity for his father to rebuke him. He would have never reached this point in life without his mother's encouragement and her belief that even the most challenged children can live a productive life. But, with intelligence like Teddy's, a career in medicine was attainable. His mother and grandparents inspired the man he had become.

Theodore sat in his wood-paneled office, reading The Wall Street Journal when Teddy entered the room. He immediately walked over to shake his father's hand.

"You are back earlier than I expected. How did you find the Hawkins family?"

"They're very nice people. I enjoyed meeting them."

"That's great news." Theodore checked his watch, and asked, "Are you ready to review the contract and make sure everything is in order? We have a nine o'clock meeting scheduled with the partners on Monday morning, and I would like to have everything ready when they arrive."

Teddy stared at the contract in silence.

His father extended his hand. "May I have the contract, please?"

"Yes. Of course."

It was Saturday afternoon on a beautiful autumn day, and this was business as usual for his father. He was a straightforward guy with an edge to his tone, and he never made time for small talk or casual conversation about where the Braves stood in the playoffs, or the Georgia Bulldogs' ranking in their season.

Looking down at the unsigned papers, Teddy understood that they mirrored his own incomplete and unfulfilled life. His marriage was crumbling, and he couldn't get away from his father's business. He sat down in one of the wingback chairs positioned in front of the antique mahogany desk. Theodore paused and looked over at Teddy before opening the envelope.

"Were you not interested in playing in the annual golf tournament this year?" Teddy asked as he looked at his watch and thought about his friends gathered at the club enjoying drinks as they finished the second day of the tournament.

Theodore removed the contract from the manila envelope and laid it on his desk. He looked at the first page of the agreement and then looked up at his son. "No, son, this industrial park is taking a lot of time. And, securing the Hawkins property is a top priority right now."

His glasses had slipped down onto the tip of his nose, and the look was one of intense intimidation. Using the tip of his pen, he skimmed each page of the contract as he pointed to the small blocks where the sellers' initials would denote their agreement, and he laid the contract on his desk. Clearing his throat, he looked over his horned-rimmed glasses and expressed the obvious.

"Teddy, they didn't sign the contract." Theodore paused and rubbed his forehead. "You know, son, I have seen this type of behavior before. I know the signs of a failed meeting."

"I realize they didn't sign it, because it appears the Hawkins Farm is not for sale."

"What in the hell are you talking about, Teddy? The Hawkins Farm is for sale; everything is for sale. They may not be interested in selling today, but they will sometime soon."

His father got up from his chair and paced behind his desk as he rubbed his temples. "Do you think they would have arranged this meeting today if they had not been interested in an open discussion? That is the reason I sent you, Teddy. You are a good-looking young man, the granddaughter may be younger than you, but you are from the same generation. She's a common-sense kind of girl, and if you can gain her trust, then this is a done deal."

Exhausted and almost breathless, Theodore looked at his son.

"So, what happened out there today?"

Teddy straightened in his chair and relayed the story to his father.

"Is that all?"

"I realize, Dad, that my opinion carries no weight, but I think Mr. Hawkins has no intention of selling his farm. His agreement to meet with me this weekend was his way of appeasing you."

Teddy paused for his father's reaction. They had never been close, and Teddy would never measure up to his father's expectations. Teddy felt he was an inconvenience in his father's life. Few people saw the real picture, the accident that killed his brother and sister was at the core of all their family's dysfunction. Wouldn't it be healthier to admit the truth than continue to hide behind lies?

Theodore slowly removed his horned-rimmed glasses and took a Kleenex from the bottom drawer of his desk. As he cleaned the glasses, he got up from his chair and walked over to the window and steadied himself. Teddy watched as his father wiped the sweat from his brow, and he wondered if his father's blood pressure was rising.

Teddy waited with patience. When Theodore returned to his desk, he picked up a shiny silver pen and walked back and forth, as he pointed the pen at his son.

"Interesting, I've never heard the history of the Hawkins Farm, and I have known Tom Hawkins for decades."

Teddy straightened the crease in his slacks to adjust his position in his chair when he said, "Well, I'm surprised. It seemed to be the story of the day. The tribal spokeswoman delivered the speech with as much drama as one could imagine."

Teddy noticed that something he had said did not sit well with his father and wondered if his sarcastic tone was stronger than he intended.

"You have a naïve attitude about our family business and a terrible understanding of life. How much money are you making from this firm?" Theodore said.

Teddy slumped in his chair and rolled his eyes in disbelief and said, "So, now we're discussing salary, correct? You pay me sixty thousand dollars a year."

"You earn sixty thousand dollars a year, and you blow off a contract like this on a piece of property central to the industrial park. And, you go out there today and fall for all that sentimentality and return with an unsigned contract!"

Theodore walked around the desk and sat down in the wingback chair next to his son. "Teddy, when are you going to get serious about this business?"

He looked over the top of his glasses, paused, and then continued. "Since my heart attack, Dr. Jackson keeps mentioning that I should retire. I have done everything but hand the real estate firm to you on a silver platter, and you refuse to accept the challenge. We need the Hawkins property, Teddy!" He hit his fist on the arm of the chair.

He paused again and took another deep breath. "Am I correct in assuming you did not introduce the possibility of an option to purchase the land at a later date?"

"No, sir, we did not discuss an option. We have enough property for the development, and I didn't want to irritate Mr. Hawkins. I am certain he would not understand the significant meaning of an option. Mr. and Mrs. Hawkins are old, and they will not be around much longer. Why don't we wait them out? We have to get the latest parcels passed through zoning, and that could take a while."

Teddy was pleased with his explanation. "Perhaps in a few days, we can meet again with the granddaughter to discuss the property. If she likes the idea, then she will persuade her grandparents to sign an option. So, let's take a deep breath and consider our choices over the weekend."

"I don't believe this, breathe and consider our choices, and see what happens? Son, there are no other choices. Their property is the largest tract of land in that area." He paused and took a deep breath as he adjusted the cufflinks on his shirt sleeve. "I believe Mr. Hawkins is a smart fellow. Remember, he is a successful farmer, and they know all about options! I'm certain Mr. Hawkins has a broader understanding of financial markets than one might imagine. The Hawkins' family didn't survive the long years of the Depression without a strong understanding of business. And, let's not forget he was a County Commissioner for many years before his retirement."

Theodore paused. The two sat in silence for a few awkward moments while Teddy watched his father stare at the pen in his hand. "However, you have made a valid point, son," he said as he looked over at Teddy. "We should consider the financial impact of holding onto those funds through the first phase of development." For the first time since Teddy arrived, his father smiled. "Time is on our side. As you suggested, we should prepare a suitable option and arrange a private meeting with the granddaughter and present her with the offer. Let's use the weekend to work out a plan and prepare to introduce this idea to the other investors at the meeting on Monday. The investors are expecting to see a signed contract, but instead, we can explain the benefit of an option. Son, will you use the weekend to draft an option for our review on Monday?"

Teddy stood up and walked to the window and looked out at the empty parking area, and then he turned around and faced his father.

"Father, we need to talk. I need to say something to you not as a son to father, but man to man." Teddy waited for his father to acknowledge for him to speak. Theodore then waved his hand for him to proceed. "First, no, I am not the person to create a plan of action regarding the Hawkins. Father, I am a medical doctor. Grandpa encouraged me to follow in his footsteps, and as a young boy, I recognized a desire to help children."

Teddy paused, and removed a smooth stone from his pocket and held it in his hand as he continued, "You know when Grandmother Simpson offered to pay my way through medical school, I realized it was because she shared in my dream to follow in Grandpa's career path. But you never encouraged my decision to go into medicine, and I never expected you to pay for medical school. But, when you had the heart scare and needed to take time off to regain your strength, out of respect for you and Mom, I agreed to help until you could return to work. When I made that promise, I never intended to take over your business. You know I have always done what you have asked of me, but I can't continue in this business." Teddy pulled out his handkerchief and wiped his brow and then continued.

"Dr. Jackson talked with me about your need to retire when you were in the hospital. Since he is your physician, please consider his advice."

"What!" Theodore said harshly, "I didn't realize you spoke with my doctor about my need to retire."

"Well, yes, he mentioned you should slow down and enjoy life," he paused, "listen, Dad, I do not want to run this business. I know this must be a tremendous disappointment to you since you have spent your entire adult life in this business, but, this isn't me!" The pitch of his voice increased to an unfamiliar level, and beads of sweat appeared on his brow as he continued to explain his reason for starting his practice. "One must have a desire to help children, and I'm well-trained and prepared to do so. To be honest, if I hadn't wanted to practice medicine in my hometown, I could've already signed with an established practice in Atlanta."

"I'm sure you've had several offers."

Teddy turned around and looked outside. "You know, Bobby would've been the perfect guy running this company. He thought he would someday take over for you. Dad, please know I agree this development is an awesome deal, but this job isn't for me. And, please don't expect me to live the life you planned for Bobby. Becoming a doctor is my life's purpose and the passion that causes me to get up each morning. Do you understand how I feel?"

"Yes, son... I recognize your passion."

Teddy turned back to face his father. "You are doing, and have always done what you enjoy, and you love this business." Teddy found himself restless, and he continued to stand next to the window with his arms outstretched on each side for balance.

"Until now, I have handled research and contracts, and now you are sending me out to negotiate contracts with clients who have relationships with you. You have established amazing credibility throughout your career, and your clients want and deserve your representation. Oh, sure the Phillips had no problem dealing with me, or selling their property. They sold to get out from under some debt and enjoy a few trips while they are still young enough to enjoy traveling."

Teddy relaxed, and his voice softened as he sat down in the chair across from his father's desk. "But, the Hawkins family are different. They don't need the money, and they are much older than the Phillips. Money doesn't mean that much to them, Dad. Their mentality is almost tribal. They have everything they need on that farm, and they wouldn't take ten million dollars in cash for their property. And why would they? Look around this town, Abington rests in the foothills of the Blue Ridge Mountains surrounded by the beautiful shoreline of Lake Lanier, a 38,000-acre recreational reservoir named for the poet Sidney Lanier." Teddy paused. "Mr. Hawkins wants to die surrounded by all of this beauty, on the farm where he was born, and I think his family should allow him to do so."

* * * * * * * *

Theodore didn't know what to say, but the lump in his throat prevented him from speaking. He looked over at his accomplished son, and although the two men were opposites, he respected him for staying true to his principles. He was one of the most trusted and well-respected men in the business community, but he had failed to earn the respect of his oldest son. The decision to bring Teddy into the family business following his heart issue was to allow them to spend quality time together and develop a stronger bond.

He looked at a family picture sitting on his desk. The photo, taken on vacation showed the sweet faces of his three young children clothed in white shirts and khaki shorts, sitting on steps leading down to the beach at Hilton Head Island. Mr. Williams noticed the love and respect on the faces of the younger children as they looked at their older brother, Teddy. Neither had ever felt any sense of jealousy toward his advanced intellect or natural good looks.

"Yes, Teddy, I know the history and geographical layout of this beloved town. And, believe me, I fell in love with this place the first time your mother brought me home to meet her parents."

Theodore realized early on that Claire's father, Dr. Simpson, was the prominent male figure in young Teddy's life, and although he had tried to carve out a niche where he and Teddy could bond following the car accident that killed his other two children, he had been unsuccessful.

Struggling to suppress his emotions and frustration, he continued, "I understand what you are saying, but you have been out of medical school for over two years, and you do not have a license to practice medicine in the State of Georgia."

Hesitating as he walked over to his desk and pulled out the middle drawer. Theodore opened a bottle of nitroglycerin tablets prescribed by Dr. Jackson, and he waited for the tablet to dissolve.

"As I was saying, you do not have a license to practice medicine in the State of Georgia, and until you get a license, you cannot open a pediatrician's office. I gave it the thoughtful consideration required, before bringing you into my business, but you needed an income, an income which would allow you to support your young wife." His father inhaled a deep breath, "and, if money is a problem for you, I will increase your annual salary. Would that help your feelings?" He could have paid Teddy any amount of money he wanted, but he wanted his son to enjoy the pride that comes from earning his position in the firm. Otherwise, his plan would have no merit.

Red blotches soon appeared on Teddy's face, and he jumped up and paced around the room while tugging at the waistband of his trousers as if they were too big. "You haven't been listening. I'm ready to find my place in the world." He paused. "Dad, we're not talking about money here. At least, I'm not! Nancy Leigh and I are managing on the salary you pay me, and we appreciate it. And, if we need more money to live on Nancy Leigh can get a job."

Theodore interrupted, "Excuse me, but I thought she was giving tennis lessons at the club."

"No. Nancy Leigh's not working."

"Every time I've been out there the past few months, she's been in the pro shop with the tennis pro."

"No, Dad. She's not working."

"You must admit, it was a natural assumption."

"I agree... Dad, are you feeling okay?"

"Yes. I just got confused, that's all."

Teddy took a deep breath and continued. "I do not want to take over your business. I want to practice medicine." The conversation now exasperated him. "Please, let's be clear, I already have a medical license. I couldn't have done a fellowship at Children's Hospital without a license to practice medicine. But, I need a business license and a corporate status with the State of Georgia. There is a three-page list of forms and applications that I need to complete before I can open my practice, but there is no time to sit down with Uncle Frederick to get started."

"I apologize, son. I should have realized you needed a business license. What was I thinking?"

Theodore stood in front of his desk and continued to stare at the picture of his children. "Teddy, I realize your life's ambition is to follow in your Grandfather Simpson's career path, and I applaud you for wanting to help people. All I know is real estate, son. We don't make our money the traditional way. I have built this business on speculative buying. When searching for properties, I look for potential growth. The level of expertise required to develop property makes us unique. It takes time to research and to develop the knowledge of the geography, along with a large measure of luck, to know which areas of the community will experience growth. Timing is everything in this business. I have made a nice living for our family, Teddy, and now I'm asking you to accept the torch and continue the family business for the next generation! Life doesn't always work out the way we plan. We have a successful business here that can sustain several generations of Williams'."

Teddy considered his father's confusion regarding the medical license. He wondered if something was going on with his dad, because he didn't seem to get that Teddy was trying to resign his position at the firm.

"Dad, I appreciate the torch you are offering, and I also appreciate the faith you have placed in me to continue your life's work. However, I cannot accept this offer. You agree that I have honored my promise to you." His father nodded in agreement. "Soon, I plan to contact Uncle Frederick for his help to establish a corporation for my pediatric practice. Once we get the legal part established, I plan to cash in the stock Grandma Simpson left me to fund my practice. I have spoken as plainly as I can, and since the Hawkins are not ready to sell, I am prepared to leave this position and establish my practice. It appears you have recovered from your heart scare and no longer need my help. Now, if you will excuse me, I'm going over to the club. My friends should finish the tournament anytime now, and I'd like to be there when they do."

Teddy picked up his briefcase and walked out of his father's office without looking back. The solid mahogany door closed much harder than Teddy had intended, and the sound vibrated the tall windows in the hallway. He stopped by the men's room and splashed cold water on his face. Beads of sweat were seeping from every pore on his body, and his face was the color of scarlet. Teddy reached up to grab a towel from the wall dispenser and rubbed his face. He looked into the mirror and the familiar feelings he got when he disappointed his father came rushing back to him. The same feelings he experienced when he didn't play little league baseball, and again when he tried out for the defensive back position instead of the quarterback position in football. That familiar ache in his stomach that he got when he and his dad disagreed had returned.

As Teddy dried his hands, he rubbed the untanned line on his finger from wearing a wedding ring for six years. The air in the restroom thickened and the pungent smell of pine disinfectant, remnants from the cleaning the building received earlier in the afternoon lingered. The nausea returned as the warm air in the room closed in on him. Teddy left the restroom and stopped by the break room and found a Coke in the refrigerator. He popped the top and took a sip as he headed toward the back door of the office building.

As soon as he stepped outside, and the sunshine hit his face, he felt better. For the first time in his life, he had stood up to his dominating father, and he wasn't about to let guilt spoil the moment! The gentle fall breeze was refreshing, and he willed himself, excited about the prospects of seeing his friends. As Teddy approached his car, he turned back toward the building, and he could see his father seated in the wingback chair where he had left him ten minutes earlier. As he started his car, he opened the sunroof, lowered the windows, and turned on the radio to the sound of *The Boys Are Back in Town,* a song by Thin Lizzy. Teddy laughed at the irony of the song. He backed out of the parking space and headed for the club. The dreaded discussion with his father completed, he allowed the powerful tension to escape his body, and his nausea slowly subsided.

CHAPTER FIVE

The Club was a beautiful two-story, white brick Georgian structure with four large columns across the front. A large door encased with beveled glass sparkled with brilliance as did the enormous, elegant chandelier hanging in the foyer. The architectural design of the 100-year-old building was a tribute to the days when structures were built to endure. The eight oversized rocking chairs on the front porch sat empty as usual, swaying in the afternoon breeze.

Teddy got out of his car and removed his jacket, and then he rolled up his shirt sleeves and locked his vehicle. He stopped in front of the car and looked at the beautiful yellow Mercedes. Mr. Williams assigned the leased vehicle to Teddy when he came on board following his heart attack. Although Teddy loved driving the car, it served as a constant reminder of the dominant control his father had over his future. He longed for his first car, a 1968 VW that he purchased for $1000 while working a part-time job during the summer months between his junior and senior years of high school. Teddy remembered the pride he experienced from having bought it with his own money. He had delayed buying the car until his father was out-of-town attending a real estate convention. Because it was his first car, he had driven it for 15 years before he had it towed off to the junkyard following an accident.

Teddy overheard his mother, laughing with a friend one day. "Little did I know the car of Teddy's dreams would be a red VW convertible! I'm ashamed to admit that I am now living vicariously through my son."

On the day he purchased the car, he drove it straight home to show his mom. She was in the sunroom reading the latest edition of her *Southern Living Magazine* when she heard the car coming into the drive. She jumped up and met Teddy at the archway in the foyer.

"Teddy, did you get it?"

"Yes. Mom, she's a beauty! Come on! We're going for a ride!"

Mrs. Williams grabbed a scarf and giggled like a schoolgirl running off with a friend for an afternoon of fun.

Teddy could never remember enjoying any time more with his mother than he did on that Wednesday afternoon in the summer of 1998. She revealed a side of herself that few people had seen since the car accident that killed her two younger children six months earlier. As they rode through town in the red convertible, they experienced freedom from the summer weather as the sun shone directly on their faces, and for the first time in a long time, he saw the fun and carefree side of his mom.

On that rare summer day, a friendship was born between a young man and his mother, and neither could have expected the beginning of the bond would sustain each of them through their most arduous struggles.

The thought of the VW convertible now tucked away in his memory, he felt an impulsive urge to talk to his mom, but he walked into the club and headed for the lounge instead. As he entered, he spotted his buddies at the large round table which they occupied regularly. They sat by the big picture window and watched while the other golfers finished the 18th hole. Teddy walked over to the table and pulled up a chair. Drew Byrd's son, Jacob, stood up and offered his seat, but Teddy motioned for him to sit still. This group had been playing golf together since their days in junior high school. During their college years, the group had agreed that they would grant their children automatic admission into their group, which would keep their coveted table secured for generations to come.

Teddy Williams was Jacob's hero. As a little boy, Jacob would beg Teddy to get on the floor and wrestle with him. Teddy and Drew played for hours until young Jacob curled up with a blanket and fell asleep. Jacob, Drew, and Teddy had established their own little sports team, as the three enjoyed playing ball in the backyard or at the park, and as soon as he was old enough, they had taken Jacob to the University of Georgia football games.

As Teddy saw the pride on Jacob's face from having played a decent game of golf, he realized that Jacob was now ready to become a permanent member of the group. He made a mental note to discuss the idea with the other guys later.

Teddy shook hands with the guys at the table and gave a brotherly hug to Drew before sitting down in the chair he had pulled over to their table.

Drew raised his hand so their waitress, Donna Gilbert could see him and as she approached the table a broad smile appeared on her face.

"While your presence adds a great deal of energy in the clubhouse, you fellows are making too much noise over here." Donna Gilbert knew more than anyone how annoyed the other members had become toward the group.

"Can I help you guys?" She asked with a smile.

"Yes please, bring us another round of beers and a cherry coke for my boy here," Drew said as he winked at his son. She turned to Teddy and asked what he would like from the bar.

"A beer will be fine, Donna, thank you."

"And where did you run off to today, Mr. Real Estate Magnate?"

"A little business meeting my father asked me to handle." Then he turned to face Jacob and said, "Well, young man, how did you play today?"

Jacob sat up straight in his chair. "Uncle Teddy, I'm sure I didn't play like you, but I shot a 76 today, and I'm satisfied with a 4 over par score considering the level of competition in this group."

"Are you serious Jacob, you shot a 76 against the so-called Tour Group here, and how did we finish the tournament, do we know yet?" He leaned back to allow Donna room to place his beer on the table. He picked up the beer and took a long swallow.

Drew glanced at Tom and then Howard, as he slid the score sheets across the table to Teddy. Embarrassed by their performance, the three guys laughed so hard that Drew spat beer from his mouth. "I knew this day would come, and frankly I'm glad it has happened before you go off to college. Jacob, I forbid you to waste another golf lesson. Your putting game is far better than mine!"

The guys at the table hollered at that comment. Drew had never been an outstanding golfer. He had taught himself the game as he played and watched his friends play. Although, he played well enough to make the golf team, his family had never invested money in lessons for him. He enjoyed the camaraderie with his friends in the lounge following the game as much as he enjoyed the game itself, and, as he often explained to his wife, the game of golf does not lend itself to too much strenuous exercise.

"Jacob, I'm proud of you, man. Thanks for filling in for me today. Did you see the article in the golf magazine last week? It was an interesting article, statistics show athletics teaches discipline and endurance, persistence, and commitment. Also, it further explained that when a young man shows interest in sports, often the relationship between a father and son grows stronger. It strengthens even the closest of bonds from their time-shared enjoying or discussing sports."

"A well-written article, I might add, and the magazine also advertised for a new putter I'd like to order. I'll show you the article when you get home tonight," said Drew.

Teddy was two years younger than Drew, and aside from their years playing on the golf team, they had played football together in high school when Drew became like a big brother to him. Drew Byrd was a man's man. If he liked you, he would do anything in the world for you, and if not, well, watch out.

The golfers were leaving for home to get ready for the formal dinner-dance to culminate the end of the tournament. As much as the wives complained about the time their husbands spent playing golf, they looked forward to the annual competitions. The occasion allowed them to dress up and enjoy an evening of door prizes, exquisite food, expensive wine, and great music.

"You know Drew, once a young man reaches maturity, he understands the importance and value of his father's support and advice. Jacob is fortunate to have a strong role model in you."

Drew and Jacob exchanged a confirming glance as they finished their drinks. Changing the subject, Drew decided this was as good a time as any to mention the medical office.

"Man, have you found a location for your practice yet?"

Teddy shook his head, "No, no, I have not," as the conversation between Drew and Teddy moved to a more serious subject.

"Excuse me, Uncle Teddy. Dad, I need to get going. I have plans later tonight. Are you about ready to go home?"

"Jacob, I can give your dad a ride home, if you need to leave now," Teddy said.

Getting up from the table, he looked over at Teddy and extended his hand, "Thanks, Uncle Teddy."

Jacob turned to his dad. "I may stay with a friend tonight if you don't mind. But, if my plans change, I'll call you, okay, Dad?"

"Sure, that's fine. Just be careful, Jacob."

As he turned to leave, Teddy said, "I'm proud of your performance today, buddy. You should play with us more often."

* * * * * * *

Jacob waved as he left the lounge and sprinted out the door to his car.

"That young man amazes me." Speaking of his oldest son, he said, "Jacob seems to have a sixth sense about him, he senses when he should leave the room or keep his comments to himself. You would have been so proud of watching him play, Teddy."

"He's a great guy, Drew, but I'm partial to his parents, aren't I? You guys have directed him into the young man he has become."

Teddy's demeanor had changed, and he could tell something was eating away at him. He asked if he had found a location for his pediatrics practice because Drew thought Teddy had spent the day looking for properties, but now he was carrying on about Jacob. Teddy had been a robust role model for Jacob just as Drew had been for Teddy in high school. But Drew understood it wasn't the same as having his own child.

Drew had sensed the tension between Teddy and his wife. As of late, anxiety was evident in every aspect of their marriage. In Nancy Leigh's defense, she married out of her league. But, being married to a permanent student was not the landscape where a woman would want to start a family. The irregular hours Teddy kept while in medical school and then going through residency would demand a lot from any marriage. Nancy Leigh wasn't strong enough to endure pregnancy and the responsibility of a newborn without Teddy's involvement. Many women could handle that challenge, but Nancy Leigh was not one of those women.

"Teddy, why don't you and I watch the football game this evening? Colleen and the girls are visiting with her parents this weekend, Jacob will be out with friends or on a date, and I'm getting hungry. How about we drive over to Harry's, enjoy a rack of ribs, and just skip the formal dinner here tonight?"

Colleen had mentioned to Drew that she and Nancy Leigh had discussed the formal dinner-dance at lunch on Tuesday. Nancy Leigh told her she would not be attending, which surprised Colleen. Everyone knew Nancy Leigh was the first to sign up as a volunteer to coordinate the door prizes. Although Nancy Leigh had spent an enormous amount of time at the club throughout the year organizing the prizes, Colleen didn't tell her husband that the golf tournament wasn't Nancy Leigh's only interest.

"Would Nancy Leigh object to your going out with your good buddy? Or, have you guys planned to attend the formal dinner?"

* * * * * * *

Remembering the argument they had over breakfast, he wondered if she was home yet. Teddy's nature was never one of suspicion, but he was noticing particular changes in her behavior patterns. Nancy Leigh's sudden obsessions with showers were cause for concern, and her unusual sleep patterns and erratic mood swings had created problems in their marriage. As of late, her daily routine involved arriving home at 9:30 or 10:00 each night, and she headed straight to the shower. Any attempt to delay her shower resulted in a verbal exchange.

"No, I'll call her. I need to find a quiet place to check my messages, anyway. She should be home by now; I'll just be a minute."

Teddy went into the business office and closed the door. He called home, and the phone rang three times, but the call went to voicemail. Teddy slammed the receiver down and shouted, "Dammit, Nancy Leigh. Where are you?"

Teddy sat down and calmed himself for a few moments before he returned to the table.

Every attempt made by Teddy to spend time with his wife had been futile. Teddy had not expected Nancy Leigh to answer the phone when he called home. No surprise, his relationship with his wife further diminished when he went to work for the real estate firm. Nancy Leigh had frequently expressed her distaste for Teddy's temporary position, and the romance in their marriage had died. It disappointed him because their romantic rendezvous were his primary attraction to her back in college.

"Let's go, buddy," said Teddy.

As Teddy and Drew left the lounge and reached the entrance to the pro shop, they saw Nancy Leigh and the tennis pro talking inside. Nancy Leigh was wearing a tennis outfit, but it was apparent she was in the pro shop for reasons other than the tennis. The young man was showing Nancy Leigh the correct way to grip her tennis racket, and she was enjoying every minute of his attention and instruction. The man stepped behind Nancy Leigh and wrapped his arm around her body while holding on to the racket. Nancy Leigh was looking up at him with those big brown eyes as if she had never played the game. Nancy Leigh had grown up in a poor family, but the owner of the home where her mother worked as a domestic staff member, installed a tennis court on their property. Upon learning that their employee's daughter was the same age as their daughter, Nancy Leigh had access to tennis lessons at a young age. After her marriage to Teddy, their membership at the Club allowed her to play unlimited games of tennis each year. He had to hand it to the tennis pro, though, he was unaware of his surroundings, or either he didn't care.

"Can you believe this, Drew?" Although he was in a strained relationship with his wife, he never dreamed that Nancy Leigh would consider an affair. The guy was younger than her, and Teddy's ego was being trampled. The nausea he'd experienced after leaving his father's office had returned with a vengeance.

As he looked around the clubhouse, it appeared to be empty. The morning, which started out as a perfect autumn day, had turned into perhaps one of the worst days of his entire life. Teddy continued to watch as the tennis pro held his wife. When he kissed her neck, Teddy stood frozen, unable to move.

Nancy Leigh turned around, put her arms around his neck, and kissed the young man with a passion he recognized. Teddy would never forget that look of wanting in her eyes as she smiled at the man. Several minutes had passed when Nancy Leigh finally turned and saw her husband and his best friend watching her actions. He was sure this event marked the end of his marriage.

CHAPTER SIX

Once Teddy recovered from the initial shock, they left the building. As soon as he felt the autumn air, he realized the tennis pro was the guy Nancy Leigh was dancing with at the club during the spring break beach trip when they were in college, the night she had lied to him about staying in with the girls.

Without warning, he turned and hit the large, white column at the end of the portico.

"Let's get the hell out of here." He walked toward his car and then stopped and turned to face his friend.

"Drew, who was that guy in the Pro Shop?" asked Teddy. "I've seen him before."

"He's the local tennis pro. His name is Brad Carlisle."

"Can you drive to Harry's Place, Drew?"

"Yes, I can drive."

Teddy pitched the keys to Drew, and then decided against it. "No, Drew, you've had too much to drink today. Give me back the keys. I can drive; just give me a minute to cool off."

Teddy unlocked the car and Drew got in on the passenger's side and waited. As Teddy stood outside the car to catch his breath, he rubbed his injured right hand. Although, his marriage had already begun to implode, the sight of Brad Carlisle kissing his wife was maddening.

* * * * * * *

Drew had consumed just enough beer to relax, but the sight of Brad Carlisle and his best friend's wife together was sobering. The situation was awkward, but the pain he saw on his friend's face made his heart hurt. Turning away from Teddy, his posture slumped as his right hand carved through his hair, holding it back and then releasing it.

As Drew watched his friend get into the car, he considered the timing for Colleen and the girls to visit the in-laws could not have been more perfect, since Teddy could not go home and would need a place to stay the night. Colleen and Nancy Leigh played tennis together every week, and he wondered if Colleen knew about the affair.

"Listen, Buddy, we can just go over to the house and order a pizza or raid the refrigerator if you'd like. I've got a full bottle of Dewar's, a Christmas gift from a client last year that may help ease the pain of your injured hand."

"Thanks, man, but no scotch for me. I'll stick with beer. I need to keep a cool head and organize a plan of action. One thing for sure, it's to my advantage I have yet to open my practice, with a pending divorce on the horizon, right?"

"Whatever you say, man." However, Drew knew his friend and thought that by the end of the evening, Teddy Williams would drink from the scotch bottle.

Lost in their own thoughts, there was no urgency to speak during the drive home.

Later in the evening, while eating a slice of pizza, Teddy pointed out, "Man, you are one of the two true friends I have had in my life, and I appreciate you being with me today."

Trying to lighten the mood, Drew laughed. "Well, I didn't know you had any friends. Who in the hell is your other friend?"

Teddy smiled. "My grandfather Simpson. Anyway, thanks for being here for me."

"Well, I guess someone has to be your friend, right?" He chuckled.

Teddy found a bag of peas in the freezer to wrap around his hand while Drew opened the Dewar's bottle and considered how best to prod his friend to file for divorce. Dealing with delicate subjects was not his forte. As a criminal attorney, he could argue and win most debates, but tact was not his strong point.

"Teddy," began Drew, "You trust me, right?"

Teddy laughed, "Oh, here it comes."

"No, no, just listen a minute, will you!" Drew continued, "We've been friends a long time and you've just admitted that we are best friends, so I can be straightforward with you, right?"

Teddy pretended to listen as he stretched out on the sofa and repositioned the bag of peas on his hand.

"Now, Teddy, you may not like what I am about to say, but someone must say it. Since we are here at my house, drinking my Dewar's, then I will say it, anyway." Drew paused, waiting for Teddy to respond.

Teddy rolled his eyes as he got up from the sofa and walked over to the bookshelf where the scotch sat next to four crystal whiskey glasses. He poured himself a drink to divert his attention from the current line of conversation regarding Drew's unsolicited advice.

"You're right; I know what you're going to say, even before you speak. We're like an old married couple, Drew. We are pathetic!"

He turned around and headed back to his spot on the sofa. Not accustomed to drinking liquor, he was already feeling the effects when he lifted his left hand into the air.

"But, first, I'd like to tell you about someone I met today."

Drew raised an eyebrow, and he showed a sudden interest in his friend's comment. He was seldom outmaneuvered during a conversation.

Teddy noticed the surprised look on Drew's face, "You know Drew, you shouldn't drink so much because it causes your inhibitions to weaken... What? You didn't think I could steer the conversation away from you?"

Drew laughed and leaned back in his chair and listened.

"Remember, I told you I went out to the Hawkins farm to discuss the contract with Mr. and Mrs. Hawkins. It seems their granddaughter, Mary Katherine, has been handling their finances for some time now, and they wanted her to review the contract. My dad asked me to lunch on Wednesday to prepare for the meeting." Teddy paused as he realized he had finished a complete thought without being interrupted by his friend.

"The agreement was to meet with the Hawkins' and their granddaughter today at three o'clock. A convenient time, wouldn't you agree? She doesn't have a clue about men and their golf schedules." He glanced at his friend to make sure he was still awake.

Teddy walked over to the fireplace and sat his glass down on the mantle. "So, here I was, Drew, inconvenienced by this meeting with the little granddaughter," air quotation marks, "and I didn't care if they signed the contract or not. Forgive me, Drew, I know this project is important to you, but since we are honest with each other, I was a little ticked that my father arranged the meeting today, of all days."

The alcohol was causing Teddy to ramble.

"And, to make matters worse, I was fifteen minutes late, and it irritated old man Hawkins. As if he had anything better to do than sit on that front porch drinking that damned iced tea. Which may be the best damn tea I have ever tasted. Anyway, Mrs. Hawkins adores the old man, and it wouldn't surprise me if she served his damn tea on a dang silver platter."

Seizing the opportunity to speak, Drew jumped up from the sofa. "My good buddy Teddy! Now, that is what I wanted to discuss with you. A wife that brings freshly brewed iced tea to her husband."

"Oh, please sit down my friend; I'm not finished with this story," Teddy said with frustration as Drew returned to his oversized recliner.

"Teddy is there a point to this story, other than the damned iced tea, or are you just trying to avoid the inevitable?"

"So, now where was I?" rambled Teddy, the effects of the scotch clearly in his speech. "Then I saw this stunning woman, perhaps 28-30 years old. You know the type, tall and willowy."

Teddy stopped and looked at his friend. "Now you hear me, Drew, this little granddaughter is not so little. Hell, she's a few years younger than me. Do you know what happened Drew?" Teddy paused and shook his head, "Yes, I froze! The sight of this gorgeous woman with a mane of auburn hair, did something to me that no other woman has ever done. She penetrated something deep within my soul."

He took another sip of his drink. "Damn, that sounds like a girly description, doesn't it? Perhaps I read that someplace, but I have no other words to describe the feeling. We had not even spoken to each other, man. But the chemistry was there, it was like finding one's soul mate. I wanted to impress her by making a profound, intellectual comment, or show off my charming, irresistible side, but as fate would have it, I could not speak." Teddy stopped and took a deep breath, and saw his friend was trying to suppress laughter. "Can you imagine my embarrassment?"

Tears were flowing down Drew's cheeks from the laughter. "I would have paid to see your performance, Teddy. Or, perhaps, lack of performance! That story is hilarious, the handsome all-American doctor, from the wealthy, prominent family found himself without words." Wiping his eyes with the sleeve of his shirt, "Perhaps being intimidated by a woman is a unique concept to you." He paused as he shook his head in disbelief. "You know, I've never enjoyed much success with women. But, you, my friend, have that boyish charm, and it has always drawn women to you like moths to a light."

"Oh, shut up, Drew."

"Well, Teddy," lowering his voice an octave as he realized he had overreacted, "Penetrate is a big college word. I like that description. 'She penetrated something deep within my soul!' I should write that down and use it on Colleen. Can you imagine her response?"

Drew crammed the final bite of pizza in his mouth as he enjoyed a chuckle. Then, he grabbed a napkin and wiped the sauce from his mouth and the perspiration from his brow. "It sounds like the lady has a brain underneath that mane of auburn hair. Is she that gorgeous?" He asked as he walked over to the bookcase to freshen his drink. He wondered if Teddy had caught his over-zealous remarks.

Teddy smiled, drained his glass of the last of his drink, and flashed that playful, boyish grin.

"She is, without a doubt, the most beautiful woman I've ever laid eyes on! It wasn't just her extraordinary looks that caught my attention, she moved with such a lovely grace." He stopped and thought for a moment and then concluded. "That's it! It's all about grace."

"Well, well, young Theodore," Drew used his professional tone for effect, "As your attorney — I am your attorney, aren't I?"

"Yes."

"Just making sure I invoke the attorney-client privilege at this point. I suggest we draw up the divorce papers right now so you can get on with your life with this lovely lady who penetrated your soul!"

"Before we get to that, counselor, there is one small detail of which I should make you aware. As of this afternoon, I am no longer employed!" said Teddy.

"What, your dad fired you, or you quit?"

"I quit!"

That remark sobered Drew, and he could not believe the dreadful events of the day. He was glad he had the house to himself for a few days because this situation would take more than a bottle of Dewar's and a pizza to resolve.

It was after ten o'clock when the phone rang, and Drew jumped up to answer it. "Excuse me, Teddy, this is Colleen calling from her parents' house, just be a few minutes." As he grabbed the phone, he turned and added. "Help yourself to more of..." he looked at Teddy's glass and said, "that iced-tea, or whatever it is you're drinking there."

* * * * * * *

While Drew was in the kitchen talking to Colleen and the children, Teddy lay back on the sofa. He envied Drew for the relationship he had with his family. Drew and Colleen enjoyed a close bond and had made a beautiful family together. He could hear Drew laughing from something Colleen said on the other end of the line, and he wished he had the same rapport with Nancy Leigh. He closed his eyes as he elevated his throbbing hand, he needed a few peaceful moments alone. Never one to drink more than a beer or a glass of wine with dinner, the scotch flirted with the onset of a migraine. He thought about going out to the car for his headache medicine but lay still instead.

He still couldn't believe Nancy Leigh would allow herself to become involved in this kind of scandal. And, a scandal, it would be when the members of the club learned of her affair with the tennis pro. In fact, he wondered if members already knew about their romantic involvement.

He reached for his phone with intentions of calling his mother before one of her friends found out about Nancy Leigh's affair and felt the need to tell her. Living in a small town made it difficult to keep a secret quiet.

As the clock in the hallway struck eleven o'clock, Teddy placed his cell back on the table and wondered if Nancy Leigh had returned to their home, or if she spent the evening with Brad. Teddy wanted to go home himself. He considered confronting her about the affair, but he knew there was no need. Her erratic behavior over the past year now made sense, and his decision to delay opening his medical practice was the last straw for Nancy Leigh. Apparently, in college, she hung around the frat house in search of a rich med student. As he continued to lie on the couch, he rearranged the pillows under his head. Teddy closed his eyes again to prevent the tears from forming. However, hard as he tried, the tears of rejection and pain continued to surface. Teddy had suppressed the raw emotions after he attacked the large column at the club, and as grateful as he was to Drew for his hospitality, he must come to terms with his emotions soon, or else he would become enraged.

He sat up and pressed a pillow to his face and decided a shower might be the perfect place to shed his emotional tension.

Involved in a long conversation with his family, he knew Drew would not notice when he went into the guest bathroom and locked the door. He undressed, turned on the shower, and stepped in. The dam within his body broke, and the pent-up emotions exploded from knowing she had been seeing the guy since college. Lastly, he mourned for the wasted six years they had spent together as husband and wife.

Teddy knew their marriage wasn't a good fit. A mutual friend introduced Teddy and Nancy Leigh during their sophomore year in college, and it became apparent soon in their relationship that their families were from different socioeconomic levels. In the beginning, their relationship was fun and casual. He murmured, "And now we're headed for a divorce."

At the end of football season, during their junior year, Teddy decided he should go home for the weekend, and Nancy Leigh invited herself to tag along.

On Friday afternoon, Teddy announced, "I'm taking my dirty laundry, and going home for the weekend. I need a home-cooked meal and some downtime, and I also need a quiet place to put the finishing touches on this paper."

His roommate laughed and said, "Well, perhaps you should think again."

"What do you mean? You know it'll be quieter at home."

"Look outside. It seems like your girlfriend has other plans."

Nancy Leigh was standing outside his fraternity house with her suitcase in hand; ready to make the forty-minute drive to Teddy's hometown.

Teddy walked outside to leave. "Hi Nancy Leigh, what are you doing here? I'm leaving in a few minutes to go home for the weekend."

"Well, I am going with you! It's time I see where you grew up. And, besides, this would be a good time to meet your parents."

What could he say? He wasn't sure how to handle the situation without upsetting her. "Listen, Nancy Leigh, my mother follows the southern rules of etiquette. She requires advance notice regarding weekend guests." But when Nancy Leigh began to rub his chest and kiss his neck, he realized the information would be foreign to someone unschooled in etiquette and manners.

However, he couldn't take the chance of upsetting her, because he couldn't stand to think about being cut off from her. So, off they went to Abington. It was during that weekend, on Saturday night after a dinner at the Club, that Nancy Leigh had slipped into his bedroom and pledged her undying love to him.

A few weeks later, when Teddy was home for Thanksgiving break, Mr. Williams called him into his study for a private conversation. "Teddy, your mother and I think you should not tie yourself down at this stage in your education. While the young lady that visited us a few weeks ago was lovely and we enjoyed her visit, perhaps you should enjoy the opportunities that college life affords you regarding other women you might meet."

* * * * * * * *

Once Drew finished his conversation with Colleen and the girls, he noticed that Teddy had left the family room. So, he gathered up the empty pizza box along with the remaining trash from the kitchen and took the cordless phone out to the garage as he placed a call to Brad Carlisle. "Hey man, it's Drew. Listen, the plan worked like a charm."

CHAPTER SEVEN

M ary Katherine awakened to the smell of coffee brewing. Sunday mornings at the Hawkins house were peaceful, without the noise from the machinery typical of farm life. Katie allowed herself the privilege of lying in bed a few extra minutes to enjoy the sounds of nature from outside her bedroom window.

She remembered having slept in the same room since the night of her parents' tragic accident twenty-five years earlier. Her thoughts settled on her home. Selling the farm bothered her much more than she cared to admit.

A knock at her bedroom door interrupted her reflections.

"Come in," she said.

"Good morning, sweetheart, I brought you a cup of hot coffee to enjoy in bed."

With an easygoing manner as she looked up at her grandmother and said, "You are such an angel, thank you."

Nora placed the coffee on the bedside table and kissed her granddaughter on the forehead.

"Give me fifteen minutes, and I'll join you on the front porch."

"No rush. Take your time and enjoy your coffee, dear. I need to wake your grandfather, anyway."

She sipped her coffee as she prepared for a quick shower. In a few minutes, she was sitting on the front porch wearing a pair of old jeans, and a faded UGA T-shirt with her hair pulled up high in a ponytail. She was looking forward to reading the morning paper while breathing the crisp autumn air and enjoying the long-awaited female companionship with her grandmother.

Nora returned to the front porch carrying a tray of homemade sausage and biscuits and a plate of fresh fruit. "What is this? No biscuits and gravy this morning." She kidded her grandmother as she took a dish from the tray.

Her grandmother smiled and said, "Please don't let your grandfather hear you say that young lady! Help yourself, but save a few for Tom, he had a restless night and is probably hungry this morning."

* * * * * * * *

Tom was awake when Nora came into his bedroom. He had awakened in the middle of the night, and could not find restful sleep. And, as usual, his thoughts returned to that pivotal day 40 years ago that altered his son's life.

It was a warm summer morning, and the crops had stopped producing because of the abundance of rain throughout the year. Only a few pods of okra remained on the stalks, and the last of the summer tomatoes hung on the vines. Although the humidity was high, the timing was perfect for running over the garden with the tractor to further cultivate the soil with the remnants from the existing plants. The various vegetables had produced a sweet bounty that summer and the long hours working in the garden were over.

Their middle son, Sammy, had turned 15 years old that year and had been driving the farm truck for several years when he showed an interest in operating the tractor. Mr. Hawkins wasn't sure Sammy's attention to detail warranted the privilege, because he was not as mature as the other children. But, Sammy was relentless in his quest to try.

"Dad, please let me drive the tractor. This is an easy chore. Please!"

More in desperation, Mr. Hawkins agreed, "Okay. Just drive the tractor in a straight line and cut the dead vines into the ground. No horseplay. Respect the power of the tractor and the tractor will show you respect in return."

Confident with Sammy's performance, Mr. Hawkins waved to Sammy and yelled, "I'm going to the house for lunch. When you finish this row, come on up and join me, son."

He turned and walked toward the house, and as he entered the back door, Nora yelled, "Tom, is that you, dear?" He chuckled to himself as he removed his work shoes and went over to the sink to wash his hands. As he turned off the water, he heard a loud noise and a shrill scream like someone in distress. He ran to the back door and saw the tractor had turned over and it appeared his son's body was trapped underneath. Without understanding what had happened, he grabbed his work shoes as he yelled to Nora.

"Call an ambulance! Hurry!" Tom then flew from the house with the speed of desperation that one finds when his child is in crisis.

CHAPTER EIGHT

Nora refilled Mary Katherine's coffee cup and poured a fresh cup for herself. "Tom and I want to give each of the boys fifteen acres of land, and we would like you to find someone to handle the legal work if you have time."

"Why is Papa negotiating with Mr. Williams if he plans to give the land to the boys now?"

Tom appeared at the door. "Because I'm old and contrary as hell, that's why!" Nora and Mary Katherine laughed at Tom's honest assessment of himself.

Nora swatted playfully at her husband. "That's the truth, old man. Now sit down, and I'll get you some coffee," she replied.

Tom walked over and touched his granddaughter's cheek with the back of his hand. "Honey, I'm an old man, and I will not sell my land. I plan to give this farm to my boys, and we want you to have the house along with the last of the acreage. The house would have been your mama's part, anyway. She loved this place."

He paused as he touched his wife's arm, "Thank you, hon," he smiled as he accepted his coffee from her.

"I don't want to burden your grandmother with the legal aspects of dividing the farm after I am gone, Mary Katherine. So, do you know any lawyers in Atlanta that could divide our property and prepare new deeds without bringing attention to the matter?"

"Yes," Mary Katherine said as she continued to sip her coffee, "I can handle it for you when the time is right, but let's wait awhile and give this situation more thought. We must think of the tax consequences for everyone involved."

"The tax consequences, hell. I'm not worried about the tax consequences. The advantage for me is that I won't have to pay any more property taxes," Tom then smiled as he placed his cup back on the saucer and pointed his finger in her direction, "but you will!"

"So this is a scheme to avoid paying your taxes in December? We should have known you had an ulterior motive behind this meeting of yours. Tell me, please, what will you complain about if you don't have property taxes to pay?" Mary Katherine said, as she laughed and winked at her grandmother.

"Haven't you noticed, my dear, I've quit complaining so much! Remember when I spent all evening complaining about a part not coming in on time, or a tractor that wasn't working, or when the hay needed cutting. Hell, I bitched about everything until I retired. One day the strangest thing happened, I realized while sitting out here on this porch that the things I enjoyed most in life were the things I had always bitched about." He smiled as he continued, "I realize that I'm not too useful at this age, but my mind still works. So, we will resolve this problem before we get too old and feeble to think straight." He looked over at his wife and winked.

A serious tone returned to his voice as he continued, "Where is Sammy?"

"He's checking on the livestock," answered Nora.

"I'd rather him wait for me to go with him."

"Well, he wants to earn his keep. So, there…"

Tom said, "Although we have written our wills to allow for Sammy's care after we die, my concern is any sudden change to his living conditions may cause a decline in his health." Every decision Tom and Nora discussed since Sammy's accident involved how the outcome might affect his health.

"If the boys hold separate deeds to this property and you hold the deed to the house along with the remaining acreage, then Mama and I can't sell it, right?"

"That is correct."

"We don't care if y'all sell the farm when we die, but we want to live out the rest of our lives on this farm. Those land developers will get this place at some point, but not while we are living."

Mary Katherine understood her grandparents' wishes, but why had they met with the developers, since they were not ready to sell their property. This industrial park had been a topic of discussion for well over a year. The recent articles which appeared in the local newspaper reported they had approved Phase One, which involved the purchase of the surrounding properties. The latest article named Mr. Hawkins and his farm as the last land acquisition.

"Grandfather, I understand your desire to live out your lives here, and I am in total agreement. However, there are many ways to approach this land sell. I'm certain none of the boys would stand in the sale's way, they would be fine if you sold the land today. Unlike Sammy, Stephen and Roger have settled in their own communities, and are not looking to gain from the sale. Perhaps we should first discuss the changes to your will with an attorney. My first concern, the same as yours, would be for Sammy's welfare and If I am able, I will make a home for Sammy."

Wondering if she should continue the discussion, or let it drop, she moved forward. "However, there are options that can secure your position without leaving the farm. I'm confused about why Teddy Williams did not approach the subject yesterday, but he somehow seemed distracted. Did you guys notice his distraction?"

When neither of her grandparents responded, she continued, "I would have thought Mr. Williams would have given Teddy some latitude regarding a contingency plan if you refused to sign the contract as written. Have you read their contract yet, Papa?

"No, I haven't seen a contract. Theo and I have met several times, but he has never offered a written contract. I'm not sure Teddy brought one yesterday, did you see one?"

"Yes, I believe he did. He removed the manila file from his briefcase when he sat down in the kitchen. But, he never presented it to you."

"Mary Katherine, what do you mean when you said, we could secure our position with the industrial park without leaving the farm until after we die?" Asked Mr. Hawkins.

"There are options to exercise if you are serious about selling your farm at the time of your death."

"Would an option require you to sell even if you and the boys keep the farm after our death?"

"No, sir. If we sold, the purpose of an option would require us to offer Mr. Williams and his partners a chance to purchase the property before listing with an agent. Sometimes, an option includes a sum of money to hold the property, like an exchange of earnest money when buying a house."

Mary Katherine looked up at her grandmother, who was pouring coffee into her cup. "Thank you. This is my last cup."

"I like the idea of an option," said her grandfather. "You know, we are too close to Atlanta for this property to remain rural for much longer."

"An option," continued Mary Katherine, "is a smart instrument for both sides. But, the developers are up against roadblocks from taxpayers, architects, zoning requirements, and perhaps the most difficult component is the weather. The process can take time to complete."

"I understand about developing the property, honey. Remember, I served as a county commissioner for over twenty years." Tom then looked over at Nora and said, "What do you think, Nora? Would you prefer dividing the property now as we discussed earlier?"

Nora considered the question. "We should contact Stephen and Roger and speak with Sammy, too. As Mary Katherine said, they will honor our decision. But, this property is part of their inheritance, and we should consider their thoughts before making a decision."

"Those are valid points, Nana. The last thing you want is to sign a contract and then ask for their opinion. That could cause ill feelings. But, remember, the option will allow you to live out your lives here and then the developers can revisit purchasing the property after you're gone."

CHAPTER NINE

Following a late night of drinking and eating pizza, Drew and Teddy awoke to an empty house and decided to go to the club for an early lunch and a game of golf. Drew's family planned to return home in the late afternoon, so the guys had most of the day to hang out. But first, Teddy needed to go over to his house to pick up his golf clubs and take a quick shower.

It wouldn't have surprised him if the tennis pro had spent the night with Nancy Leigh. The thought filled him with equal parts apprehension and anger, but when he rounded the curve and approached his house, there was only one car in the driveway.

As Teddy entered through the backdoor, Nancy Leigh was coming out of the bathroom with a towel wrapped around her hair wearing only a terrycloth robe. She looked stunned when she saw him.

"What are you doing here? I wasn't expecting you to come back," she said.

"I didn't expect you to be here either." He couldn't help but notice her body was still damp from the lotion she religiously applied after each shower. But, just the sight of her now conjured up several layers of disgust. "I've come home to take a quick shower, change clothes, and pick up my golf clubs." Teddy walked toward the bathroom.

Nancy Leigh raised her voice. "You can't go in there!" She pointed to the bathroom door.

"Of course, I can." He placed his hand on the doorknob but hesitated when he heard a sound coming from inside. *So, the tennis pro had spent the night, after all*, he thought. Not wanting to cause a scene, Teddy sighed and turned and went into the bedroom.

Nancy Leigh followed him. "Listen, Teddy, you need to leave. You can't be here."

He hesitated as he made a mental note of things he would need for the day. Although he really didn't want to get into an altercation with his wife's lover, he felt a sudden urge to make him nervous by hanging around longer than necessary. "I'll leave when I'm damn good and ready! The last time I checked, this house belonged to my parents, and I will stay here until I'm done!"

Teddy searched for his golf shorts and went over to his closet and found a shirt and his golf shoes. He pulled the golf clubs from the closet and placed them in the doorway to prevent anyone from coming into the bedroom.

"I have a question."

"What is it?" Nancy Leigh replied as she fidgeted with a headband she had picked up from the dresser. Her eyes shifted back and forth from Teddy to the bedroom door, expecting Brad to come out of the bathroom at any moment.

"Is this tennis pro the same guy you saw in college? You know the guy you were with at the bar on spring break?"

"Who told you that lie?" She said effortlessly as she continued to fidget with the headband.

Of course, he could see right through her, and he knew she was lying. There it was… she chewed away at the corner of her lip, which she always did when she lied. He wanted to laugh, but instead, he gave her an icy stare and with a deliberate tone in his voice said, "Remember the time during spring break when you told me your girlfriends were staying in the condo for a movie marathon? A pizza and beer night, I believe is how you spun it. Isn't that the same guy in the pro shop you were making out with yesterday?"

"I don't know what you are talking about, Teddy."

"Of course, you do. Even though I could tell you were lying about staying in with the girls, I encouraged you to go with your friends because I was going out with the guys."

"Well, since you remember this so well, please tell me what happened that night, because this story is ridiculous?"

Teddy sat down on the side of the bed and looked through the nightstand drawer and said loud enough to be heard in the next room, "That night, my buddies and I went down to the boardwalk until the sun went down, and then we walked across the street to that bar where you and I went early in the week. It was dark inside the bar with large colored lights spotlighting the band. I remember the band was nearing the end of a set, the lead singer was doing his best with 'Brown-Eyed Girl' by Van Morrison. We found a table at the back, and while we placed our orders, Tom pointed to a couple across the room, and mouthed, what the heck? Even though it was dark inside, I got a good look at your friend. And, I'm sure it was the tennis pro at the club."

"Well, how did you know it was me? It could have been any college girl."

"Oh, no. It was you. You wore that sundress you bought for the Jimmy Buffett concert the previous summer."

"This is a great story, Teddy. What happened then? Did you knock the hell out of the guy, or did you pick me up and storm out of the bar?"

"No. No... you know I don't like confrontations; I looked over at Tom and said thanks. Then I dropped a few bills on the table to cover the cost of the beer and left the bar without being noticed by you or your fellow."

Nancy Leigh went pale, and her lips began to quiver. "And, you never said a word to me about that night. . . You didn't even care that I was with another guy."

Teddy saw the hurt in her eyes and said, "Nope, and I don't like being lied to, either!"

"Teddy, I want a divorce. I don't love you anymore."

He turned and stared at her, "You think! I doubt you ever loved me, Nancy Leigh. You went to college to find a med student to latch onto, didn't you? That's it, isn't it? You never loved me; you just wanted to marry well!" The last remark was said louder than he had intended.

"What's the use of having this discussion? Let's just split everything and go our separate ways, okay?"

Teddy whirled around and yelled, "Split what, Nancy Leigh! You're driving a car that's perhaps worth five thousand dollars. We have twelve thousand dollars in our bank account. That's the money I saved from the funds my parents gave us to live on when I was in school. You haven't worked a day since we got married, and you have contributed nothing to my education, or to our lifestyle. Hell, you wouldn't even work to help buy groceries. How much do you expect to get from me?"

Teddy leaned over to pick up a book that had fallen from the closet shelf. The name of the book was *A Dance with the Devil* by Barbara Bentley. He noticed that it was based on a true story about being married to a psychopath. When he read the title, he said, "And, which one are you Nancy Leigh, the dancer or the devil?" Then, he pitched the book to her and laughed.

"How about that new Mercedes you've been driving since you went to work for your dad?"

"Are you serious? That's a lease vehicle, paid for by my Dad's company! We don't own it." Teddy looked at the nightstand next to the bed and asked, "Where is my phone charger? It was on the nightstand yesterday morning."

"I think it's in the bathroom."

"Well, go in there and get it for me, will ya?"

When she came back out with the charger, she threw it at him. Teddy reached for a tote bag from the top of his closet and crammed his clothes and charger in it, and then picked up his golf clubs and stormed out of the house.

Nancy Leigh followed him to the car. "Your parents never liked me, Teddy."

"Good, lord! If I had a dollar for every time you have said that during our marriage, we would be rich," he paused. "Let me ask you something. If they didn't like you, why did they pay for our wedding and our living expenses while I was in medical school? Could it be that you are the one who doesn't like my parents?"

"I want to ask you a question."

He asked, "What is it?"

"If you knew I was seeing someone else in college, why did you keep dating me? Did you not care?"

He opened his car trunk and threw in his stuff, he turned back to face Nancy Leigh, "It was because of your pretty face and sexy little body. Because that was all you had to offer. For the first time in my life, I found myself addicted to something that I couldn't walk away from."

Teddy noticed her eyes moistened with tears.

He softened when he realized that maybe he had gone too far in his accusations. "I'll give you a divorce, Nancy Leigh and I'll split the twelve thousand dollars with you. Perhaps both of us married for reasons that were less than honorable, so this situation should be of no surprise."

"Oh, no Teddy Williams, I'm getting more than that out of you!"

"We'll see about that."

"You haven't heard the last of me, mister!"

* * * * * * *

As Teddy drove away, Nancy Leigh stormed into the house and went straight to the kitchen and poured a glass of water.

Brad came out of the bathroom with a towel around his waist and found Nancy Leigh in the kitchen, "Is the coast clear?"

"Yeah, he's gone," she said as she wiped the tears from her eyes.

"Well, that was interesting." He dried his hair with a kitchen towel he pulled from a drawer, and grinned.

"He acts like we only have that junky car I'm driving and twelve thousand dollars. Can you believe it? Now you see what I've been talking about. He's a jerk."

"It's hard to believe you guys only have twelve thousand dollars between you. For the record, I have more money than that, and I don't have a medical degree."

"Well, I don't believe it for one minute. His family's got boat-loads of money." she said.

"I just knew he would come into the bathroom. Can't you just imagine the headlines in the local paper, 'Naked man found dead in the shower'? What a story for the gossip columnists," Brad chuckled.

Nancy Leigh walked over to Brad and gently massaged his chest. "I'm so glad we can be together now. We need to eliminate his entire family. I'm ready to get rid of them."

Brad stepped back from her reach and looked at her with furrowed eyebrows.

"What are you saying, Nancy Leigh?"

She nestled up to him and kissed his neck. "I'm just ready to collect our money and get away from these people."

CHAPTER TEN

The sounds of children's laughter awakened Teddy, and the noise from the local radio station blasting through Jacob's bathroom walls was deafening. He had stayed at Drew's house for two nights. The sound of the telephone and a sudden bang at the door blasted him out of his dazed state.

"Hey, Teddy, you awake?" Drew asked as he knocked on the bedroom door.

"Do you think anyone could sleep through this damn noise?"

"Listen, man, Nancy Leigh's on the phone, and she wants to talk to you. She left you several messages last night," Drew laughed, as he heard the loud noise coming from his son's room down the hall.

As Teddy rubbed the sleep from his eyes. "Okay, Drew, thanks. Can I take the call in your study?"

"Sure, make yourself at home and lock the door behind you. This crowd has no regard for privacy."

Teddy slipped into his shirt and slacks and found his shoes in the room's corner behind the closet door. As he started down the hall to his friend's study, hoping the noise level at the east end of the house would be more bearable, he ran his fingers through his hair in a nervous gesture. Teddy found the light switch and locked the door behind him. Thankful for the privacy the room provided, he sat down at Drew's desk and cleared his throat before picking up the telephone.

"Hello."

Nancy Leigh hesitated a second before she spoke as she waited for Drew to hang up the phone from the kitchen.

"Teddy, this is Nancy Leigh. Your mother has tried to get in touch with you, and I thought you might have stayed over there. Claire seemed upset last night when she called. I've just hung up from talking with her again this morning, and she needs to talk with you. Perhaps you should charge your phone sometime soon."

Teddy realized how wrong he had been in not contacting his mother on Saturday. He should have told her he was staying over at Drew's house.

"I appreciate the call, what seems to be wrong? Did she give any explanation?"

"She said she had taken your father to the hospital and wanted to let you know, but her voice kept breaking, and I could tell she had been crying. You should check on them before going to the office. And, Teddy?"

"Yes."

"I'm sorry. I'm sorry for everything!"

Teddy could hear his wife's sniffles on the phone. Any other time, Nancy Leigh's tears may have touched a tender spot within him, but he didn't dignify her with a response. However, as he sat in his friend's study, his thoughts returned to the unpleasant discussion between him and his father, and the guilt slowly returned.

"Thanks for letting me know, Nancy Leigh." He hung up the phone before she could say any more.

Teddy sprinted back to the bedroom, hurried through the shower, and put on the same clothes he had worn to play golf. Ready to face his mother, he ran downstairs, thanked Drew and Colleen for their hospitality, and gave them the news of his father's hospitalization. As he was walking out the door, Colleen handed him a cup of coffee and a bagel to eat on the way to the hospital.

"Teddy, we love you, and you are welcome to stay here for awhile if you don't mind being surrounded by children and noise."

"Thanks, Colleen, I've stayed long enough already, but I'll keep it in mind, just in case."

"I realize this isn't the best time for you, but I'm closer to Nancy Leigh than anyone. Aren't you concerned about her behavior as of late? Based on her recent sleep habits and mood swings, it appears she is suffering from depression."

He didn't respond but removed his keys from his pocket.

"Teddy, I realize I am not a medical doctor like you, but I think she needs an evaluation by a psychologist to determine if she has developed a chemical imbalance."

"I appreciate your diagnosis, Colleen, but a chemical imbalance doesn't excuse the affair."

"Fair enough. But, I should probably tell you that the girls on the tennis team are talking," Colleen said.

Teddy shot a sideways glance at Drew and said, "Isn't that what girls do?"

"Sometimes, yes. But, I overheard one of the girls saying that the only thing worse than a poor girl marrying a well-educated, prominent doctor from old money, is a beautiful psychopath from no money."

He smiled as he leaned down to kiss Colleen on the forehead and he turned to hug Drew. "Thanks for everything, guys. I appreciate you putting up with me this weekend. Now I need to get to the hospital and check on my mom and dad."

The Monday morning traffic was heavy as everyone was in a rush to get to their respective destinations. The wind from the night before had blown leaves onto the paved streets. Still wet from the morning rainfall, they papered the streets with an array of varied colors. As he reached the hospital, he found the parking deck was already full of vehicles.

As Teddy circled the parking deck looking for a place to park, he thought about Colleen's remark regarding Nancy Leigh's need for a psychological evaluation.

He parked his car and sprinted to the entrance of the medical center. When reaching The Medical Center Cardiac Care Unit, Teddy spotted his mother, who looked as if she had been awake all night.

"Mother, are you all right?"

"Oh, Teddy, thank God you are here!" Mrs. Williams hugged him.

"Dr. Martin needs to talk with us as soon as he examines your father; he asked me to wait out here. We're going down to the cafeteria to discuss Theo's condition over a cup of coffee."

She dabbed her eyes with a fresh Kleenex. "I must caution you, son, it doesn't look good."

Teddy, realizing the gravity of her remark, bit his bottom lip and pinched the area between his eyes with his forefinger and thumb.

Claire reached for her son's hand. "Your daddy loves you, son."

He attempted a partial smile because he knew his mother expected him to be strong. "I know he does, Mom. And I love him. We just have an unusual way of showing it."

He shifted in his chair, "What happened to Dad last night? What was he doing when he became ill?" Inhaling as his chest expanded from the increased air in his lungs.

"Sit down, son, and rest a minute. You are breathing as if you ran from Drew's house this morning." Teddy obeyed his mother and sat down, taking a cleansing breath.

"He didn't feel well all weekend. It was after seven o'clock when he came home from the office on Saturday evening; I was getting worried about him. When he got out of the car, his face was pale and the color of ashes. He looked exhausted, and I noticed that he didn't come straight into the house when he parked in the driveway. He paused several times to catch his breath. I didn't let him know I had watched him because you know how that would have bothered him. I suggested we cancel our dinner with Andrew and Daisy. He never argued with me and said to give them his regards."

"Did he rest okay Saturday night?"

"Yes, he slept well Saturday night, but he was sluggish yesterday morning, so we sat around and read the morning papers until around 11:30. We went over to the club for lunch and spent the afternoon watching football and talking, much like we did during the early days of our marriage," She smiled at the thought of the memory.

"Then, around eight o'clock last night, he complained of chest pains. Unlike the symptoms of his first heart attack in 2010, he couldn't get his breath well, and the pain kept getting worse. He took the nitroglycerine pills, and we thought the pains would subside after a few moments, but the pain continued. Once Dr. Jackson confirmed that he had a mild heart attack, they admitted him to the cardiac care unit, and we've been here ever since. The nurses have been nice and helpful, dear, and they let me check on him every few hours so I could keep up with his condition throughout the night. It has been a touch and go situation. I'm not sure if he has suffered another attack since last night, but they called the cardiologist about six o'clock this morning, and then Dr. Jackson arrived around seven. We should have more information soon."

Teddy hesitated before asking his mother the inevitable question, "Was Dad upset about anything recently that could have brought this on?"

"No, not that I know of, son. Your father didn't feel well last week. Dr. Jackson has been encouraging him to slow down, so maybe this will convince him it's time to retire."

Claire looked at Teddy with a look of concern on her face.

"Theo mentioned a year ago that a guy contacted him about buying the real estate firm. I wish your father would reconsider and sell the business." Teddy was not aware that a potential buyer had approached his father; and hoped he was not holding on to the business for his sake.

"Teddy, please help me remember to tell Dr. Martin about your father's slurred speech. It happened Saturday morning again while we were eating breakfast. We were talking about the fall golf tournament at the club, and I asked him if you were playing in the tournament this year. When he responded to my question, his speech was so slurred I couldn't understand him. I also noticed that his mouth drooped. Then, just as fast as it happened, it cleared up. We finished our discussion of the tournament, and he was back to normal."

Claire squeezed Teddy's arm as her breathing increased, "Son, I had my hand on the phone ready to call 911. I thought he was having a stroke sitting right there at our breakfast table."

Teddy placed his arm around his mother and pulled her to him to comfort her. "Mom, it's okay to cry, you've had a hell of a night in this dreadful place, but Dad will be fine. He's a tough old bird, and he'll fight like hell to get better. He's got a lot to live for, and he's got that industrial park to complete. I'm so sorry I wasn't here for you last night, but I'm here now. We will get through this together."

In the hospital waiting room, Teddy watched the clock which hung on the wall with attention to every movement made by the second hand on the large white face. The exercise was maddening!

"I love you, big guy. What would I ever do without you?" Claire reached up and patted her son's cheek.

The longer he looked at the wall clock, the further down the chair he slid until his neck rested on the back of the hospital chair. The tic-tock of the clock drowned out the sounds coming into the emergency room, which was two floors under the waiting room they occupied. And, with each movement of the second hand, the shallower his breathing became.

Claire and Teddy sat in silence, waiting for the doctors to complete their examination.

"Are you all right, son?"

"I'm fine, Mom, I'm just having personal problems. But, I'm sure everything will work out. I should have been here with you last night." He held his fist under his nose and fought back the tears.

"Don't worry about it, son, you are here now." She smiled at him and continued to chatter as she often did when she was nervous.

"Mom, Nancy Leigh and I have separated."

"Yes," she rubbed his forearm. "Nancy Leigh told me this morning that you had not been home in two nights. I'm certain she is hurting, too."

"Yeah, I'm sure." Trying to keep the sarcasm from his voice. "Listen, I'm going for some air. Do you want a cup of coffee or a Diet Coke from downstairs?"

"Oh, dear, here's Dr. Martin and Dr. Jackson!" She stood up to meet them.

"Good morning, Claire, how are you?" Dr. Jackson hugged her before making the introductions. "Dr. Martin, this is Teddy Williams. Teddy, Dr. Martin is the cardiologist we called in when we discovered Theo had a heart attack." They shook hands, and with a cracked voice, Teddy asked the condition of his father.

"Claire and I were going down to the cafeteria for coffee, would you guys like to join us? We can talk better down there."

Dr. Martin chose a table away from the other customers, and began the conversation, "Teddy, your father experienced a heart attack last night. We've monitored his heart throughout the night, but his heartbeat has been erratic and is not as strong as we would hope. We ordered the routine blood work and diagnostic testing to get a better feel for his condition, and the test results confirmed our suspicions of a heart attack. What concerns us now is the possibility he may have also suffered a stroke. There seems to be paralysis on his left side that did not exist last night. We have seen this happen before with other patients in the same condition, where the paralysis will go away in a few days. In others, it remains. This is a wait-and-see situation regarding the paralysis. We would like to run a few more tests to determine if there are blockages in areas the previous tests did not pick up. We've ordered an MRI and cerebral angiography to help us better evaluate brain activity. And, we have also ordered a carotid ultrasound to check the veins in his neck."

He looked at Claire and continued, "Claire, have you noticed any unusual behavior, such as different sleep patterns, excessive indigestion, swelling in the extremities, loss of appetite, dizziness, or anything out of the ordinary that might help us better understand his condition?"

Claire explained to the doctors about the slurred speech and the other changes she had noticed in Theo over the last few weeks.

Dr. Martin continued, "Well, Claire, if you don't object, we will start extensive testing this morning?"

"No, no, I don't..." She said as she cried. Teddy intervened, realizing his mother was too emotional to talk.

"Dr. Martin, would it be possible for Mom and me to check on my father before we run home and clean up? We will return in a few hours, but I'm sure Mom will feel better once she gets a shower and a hot meal." Reaching into his pocket, he pulled out his wallet and found a business card. "I wrote Mom's phone number down for you. Please call us if there are any changes."

"Go on up and visit with your dad a few minutes; however, I must caution you against encouraging him to talk just now, Teddy. We're not sure if he knows of the paralysis," explained Dr. Martin.

"Claire, try to rest today if you can. Waiting in a hospital can be exhausting. These tests will take most of the day to complete since we will fit him in between patients already scheduled for testing. You understand Theo may be here for some time."

"Thank you, Dr. Martin," said Teddy. "After we check on my dad, we'll be leaving for a few hours. Please ask the nurse to call us if there is any change in his condition."

Although Teddy was familiar with sick patients because of the years he spent at the hospital during his residency and fellowship, no amount of training could prepare him for what he saw as he looked at his vulnerable father lying in the hospital bed.

When Teddy opened the door of the unit, he could see straight into his father's area. "Oh, my God," is all he could say as he reached for his mother's hand. As they moved closer to the bed, Teddy fought back the tears from the sight of his dad lying under the bright, fluorescent lights which emphasized the grayish color of his skin.

Claire said. "He wouldn't appreciate being seen in that hospital gown."

"You're right. But, it's necessary to allow the nurses to attend to his needs with greater ease."

Claire clung to her son's arm as they reached the side of his bed, both trying to avoid looking at the saliva running from the left side of his mouth.

Teddy reached for his father's hand and said, "Dad, Mom, and I are here, okay?" He felt no response from his father as he spoke.

As if Mr. Williams sensed their presence in the room, his eyes fluttered for a brief second. After a few moments, a nurse appeared in the doorway and asked them to step outside while they worked with the patient.

"Dad, these nurses are kicking us out of your room. Mom and I are going over to the house so she can take a shower, but we'll be back shortly. You hang in there, and do what these ladies tell you, okay?"

It saddened Teddy that he had not tried to be closer to his father. But, Mr. Williams was a complicated man who used his passive-aggressive personality as a manipulative tool.

His dad became agitated as he struggled to speak, and Teddy bent to hear what he was saying. All he could make out was the word "park." Teddy looked into his father's moist eyes, and it grabbed at his heartstrings. Teddy had seen patients in this condition too many times during his years of training, but he was gaining a different perspective now that his own dad was the patient.

"Dad, I promise to handle the industrial park project until you can get back to work. But, please don't take too long. You know, Dr. Gilbert is retiring, and the children in this town will need another doctor soon." He winked at his dad and gave him a reassuring smile. He removed the tears from his father's face, and then he turned away from his father's bed as he wiped tears from his own eyes.

* * * * * * * *

Claire leaned over and kissed her husband. "I love you, Theo," She whispered in his ear while smoothing his gray hair. Suppressing her tears, Claire refused to let her husband of 40 years hear the sadness in her voice. Then she turned and walked with Teddy out of the room.

Claire and Teddy were each lost in their thoughts as they drove the short distance to the Williams' home. Their friends referred to her as a sweet lady, and she was, but the real Claire Williams had an inner strength that enabled her to survive these painful times. Claire loved her husband, the father of her children. It wasn't a worshipful love or even submissiveness that some women her age felt for their husbands. She had realized early on that she and Theo were not compatible in the real sense of the word. They led separate lives but lived under the same roof, and their conversation revolved around the children's financial needs. He had never included her in business or financial decisions, but he had provided her with a good life.

It was when her children came along that she found the fulfillment she was missing in her marriage. Teddy, her firstborn, was a sweet and happy baby, and Claire spent most of her time in the nursery with her son. When Teddy was three years old, she discovered she was pregnant again; she was ecstatic. The second pregnancy brought about mornings of nausea that didn't happen with Teddy, but it diminished by the second trimester. She gave birth to a precious baby boy named Robert Theodore Williams. Claire was unaware of her third pregnancy until the night before Christmas Eve when she became ill. By the time the blood work revealed her pregnancy, the doctor had put her on bed rest and prescribed strong medications to fight the flu-like symptoms. Her temperature rose to 104 degrees before the medicine had worked. Otherwise, she had a healthy pregnancy and later gave birth to a beautiful baby girl. And, although their daughter, Elizabeth SanClaire, named after her family, was born with mental challenges which included hyperactive behavior, disobedience, temper tantrums and aggression, Claire's life was then complete.

Theo and Claire seldom discussed their problems, and when together with friends, they appeared as the happiest of couples. Theo's strength lay in his ability to provide for his family. He was a generous man and met their every need, but his generosity did not make up for his lack of fathering skills. He did not take the time to appreciate the differences in his children, and this lack of understanding had created an almost unbearable cost to his family. But, now she should not reflect on the tragic day that took their two younger children from their lives. As Theo was fighting for his life, she realized the need to maintain a clear head.

CHAPTER ELEVEN

T eddy sat at the breakfast table and sipped on a glass of ice water and glanced through the morning papers while his mother was upstairs resting. The sound of a car door caught his attention, and he looked outside the bay window. Nancy Leigh was walking toward the back door with several hangers of clothes folded over her arm.

He took several deep breaths, trying to calm himself as he walked to the back door and opened it. In a cold tone, he said, "Nancy Leigh, what are you doing here?"

"I thought you might need a fresh change of clothes. When you came by yesterday, I noticed you didn't take much with you."

"Thanks for calling me this morning. My mother was at the hospital last night by herself." He paused and looked back toward the kitchen. "I plan to stay here while my dad is recovering in the hospital."

Nancy Leigh gently rubbed his arm and said, "Teddy... is your dad going to be okay?"

"I'm sure he'll be fine, although he has suffered a heart attack and a stroke." Teddy raised his arm over the door frame and continued, "he has paralysis on his left side, but we are hoping the condition is only temporary."

Claire yelled from upstairs. "Teddy, are you talking to someone at the hospital?"

"No, I'm talking with Nancy Leigh. She brought over some of my clothes!"

"Okay, I'll be down in a minute!" said Claire.

Nancy Leigh hesitated and said, "Listen, Teddy, I realize this is not the ideal time to bring this up, but I have plans to see a lawyer on Thursday. I would like for us to work out the details of the divorce as soon as possible."

As grateful as Teddy was to her for bringing the clean clothes, he became irritated and sat down at the breakfast table. How could she be so insensitive? His father was fighting for his life. He couldn't believe she dared to bring up the subject of their divorce again this morning.

"Are you sure this is what you want, Nancy Leigh? Shouldn't we give our marriage a little time before running off to an attorney's office?"

Nancy Leigh's demeanor changed, "I'm sure your lawyer gave you advice over the weekend. And, I'd like a quick settlement."

Sensing her urgency to file for a divorce, he said, "I see what you mean.... Of course, you want to confer with legal counsel, and you are correct I have already consulted with mine. But, don't fret, our divorce should settle quickly. You realize we have gained no assets to speak of during the short period of our marriage. And, remember Nancy Leigh, we don't own any property. The divorce will settle much quicker if we use the same attorney, and it should not create a financial burden for either of us."

A look of concern appeared on her face, and she said, "I'll agree to that if you let me choose the attorney."

Teddy got up from the table and walked toward the back door as he said, "I'll give it some thought. However, right now, my head is spinning from all that has happened over the last forty-eight hours. But I'll think about it and try to give you my answer before the end of the week."

She said, "Let me know when you want to come by for your other things." Nancy Leigh paused at the door. She reached up and to his astonishment, gave him a quick kiss on the mouth. "I hope everything works out for you, Teddy. You'll make a great daddy one day!"

Teddy tried to suppress his emotions as his wife walked out the back door of his parents' home for probably the last time. She had been adamant in her decision to postpone having children until he finished medical school and was making a decent salary. Their latest discussion about starting a family had ended with him telling her if they waited to have a baby until they could afford children, they would never start a family. He wondered if her unwillingness to bear his children was at the very core of their failed marriage.

* * * * * * * *

Claire found Teddy sitting at the kitchen table apparently wiping tears from his face. Her first instinct was to wrap her arms around him, but she knew she should ignore his tears until he was ready to talk.

"Did Nancy Leigh leave already?"

"Yeah, you just missed her. She brought over a few clothes to get me through the next couple of days."

"That was thoughtful of her," she said.

Teddy blew his nose and hesitated before responding. "Mom, do you mind if I stay here with you while Dad's in the hospital?"

Smiling, Claire said, "You are welcome to stay here as long as you want."

Claire wasn't in the mood to discuss her daughter-in-law. She had been compassionate and respectful when she had spoken to her on the phone about Theo's condition. But, the sadness she saw in her son's eyes when she walked into the kitchen broke her heart. Claire didn't understand the nature of their problems, but she was sure it was too soon for him to discuss the situation with her.

"Son, I called Daisy while I was upstairs resting, and she told me that Andrew had a nine o'clock appointment this morning in Athens. He's not expected back in the office until after lunch. Do you know where your father keeps his personal papers?"

"Have you looked in the study?"

"Yes, I've looked in his desk, but I couldn't find a thing with Byrd, Whelchel & Byrd law firm's name on it. Would he keep those documents at the office?"

"What exactly are you looking for?"

"When we arrived at the hospital last night, they asked about healthcare directives. And, Dr. Martin asked me again this morning, before you came to the hospital if your father had a Power of Attorney or a Living Will. I can't remember if he has either of those documents. Daisy will ask Andrew to call me tonight; he should know since he handles Theo's legal matters."

"Drew should be able to check the office files for you, Mom. I'm sure Andrew keeps a copy in his files."

"I called the office before calling Daisy, but Drew is in a meeting. They don't expect him back in the office until this afternoon."

"Don't worry about it, Andrew will call you the minute he returns to town, and he'll know where Dad keeps his personal papers. I hope for your sake that Dad prepared a Living Will and Power of Attorney. It looks like you might need them."

Claire's eyes moistened, and her bottom lip quivered, "What do you mean, son?" Teddy explained that because of his dad's incapacitated condition, he could not sign any medical documents.

"A Health Care Power of Attorney is a legal document which allows you to decide on Dad's behalf, regarding medical procedures you feel are necessary. A Living Will explains Dad's wishes regarding any measures used to prolong his life, such as the use of a ventilator. Both documents are critical in situations such as this. They will protect you if a conflict arises regarding procedures that are against Dad's wishes."

"What happens if we can't locate the documents? Can Andrew prepare them for us now?" Claire asked.

Teddy shook his head, frowning. "Not at this late date. They must prepare those forms while the person is lucid and can understand what they're signing. Dad can't communicate his wishes now."

"Shouldn't I know if he had named me his Power of Attorney?"

Teddy paused, "Yes, typically one would discuss the contents of those instruments, but considering the way Dad protects you, perhaps he postponed the discussion. And, he probably didn't expect to need them so soon."

Claire's breathing grew heavy as she clenched her fists; upset that she could not locate the documents.

Teddy continued the conversation, "There's also a Power of Attorney for financial matters. Someone will need to transact business, other than signing checks, for the real estate firm until Dad can return to work."

"I don't understand why Theo never involved me with his business. He took care of the money and paid all the bills, and he made deposits into my personal checking account to cover any incidentals I might need, but other than that, I don't even know how much our power bill runs each month." She sighed and looked down at the Kleenex she held in her hand. "I can't believe I've been so naïve over the years! Here I sit with no knowledge of our finances, either personal or business, and my husband is in the hospital unable to speak." Claire extending her open hands in front of her, "What am I to do?"

Teddy walked toward the sink and asked, "How about a nice cup of tea, Mom? We'll get through this. At least I can sign on the checking account and keep the lights on at the office, and together we'll figure it out. I'm sure Andrew will provide guidance when he calls this afternoon, so let's not jump to any conclusions." He filled the kettle with water. "So, how about that cup of tea?"

Slowly, calm returned to Claire's voice, as Teddy tidied the kitchen. Claire found the morning paper and went into the family room and sat down in her recliner. Teddy gathered the clothes Nancy Leigh had dropped off earlier and started up to his old bedroom.

Teddy sat down on the side of the bed, and he looked at the picture his mom had taken when they returned from their ride in the red VW on the day he made the purchase. He vividly remembered the events of the day and was grateful for the memory of that afternoon he had spent with his mother.

As Teddy lay back on the bed, he thought about his mother's anxiety about finding their healthcare directives. Then, Teddy considered the promise he had made to his dad earlier in the day and knew he had to complete the project his dad had started. Teddy owed that much to his parents, and knowing how little his mother knew of their business dealings, he couldn't help but feel sorry for her. At least, he could keep the real estate office open.

As he headed down the steps to the study, Teddy thought if his father had discussed their conversation on Saturday with his mother, she would have mentioned it by now.

When he walked into his father's study, the sweet smell of pipe tobacco permeated the room. As he sat down on the sofa, he got a whiff of the beautiful leather furniture, along with the strong scent emitting from the bourbon decanter sitting on the credenza. All these things were reminders of the time his father had spent in this room.

This was Theo's retreat. A wood-paneled room that included hunting pictures which hung above the credenza and his grandfather's gun displayed above the mantel were all key features of the study. The room's furnishings differed from the elegance which graced the halls of this 19th century-style home. As he basked in the familiar aromas and studied the contents of the room, Teddy's gaze returned to his father's desk. There was a framed picture of his parents' sitting in front of the desk lamp, he picked up the picture and said, "Dad, it looks like I won't be leaving your real estate business just yet. I won't let you down. I'll finish your industrial park project."

Teddy searched the desk drawers, finding the same meticulous filing system in his study, which his father maintained at work. It surprised him that the household checkbook was not in the desk drawer, nor did he find their health care directive.

CHAPTER TWELVE

I t was an afternoon late in August of 2014, when Katie heard the telephone ringing as she unlocked her apartment door. She threw her purse and car keys on the table as she hurried to pick up the phone before the answering machine turned on. It was too late, as Katie listened to the identity of the caller with her eyes closed. She recognized the voice of Tyler Brock and was glad she had let the machine take the call.

Tyler Brock was a financial planner she met at Kim and Staten Fuller's Halloween party the previous fall. Later, when Tyler invited Katie to lunch, they discovered they worked in the same office complex. He was a few years older than Katie, and she enjoyed the friendship of a male companion. However, she desired no more than this because platonic relationships were her specialty.

When they met at the Fullers, Tyler was in search of another wife, he had gone through a painful divorce the previous year. Katie knew he was lonely because he had started calling her several times a month to go to dinner. As she listened to his voice on the answering machine, she thought, *I'm tired and not in the mood for a late dinner tonight. I just want to take a nice warm bath and go to bed.*

As she rinsed out the bathtub, her mind began to wander back to the day she met Teddy Williams, although she had tried not to allow her mind to dwell on him. She was no longer an immature schoolgirl and had long since outgrown the teenage crush stage. However, there wasn't a day that passed that the memory of his handsome face and boyish charm didn't come to mind. After she left the farm earlier in the afternoon, and as soon as her car reached Interstate 85 South, her mind returned to their flirtatious conversation in the driveway two years earlier at her grandparent's farm. If Teddy had been on the phone just now she would have picked up the phone and accepted an invitation to dinner. Unfortunately, Teddy had not called her since they last met. When she told him that her family's farm was not for sale, she had cut off the need for communication with him, and it saddened her he had not tried to make contact.

As the bathwater ran, she poured a glass of wine and then returned to the bathroom and slipped into the bubble bath. She lay back and sipped the chilled wine. Her thoughts returned to Teddy, and warmth filled her body with a sweet, wholesome feeling that one experiences from finding love for the first time. His golden blonde hair, his penetrating deep blue eyes, his cute boyish smile, were all the things that made him attractive and desirable to her. She ached the slow, hard ache of a woman desiring a man, she knew in her heart that somehow their paths would cross again.

The clock on the vanity showed nine o'clock. Katie had been in the bathtub for over an hour. She shivered from the chill as she stepped onto the tiled floor, wrapped herself in a long terry-cloth robe, and went off to the kitchen to deposit the wineglass into the dishwasher. As was her nightly habit, Katie secured the locks on the door and turned off the lights. As she headed to bed, she did so with a dreamy satisfaction.

The next morning, she chose a black Ralph Lauren suit and peach-colored blouse with tiny tucks down the front. A strand of cultured pearls and a simple gold ring that had belonged to her mother completed her signature outfit for the office. The first appointment of the morning was 9:00 a.m., with the owner of a distinguished law firm in Abington, Georgia. Andrew Byrd sounded troubled when they spoke on the phone the previous week, and Katie recognized the fact that he was an elderly gentleman. Although he had contacted her for assistance, the age difference would require her to show great respect toward him. As she dressed, she achieved her goal to look professional and a bit more mature than her age.

Katie had interviewed with Clayton Thomas who owned the accounting firm the year she graduated from the University of Georgia. She knew being single was an advantage and was perhaps the deciding factor in him hiring her from the large pool of applicants. This allowed her to work long hours to meet the demands of their growing business. The firm had tripled the number of clients since she came on board.

Mr. Thomas stood inside her office and pointed to the conference table saying, "I noticed the fresh bouquet, which is your trademark for entertaining clients. Another potential client coming in for a meet and greet this morning?"

"Yes, sir. You have always said the first meeting is to establish a rapport, and when done well, the business will follow."

"You are very teachable, Katie... Good luck with Mr. Byrd, I'm sure you will add him to your roster of clients before the end of the meeting."

"Thank you." She raised her crossed fingers in the air.

She had removed the files she had been working on earlier in the morning. The top of her desk was spotless as she glanced at the appointment book and glared at the name scheduled for the nine o'clock appointment, Byrd, Whelchel & Byrd law firm. The receptionist had placed two legal pads and several pencils on the conference table, along with a pitcher of ice water. Her office reflected her meticulous personality trait. She smiled as she moved the napkins next to the glasses in the center of the table.

The receptionist walked into her office, "Katie, Mr. Byrd is waiting in the reception area. I've already served him a cup of coffee, so whenever you are ready..." Katie felt a twinge of excitement in her stomach as she walked out to greet him.

"Good morning, Mr. Byrd," Katie said as she extended her hand. "I'm Katie O'Neill, it's a pleasure to meet you."

Mr. Byrd moved forward to shake her hand. "It's nice to meet you, Ms. O'Neill," he said as his relaxed manner calmed her nerves.

"How is your grandfather?"

"He is well. Thank you for asking, Mr. Byrd."

"Glad to hear it. He's a good man. I served as the county's legal counsel while your grandfather was a commissioner, and during that time, we got to know each other well. I trust he is enjoying retirement life?"

"Yes, he's loving retirement. He has expanded his hobby of tinkering with small engines, which isn't a bad thing, but we've had to replace the riding mower and the tractor in the last month because of his tinkering."

"That's a great story, and it sounds just like him! I enjoyed getting to know Tom. He made many friends in our county and was a strong presence on the board."

During their meeting, Katie learned Mr. Byrd's firm had experienced a decline in revenue despite their continued client growth since his partner's death. He used an accounting firm for all quarterly and annual tax reporting. The firm had invested in an accounting software package intended to document the billable hours created by each attorney. Mr. Byrd thought someone within the firm was embezzling money or was misrepresenting the billable hours in the system, and he intended to find out whom.

"Ms. O'Neill, my good friend, Henry Whelchel, and I began our law practice in 1976, and I am now the surviving partner. Who would have thought Henry would have died so young? I still find it hard to believe." He said as he shook his head.

"I'm sure it's been hard on you, sir. But, you have built a sizable firm, and one you can be proud of."

"You know, Ms. O'Neill, we attribute the success of our firm to the high-profile criminal cases Henry handled during the early years. It was Henry's belief and mine, too, that every person deserves an advocate when standing in front of a jury of one's peers. He often said that proving one's innocence was the sole job of a criminal defense attorney, and he could not let his judgment become clouded by his own opinion."

Katie asked, "Mr. Byrd, does your firm only handle criminal law cases?"

"No, dear. We have handled a wide variety of cases throughout the history of our firm. However, the clients I represent come from the business sector. Mainly, I handle corporate lawsuits and workers' compensation cases. I have also handled a few wrongful deaths and divorces along the way, but my preference is corporate law."

He explained that although he did not have the ambition to excel like his partner, as it was Henry's contagious drive had pushed both he and the firm to limits he had never expected to attain. Together, they had made a successful team, building a reputable law firm, and he was proud of their success.

Katie had spent a few days the previous week reviewing his financial statements, and she had prepared a list of questions for Mr. Byrd.

While he enjoyed a fresh Danish and a cup of coffee, Katie took a moment to articulate her words.

"Mr. Byrd, I reviewed the reports you faxed over, and there seemed to be quite a few discrepancies within your monthly statements," she said after she'd sipped from her water glass.

"For instance, the general ledger balance does not agree with the operating account reconciliation. Also, the revenue generated from the retained accounts fluctuated from month to month. Perhaps revenue is not being recorded properly by your staff, or the ledger entries were not coded correctly. Audit trails are important, so checks and balances are necessary to prevent errors. If the problems in your financial statements are because of erroneous posting entries, your previous audit should have revealed the problem."

"I think you should know there were no irregularities reported in the last audit."

She watched Mr. Byrd as he continued to sip his coffee, "If you want a second opinion in the form of another audit, let me explain how this would work."

After Katie reviewed the procedures to get started, she said, "Does this make sense to you, Mr. Byrd?"

"Yes, ma'am, it makes perfect sense. My company has been audited every year, but I'm just not comfortable with the results of the last audit."

"Did the previous auditor check the setup of the billing module in your accounting software?"

Andrew rubbed his forehead and remained quiet for a few moments. "I can't answer that question, but I've been working long days, and I go in on Saturday mornings to fulfill the executor role for Henry's estate."

"Have you discovered anything while working on Henry's estate that would add to your suspicions about the firm's financial condition?"

"No, I have found nothing at all. Henry left everything to his wife, Laura. He had taken out a large insurance policy, but most of the proceeds of the policy went to cover his personal debt."

Katie looked up from the file and asked, "Mr. Byrd, when did you discover the problems with your accounting system?"

"It wasn't so much a problem with the accounting system as a problem with our cash flow," he sighed. "When our banker called about the overdrafts, my suspicions increased because our accounting firm had just completed the annual audit. The firm, although reputable, could not satisfy my concern regarding our financial shortfall. Also, the person handling our account is a close friend of my son, Drew."

Katie considered the information provided by Mr. Byrd, and none of it made sense. Here sat a successful corporate lawyer with a long roster of clients, and his business was showing very little profit. She knew from experience that she must start with testing the accuracy of the software. Katie studied her packed calendar and considered moving some appointments around to make room for the audit. She smiled at the thought of working in Abington because of the proximity to Teddy Williams.

"Mr. Byrd, did the death of Mr. Whelchel cause the firm to lose any accounts on retainer?"

"Oh no, dear, Henry released his cases as soon as his pain interfered with his focus. My son took over his active criminal cases when he began the chemotherapy treatments. When he felt like it, Henry came in for a few hours each week and focused on finance."

Katie removed a list of information needed to get started, and she looked across the table and smiled, "Mr. Byrd, this audit will help us determine the source of the problem. Aside from the alleged software problems, it appears your firm has not been following Generally Accepted Accounting Principles."

"But, we can correct that during the audit, right?"

"Yes, we will get with your accountant and document the procedural changes."

"Okay, when we decide on a date, I will ask my assistant to make reservations for you at a local hotel."

"Thank you, sir. But, no need, I have friends and family in the Abington area, and I can stay with them while I am involved with the audit. However, I will need to do most of my work on weekends, because my calendar is already full for the next six months. Are you okay with me coming in on Saturdays?"

"Of course, that will work well for me also, as I plan on being in the office while the audit is underway. When will you begin?"

Katie responded, "I must clear the date with Mr. Thomas. You can expect a call in a few days to discuss the exact date."

Andrew smiled and said, "Fair enough. I appreciate you meeting with me today. Perhaps you could join my wife and me for dinner before we get started. I'm certain she would enjoy meeting you."

Satisfied with the way the meeting ended, Katie walked with Mr. Byrd back to the reception area.

CHAPTER THIRTEEN

Drew and Colleen Byrd lived in an old established residential neighborhood. A tall, stone chimney stood at each end of their modest, two-level, stone and brick exterior home. The four large windows on the front of the house, along with the cedar roof and gables created a look of Old-World European distinction. A beautiful home by anyone's standards that included a well-maintained yard, multiple flower gardens, and a rock garden which Colleen started the year they bought the house.

When the girls finished their dinner and had gone off to complete their homework, Drew and Colleen enjoyed a few minutes alone at the kitchen table.

Sipping the last of his coffee, Drew said, "I want to run something by you."

"Okay. What is it?"

Drew asked, "What do you think about selling this house?"

"Are you serious, Drew? Why would you think I would ever want to sell this place?"

"Well, Jacob will leave for college soon, and I thought it might be a good time to move into a smaller house."

Colleen said, "This old house fits our lifestyle complete with the hardwood floors and the ceiling-to-floor windows which line the back of the house. It's filled with wonderful memories, and I can't imagine living anywhere else." She walked toward the back of the house and remembered a comment made by her mother the previous Christmas. Her mom had said *the beautiful gardens appeared to extend the kitchen out into the yard, and they were lucky to enjoy such a panoramic display of colorful flowers and foliage from early spring through late fall. Yet, in the winter as the snowflakes began to fall, one could imagine a few flakes just might touch the tip of one's nose while standing in front of the fireplace.*

"It's just a thought," he said, "we could pull some equity out of the house to pay off some bills and still have enough to make a decent down payment on a smaller house."

Colleen didn't respond. She thought about how they had furnished their home with vintage pieces that often-required refinishing, a talent she had perfected.

"Do you remember early in our marriage you referred to one of my treasures as an old piece of junk? But, one day, you stopped making light of my hobby. What changed?"

Drew laughed and said, "When I saw the satisfaction on your face as you worked to bring life back to the distressed furniture, that allowed you to discover the beauty of the original wood, I knew I was wrong to make fun of your work."

Colleen looked around the house and said, "Although our home is older and smaller by many standards, we have filled it with objects we both love, and I would hope to stay here until the girls grow up. Moving to a small house now makes little sense to me."

A cross-stitched sampler that hung in her kitchen read: *The Quality of One's Home is Determined by Those Who Live Within.* Colleen had lived by this motto for almost twenty years while creating a home filled with warmth, love, and beauty from restored antiques.

While clearing the table, Drew changed the subject and mentioned that he had to work the following Saturday.

"Drew, what is going on? Have you landed a big case you did not tell me about?" Drew had been practicing law for 14 years, and she had never known him to work on a Saturday unless a critical case warranted the extra hours. He often spent his weekends on the golf course with his friends.

"No, I have work to do, and Saturday is a good time to catch up without the interruptions from phone calls and appointments," Drew stated. "Also, Dad has hired a CPA firm from Atlanta to conduct an on-site audit, and I think I should hang around in case they have questions," Drew explained.

"An on-site audit... That sounds serious. What prompted Pop to hire a firm from Atlanta? Why aren't you using a local accounting firm?"

Drew explained his dad's concerns over declining profits over the past few years as his main reason for the audit. Concerns that Drew thought were unwarranted since his dad had agreed to hire his friend's firm which included annual examinations. Drew pointed out that Henry had been the financial brains of the business, and since the recent audit did not reveal any unusual problems, there was no reason for his dad to hire a firm from Atlanta.

"I could have saved him several thousand dollars and explained it to him in less than 15 minutes, but he thinks we have a cash flow problem. Now since Henry died, Dad feels it is his responsibility to get a second opinion. It looks like we will be working on Saturday until the audit is complete."

Colleen was quick to come to her father-in-law's defense. "Pop is a smart man, and if he suspects a cash flow problem and has noticed the profits are down, then this is something that causes him concern. Remember, he is the managing partner."

She and her mother-in-law, Daisy, had already discussed the upcoming audit. "Pop works too hard. He's getting some age on him, Drew, and you need to insist that he slow down. You could take some of his cases and lighten his load."

Colleen and her father-in-law hit it off the first time they met. It didn't take much to entertain either of them whether it was reading a good novel, watching a sporting event, or perhaps seeing a good movie. Any of the above provided the perfect afternoon for her and her father-in-law.

"Drew, when you question your father like you did a few minutes earlier, you are showing a lack of respect. Why do you doubt his motives?" She stared at her husband as she waited for an answer that never came. "You realize the other attorneys in the firm watch you."

"Seriously, Colleen!" Trying to control the high pitch in his voice, "Dad works long hours because he wants to work long hours. He feels like the senior partner should be the first to arrive at the office each morning and the last to leave each evening. He is a classic example of a workaholic. The man doesn't know when to stop.

Colleen patted his arm, "Honey, it's okay. We're just having a conversation here."

He shook his head and softened his tone, "I agree with you he should slow down and delegate some of his work to other people, but he doesn't trust anyone to handle his client files. Do you realize that Dad has been a counselor to most of his clients for over 30 years?

"Why would your dad have trust issues?"

"You tell me. Dad remembers the dates of his clients' birthdays, anniversaries, and the birthdays and christening dates of their children. I would bet this house he already knows more about the clients he inherited than Henry ever knew."

"It sounds like your dad is very thorough in his job."

"Yes, he is. Do you know what is ironic? Henry enjoyed more notoriety than Dad. Henry was a hell of a criminal lawyer, and he had a very analytical mind. That probably explained his financial astuteness and his decision to switch to tax law half-way through his career. Dad is a superb lawyer, too, but not as well-known as Henry because he handled the high-profile cases. However, the business leaders in this community respect Dad and he has established a stellar reputation as a corporate attorney. When his clients need legal advice, they expect it to come from Dad."

Colleen tilted her head to one side as she listened to her husband. "But, Drew, you are also very personable, so he should have a few clients who would enjoy working with a younger guy like you. I would want you to be my attorney if I needed legal representation or advice."

Drew grinned and said, "Yeah babe, but you're partial, aren't you?"

Colleen leaned over, kissed her husband's cheek, and ran her fingers through his hair. "Yes love, but you have a dilemma on your hands. Daisy has suggested you talk with your father about him delegating more. They'll never get him to retire if he keeps working these hours."

Drew said, "You know, Mom's got a point there. Some attorneys continue to work for way too long even if they are not able."

"But your Dad isn't like that. He's been talking about retiring for a while now, Drew."

"I know. Perhaps, Henry's death changed his mind."

"What would happen if Pop developed health issues the same as Mr. Williams? Who would handle his clients in that situation?" Drew considered the question. But, he did not respond.

Colleen continued. "I was thinking the other day about how sudden one's life can change. Nancy Leigh and I had lunch at the club a week before Mr. William's heart attack. He and Pop and a few of their friends were at the café enjoying lunch that day. The following week Mr. Williams went into the hospital and left a different man. Life is precious and in a blink of an eye one's world can fall apart."

"I know, and you think the same thing could happen to Dad. Believe me, I have given that a lot of thought, too. However, all we can do is hope he slows his pace once this audit is over. Mom called me at the office that Monday morning after they hospitalized Theo, and I've never heard her talk so fast. When Claire couldn't reach Teddy by phone, she tried to get in touch with Dad about some of Theo's legal papers. Dad was out of town that morning, and I was in a meeting. Mom almost went ballistic just because Claire couldn't get in touch with either of us. To make matters worse, once we spoke it disturbed her I knew nothing about Theo's affairs."

Colleen looked at her husband and shook her head, "That is so unlike your mother as she rarely gets so worked up. What kind of legal papers did Claire need?"

"When they arrived at the hospital someone asked for historical information, and Claire did not know where to locate the documents they requested. When she couldn't get in touch with Teddy on Sunday night, she called Dad first thing Monday morning. When he was unavailable, she panicked and called Mom at the house."

"Did Pop have the documents at his office?" asked Colleen.

"Hell yes, what do you think he keeps in that big safe behind his desk?"

In a concerned voice Colleen asked, "Is it normal behavior for an attorney to store their clients' important documents in their office?"

Drew continued to rub the back of his neck, "No. It is not normal behavior."

"Let's hope the firm from Atlanta will determine the financial discrepancies within the books. I didn't realize you were so stressed out. You hide it well."

"I guess I do, but we will get through this. When was the last time you spoke with Nancy Leigh?"

"We played tennis this morning at the Club. She scheduled an appointment for this afternoon with her primary care physician about her mood swings, and it's not helping any that Teddy isn't cooperating as she thinks he should. I'm worried about her."

"She's ruthless, Colleen. If you are smart you will distance yourself from her. I realize you guys are friends, but this isn't something you should get involved with." argued Drew.

Colleen shot her husband a look of dismay. "Excuse me?"

"I'm sorry, Colleen. I shouldn't have said that, because you are the only friend she's got. However, I must warn you about discussing the divorce. Anything you may hear Teddy and me discuss in your presence is confidential, okay?" He paused, and then questioned his wife about how much she knew about Nancy Leigh's affair with Brad. "How long has she been seeing Brad, do you know?"

"I'm not sure. I know Nancy Leigh met Brad when she was in school at UGA." She hesitated, "but, we shouldn't talk about this subject anymore because it'll only make us upset with each other."

Drew got up from the chair and started clearing the dishes from the table. Colleen asked Drew about the industrial park as they cleaned up the kitchen. Drew explained that they still needed one more tract of land, and it looked like Mr. Hawkins may decide not to sell. He said that Theo had been unsuccessful in getting the property. The investors had met and were pondering a decision to proceed without the Hawkins' farm.

He finished drying the dishes, then picked up the trash and took it out to the garage. While he tied up the garbage bags, he noticed a box from Amazon addressed to Colleen. Drew wondered how she would react if she knew they were late paying their mortgage. When he came back into the house Colleen asked, "Who's taking Henry's place in the investment group? Will you need to find another investor, or can you handle it without bringing in anyone else?"

"Teddy and I have discussed this more than once. It would be less stressful if we had someone with Henry's financial knowledge to step in and given us some advice. Of course, he will look out for his father's interests, but he also wants to limit the number of partners in the project. Do you think one of your brothers would be interested, Colleen?"

She looked surprised, "I don't know, Drew. They are both extremely conservative with their money. It would take a lot of selling on your part to convince them to invest in a project in another town. But, you could certainly ask them if you like."

"Tyler and I talked about the project last Christmas. He would be a perfect fit because of his finance background. At first, he seemed interested, but since the divorce settlement turned out as it did I doubt the guy has much money left for investing."

"How do you know about Tyler's divorce settlement, Drew? My parents asked us not to discuss the results of the divorce with anyone, so who told you about it?"

"Well, Tyler told me about it," he paused. "He mentioned it last Christmas when we were playing golf, and he's called me at the office several times during the year to ask for legal advice."

Drew's voice increased an octave, "I didn't realize your family didn't want me to know about the settlement! Do they expect you to keep information of this nature from me?"

"Calm down Drew, your face is blood red. They would never ask us to keep secrets if that is what you mean. Since the Mackenzie's are my parents' dearest friends, we have limited our discussion about their divorce to minimize any negative comments from getting back to Deborah's family. You seem to know more about Tyler's divorce settlement than anyone in my family. I'm really glad Tyler felt comfortable in seeking your counsel. Since you consider this client-attorney privilege, I will not question you further."

"I appreciate it Colleen, it would be best if Tyler told you himself."

"What do you mean?"

"Well, keep in mind honey, you are his sister and he may never want to talk to you about the divorce. He wants to put it all behind him and look to the future, which is the best thing he can do for himself. He told me the other day he has been seeing a girl he met at a party. They have developed a friendship, and it allows him to get out and meet people. It's tough being single these days, and I'm glad I'm not him." Drew brushed against his wife and kissed the back of her neck as he realized he should be spending more time on his marriage.

CHAPTER FOURTEEN

Tyler said, "Katie I'm sorry I was late picking you up tonight," he explained as he placed the napkin in his lap. "I stayed at the office later than normal to complete a portfolio review. Time got away from me, and I didn't allow enough time to go home and change from my work clothes. Hope you don't mind?"

The candlelight from the small votive in the center of the table was flickering light from Tyler's sultry, black eyes. His sexy smile had caused heads to turn earlier when they walked into their favorite Chinese restaurant.

Smiling, Tyler said, "While scanning through the AJC this morning, I found a few advertisements from antique stores we've never visited. I thought we could visit some of them on Sunday afternoon on the way home. Perhaps we will find a rare book or one of those small silver trays you love. Afterward, we can stream a video from the latest list of movie releases to watch after dinner."

"That sounds like fun, but I won't be able to join you this weekend."

Tyler had been suggesting a weekend getaway for several months, but Katie had used every excuse she could think of to keep the relationship platonic.

He had endured several difficult months following the divorce, and Katie had been a true friend and allowed him to talk about the split up. Tyler had told her she made their time together fun and exciting. He thought their relationship included a level of compatibility absent in his marriage, and he could relax in her presence.

"That is disappointing news."

Tyler had been planning the special weekend to make his feelings known to her. He planned to visit a waterfall in the area on Saturday afternoon and had arranged for a table to be waiting close by complete with champagne and violin music playing in the background. The plan had taken a great deal of time to put together, but he thought the romantic venue would show Katie how special she had become in his life. However, in the last couple of weeks, Katie had delayed returning his phone calls and was even more withdrawn than usual. As he watched her from across the table, he wondered if she was seeing someone else. He thought that although they hadn't been dating for long, he'd fallen for her and was ready to commit to a future together and thought she might be too.

Katie smiled. "I know. But I can't help it... maybe another time."

Tyler felt she enjoyed dining in restaurants where soft music and lighting created an intimate atmosphere while they dined on gourmet foods paired with complimentary wines. Spending almost every Sunday afternoon together allowed him to get to know her better. During those evenings, they usually dined out. But, on a rare occasion they enjoyed cooking a light dinner in Katie's small and well-organized kitchen.

He suddenly wished that they were dining at her place, since he wasn't sure now how she would respond to his plan.

"You may want to reconsider because I've planned a special weekend for you," he replied. Katie was holding the stem of her wineglass, staring into the crimson liquid as if her thoughts were a thousand miles away.

Tyler reached across the table and tapped her glass with his forefinger. "You're not even listening, are you?"

Something he said caused her to look up.

"Hello, there... a penny for your thoughts."

A slow smile appeared on her face, and she said, "I was thinking of the upcoming weekend."

"What are you doing this weekend?" Tyler was careful to hide his disappointment.

"I'm going up to Abington tomorrow after work to start an audit for a new client on Saturday. I rarely conduct a weekend audit, but my schedule is full, and I can't work around it." Katie paused as she sipped her wine.

"What company are you auditing in Abington, may I ask?"

"You know I can't tell you the name of the company I am auditing, but I admit I'm looking forward to this challenge. The client is an older guy... a perfect southern gentleman and a charmer."

"Yeah, he sounds like a real prince."

Katie detected a hint of sarcasm in his voice. "He's old school. He's looking forward to retiring next year, and I imagine this audit is another box to check off before the big day."

"I would assume you receive quite a few referrals from Abington?"

"Not really. It would surprise you at how few referrals I receive from my hometown. As a matter of fact, this is my first."

Tyler said, "That's hard to believe."

"You know how much I cram into my weekends, and this will provide the perfect opportunity to blend business with family. My grandparents are in their eighties, and I'm looking forward to spending time with them."

Tyler said, "Are you sure I can't change your mind about the weekend?"

"Sorry, it looks like I must pass. Are you still determined to hike up a mountain and sleep under the stars?"

Tyler shook his head and laughed for creating this image in Katie's mind. He thought, *no wonder she wasn't interested in going away for a weekend.*

"My dear, Ms. Katie, I'm ashamed of you. Do I look like a rugged outdoorsman type guy?" They both laughed as Tyler changed his voice to sound much older than his actual age.

"You don't know me well, do you?"

Her tone turned serious. "Well, yes Tyler, I know you very well."

Tyler touched his lips with his napkin as he tried to hide a grin. "My idea of a perfect weekend is finding a charming little bed-and-breakfast with beautiful antique furnishings. And, perhaps a veranda on which to sit and enjoy a leisurely cup of coffee in the morning. I visualize a place where the housekeeper leaves a mint on the pillows each night. Now that is the perfect mountain getaway. You know how I enjoy being pampered? I'm not exactly a Jeremiah Johnson guy who survives on beef jerky and stewed rabbit."

Her neck and face turned red as she scrunched her nose. "I apologize, and it seems I have stereotyped you as a rough outdoorsman. Of course, the quaint example of the B&B now seems perfect for someone like you."

"No worries. Will you be home on Sunday? Perhaps you could come over to my place late in the afternoon. If the weather is cool enough, I'll build a big fire while we cook dinner. How would you like a rich pasta dish and a loaf of crusty bread?"

"That sounds nice."

"I'll even pick up your favorite amaretto cheesecake. We can sit around and enjoy a Sunday night meal together." suggested Tyler.

"Oh, my goodness, Tyler. Are you ready to order dinner? This discussion of food has suddenly made me hungry."

Tyler was more talkative than usual during dinner, and it pleased Katie he hadn't pouted. He often withdrew from the conversation when things had not gone his way, but he worked through it in due time. He was a sweet and kind man, but romantic chemistry did not exist between them. Katie had experienced that romantic feeling with only one other person in her life. Her mind wandered, as it often did these days, to Teddy Williams. She'd been having a hard time getting him out of her thoughts, even more so since she hoped they'd somehow run into each other over the weekend.

The conversation as they left the restaurant was light and playful, and Tyler made sure their discussions didn't turn serious. On the drive home, he noticed Katie had drifted into a quiet mood. Perhaps it was the rich food or the two glasses of wine, but she was more subdued than usual.

Tyler pulled into the apartment complex and parked the car. He turned in his seat to face her. "Katie, we need to talk," he said as he reached for her hands and held them between his own. "I care a great deal for you. In fact, I'm in love with you. But I feel you are building a wall around your emotions to distance yourself from me. What are you afraid of Katie?"

She sat in silence and never responded to his question, but neither did she look away. He continued, "I don't know if I have ever shared this with you, but please know that my parents arranged my first marriage. Mine and Deborah's parents matched us together at a young age. Although, we were fond of each other and knew each other well from the many years our families spent together, the chemistry did not exist between us. We cared for each other, but you know one can't fake that attraction between two people in love."

Katie continued to listen to Tyler as she squirmed in her seat and released her hands.

"The past year has taught me a great deal about life, and I now realize that friendship is the one element I want in my marriage. Our relationship contains this important ingredient, Katie. We have a great time together, whether we are reading the paper in front of a warm fire on a cold day or sailing the waters of Lake Lanier beneath the scorching Georgia sun. We are at ease with each other, and when we hang out, promoting conversation isn't necessary, it just happens."

As Tyler paused and adjusted the heater, he wondered what was going on in her head. He thought, *if she would just say something, anything at all.* Gauging her thoughts at this critical moment would be helpful. But, he knew his gut feeling was accurate: Katie O'Neill offered an element of security to his world, and he could easily spend the rest of his life with her.

He watched as Katie picked at her fingernails, but her eye contact made it clear she was listening to him.

"Please understand this isn't exactly how I envisioned this happening. I want to ask you a question, and I don't expect an answer tonight. But, promise me you will think about it while you're in Abington this weekend." Tyler reached up and touched her cheek with his fingertips.

"What is it, Tyler?"

"Will you marry me, Katie? I love you, and I have never felt as complete as I do when we are together. I believe the two of us can build a great life."

There was stone silence from Katie.

"Please, give it some thought, and we'll talk about it again when you return to Atlanta on Sunday." He kissed her on the lips, smiled a weak, bashful smile, and said, "Goodnight, Katie, and remember while you are working in Abington, I will be here counting the minutes until you come home."

* * * * * * *

Katie's body went limp. She knew it was time to get out of the car and go inside, but her stomach was flipping, and she grew nauseous. She was ill-prepared for what Tyler said, but as her heart pounded in her chest cavity she was holding her breath and could not speak. As awkward as this situation was, she was thankful she hadn't agreed to go off for the weekend because he had probably planned a proposal on a much grander scale.

The warmth from the car heater en route to the apartment caused Katie to sweat. She felt like the oxygen had been sucked from her lungs. Yet, she took a deep breath as she grabbed her pocketbook and got out of the car. She reached the front of the apartment and unlocked the door and entered the dark living area. After switching on a few lights, her head spun, and she fell on the sofa.

Katie had not seen this coming. She was unfamiliar with the signs of a man falling in love with her. She had enjoyed spending time with Tyler, but this relationship did not fit her lifelong expectations of falling in love with the perfect man. Her mind went back to one summer afternoon, while stringing green beans on the front porch, her grandmother tried to have "the talk," with her. And, during their intimate conversation, she told Katie "that when the right man came along you will know it in your heart before you can admit it with your head. The mere thought of losing someone so dear will be like losing half of your body, so the remaining half will feel worthless."

Was this what her grandmother had meant? She could not bear the thought of never seeing Tyler again. They enjoyed a beautiful friendship, which she cherished. However, there was Teddy Williams and the sight of him made her tremble. *Was that love, or was that lust?* She thought, *how can I be sure?*

Katie intended to pack her suitcase for the weekend in Abington, and she considered the items she should lay out. She ran the water for a bubble bath instead.

As she stood in her kitchen, pouring a glass of ice water to enjoy while in the tub, she thought, *how could I get out of this situation without hurting Tyler?*

In the bathroom, she slipped into the warm water and closed her eyes as she bathed in the sweet fragrant bubbles. While relaxing her body and mind, she thought about Tyler. He's smart and kind. Although his attributes checked every box on her requirements for a husband, she knew in her heart he wasn't right for her.

Katie's mind immediately went back to Teddy. Her heart pounded at the thought of his charming smile, and she reached for the ice water and rubbed the cold glass over her flushed face. When her skin had cooled off, she opened her eyes. The answer was as transparent as the water in the glass she held. Had the proposal come from Teddy Williams, her immediate response would have been an immediate yes.

CHAPTER FIFTEEN

(Flashback – Summer 2012)

I n the summer of 2012, Theo Williams and Henry Whelchel had discussed the possibility of finding a partner to finish financing their project. Since both men were close to Andrew Byrd, they never hesitated when his son, Drew, approached Henry about his participation in the real estate deal. They needed another partner with capital, and Drew's father had the wherewithal to complete the financing for their project.

The guidelines required each partner to invest a quarter of a million dollars in the project. Costs included various fees such as zoning requirements for industrial properties, infrastructure, and architectural studies. Theo and Henry had discussed the project many times with Andrew, but he never showed interest in taking part. However, he offered to call in a favor from a good friend serving on the board of county commissioners if needed.

After Drew met with Henry to express his interest in the project, the partners assumed that he had involved Andrew in the decision. Wary of dipping further into their personal funds, Henry and Theo decided that Drew's involvement would eliminate the need for using more of their money. As a precaution, they continued to approach local businessmen with the means to invest in their project.

As weeks passed, financial pressures mounted, which often occurred when a project begins without all the financing in place. Moving forward, they contacted most of the landowners about purchasing their land, while keeping enough funds in reserve for the unexpected expenses reasonable for a project of this size.

"I don't know Theo," said Henry. "I find Drew's suggestion aggressive and even risky for a firm of our size. I'm certain Drew must act upon approval from Andrew, and I have not yet expressed my concerns. I plan to discuss the idea with Andrew at our next partner luncheon."

"Perhaps we should arrange lunch with Andrew, so we both can be present," suggested Theo.

Henry said, "Good point, I've spent hours reviewing the ROI for the project, and I'm certain the law firm can sustain a certain amount of risk without jeopardizing our financial security. But, I'm not in favor of pledging the law firm's assets as collateral, and I'm interested in finding out if Andrew would pledge his personal funds."

* * * * * * * *

Drew considered it a significant achievement to be in a partnership with a prominent businessman like Theodore Williams. At first, Drew's friend, the architect for the industrial project, encouraged him to take part and hinted that he would consider bartering architectural fees or could find enough funding to complete the initial stages of their project. Drew continued to be optimistic about the plan and had mentioned to Henry that they might consider financing the remaining amount through the local bank by pledging the furniture, fixtures, and real estate of the law firm.

Drew had financed his part of the deal with his friend Tom Jackson at the local bank. Tom had cautioned him about the risk of pledging his house and every asset he had accumulated as collateral.

"Tom, I realize this is a risk," said Drew. "But, you know Theodore Williams and Henry Whelchel are both savvy businessmen. I'm certain neither one of them would invest their personal money if they weren't certain of their success."

"You're right Drew, but you're a young man with three children to educate and a mortgage to pay. Those guys are looking for partners with deep pockets, who can afford the risk."

"Okay Tom, I appreciate your concern. If it will help, Colleen has some shares of Coca-Cola stock her parents gave her when she graduated college. We can pledge those shares if needed."

"We aren't interested in using the stock as collateral, Drew. In fact, encourage Colleen to hang on to that stock, that may be the best investment you ever own." Drew was confident that Tom would never agree to take the request to the board of directors unless he was sure the board would agree to the loan.

With Christmas Day just a week away, Drew worried about the bank's approval for the loan. He and Colleen had taken a day to finish their Christmas shopping at The Forum, and as they entered the restaurant for lunch Drew received a call. While Colleen went to sit down, Drew stepped outside to take the call from Tom Jackson.

When he returned to the table, he smiled at Colleen, "Well, honey we have just received an early Christmas present."

"What are you talking about, Drew?"

"That was my banker, Tom Jackson, on the phone. He called to let me know the board of directors approved our loan for the industrial project."

Colleen reached for her husband's hand and with a look of relief said, "Thank God! That news could not have been better timed."

He winked at her as he lowered his voice. "Babe, this deal will make us some serious money. You mark my word."

While Colleen was shopping, Drew sat on a bench and watched the shoppers in the mall. When he first considered the industrial park project, he was sure his father would go along with the investment when he pointed out the ROI.

However, when Drew mentioned the deal to his father, he squashed the idea without examining the specifics of the agreement. Andrew had said in no uncertain terms that he would never invest in a speculative land deal. He gently encouraged Drew to stay out of it, too.

Drew had a way of convincing people of what he wanted them to believe, so he had inferred to the partners that his decision involved his father's agreement. The day they completed the deal, Drew showed up at the closing alone and signed his name on behalf of the law firm. He had excused his father's absence by explaining that he was out of town. This single act involved the law firm as a significant player in the world of speculative buying which his father had warned him against.

* * * * * * * *

After the partnership meeting, Henry and Theo went out to lunch. Henry could not wait to speak with his friend in private. "I have known Andrew for almost forty years, and I have never known him to become involved in a project without great fret and worry. Do you realize he just invested two hundred and fifty thousand dollars in this project and has yet to sit down with either of us?"

Theo responded, "That is so true, Henry. I was thinking the same thing on the way over here."

"Andrew has spent more time pondering a ten-dollar lunch than he has seemingly spent on this investment. Theo, have you talked with Andrew lately? Is he acting normal to you?"

"Yes, we've had lunch several times over the past month, and we were together again over the weekend. He seemed fine, but perhaps we have all been skeptical about opening a line of discussion concerning the industrial project because we don't want him to think we are undermining Drew."

Theo paused for the waitress to serve their lunch. "Besides, he may have asked Drew to handle this transaction for him. Remember, we have brought up the subject of investors to Andrew before. If you recall at our last meeting, the architect asked Drew if his father knew of his involvement. He inferred he did. In a partnership situation one must trust the people involved or the partnership will not work. Besides, it's easy for me to understand what Andrew is thinking. Henry, we are getting older and we need to let the younger generation take on a heavier load. Andrew hasn't mentioned when he plans to take retirement, but we can't work forever."

"Perhaps you are right."

"Claire and I would enjoy taking a few trips before we get too old to enjoy traveling, if you know what I mean?" Theo picked up his fork, "Between the two of us, I wish Teddy showed as much enthusiasm and assertiveness as Drew. I'd turn over my business to him today, and Claire and I would be in the air by morning to some wild and exotic place."

"Theo, Claire would declare you'd lost your mind if she heard you say that. You're not a wild and exotic type of guy," replied Henry with a loud chuckle. "And, let's be honest, you will never relinquish your company to Teddy or anyone else."

CHAPTER SIXTEEN

In August of 2014, a year and a half into the project, Drew was feeling the effects of overextending himself. He had just lived through one of the worst weeks of his life, beginning with the audit the previous Saturday. Katie had just learned her way around the office and memorized the server codes on the one day she had spent in the office preparing for the audit. Between conversations with Andrew and an hour and a half lunch break, it would take her months to complete the examination.

On Tuesday, Drew called Teddy and asked to meet him for lunch at the Club. "We need to review the insurance certificates for the subcontractors we are using. We can also go over anything you need to discuss." Drew's tone was curt and hateful as if he didn't trust Teddy to monitor the certificate dates.

Teddy said, "No problem, I have reviewed the certificates for the subcontractors every month and they are up to date. However, we need to forecast the exact completion date for construction if that's possible."

Drew's mood was dark but he continued, "Jacob fell last night and broke his collarbone while playing football in the backyard with his friends. We spent the evening in the emergency room at the hospital, and the x-rays confirmed a broken bone."

"Damn, I bet he's sore this morning. Is there anything I can do for you guys?"

"No. Jacob's good. I just thought I'd let you know. I've had very little sleep."

Now with Henry gone and Theo incapacitated, Drew was the only partner remaining of the original three. Teddy watched the purse strings and handled the certificates for the insurance company and lined up tenants to fill the space... and, although Drew had helped with securing and managing the contractors, Teddy felt that the obligation to his father required him to meet with Drew about the construction of the project. He wanted to make sure they were staying on target for budgetary reasons. Drew agreed Teddy had a right to question the timeline of the development since he was working on behalf of his father.

In the meantime, Drew was in constant contact with the bank, trying to intercept the interest bill that was due to arrive in the mail within the next few weeks.

At each month's end, Drew stayed after the office closed and made ledger entries to hide the interest payments to the bank. Although, Henry had handled the financial dealings for the firm's partnership until a few months before his death, Drew had worked with the accountant to continue to classify the interest payments in a way that would not be obvious to his father. Now with the law firm in the middle of a financial audit, he felt sure that his days of moving money around and altering financial reports would be difficult. Katie O'Neill was one of the smartest accountants with whom Drew had ever worked. He nervously paced the halls of the office waiting to see if she discovered the distorted accounting practices he had created since Henry's death.

Drew sat at his desk staring at the dark morning sky, which reminded him of the weather on the day of the partners' luncheon when the architect suddenly decided against investing in the project.

Drew said, "Listen, either you plan to invest or not. We can't go on like this forever." He looked over to Theo Williams to back him up, but he remained quiet.

The architect inquired, "Is there anyone else interested in the project?"

Theo responded, "Not at this time. Henry and I have spoken to several people, but I agree with Drew we do need an answer. If you aren't interested then we must consider other options.

"Drew, is your dad still showing interest in becoming a partner?" asked the architect. "If so, perhaps he would take my place."

"Yes, of course, he's still interested."

"Okay, then I'll step aside and let Mr. Byrd take my place in the partnership."

Drew was concerned with gaining the respect of Mr. Williams, and since he had implied his father was interested in the project he jumped in with both feet.

As he watched the cold rain pouring down from outside his office window, it became clear he should have listened to his father's advice. He remembered the conversation with his dad as it played over and over in his mind.

(Flashback to Christmas Eve 2012)

Drew and his father were in the family room at Drew's house on Christmas Eve after the church service. They were stoking the wood in the fireplace and enjoying a cup of eggnog while his children were upstairs preparing for bed. Andrew had recited 'The Night Before Christmas' to his grandchildren on Christmas Eve night since the year of Jacob's birth. The tradition was as much a part of the Byrd family Christmas festivities as the candlelight service at the Methodist church.

While the ladies and the children were upstairs, Drew approached the subject with his father. "Dad, what are your thoughts regarding the industrial park project that Theo and Henry are planning?"

"Son, I'm not much for speculative buying. Henry has sunk a lot of money into the project, and so has Theo. They have not come out and asked me if I would join the partnership, but they have said enough for me to know they would welcome me as an investor. Speculative buying is a perilous business, son. I have a great deal of respect for both of my friends for different reasons, and I value their friendships more than the potential profits from the project. Some of the best friendships in the world have dissolved over business partnerships, and I'm not willing to take that chance."

His father sipped his eggnog and continued, "I realize you've been discussing a partnership with Henry, and I can't tell you how to handle your finances, but perhaps establishing a fund for your children's college education would be a wiser investment. More often than not, these kinds of partnerships don't turn out as investors may lead you to believe. With three children to educate and one entering college next fall, you've got your hands full."

"That is a valid point Dad, but it sounds like the partners will make a nice return on their investment."

"I'm sure they will make some money, son. I've known of only one incident when Theo Williams invested wrong, and he lost a year's salary. He almost lost his business, but with a little creative financing and restructuring of debts, he worked through it. In every other situation he profited, and I venture to say he profited handsomely. But Drew, a man your age could lose his home and everything you and Colleen have built together. I'm not trying to tell you what to do. I'm just giving you a few words of caution. There have been many times during my life when I would have appreciated advice from my father, but he died when I was a young man. Therefore, I've had to rely on my gut instinct and several long talks with the good Lord. Some folks are natural winners in the world of real estate, as they have that innate ability to spot a successful opportunity. We are not developers, but we are in a highly respected profession."

He paused, and then continued, "During the early years we worked long hours building our firm, and I often remembered "The Moon Speech" given by President Kennedy. Whereby, he stated during the 20th century we are going to the moon, not because it is easy, but because it is hard. Drew, we have built an established law firm, and it has not always been easy. There were many lean years along the way, but if we continue to spend our time well and concentrate our energies on that which we know, then we will continue to build and strengthen our firm for the next generation."

Drew and his father went upstairs to the children's room where the young girls were preparing for bed in their Christmas pajamas with matching bathrobes and slippers.

Andrew looked from his beautiful granddaughters to his son. "This, my son, is the most important investment you will ever need. If you invest your spare time in your children, the rewards will be far greater than any amount of profit from a real estate project. Your family," as he opened his arms towards his grandchildren, "is all that really matters in a man's life. Son, these children watch everything you do and say. You have a tiny window of time to influence your girls while they are living under this roof. Make sure these years count."

The two men lifted the little girls onto their backs and took them downstairs for the traditional Christmas Eve bedtime story.

Colleen, Drew, and Daisy sat on the sectional sofa in front of the fireplace, along with Angie and Rebecca. Jacob sat on the hearth next to his grandfather, as he read the story about the birth of baby Jesus. At the end of the story, everyone joined hands as Andrew said a prayer of thanksgiving for his family and for the joyous season. Andrew was a man of firm religious conviction and used every opportunity to tell his family how much they meant to him.

While his father prayed, Drew felt as if the words of the prayer were intended for his benefit.

At the conclusion of the Christmas Eve prayer, Andrew said, "And Lord, please let us never forget the responsibilities of parenting. Thank you for my family and for the love and warmth we experience when we are together. May the joy and love of that very first Christmas live within our hearts throughout the entire year."

The prayer caused the adults to wipe tears from their eyes. Andrew was an influential figure within his family unit, and his love enveloped his family as a blanket provides warmth on a cold winter's night. For as long as Drew could remember, his dad only wanted to be a good husband and father. Although, practicing law was his occupation his family was of foremost importance in his life.

Drew was the first to break the silence as they sat in front of the fireplace. "I'd like to say I feel blessed that you are my father. Thank you for making this an evening we look forward to each year. We love you, Dad."

"I love you, too, son." Rubbing his hands together as his eyes danced with excitement. "And, now it is time to read 'The Night before Christmas' by Clement Clarke Moore." Andrew winked at his son as he handed him the book. The gesture was a significant passing of the torch as he slid between Daisy and Colleen and put his arms around each of them.

Colleen snuggled up to her father-in-law and said, "Thanks, Pop."

He kissed her forehead and said, "Thank you, dear. Without you we wouldn't have this beautiful family."

* * * * * * * *

A visceral pain developed as Drew pondered the poor decision he made to partner with the industrial park group. As he placed his face in his hands, he remembered the look of awe on the faces of his children and the contentment of his adoring wife as his family gathered around the hearth on that Christmas Eve night. The memory was as real as if it were yesterday. As the problems of the deal manifested, Drew would reach into his memory bank and recall the picture of that special Christmas when his three children still lived under his roof.

He wondered how different things would have turned out had he only listened to his father and not committed the firm to the deal.

Because of his bad choices, he tried to stretch every dollar he made, and also every dollar from the firm to meet the operating expenses and to make interest payments on the loans to cover his investment. The leisure time he had enjoyed with his family had dropped to a bare minimum. Colleen didn't seem happy anymore, not that their change in financial status would hinder her happiness, but she resented the time Drew spent away from her and their children.

With the expense of college for Jacob and the additional burden of a third vehicle, any day now, Drew's world could implode. The bills were past due and nothing in Drew's life appeared as it seemed.

CHAPTER SEVENTEEN

(August 2014)

When Katie returned to her grandparents' farm following a day at the law firm, her feet were aching. She forgot how much she had missed her Saturday morning sleep.

One doesn't expect to discover anything amiss on the very first day of an audit. However, before they left for lunch she ran a report of month-end entries for the past twelve-month period. There were four repetitive $7,000 entries that stood out on the report which appeared to be payments to the local bank. The classification of the offsetting entries made the audit trail harder to follow. She made a note on her pad to ask for copies of the loan documents. The three had enjoyed a leisurely lunch over at their Club, which lasted longer than she intended. Although, Drew continued to offer his help with the audit, Katie sensed his discomfort regarding her questions about the interest payments.

I can think of this audit later, but now I am going downstairs to enjoy a home-cooked meal with my grandparents, she thought as she tied her hair back with a rubber band. She ran down the steps to the country-style kitchen where the smell of pan-fried pork chops smothered in onions greeted her.

"Oh Nana, this is my favorite meal. Are you planning to throw in a few slices of potatoes as well?"

Nora turned to face her granddaughter with a huge smile on her face. "Of course. Pan-fried pork chops aren't as tasty without a few potatoes."

Katie relaxed as she strolled through the kitchen in search of a glass of iced tea. "Oh, my goodness, this tastes so good. Of all the many things I miss from your kitchen, this tea is at the top of my list. Nana, this sweet nectar is addictive."

"Your mother loved my sweet tea, too. She would invite her girlfriends over on Friday nights when the boys were out, and the six of them would drink two gallons in one evening. I'm not sure if her friends enjoyed staying here because we ate well or because Katherine had four brothers," she chuckled. "Those were fun times just the girls and me. The kids gave me a pizza cooker for Christmas one year and the girls enjoyed making homemade pizzas. We made French fries and peanut butter fudge for dessert, and I remember one night after their Homecoming Dance, the girls and their dates came back over here. We made biscuits and gravy with sausage, eggs, and grits. It was such a fun time for me! They laughed and told stories about their classes and teachers many of which I had heard numerous times. You know how it is with stories, they get bigger and better each time they're told. Then, after Sammy's accident and Ben's death I suffered some bouts of depression. Once I got myself back together, all those sweet girls had graduated and left the area. I have received notes from several of them down through the years, and I have kept each note as they continue to bring me comfort."

"Nana, I've never asked you about Sammy's accident for fear it would upset you, but sometime when you are feeling up to it, would you mind sharing the story with me? Is it true that my mother caused the accident?"

Nora turned to face her granddaughter. "No dear, your mother wasn't even home the week the accident occurred. She was away at 4-H camp at Rock Eagle in Eatonton, Georgia."

"Seriously?" asked Katie.

"Yes seriously. Katherine and her friends were members of the local 4-H club and had taken part in the state competition. Katherine had a love for horses, and she was an excellent rider, too. Like

Sammy, Katherine always had a passion for horses and often competed in local equestrian events around the area. But, your mother was at that age where she thought about boys, so she decided sewing would be a better project for her to undertake. One of the older girls in the club took on a few girls Katherine's age as her 4-H project. She taught them the techniques of sewing. Every Saturday morning the girls would pack a lunch and go over to Carolyn's home for a four-hour lesson in sewing. You know, those young girls did well, too, they each made a well-tailored suit complete with lining. Your mother excelled in sewing, and she made her formal for the homecoming dance her senior year."

"Nana, why did I think Mom was responsible for Sammy's accident?" Katie asked.

"I don't know, sweetheart. I was just wondering the same thing. She and her friends were excited about the camp and wanted Sammy and Roger to go with them. Katherine, Sammy, and Roger were very close and hung out together. Some of their friends within the county named them the 'silver circle.' Please don't ask me how they came up with that, but my children were known countywide by that name."

Nora became pensive, and then Katie saw the fresh tears forming in her grandmother's eyes. She thought it was time to change the subject, but Nora forged on with her story.

"Roger, Katherine, and Sammy were each ten months apart in age, and they grew up close. Katherine begged and pleaded with her brothers to go with her to camp that year. Your mom had never been away from home, much less without her brothers, and she got homesick easily. She kept bugging them until both Sammy and Roger decided they would rather stay home than go off to an organized camp. Roger had just passed his driving test and did not want to spend five days without driving a car. They understood the outdoor activities would be fun and well organized, but they didn't much care for being dropped off on Monday morning and picked up on Friday afternoon without as much as a break in between. So they stayed home and let the girls enjoy the camp with a promise they would consider going the following year. You can imagine how that turned out."

Nora poured herself a refill of tea and sat down at the table opposite her granddaughter while the potatoes continued to cook in the large black frying pan.

"Several years later, Katherine told us that at about the same time of Sammy's accident, she had experienced an extreme pain on the side of her head that felt much like a blow to her skull. When the tractor turned over, it trapped Sammy's body, and it applied pressure at the same location on his head, which caused the concussion. The time of that accident was a few minutes after noon on Wednesday when Katherine was away at camp. Your mother experienced the same piercing pain at the exact time of day the accident occurred."

Katie rested her glass on the counter so suddenly, drops of tea splashed onto her hand. She'd heard of these kinds of connections happening between twins, but it had never occurred to her that regular siblings could have that kind of relationship, too. Katie looked up at her grandmother's face. It had paled considerably since she'd told the story, and Katie wanted to reach out and hug her, but she'd waited years to hear the truth about what happened that fateful day and she wanted to hear more. Katie covered her grandmother's shaking hand with her own, then asked softly, "How did my mom react when she heard about Sammy's accident?"

Nora walked over to the stove to check on dinner. She turned the potatoes and wiped her hands on the dish towel which hung over the oven rail and said, "Well, she didn't respond as I would have expected, that's for sure. After the medics had completed their assessment, they determined that they should fly Sammy to DeKalb General in Atlanta, where a specialist in traumatic brain injuries could better diagnose his condition. We were all in a state of panic with other children to think of and three of them were out of town. We were just trying to make sure we notified everyone before they heard of the accident second-hand. Sophie had already passed at the time of

Sammy's accident, and Ben was serving a tour in Vietnam. Our minister agreed to contact the military authorities to get a telegram to his commanding officer, and we were skeptical that he would receive the news in due time. Stephen was attending summer classes at the university. He had returned to his apartment between classes when your grandfather reached him. As you know, Stephen was protective of your mother, and he immediately offered to drive to Eatonton, Georgia, to deliver the news of Sammy's accident in person." Nora had a distant look in her eyes as she remembered the events of that painful day.

She then smiled and continued. "It was during that week at 4-H camp when your parents met for the first time. One of Donald's friends came down with the mumps, and his friend's parents offered for Donald to go to the camp in place of their son. Imagine had Donald's friend not got the mumps they may had never met. Katherine and Donald met the first afternoon of camp while riding horses on the trails surrounding the lake. Donald told us later that when he met your mother, he knew immediately that they would marry and spend the rest of their lives together. And they did just that."

"You realize some people don't believe in love at first sight."

Nora continued, "Yeah, well, I do. Stephen drove to the camp as soon as his class ended without as much as a stop for food. When he got there, dinner was over, and the kids were roasting marshmallows while singing campfire songs around a fire pit. Not wanting to disturb his sister, Stephen returned to his car and waited until the night session ended. As soon as they dismissed the campers for the evening he walked over to the administrative building and explained the reason for his visit. Someone sent a young staffer over to Katherine's cabin and walked with her back to the administration building. Katherine told me later that she knew something was wrong when she saw Stephen sitting on the sofa in front of the fireplace. She hesitated at the door as she wasn't sure she wanted to know the cause of his visit for fear she would have to leave Donald."

Katie said, "She was love-struck, wasn't she?"

"Keep in mind Katherine thought Stephen was the best big brother ever. He was always the first to reach her side when the need arose."

"Nana, I realize how much I missed by not having my little brother in my life. Mom and Uncle Stephen shared a special bond, didn't they?"

"Yes dear, sibling bonds are strong. Stephen wanted to get to Katherine before she heard about the accident from anyone else. He also understood the unique closeness that existed between her, Sammy, and Roger, the *silver circle*."

"What did you mean earlier when you said Mom did not react to the news of Sammy's accident as you would have thought?"

"We thought Katherine would pack her things and return home with Stephen that night. She chose instead to finish the week of camp. Understand, dear, your mom had just met Donald, and they were experiencing the start of a young romance. She couldn't leave that night, and it was best she stayed at the camp because we were back and forth to Atlanta all week. I'll never forget seeing Sammy on the life-support machine along with the brace around his neck. It was a disturbing sight for all of us, but it would have been traumatic for a young girl. Sammy was a good-looking kid, with the sandy blonde hair, and those gorgeous blue eyes, and you know that special spirit of his. He was such a sweet guy and was always looking out for his buddies. Perhaps the worst part for him was the rehabilitation, but, he handled it with such grace. We always said it was his spirit that pulled him through. The accident had changed him as his broken leg healed quickly, and fortunately, he didn't suffer any physical deformities. The impaired vision and headaches that resulted from the concussion also healed, but when he finished rehab we knew that his mental disabilities resulting from his traumatic brain injury would prevent him from living alone."

Katie smiled at her grandmother and said, "Thank you for sharing this story with me. I now have a better understanding of what happened, and how impactful those events were in the lives of my family."

CHAPTER EIGHTEEN

(November 2014)

While looking out of the window at the real estate office, Teddy thought of the man whose desk he occupied. He had served as interim CEO since his father's illness had left him incapacitated. It had been a tough transition for Teddy, but as promised, he'd facilitated the team to complete the industrial park project.

His divorce from Nancy Leigh was not final, so he was not yet free to move forward regarding relationships. The separation was liberating, but Teddy continued to feel that he had failed. In his heart he always knew their marriage wasn't a good fit. However, Teddy had hoped that his marriage would mirror the relationship enjoyed by his maternal grandparents.

As he realized the time, he buzzed the receptionist. "Would you try to get my mother on the line, please?" He needed to discuss the upcoming holidays with her. Andrew and Daisy had extended an invitation for Thanksgiving dinner, and he wanted to find out his mother's plans before accepting their invitation. He was grateful to the Byrds for their support to his family throughout the years.

"My parents have invited a new friend to Thanksgiving this year. Colleen and I were thinking you might enjoy meeting her that day. Since it's a big holiday dinner and they'll be a bunch of people around, if you don't hit it off it wouldn't be so obvious."

Teddy thought it strange that Drew was so secretive about the name of the woman. He knew nothing about her other than she was auditing the firm's books. Teddy made sure she wasn't another member of Colleen's sorority. Since the separation, it seemed he had met every available Phi Mu member in the state. However, with the divorce proceedings almost completed, he was ready for female companionship.

Clearing his desk of work, Teddy noticed it was almost time to meet Drew for lunch. He reviewed the land option he had prepared earlier in the day and placed it inside his briefcase.

As he left his office he stopped by the receptionist's desk. "I'm meeting Drew for lunch to discuss updates on the industrial park project, so I won't be back this afternoon. If anything comes up, you can reach me at the club.

"Your mother didn't answer the phone. Should I continue to call her?"

"No, but thanks for the offer. I left a voicemail on mom's recorder at home. She checks her messages throughout the day. I appreciate you trying to reach her."

The lunch with Drew would not take long, but they had several issues to discuss regarding the industrial park. Once they finished, perhaps they could spend the afternoon on the driving range hitting golf balls.

Teddy was sitting at their table at the club, checking his phone and oblivious to Drew's arrival. "Hey man," Drew said, as he slapped Teddy on the back while pulling out a chair. "Why didn't you order lunch when you got here? Now it will take Donna ten minutes to get back over to us."

A slow smile appeared on Teddy's face as he finished typing a message on his phone. "Calm down, Donna will be over here any minute with our order." As if right on cue, Donna appeared with two turkey club sandwiches and fries.

Teddy asked, "Where have you been?"

"Dang, she entertained you while I drove over here, didn't she?"

Teddy looked confused, "What in the heck are you talking about, Drew?"

Drew laughed and said, "Colleen called the law firm just as I planned to leave for lunch. She asked me to run by the bank and make a deposit into Jacob's account. I knew if the traffic was bad, going by the bank would cause me to run late, so I placed a call to the club to let Donna know I would be late. She promised to keep you entertained until I got here."

Teddy shook his head as he considered his friend's dramatic imagination that always ran amok.

Over lunch, they discussed the progress of the project. "Drew, what are your thoughts on approaching the Hawkins about an option agreement to execute upon their death?" Teddy had prepared an option that required signatures of Mr. and Mrs. Hawkins and the granddaughter. He slid the manila envelope across the table for Drew to review.

"Well, aren't you the pro-active administrator?" Drew opened the envelope and read the document which did not include a financial offer to hold the property. Teddy noticed that Drew paused at the last page when he read the names listed for signature.

"Who is Mary Katherine O'Neill?"

"I've told you, Drew, she is the granddaughter. That gorgeous woman we discussed the day I met with the Hawkins the weekend my dad got sick."

As Drew reviewed the document, Teddy asked if he thought the language would cause a problem for either side.

"Nope. The document is well prepared and should not present any problems."

"Why do you have that dumb look on your face? What the hell?"

Drew shook his head as he moved the document back to Teddy, "Nothing, man, I... I suspect I may have met Mary Katherine O'Neill."

"Oh please, Drew you know every Phi Mu member in the state. I've met most of them, thanks to you and Colleen trying to fix me up. Believe me, if you had met Mary Katherine O'Neill you would remember it, buddy."

Drew shook his head as if dismissing a lousy thought and laughed at the uncharacteristic emotions expressed by his friend.

"Okay, Teddy, let's go with this. May I suggest you schedule the meeting with Mr. Hawkins and the granddaughter? I'd leave Mrs. Hawkins out of this meeting."

"And how do you suggest I do that, Drew?"

"You know how women are. They get emotional about these types of decisions and could derail our efforts to move forward." Redirecting the conversation, Drew said, "I feel certain we can complete the current phase within the next couple of weeks, but it will be great having a contingency plan in place."

Teddy checked the calendar on his phone and suggested the next Saturday afternoon. He explained the granddaughter lived out of town and would require a few days to confirm a meeting.

Drew motioned for Donna to come back over to the table while asking Teddy if he had time for another beer. Teddy responded that he had penciled in the entire afternoon on his schedule and wasn't planning to return to the office until the next morning.

"Seriously. You scheduled an afternoon for this meeting. Do we need that much time?"

"No, but I have no appointments scheduled this afternoon, so I thought we could just hang out and perhaps hit the driving range in a few minutes. If you need to get back to work, then please go ahead, and I'll just sit here and let Donna entertain me."

Donna stopped at the table and placed her hand on Drew's shoulder. "Drew, you have a phone call. If you like you can step into the business office to take the call in private."

"Dang. I left my phone on my desk." Drew said as he reached in his pocket.

When Drew completed the call and returned to the table, he appeared shaken.

"What's wrong with you? You look like you've just run a marathon, what's up?"

Sweating profusely, Drew reached for his beer and guzzled half of the drink and then wiped his mouth with the cuff of his shirt sleeve. "Man, I've got to talk to you about a situation that's about to explode. The kicker is I've got until tomorrow to come up with a solution, or I'm toast."

Teddy knew something was going on with Drew. He had thought so for some time.

"This may take a while. Do you need anything?"

Teddy said, "No, I'm good."

"That was our accountant on the phone. She called to let me know that the deposit we made today wasn't enough to cover the overdraft at the bank. Please understand what I am about to tell you is confidential. You should not discuss this with anyone."

"Okay, what is it?"

"When we borrowed money from the bank on behalf of the firm, we used the real estate and accounts receivable to secure the loan. If you remember, Henry was still alive. He had learned of his terminal diagnosis, and Dad immediately named me a full partner in the firm and gave me most of Henry's criminal cases to handle. He also gave me signing privileges for the operating account and updated the corporate documents to allow me to transact business on behalf of the firm. It has been a policy of the firm that any check written for more than $5,000 required two signatures. So, we already have limited checks and balances in place to prevent fraudulent activity."

Drew stopped and took a deep breath and took another gulp of beer from his glass. He realized that using the term 'fraudulent activity' admitted guilt on his part.

Teddy was silent and looked at Drew with concern.

"When the architect finally told us, that he would not invest in the deal, we needed another quarter of a million dollars. I thought the firm could step in and help. Being very naïve, I did not run the plan by my father before signing my name to the banknote, which involved the firm in the industrial park. The additional burden of interest has created a challenging situation for the firm."

"Wait a minute, Drew," Teddy said. "You used assets from your dad's law firm as collateral for the loan to invest in the industrial park. Is that correct?"

"Yes, that's correct. The phone call I received was from our accountant. She received a call earlier from the bank. We accessed our line of credit, which our banker started when the first overdraft occurred. The interest payments for the $250,000 loan are huge, around $2,000 per quarter. The bank requires an annual principal reduction of ten percent, and we had to tap into the credit line to cover the payment."

"You're telling me you still haven't gone to your Dad? Drew, you're not naïve. You're an attorney, for God's sake."

"I know. Just let me finish. We are a solid firm, but this new liability has created a problem. The bank requires us to pay back the total line of credit by noon tomorrow, or the banker will notify my dad. Teddy, I have really screwed up. I should have never agreed to let the firm get involved with the industrial park without first discussing this with my dad. Now that Henry is dead, I'm carrying this burden alone." Drew's voice quivered, and as he finished he covered his face with his hands.

Teddy ran his hand through his hair and let out a deep breath and said, "Whew, that's a lot of information to absorb. I guess we need to figure out a way to pay the money back. But, first, I need to go to the restroom." While he was washing his hands, Teddy realized this was the reason he had scheduled the afternoon to spend with Drew.

When Teddy returned to the table, he said, "I knew there was a good reason the deal with the Hawkins's property didn't go through.

We have a sizable balance in the industrial park account that we can use to pay back the credit line. Perhaps, I can access funds from Dad's real estate company to repay the banknote until we can secure financing. Once the project is complete, I will replace the money. However, we need to remove the Byrd Law Firm's name from the project and eliminate the cash flow problem created by that loan. Once we do that, I suggest we both approach your dad and explain what has happened. He's a reasonable guy, and it will relieve him to know the reason for the cash flow problem."

Drew looked at his friend with a look of disbelief. "Man, are you sure you want to do this? Your dad has invested a fortune into this project. Would he approve of your using funds from his real estate account to cover that note?"

"Let's not forget, this was Dad's project, and he would have secured financing for the entire deal if you guys had not shown an interest. The industrial park was a dream of his, and I consider it his legacy if you will. Do you have online access to your loan account? If so, let's go online and find the amount of interest already paid by the firm."

Drew shook his head and said, "Yes. But, I left my phone on my desk."

"Well, just use the business office phone and call your bank and ask for a printout of interest already paid. Let your banker know we intend to cover the overdraft by the end of the day." Reaching for his briefcase, Teddy opened and removed the checkbook from the side pocket. "Drew, we'll cover the overdraft this afternoon. Tomorrow we will repay the credit line with a check from the industrial park so the banker will back off. My dad would expect me to repay every dime of interest paid by your firm, and that is what I intend to do. Perhaps the bank will transfer the original loan to Dad's company, and if that isn't a viable option, we will think of some other way to clear your dad's firm of this liability."

Drew returned to the Club's business office to place the dreaded call to his bank. As he dialed the phone number, his breathing became irregular and a wave of nausea swept over him. Once again, he practiced the deep breathing technique that he read about in his health magazine. Deep breath, hold eight seconds, release for eight seconds, and then repeat. He was thankful that Teddy had remained calm throughout the lunch and had offered to repay the line of credit as well as interest from the industrial park account. The breathing exercise worked, and he was feeling much better when the banker got on the line. Drew was cautious in choosing his words as he spoke to the banker, but he showed no alarm when asked about the total amount of interest paid to date.

"Listen Don, I will cover the overdraft by the end of the business day. If you are available tomorrow morning, my partner, Teddy Williams, and I would like to schedule an appointment to repay the credit line and discuss retiring the loan."

The banker placed him on hold as he gathered the information. Drew listened to classical music as he continued to practice the breathing technique which had proven to calm his nerves only a few minutes earlier, but he wondered if another train wreck was around the bend.

CHAPTER NINETEEN

D riving home from the assisted living facility, Claire looked forward to getting back home and making a cup of tea. She had visited Theodore every day since they dismissed him from the hospital following the second heart attack and subsequent stroke. The diagnosis was grim, and Claire recognized that each day Theodore lived was a special gift. Although he was confined to a bed and could not communicate, she insisted that he be treated as if he could respond. When she wasn't with Theo, she hired people to come in and read to him, and she played soft music in the background, which had been proven to promote healthy levels of serotonin. Finding a room in a facility usually took months, but with Teddy's contacts in the medical community, they had navigated through the health care system at a much faster pace than the typical family.

The amenities offered by The Summerhouse Assisted Living and Rehab Facility was exactly what Teddy and Claire wanted. A beautiful gray sided building perched on a hill overlooking a lake on one side and a picturesque view of the Blue Ridge Mountains on the opposite end. The architect had designed the facility to house modern exercise and spa rooms complete with well-appointed private suites on the second floor for overnight guests. Although the plan had been perfect, the economy at the time hadn't been able to support the extravagance. A developer from North Carolina riding through the area on his way home from Atlanta, one autumn weekend spotted the gray structure from the highway. As the developer steered his way up to the property, he was confident he could convert the high-end spa into an assisted-living facility. He had completed his fifth such facility the previous spring and was already planning to get started on another.

Claire found navigating the late afternoon traffic stressful. The gentle rain that had fallen since early morning had stopped before she left The Summerhouse. The roads were wet, but as the streetlights appeared at dusk, the streets took on a festive appearance. The Halloween Jack-o'-lanterns, which illuminated the front porches in town the previous month, had turned black as they shriveled and rotted. Claire looked forward to the approaching Thanksgiving holiday followed by the season of Advent. In eight weeks, they would attend the candlelight service on Christmas Eve night at the Methodist church. Claire and Teddy had spent the previous two Christmas Eve afternoons with Theodore until time to leave for church, and following the service joined the Byrd family for a festive meal.

She needed to call Daisy to accept the invitation to Thanksgiving dinner. In the previous two years Claire had spent the holiday with Theodore and enjoyed a turkey feast with the other residents at The Summerhouse. Recently though, Theodore's condition had declined to a comatose state, and he no longer responded to her or the staff.

When Claire checked her voice mail after lunch, there was a message from Teddy inquiring about their plans for Thanksgiving. Considering he and Nancy Leigh had separated and continued to negotiate the divorce settlement, Claire smiled as she listened to the upbeat message realizing her son was moving forward regarding the upcoming holiday plans.

As she drove down the familiar street in the well-established neighborhood, she spotted Teddy's car parked in the driveway.

"Good evening, son!" she said as she entered the kitchen. "It is such a welcoming sight to see the lights shining from the interior rooms as I pulled into the drive. I wasn't expecting you home so soon, but I'm glad you are here." She had considered calling a friend to go downtown for a nice meal at Scott's, but a dinner with Teddy would provide the perfect opportunity to discuss their plans for the holidays.

Teddy was addressing an envelope when Claire walked into the kitchen. "What are you working on there, son?"

"This envelope contains an option for the Hawkins' property which I asked Drew to review. Mr. Hawkins suggested since it was raining, to mail the option to his home as opposed to dropping by his house since his granddaughter will be back at the farm over the weekend."

Excited to see her son, but uninterested in an option for the property Claire began a lively chatter about the events of the day at the assisted-living facility.

"Mom, I need to go back over to the post office to mail this envelope. Would you like to ride with me downtown and grab a bite of dinner?"

"Oh Teddy, that sounds wonderful! I need to pick up a gift while we are in town if you don't mind. Just give me a moment to run upstairs and freshen up. I need to change into something more appropriate for dinner."

"No problem, take your time. We're in no rush."

The congested street on the way to the post office was a sign the holiday season was approaching. Individuals were leaving work, picking up children, meeting friends for dinner, and living life in a small town. The city was ablaze with Christmas decorations, including the twinkling of thousands of tiny white lights on the many trees and lamp posts encircling the city.

The tall, magnificent holly tree draped in multicolored lights at the intersection of Academy and Green Street, near the local Chamber of Commerce was in clear view of the post office.

"Teddy, do you see that beautiful holly tree? It has provided an annual announcement of the expected Christmas season for many decades. And each year, I think the tree is even prettier than the previous." There were large wreaths hung on the doors of the many businesses along the main thoroughfare throughout the city. Having grown up in town, Claire remembered with fondness the view from a child's lens of pure magical delight.

When he pulled out of the post office, Teddy headed toward the town square and parked in front of his mother's favorite restaurant, Scott's. He then turned to his mother for confirmation and Claire smiled with approval.

The captivating aromas of baked bread and roasted chicken were emanating from the kitchen as they entered the front door of the restaurant. As soon as the waiter appeared at their table, Claire ordered a cup of hot tea while Teddy ordered a cup of coffee. A basket of hot rolls and cinnamon butter arrived in time to enjoy as they watched the light snowfall from the restaurant window. The locals were assembling into the downtown area to admire the seasonal decorations and enjoy a meal from one of the many eclectic restaurants popping up around the square.

Claire had served on the beautification committee appointed by the city government. She worked closely with the downtown merchants' association to interject increased traffic into the downtown area. The city restored the extensive damage suffered during the 1936 tornado, but few modifications had occurred since that era. They determined a complete upgrade to the town square would be necessary if the city government intended to bring new life into the area.

"Daisy and I enjoyed serving on the beautification committee. We spent three years planning and scheduling meetings with leaders of other towns and municipalities as we gathered information which had proven successful in rebuilding their own downtown areas. We met some of the nicest people from around the state."

"Well, you can be proud of your work, Mom. The businesses in the downtown area are booming. And I must admit, the addition of brick streetscapes adds an old world feel to the square."

"One topic expressed by the merchant association members was their concern about the large millennial population continuing to travel to more populated areas closer to the Atlanta corridor. Those areas feature an array of shopping venues and upscale restaurants they view as more sophisticated."

"That was a valid concern. I can attest that my friends enjoy going to The Avalon and The Forum areas to shop and dine. There's something exciting about going to the "big city" on a Saturday afternoon."

"Such is the benefit of living close to a larger metropolitan area. Of course, young people also migrate to those areas because of the many job opportunities. The recent census shows they are better educated than any previous generation and have a greater appetite for high-end goods and services."

"Understandably so. We're a generation of self-declared foodies."

"That's a fair assessment. Unlike my generation, your friends take their children and dogs everywhere they go. So, babysitters are no longer needed."

"Look around outside. Everywhere you look, there are young adults with children and dogs of all sizes. I would say your committee nailed it, Mom."

"Thanks Teddy. The committee recognized the success of the downtown area depended on the financial support of the younger generation. Thankfully, it was just a matter of attracting businesses to entice us to shop locally, as opposed to spending our money in other towns."

"Well, I would say you were successful. This restaurant has made a huge difference in this area."

"Our committee worked to improve the footprint of the town to include green initiatives while continuing to support the local arts." Claire's interest included a vision of the future as she imagined herself and Theodore with their grandchildren enjoying the town area as a family. On this cold November evening, as she enjoyed a delicious gourmet meal with her son at this upscale restaurant, she felt a wave of pride while watching the young families meandering along the exquisite brick streetscapes.

As their waiter cleared the table Teddy asked, "Are you sure going to the Byrds' house for Thanksgiving this year is what you want? If not, we can make reservations here at Scott's."

Claire was careful in her response. She recalled the excitement in her son's voice on the message he left on her phone earlier in the day. "It will be fun. There's nothing like an elaborate Thanksgiving meal of turkey and dressing served in an elegant dining room, surrounded by family and friends." Claire glanced at the massive mirror on the wall, which provided a view of the satisfying smile on her son's face. "If that's settled, I'll call Daisy tomorrow and let her know we plan to join them for Thanksgiving dinner this year."

"That sounds good. While we are discussing holidays, which Christmas Eve service shall we attend this year?"

Claire shook her head and smiled. "I remember the Christmas Eve service your father and I attended the first year we married. There were two services held, and we attended the five o'clock service so we could get back home and enjoy the evening together. It was held in the original church building downtown, before they finished the new church out on the lake. The stained glass in that building was exquisite, and the light from the candles during the service danced off the various colors of the glass. It was a beautiful and surreal experience ... Let's mix things up this year."

"What do you mean?"

She thought back to the first year attending the service without Theodore. It was difficult, but Claire felt strongly about continuing to honor a tradition they had started together.

"What do you think about attending the late-night service? We can have a nice dinner around eight and have plenty of time to get to the church at eleven o'clock. And when the service is over, it will be Christmas morning."

"Sounds like a great idea! Let's do it."

Claire said, "I mentioned earlier that I need to pick up a gift at the Book Exchange. Do we have time to go over there when you finish your coffee?" She also wanted to hear the holiday music they piped in for the season.

"Sure. Let's spend a few minutes walking around the square. I haven't seen the decorations yet," said Teddy.

The Book Exchange was a gathering spot for book club members to discuss their latest purchases, while snacking on small plates of assorted fruits and chocolates. The younger adults discovered the carefree pleasure of the outdoor seating as they dropped by The Exchange, following an art exhibit or musical performance at the Coliseum or the Arts Center.

Claire smiled as they left the restaurant and walked toward the square. "This is a perfect November evening in Georgia. The air is crisp, and the holiday atmosphere is festive." The scents of hot chocolate, spiced tea, and Frasier fur escaped the many shops and bakeries. As Claire and Teddy found their way to The Exchange, couples of all ages were perched along the window seating while enjoying the holiday decorations and music.

"Mom, it's downright cold," Teddy said as he wrapped his scarf around his neck.

Claire laughed as she wandered in the door of the bookstore to pick up her gift.

She completed the purchase and turned to find her son, who was reading a menu in front of the big picture window. As she headed to the table, she stopped and chatted with a couple she and Theo had met at the Club.

* * * * * * * *

Teddy looked up as he heard his mom greeting her friends. The noise from the entrance of the building caused Teddy to shift his attention to the front door where a beautiful woman stood. Although, he had not seen her in over two years; he recognized Katie O'Neill at once. Teddy watched as she rubbed her gloved hands together and then dusted the moisture from her coat as she scanned the room. She was obviously looking for someone as she gazed from table to table. And then it happened, her face lit up as she bit her lower lip when she saw him. Teddy's eyes never left her face as he stood up and walked toward her.

As he approached, she looked at his extended hand, tilted her head, and with a sassy tone, she said, "Now, Mr. Williams, so you would like to shake my hand again? If I remember correctly, the last time we met my grandfather reprimanded you for holding on to my hand too long."

Teddy's head went back as he burst into laughter. "I had hoped you had forgotten that awkward moment. I don't understand what happened to me that day."

Katie squeezed his hand and reached up to give him a quick hug and a kiss on the cheek.

"It's good to see you, Teddy," she said as she looked over her shoulder to the area where Claire had purchased her book. "I'm supposed to meet a client, but he isn't here yet."

"Please, come and sit with us until he gets here. We've just come from Scott's and dropped by for a quick champagne cocktail." Teddy chuckled as he whispered in her ear, "Actually, Claire needed to pick up a gift, but I came for the champagne cocktail."

"Oh goodness Teddy, are you with someone?"

As Teddy directed her to his table he noticed Katie's face showed a slight disappointment. "Yes. But, no worries, she'll enjoy meeting you." Teddy motioned for Katie to sit down as he glanced back at his mother who was still engaged in conversation with her friends.

Katie stole a quick look at his left hand and noticed he wasn't wearing a wedding ring. "Should we grab another chair?"

An attractive woman approached their table and extended her hand to Katie and said, "Hello, I'm Claire Williams."

Teddy watched the surprise in Katie's face as she recognized the family resemblance between mother and son. As expected, he watched her graceful movements as she rose from her seat and accepted Claire's hand in a gesture of genuine warmth.

"Hello Mrs. Williams, such a pleasure to meet you." Katie cut her eyes at Teddy realizing he had tricked her into thinking he was with a date.

Teddy winked at her and flashed a huge smile as he watched the previous anxiety melt from her body. Katie and Claire talked like old acquaintances as Teddy offered his mother a chair and left the table to grab a chair for himself. He watched Katie engage his mother in conversation which endeared herself to him even more.

The waiter appeared with the two cocktails he had previously ordered, and he looked to Teddy for direction. Teddy nodded toward the ladies and motioned to prepare one more drink. During a lull in the conversation, Claire turned to Teddy. "I think meeting Katie is cause for a toast, but you don't have a drink."

The waiter appeared and placed the cocktail in front of Teddy. "Well, I do now." He lifted his glass and winked at his mother, and when he looked at Katie he noticed the twinkle in her sparkling eyes. He wondered if his mom had seen that, too. Claire smiled and said, "Here's to a lovely evening and a new friendship."

As they toasted, Teddy thought he couldn't have been more pleased had he planned the meeting himself. The first introduction to his mother played out like a scene from a classic movie, and it could not have been better orchestrated. Nor, could it have been any more different from the time he introduced Nancy Leigh to his parents.

CHAPTER TWENTY

A s Katie left The Exchange, warmth radiated throughout her body as she recalled running into Teddy and his mother. She and Claire had hit it off well, and as they were leaving the bar Claire had invited her to lunch the following Monday at Scott's. Delighted by the invitation that created some anxiety, she hoped Teddy would also join them.

An opening in Katie's schedule had allowed her to spend the day at the law firm working on the audit. Throughout the day she had noticed Drew had walked the halls, and she wondered if he needed to speak with her.

"Excuse me Katie, I don't mean to bother you but there is something I need to talk with you about," Drew said as he continued to glance up and down the hallway.

"Sure, come on in, I'm just wrapping up a review of the loan documents."

Drew had walked over to her desk and spoke in a low voice, "it's rather private and I wondered if you could meet me around eight o'clock at The Exchange downtown?"

Katie usually wouldn't have agreed to meet a married client after hours without another colleague present, but as Drew stood in her cubicle he nervously watched the door and spun his wedding ring on his finger. After some thought, she decided The Exchange was a safe place for them to meet.

As she walked around the square to her car, she thought back to the conversation with Drew earlier in the day. She examined their discussion word by word and was careful to recall anything in the conversation that should have caused alarm. He had seemed so nervous and fidgety, but she reasoned that something could have happened at home that prevented him from meeting her as planned.

She adjusted the heater in her car when she looked at the digital clock on the dashboard. The display showed 9:45 p.m., and she was toying with the option of driving back to Atlanta or finding a hotel room for the night. Prepared for the unexpected, Katie carried extra business clothes and toiletries in her car for situations such as this. After she fastened the seat belt, she realized by driving back to her apartment it would be late when she got into bed. The rain that had begun to fall earlier had turned to a mixture of rain and snow. Experiencing a sudden urge to see her grandparents, Katie made a split-second decision to spend the night at the farm. She had planned to spend the upcoming weekend at the farm, but with no place to stay the night the thought of snuggling down in her childhood bed was very appealing.

Thoughts of a relationship with Teddy Williams had occupied Katie's mind since they had met. The meeting at the bar was a random occurrence, and she could only consider that fate had directed her to the bookstore at the exact moment Teddy and his mother had picked up a Christmas present. Katie thought, *What were the chances of that happening?* As she turned into the driveway of her childhood home, she noticed a light in the kitchen area.

Good, she thought. *Nana is still up, and I would really enjoy a cup of hot tea while sitting in front of the fireplace in the kitchen.* Katie parked her car and removed her luggage from the trunk. As she slammed the trunk lid, Katie looked up to see her grandfather approaching the car with a gigantic smile as he held a cigar between his teeth.

"Papa, what are you doing up this late?" Katie asked. She dropped her suitcase and placed her arms around his neck.

"Well, sweetheart, I might ask you the same question." He laughed as he picked up the suitcase, and they walked toward the house with their arms linked. Katie knew there would be no more questions. Her grandparents had always respected her privacy.

Katie watched her grandfather's gait as he ambled toward the front porch in the cold rain. The dampness and the chill caused additional pain in his old joints, but she didn't draw attention to his pace. Instead, she asked him if he had enjoyed his day.

"Yes, I had a good day. I spent much of the day by myself while your grandmother went to Emory Hospital in Atlanta with one of her friends. It's unlike your grandmother, but she has said very little about her friend's health problems. So, let her tell you about it when she is ready, okay?"

"I agree. She'll tell us when she's ready."

As they continued toward the house, "you know how these ladies are sweetheart, they like to keep a few secrets between themselves, and I've learned through the years to let it go. I may not want to know about her friend's health issues, come to think of it."

Katie laughed at her grandfather but knew it amused him. Her grandparents had always shared everything with each other, and this situation was an exception in their marriage.

As they reached the steps at the front porch Tom stepped back to allow Katie to continue up the steps in front of him. "I know one thing, you are a sight for sore eyes. Nora was just saying at supper, she would love to sit down and share a nice cup of tea with you. I think she needs a little Katie time, sweetheart."

"Well, I'm glad I came by."

"While you're here, I need to go over a few items of business with you about the farm. So, please don't slip out in the morning before we talk, okay?"

"I plan to be back this weekend, so if we don't find time in the morning we can have that chat when I come back on Saturday."

Tom paused and then nodded his head. "Well, that sounds like a good plan."

Katie and Tom were laughing as they walked inside. "Nora, Mary Katherine's here!"

As their laughter awakened her, Nora jumped up from her chair and hurried through the kitchen. Her eyes moistened as she approached her granddaughter. "Oh, my goodness, I've been hoping you would stop by for the past week. I'm so glad you're here, and I see from your luggage you intend to spend the night." She wiped the tears from her face as she clung to Katie's hands. "Honey, your hands are freezing."

"Yes, it's cold outside. I noticed on the way over the rain is now mixed with snow. I believe I'll stand in front of that fire for a minute and get warm," said Katie.

Nora turned to her husband. "Tom, please take Mary Katherine's bags up to her room, and I'll make us a pot of tea."

Katie hugged her grandmother and inquired about her sudden show of tears, which was uncharacteristic.

Nora made a dismissive wave. "Oh, don't worry about me. I'm going through a teary-eyed phase. Go on upstairs and change your clothes, and I'll have a hot cup of tea ready when you come back downstairs."

Once in her room, Katie turned to her grandfather and asked what was going on with her grandmother.

Tom said, "Well, she has been acting a little different the past couple of weeks, but I believe she's worried about her friend's trip to Emory Hospital. The news may not have been what they had expected. I'm sure she will tell us when she is ready. Like I said earlier, let's act as normal as possible and not push her for an explanation, okay?"

Katie looked at her grandfather and smiled. "You are such a gentleman and a diplomat. No wonder she loves the ground you walk on. I hope one day to find a guy that is just half the man you are."

She reached up and cupped her grandfather's face in her palms and kissed his nose, a gesture he had often shared with her while growing up. Tom had dried thousands of tears and calmed many anxious moments by cupping her face in his large palms. Now, Katie used the same sweet gesture with her grandfather, and realized as she did that their roles had reversed.

The conversation between the three was light and fun, as they sat by the fire and enjoyed their tea until Katie began to yawn. "I'm ready to turn in. It's been a long day."

Nora asked, "Would you like a breakfast of blueberry pancakes and bacon before you head out in the morning?"

"You know I can't resist my favorite breakfast. But, I need to be on the road early to get through the morning traffic." She kissed her grandparents and went up to bed.

Katie looked around with nostalgia at the place that had provided a safe haven for her while growing up. When Katie opened her dresser drawer to remove a set of pajamas, she got a whiff of the 'Tommy Girl' cologne. Her best friend had spilled the cologne years before, during one of their sleepovers. Remembering how her life was much more straightforward then, Katie got into her bed. Then, she reached for the lamp switch when her eyes rested on the silver-framed picture of her young parents. She picked it up and looked at her mother's face, and wondered if her mother and Claire would have become friends.

She turned off the light and as she snuggled into her bed, her thoughts returned to Teddy Williams. Earlier in the evening, as she walked around the square to the bookstore she could see Teddy sitting at a small table in front of the window and he appeared to be alone. She remembered his solemn demeanor as he looked at the menu. Warmth permeated her body as she remembered the boyish smile which appeared on his face as he acknowledged her presence.

Their conversation was engaging, and the interest Claire showed in her seemed to delight Teddy. Katie wasn't sure what to make of the coincidental meeting, but, she was grateful that Drew had suggested meeting there. She decided that whatever force directed them to The

Exchange, she said a simple thank you as she fell asleep praying their paths might cross again soon.

Katie welcomed the restful night's sleep, and she jumped out of bed at the sound of her alarm clock. She went downstairs to get a cup of coffee, and her grandmother was already in the kitchen frying up a pan of bacon. Katie hugged her a little longer than usual as she realized she was shouldering a concern regarding her friend's health.

"I asked Papa last night if you were okay, and he told me about your trip to Emory yesterday with your friend. I want you to know that I'll be praying for her."

Nora wiped her hands on the kitchen towel and looked at Katie with a pensive expression. "Thank you, dear. One can never have too many prayer warriors."

Katie squeezed her shoulder. "That's true."

Nora's focus had returned to the pan of bacon frying on the stove.

"I will go back up and run through the shower and be back down in a few minutes to enjoy a stack of those blueberry pancakes you promised me last night."

As Katie dressed, the worried look on her grandmother's face concerned her. She appeared to have lost a few pounds since the last time she was home. When Katie finished dressing and was placing her clothes in her luggage, she noticed her parents' picture was not positioned as it was the night before. Then, Katie paused and picked up the frame once again and looked at the beautiful couple. That's when she saw it. The striking resemblance that Teddy Williams had to her father. His hair was close to the same color as his, but it was the charming smile and the sparkle in his eyes that tugged at her heartstrings. It was the same expression Teddy had on his face when he saw her standing at the front door of The Exchange.

This was an omen, Katie thought as she turned off the lamp. Perhaps the similarities were a sign from her dad that he approved of Teddy. Feeling a sudden closeness to her parents as if they were sitting on the bed and had just learned that she was in love for the first time, made her feel like they approved of him. Closing the bedroom door and stepping into the hallway, the familiar smells of brewed coffee and fried bacon conjured up memories of growing up at the farm. Halfway down the stairway, Katie stopped to inhale the comforting scents coming from the kitchen. Then, remembering the similarities between Teddy and her father, she bounced into the kitchen with a joy she hadn't known in months.

Pouring herself a cup of coffee and noticing the pancakes were almost ready, she was thankful the rain had cleared overnight because she wasn't looking forward to facing the morning traffic on I-85 South.

When the food was ready, Katie and Nora sat down to enjoy their breakfast. Katie devoured her pancakes, while Nora sipped her coffee and nibbled on a single slice of bacon. Hearing a noise, Katie stopped chewing and turned her head toward the kitchen window. "Nana, did you hear something?"

Nora nodded.

Picking up her coffee with one hand she reached for a slice of bacon with the other. Katie walked over to the kitchen window. "Is it normal for Sammy to be alone in the fields this early in the morning?" As she watched Sammy looking down at something on the ground.

Nora jumped up and went over to the window. "No. After he finished his breakfast he went out to the stable to check on the mare… What is that on the ground? Oh, my God! Mary Katherine, please run upstairs and wake your grandfather!" Nora then ran out of the kitchen door toward Sammy.

When Katie reached the top of the landing, she stopped outside her grandfather's room and listened for any sound of his snoring. Hearing none, she knocked on the door. While turning the doorknob, there was a hysterical scream from the yard.

CHAPTER TWENTY-ONE

Teddy and Drew met for breakfast to discuss reimbursing the interest paid by the law firm. The sum was a considerable amount of money, and Teddy could never have settled the score with Drew had his father not managed the funds for the project with such precision.

While munching on a slice of fruit, Drew asked, "Teddy, when do you plan to transfer the loan to your name and remove the law firm of the liability?" Teddy stopped writing the check and glanced over at Drew with a look of disbelief.

"Drew, I never intended to assume the loan personally. You know I don't have the assets to take on that kind of debt. What were you thinking?"

"Well, you sure talked like you had the money yesterday afternoon when you explained your plan to eliminate the liability, that I assumed to help your dad out of a jam."

Teddy felt a sense of anger welling up inside his body as he placed his pen on the table and looked out of the grimy restaurant window to absorb the impact of the remark.

After a few awkward moments, Teddy said, "Let's be clear, your decision to involve the law firm in the industrial park was never a result of a financial shortfall by the partners." He considered his words carefully and continued. "Believe me when I tell you, Drew, my dad and Henry were doubtful your father would ever agree to you becoming a partner, and they continued to seek additional financing. But, they were all friends, so when you gave them your money, Dad and Henry arranged a lunch meeting with your father and approached him about discussing the project, because an investment of that size warranted full disclosure as a partner." Teddy waited for Drew to comprehend his words. "On the day they met with your dad, they tried to disclose complete transparency. But, he brushed them off and refused to discuss it."

Drew looked surprised and said, "So, you're saying Theo and Henry didn't trust me?"

Teddy raised his voice, and then he paused and took a deep breath. "I didn't say that, Drew. They felt they owed him full disclosure on the deal. However, as we now know, not only was your dad unaware of your personal involvement, there's no way he could have known that you had leveraged his law firm." Teddy walked off to the men's room to cool off. He returned to the table scowling but sat down to write out the check to repay the interest the law firm had paid to the bank.

The tension between the two was still thick but Drew asked, "Nancy Leigh has been badgering me about the divorce. Have you heard from her lately?"

Teddy closed the briefcase and turned in his seat as he placed his elbow on the case, showing his indifference in hanging around. "Nope, I've not spoken to her in over two years. I really can't blame her for badgering you at this point, Drew."

"Teddy, it's just part of the process."

"Oh, yeah, part of the process. How could anyone drag out a divorce proceeding for this long? We were together a little over six years, and considering our limited assets, it shouldn't have taken long to settle. Tell me, Drew, what exactly are you hoping to find?"

Teddy looked away from the table as if searching for someone to redeem him from the current situation. He drank the last of his coffee and said, "I'll tell you how to resolve this issue. Prepare a settlement and include an offer of the car which she has driven since we married, plus $5,000 cash, and we can complete the divorce settlement this week. However, there is one caveat. She must accept the settlement by midnight Saturday, or otherwise, the deal is off. You have searched for assets owned by Nancy Leigh and me, and you have found none, correct?" Drew nodded.

"That's because there are no assets in my name. Except for the time working with my father, I have been in school, and if anybody should understand that, it should be Nancy Leigh. Please make this known to her. When we married, she had little more than the shirt on her back and shoes on her feet. My offer is a generous settlement considering the way she has disrespected my family."

Teddy cleared the table of the breakfast trash and looked over at Drew. "I'll meet you at the bank at eleven-thirty."

* * * * * * * *

It angered Drew as he watched Teddy leave the restaurant. With elbows on the table and his face placed in his hands, he rubbed his temples hoping to relieve the pressure inside his head. He couldn't understand why he had allowed himself to make such a blunder in front of Teddy.

He had always considered himself savvier than his friend. Teddy's soft-spoken voice, quiet demeanor, and noncommittal body language allowed him to mask his frustration. However, he could now see a resolve in Teddy that perhaps he had never noticed before, and Drew now thought he had miscalculated his inner strength. Teddy had also developed a degree of assertiveness, and wasn't taking any crap from him regarding the industrial park. He had shown true friendship in orchestrating a plan to redeem the firm of the liability that Drew had so carelessly incurred because of his extreme greed. He had to meet with the banker and then, later, his dad, and was unsure of the outcome.

* * * * * * * *

Don Johnson sat in his office and watched the front door, as Drew told him about Jacob's broken collarbone. Their sons were the same age but attended different schools, and the two dads had bonded over the years by sharing stories about their boys. But, as soon as Mr. Johnson spotted Teddy, he excused himself and went to greet the man whose family's business he had pursued for many years. There were individual families in a community whose business could make a big difference in one's career, and Mr. Johnson saw this as an opportunity to showcase his bank to a man whose family's wealth preceded him.

Once inside Mr. Johnson's office, Teddy greeted Drew and extended his hand. Although he measured his words, his professionalism was firmly intact. Mr. Johnson asked how he might assist the gentlemen, and Teddy was the first to speak. "Mr. Johnson, as you know, Drew took out a loan on behalf of his law firm to invest in the industrial park my dad developed, and now with the properties secured, we need to rid the law firm of its liability. We want to assume the loan in the industrial park's name, and by doing so, we can pay the note off when the park is complete. Hopefully, we can complete the transaction quickly."

Mr. Johnson removed a handkerchief from his jacket and began to clean his glasses. "So, gentlemen, if I understand you correctly, you want to pay off the loan incurred by the law firm and sign a new note for The Abington Industrial Park, LLC. Is this correct?"

Teddy said, "Yes, sir. That is correct."

"Yes. Yes, sir," said Drew.

"Let's look at the collateral securing the note, shall we?" He opened the folder and withdrew a sheet that itemized the collateral used to secure the $250,000 loan. The two guys leaned forward to view the document, and as soon as he saw Teddy's reaction to the items listed securing the loan, he suspected a problem.

Mr. Johnson gave the guys a few moments to review the collateral, and then he noticed Teddy had closed his eyes and leaned back in his chair. He turned and looked over at Drew, and he wondered if Teddy thought Drew could be of any help. As his banker, he knew his financial situation, and the only reason Teddy Williams was sitting in his office was because of Drew's financial problems.

Teddy looked up from the list of collateral. "Mr. Johnson, thank you for taking the time to meet with us this morning. Until now, I was not aware of the extensive collateral used to secure this note. I need a few days to consider my options before we discuss converting the note."

Mr. Johnson measured his words but knew he could work with Teddy. "Mr. Williams, you are a man of character, and I appreciate your honesty. For reasons beyond my control, the bank directors are concerned the law firm hasn't paid down the principle note. Also, there is a concern that the liability is... causing an undue strain."

"How much time do we have?" Teddy asked.

He folded his handkerchief with precision as he said, "I consider Drew Byrd a loyal customer and a good friend." The banker glanced at Drew and then turned his attention back to Teddy. "I would never want to betray his confidence by going to his father. However, the directors of this bank do not share my sentiment. Failure to resolve this issue by the end of the month will leave the bank with no other recourse but to involve Mr. Byrd."

Recognizing the tension between the two men, Mr. Johnson gave Drew a helpless look.

"Drew, I'm sorry. It is in your best interest to work with Mr. Williams to resolve this matter... as soon as possible."

* * * * * * * *

The dreaded meeting was over, and Teddy left the bank while Drew stayed behind for a few minutes to talk with the banker. As Teddy's head began to clear, he realized that he needed time alone. He considered contacting his great uncle Frederick, his grandfather's youngest brother, for advice. As the treasurer of the various corporations and LLCs owned by his family, they involved Uncle Frederick in forming trusts for three generations, and he oversaw the bookkeeping of each entity. Teddy knew his family had the wherewithal to absorb the debt, but he needed his uncle's help to work out the details.

When Drew came out of the bank, he approached Teddy in the parking lot and said, "I thought you were ready to convert the note."

Teddy looked at Drew. "What? How could you have put your family's business in such a precarious financial bind to invest in this real estate venture? I suppose you have pledged every asset owned by your dad's firm, Drew. I don't know the specifics yet, but we can't speak with your father until we have this sorted out and are certain of our options." There was an awkward pause, and then he continued. "I will get back with you in a few days." Teddy then turned and headed toward his car.

"Man, you can't leave this up in the air like this," Drew followed. "We need to put our heads together and get this resolved. I've already told my dad we would need a few minutes of his time this afternoon. He's expecting us around five o'clock. We need to straighten this out now."

With his hand on the car door, Teddy turned to Drew. "Oh, yes. We can leave it for a few days. Mr. Johnson and I have just entered a gentleman's agreement. He has given me to the end of the month, and I intend to make this happen. When we sit down with your dad, I'll have a viable plan to present."

Teddy got into his car and angerly slammed the door. As he backed out of the parking space, he turned on the radio. The twelve o'clock news had just started when the news reporter announced, "Breaking news report for Abington, Georgia: We have just learned that prominent landowner, Mr. Tom Hawkins, was found dead at his farm earlier this morning." Still in the bank parking lot, Teddy stopped the car and lowered his head as he thought of Katie. The reporter continued, "Mr. Hawkins was a county commissioner from 1974 through 1990 and was instrumental in the completion of I-985, which connected Abington to Cornelia, Georgia, in 1986. His one-hundred-acre farm has been pursued by local developers as part of an industrial park in southeast Abington. As of this news release, the funeral arrangements are incomplete."

CHAPTER TWENTY-TWO

Early in the planning stages, the family determined they would need a larger venue to accommodate the number of people planning to attend the funeral. Mr. Hawkins was never one to attend church regularly, but when he did, it was at a small country church with his wife and children. As soon as the funeral director learned of the governor's plans to attend, he approached Nora and offered his help in finding an appropriate size venue by contacting the ministers of the larger churches in the area.

On the day of the funeral, they filled the chosen First Baptist Church on Main Street to capacity as every prominent person in the area was in attendance.

Claire and Teddy arrived early, and as they waited for the funeral to begin, they noticed that several U. S. Representatives and both U. S. Senators representing the State of Georgia were in attendance along with local government officials, including the mayor, city council members, and county commissioners. The governor of Georgia, who practiced law in Abington before entering politics, also arrived at the church, surrounded by his secret service detail, who traveled in a caravan of black Cadillac Escalades.

The long black hearse, which carried the casket to the church, was as it always is, a sobering sight. On this day, while the soft billowing clouds floated over a canvas of vivid blue sky, a stark silence prevailed in the churchyard as the community stopped to pay tribute to the man whom many had known for decades.

The service began with the local minister, a pleasant young man with a resounding voice, reading from the book of Ecclesiastes followed by a song by Mr. Hawkins' son, Roger, sang while sniffles echoed throughout the crowd.

As Roger completed the song, his older brother, Stephen, made his way to the lectern and spoke briefly about his father.

In conclusion, Stephen said, "Together, as a family, we decided that it was only fitting for 'our Katie' to deliver the family eulogy."

A man of towering height, Stephen was the spitting image of his father. Teddy leaned over to his mother and whispered, "Stephen could pass for a younger version of his dad and is equally comfortable in his own skin."

Stephen waited as Katie made her way to the lectern. He kissed the top of her head while giving his niece a heartfelt hug before returning to the vacant seat between his mother and his wife on the first pew of the large sanctuary.

Katie appeared graceful and regal as she stood in front of the large congregation and showed no visible signs of nervousness. Katie looked out over the group with a look of satisfaction, as she observed the vast crowd in attendance to celebrate the life of her grandfather. She saw Tyler sitting on the left side of the church in the back, as she spread out her notes on the lectern and began…

"Just like there are seasons in the weather, there are also seasons in our lives. My grandfather weathered many seasons through eight decades, as a family man, a prominent landowner, and a political figure.

He was a large, imposing man, and some might even call him a hard man. However, I knew his compassion and his gentle spirit. He was comfortable with himself, which allowed him to put everyone at ease while in his presence, as he made one feel that their opinion was the only one that mattered.

Many of you may remember that lightning killed my grandfather's oldest daughter, Sophie, during an electrical storm. And, his oldest son, Ben, served in the military during wartime, where he died on foreign soil many miles from here in the jungles of Vietnam. One of the highest honors of my grandfather's life was when he accepted the Purple Heart our country awarded posthumously for the unselfish valor Ben exhibited while serving in a war he did not understand.

A few years later, when I was four years old, a tragic automobile accident occurred, which involved my mother, father, and baby brother and me. I was the only survivor. What are the chances, right? My dear grandfather was asked to identify the bodies of my family members. How hard that must have been for him. He had already lost his firstborn son and oldest daughter, and now suffering the loss of a third child was especially hard. I remember riding home from the hospital following the accident with my grandparents and me in the car. My grandfather drove over to my home and went inside as he left my grandmother and me waiting in the car. When he returned, there was a pillowcase full of items in one arm and Prissy, my little cocker spaniel, in the other. He had grabbed everything he thought I might need for the night, along with Prissy's bowl and food. They took me to their home on that night that forever changed my life. I remember walking inside that familiar old farmhouse, and we all sat down in the big country kitchen, while I held my dog Prissy in my arms, clinging to the last trace of a childhood which was only a memory. My grandfather cupped his large hands on the sides of my face and looked into my eyes. I will never forget the words he spoke that night, 'Mary Katherine, from this day forward you will live here with us. This is now your home.'

Faced with the three greatest tragedies of his life, my grandfather rose above the pain and grief and showed us all how a man of faith lives. He refused to focus on the loss. Instead, he focused on the blessings he had received from each of his children. Each child was a precious gift, and he appreciated their presence in his life. Please understand a smaller man, a weaker man, may have withdrawn from society and slipped into a deep depression. However, my grandfather was neither small nor weak. He was a tower of strength in the face of adversity, and it was through his strength and example that his family found comfort and survived.

Tom Hawkins was a man of integrity, a man of honor if you will. He suffered extreme loss in his life, but he also experienced great joy. He has three living sons, and all are pillars of their respective communities. All three are thriving in their chosen occupations, Sammy, who trains horses on the family farm; Roger, an accomplished musician and music professor in Athens; and Stephen, a successful contractor in Atlanta. Each of his sons has chosen a life of substance patterning themselves after their father's strong work ethic and displaying the same moral code of conduct. My grandfather leaves behind a large, loving family and a wife, I often say, 'who worshipped the ground he walked on.' They had a beautiful marriage, and they shared everything. He once told me, 'Your grandmother, and I formed a covenant with God on the day we married, and we don't take our union lightly.' Believe me when I say, he never did. My grandmother was the sunrise in his mornings, the sunset at the end of each day, and together they raised their family, worked their farm, and faced the tragedies and joys of life, while their love remained steadfast and strong.

My father, the man whom I adored, died when I was just four years old. I am told that he called me 'my Katie.' I was one lucky little girl to have a father like mine who was more significant than life. Even in losing my father, I was luckier still because of Tom Hawkins. As I say my prayers each night, I offer an extra prayer of thanksgiving for the man responsible for picking up the pieces of my shattered life."

When Katie finished the eulogy, business acquaintances told stories about Tom's love for the town of Abington. "He was a political activist with a progressive mindset to the very end," one political figure said, as he remembered his last discussion with Tom regarding ways to improve the community.

As the attendants removed the casket from the sanctuary, Roger sang an operatic version of 'Amazing Grace.' The powerful music was the perfect conclusion for a celebration service for a man of Mr. Hawkins's prominence.

Trailing the casket down the long aisle was Nora and her son, Stephen, followed by Sammy and Roger. Then, last to leave the family pew was Stephen's wife, Amanda, and Katie, followed by the other grandchildren, their spouses, and members of the extended family.

Teddy and Claire had positioned themselves at the end of a pew where Teddy could watch Katie from his angle. As Katie walked with her aunt Amanda down the aisle of the church, Teddy and Katie's eye locked from a distance. Teddy waited until Katie was a few feet away, then he winked and mouthed 'good job,' and Katie lowered her head and gave him a bashful smile and patted his shoulder as she walked by.

When Teddy and Claire arrived at the cemetery, they parked a few cars behind the Byrds. They walked behind them toward the grave site, when Teddy noticed Nancy Leigh and Brad Carlisle standing off to the side. Then Drew left his family and walked over to greet the couple who had caused his friend enormous pain. As Drew got closer, Nancy Leigh reached up and hugged him, and the embrace ended when Drew shook Brad Carlisle's hand and placed his left arm around his back resting on his shoulder. Teddy froze as he witnessed the friendly gestures of his best friend, soon-to-be ex-wife, and her lover.

CHAPTER TWENTY-THREE

C laire awakened early. She continued to toss and turn in her king-size bed for over an hour, until she finally got up and made a pot of coffee. The news of Tom Hawkins' death on Thursday had played havoc with her emotions, and Claire wasn't sure why the loss of a person whom she had never met would cause her such personal unrest. One might suspect because of the property Theodore wanted to purchase as part of the industrial park, but she couldn't be sure.

Theodore had been away from his business for three years, including the year he took off following his first heart attack. The industrial park was a project Teddy vowed to complete, but they had never involved Claire. So, neither her husband's investment nor the death of a potential client should cause emotional unrest in her life.

As she stood next to the counter waiting for the coffee to brew, she thought *Teddy is in love with the Hawkins' granddaughter*. Mothers just know these things, and after carrying a baby around inside her body for nine months, they develop a sixth sense about their offspring.

It's the same as knowing when a child has lied or misrepresented the truth. It's part of an innate sense that's awarded to mothers during childbirth. But, one thing Claire knew for sure, Katie could not hide her love for Teddy. After meeting Katie at The Exchange Claire had never seen Teddy react to anyone with the same level of tenderness as he exhibited that evening. His insistence on attending her grandfather's funeral to show support, and the intimacy shared as they acknowledged each other's presence when Katie walked out of the church, once again confirmed their feelings were mutual.

171

As Claire sat down at the breakfast table, she began to reminisce. Neither she nor Theodore thought Teddy had married Nancy Leigh for love, and even now, their initial assessment of Nancy Leigh had not changed. Teddy brought Nancy Leigh home one weekend from college unannounced. At the end of the weekend, as Teddy backed his car out of the drive heading back to college, Theodore turned to Claire and said, "That girl is nothing more than a gold-digger." Sadly, Claire knew her husband was right.

Claire's thoughts kept returning to Nora Hawkins. She had met Katie's grandmother at the funeral on Sunday and immediately noticed her humble nature. She wanted to reach out to Nora, perhaps take food and share lunch with her, or just go down to her home and be neighborly.

When Teddy came downstairs, Claire mentioned her plans to visit Nora. She explained her concern about how it might look, considering their connection to the industrial park. But, Teddy had encouraged her call and arrange a visit.

Once she finished the breakfast dishes, Claire went upstairs to shower and dress. As she was leaving the house, she stopped by the kitchen to gather the basket of food items and turned off the lights.

Teddy had written detailed directions to the Hawkins farm, and Nora was waiting for her on the front porch when she arrived. Following a few minutes of small talk, Nora appeared to be relaxing as the conversation flowed.

"Claire, let's move inside and make a pot of tea."

"I'd love a cup of tea." They continued to discuss the people who attended the funeral on Sunday. Claire shared that, like her, she had also buried more than one child. Nora could not keep her emotions in check as she admitted to Claire that she had received a special gift in her marriage to Tom Hawkins.

When Claire noticed the tears forming in Nora's eyes, she reached for her hand and said, "Oh, dear. I know your emotions are still raw."

After a few moments, Nora excused herself in search of a Kleenex. When she returned, the water was hot, and she prepared mugs of tea for herself and her guest.

Nora took her tea and stepped over to the window in front of the kitchen sink, where she had watched several tragedies occur throughout her life on the farm. She turned to Claire and said, "Step over here beside me, Claire, I want you to see something."

Claire placed her mug on the kitchen table and joined Nora in front of the window. Nora pointed out to the pasture and said, "Do you see that area of the pasture?" And she told the story of Sammy's accident on that dreadful summer day many years ago, and as she did so, tears moistened her wrinkled face.

Claire wondered why she recalled the tremendous pain by reliving that day, so soon following her husband's death.

When she completed the story, Nora looked at Claire and said, "And, Claire, that is the exact place where we found Tom on Thursday morning. Who would believe Tom died in the same spot where Sammy suffered his accident?" As she told how they found Tom's body, Claire understood the pain she had experienced and marveled at the inner strength she had displayed throughout the previous days. Nora then placed her mug on the kitchen counter, covered her face with her hands, and sobbed. Claire put her arm around her new friend and cried, too.

Once they regained their composure, Nora turned to Claire and said, "I'm so glad you're here. The boys headed back yesterday afternoon. Katie had a few errands to run this morning, and I dreaded being here alone today. It's hard to explain, but even surrounded by all the family and friends the past few days, I have never felt so alone."

Claire hugged Nora and said, "After living with Tom for such a long time, I'm sure you are feeling an unbearable loss."

Realizing that Claire had just read her mind, Nora smiled at her and said, "I believe I have a new friend in you, Claire Williams."

They busied themselves by refilling their tea mugs and settled into chairs at the kitchen table when they heard a car coming up the long drive. A few moments later, Drew appeared at the back door. Nora opened the kitchen door and invited him into the house. However, it was apparent she wasn't expecting him.

The three exchanged pleasantries. Claire thought Drew was there to probate Mr. Hawkins' last will and testament. Nora's demeanor had changed from humble and sad to agitated, so Claire said, "Nora if you don't mind, I will take my tea out on the front porch so you and Drew can spend a few moments in private." Nora nodded her head as she continued to watch Drew.

Claire hesitated when she reached the front door. Nora's reaction to Drew caused her concern and, she thought it unusual for an attorney to make a house call. She stepped out onto the front porch and sat in one of the large rockers. As she looked out upon the rolling fields, Claire thought about a childhood surrounded by the beautiful landscape. She spotted a few horses in the pasture and wondered if Katie had grown up riding.

When Claire walked out to her car, she noticed Drew had parked behind the house instead of in the driveway. She saw movement in the front seat of his car, and she moved closer to get a better look. The lady in the car turned her head, and she saw it was Nancy Leigh. Claire muttered to herself, "that's odd," as feelings of suspicion overtook her.

CHAPTER TWENTY-FOUR

(Flashback)

Drew's parents and Mr. and Mrs. Williams were the best of friends. Although Drew considered Teddy, to be his best friend, he had always been envious of his natural charm and ease with the ladies. Teddy appeared to be born with a silver spoon in his mouth, and education had never been a struggle for him. Drew knew of the success Mr. Williams had enjoyed because of his real estate dealings and the significant wealth of Dr. and Mrs. Simpson, whose only child was Teddy's mom.

Drew was two years ahead of Teddy in school. He also wanted to be a doctor, but not with a passion that most people have when they declare a profession at a young age. Still, he wanted the prestige and wealth associated with the lifestyle of a medical doctor. Unfortunately, his grades in mathematics and science weren't as good as Teddy's, and Drew realized getting into medical school was a crapshoot. Although, his parents were comfortable, he wasn't sure they had the wherewithal to handle the expense of twelve years of higher education. But, in the end, it had not mattered, because his GPA and the Medical College Admission Test scores, were below the necessary requirements, and his list of civic and leadership involvements weren't strong enough to be accepted into a medical school. On the day he received the letter from the M.C.A.T., Colleen told him she was pregnant and wanted to get married. Hence, he changed direction and had applied to take the Law School Admission Test, passing it on the second try.

* * * * * * * *

When Drew met Nancy Leigh, it took him a while to figure her out. She wasn't the typical sorority girl he would have expected Teddy to date in college. She didn't have the financial means to support an affluent college lifestyle. She was different.

Teddy had introduced Nancy Leigh to Drew and Colleen the weekend he brought her home to meet his parents. The first evening at the club while the four were at dinner, Drew made two remarks to Nancy Leigh about Teddy's family's wealth, and it should have been evident to everyone present that Drew had a motive for sharing this information. Once Drew realized the socioeconomic level of the family Nancy Leigh had been born into, it would be just a matter of time before he would bring her into his confidence to assist him in his plan. However, he would need to take it slow so as not to bring attention to his scheme.

At the end of the weekend, after Teddy and Nancy Leigh had returned to Athens, Drew pondered how best to approach her. He had heard through Colleen that she had dated a tennis player by the name of Brad Carlyle. While she continued dating Teddy, she had continued to meet Brad at an obscure bar on the edge of town.

Drew hooked up with Nancy Leigh one Wednesday night at The Nighthawks Bar, a local hangout for college students. As Drew entered the bar from the quiet side street, the heavy smoke engulfed him and caused him to cough. The music from the jukebox was playing a song from an American rock band when he spotted Nancy Leigh sitting alone in a booth. She looked at the front door and saw him, then she cut her eyes from one end of the bar to the other and back to the front door. Drew looked around the bar, and then he strolled over to her booth. "Hello, Nancy Leigh. What a coincidence meeting you here tonight." Drew had done his homework and knew she met the tennis player every Wednesday evening at the bar. He also identified The Nighthawks Bar as an establishment that Teddy Williams would never frequent.

"Hi, Drew," she said.

"It's a damn small world, isn't it?" Drew wondered why he had made such a ridiculous statement.

Nancy Leigh folded her leg and pulled it under her which provided a better view of the front, she shifted in her seat and continued to watch the front door and said, "What, what are you doing here?"

Drew said, "I'm hoping to meet a local tennis instructor by the name of Brad Carlisle, about lessons for a friend's sister. Her birthday is next month, and my friend wants to hire him to teach her to play. Someone told him I could find him here on Wednesday evenings."

Nancy Leigh responded, "This guy must be a good friend for you to drive all the way to Athens to find an instructor for his sister. Is he a fraternity brother?"

"Yes, yes, he's a fraternity brother. He lives out of town and has asked me to meet with Mr. Carlisle and make sure he's a decent guy to instruct his little sister."

After a second beer, Nancy Leigh relaxed and brought up the previous weekend at Teddy's home. "Teddy's such a down-to-earth guy. It surprised me he came from such a rich family."

"Yes. The Williams are prominent members of the community, as I mentioned the other night at dinner. They're well-off."

Tilting her head, Nancy Leigh asked, "I never understood the phrase, well-off. What exactly does that mean?"

Drew ignored the sarcasm but used the moment to introduce his plan. "Teddy's grandfather was a prominent doctor, who was loaded, and Teddy will inherit millions from his grandparent's estate."

"How do you know so much about Teddy's financial business?"

"Remember, I passed the bar exam, and attorney's get paid to know these things about people."

"And, why are you telling me this?" she asked.

"You're in college to get an education, aren't ya? Education comes in varying forms. If you marry well, you could stand to gain a lot of money. If you marry a bum, not so much." He raised his eyebrows and smiled.

"So, are you suggesting Teddy and I get married?"

"Yes, that's exactly what I am suggesting. And, then once the inheritance has been distributed and you and Teddy have been married a few years, you could divorce him and walk away with half of his inheritance. Unless you have a better idea," said Drew.

She sat up straighter and said, "What's in it for you, counselor?"

Drew saw the trust developing between them and said, "As your attorney, I'll settle the divorce and get a percentage of your settlement," he said.

He had piqued her interest when Nancy Leigh waved at a guy who was standing at the door. When he reached the booth, he leaned over and hugged Nancy Leigh before shaking Drew's hand. "Hi, I'm Brad Carlisle."

Nancy Leigh said, "Drew, and I were just discussing a plan for us to make some quick cash."

"I could use some extra cash. But, right now, I want to eat supper," said Brad.

Nancy Leigh nibbled at her food while Brad finished his plate of ribs. When Drew finished his meal, he noticed a young lady in a saddened state sitting alone at the bar who controlled the jukebox with a stream of quarters as she played songs from a newly released album. However, the song that spoke to her inebriated state was a love ballad. And she played it over and over while nursing her drink. Although Drew found the repetitive music annoying, he saw the irony in the words which related to their plan of Nancy Leigh keeping her relationship going long enough to get the money.

As the evening progressed, Drew explained the multi-million-dollar inheritance Teddy would receive from his grandparents' estate, and the three devised a long-term plan which involved Nancy Leigh and Teddy marrying. Nancy Leigh told them she thought she could pull it off, provided she could win the hearts of Mr. and Mrs. Williams. The plan involved the couple living together long enough for Teddy to receive the sizable inheritance from his grandmother Simpson, and then Nancy Leigh could divorce Teddy and walk away with at least half of his estate. The agreement also included giving each guy a 25% cut of her divorce settlement. When Drew left the bar at the end of the night, Nancy Leigh and Brad had agreed to meet with him every month to discuss their plan. Nancy Leigh first made Brad promise they would continue their relationship after her marriage to Teddy Williams. The words of the song now etched in Drew's mind, and the mention of the tennis lesson for his friend's sister was long forgotten.

CHAPTER TWENTY-FIVE

K atie had planned to return to the city on the day following her grandfather's funeral. But, as the other family members left, she could tell that Nora needed someone to stay with her for a while longer.

She watched as her grandmother tried to function in a world without the person whose life she had shared for over sixty years. The grief in her life was intense and the void so profound, that it seemed to have manifested into a physical illness. It made it difficult for her to focus on simple tasks: namely, locating copies of Tom's last will and testament.

Katie had set a basket in the parlor to collect the newspapers and mail until after the funeral. As life on the farm returned to a natural pace, she eyed the growing stack of papers but had not found the time or energy to sort through them.

After breakfast, Katie made a quick trip to check on her apartment and pick up some files from the office to work on while staying with her grandmother. When she returned to the farm in the late afternoon, she noticed an unfamiliar vehicle parked outside her grandmother's house. Her grandmother was sitting on the front porch involved in a serious conversation with someone Katie could not see, the angle of the chair impeded the identity of the visitor. Katie saw her grandmother dabbing her eyes with a Kleenex, and wondered if this had been another stressful day. She gathered her clothes and other items from the trunk, and as she approached the front porch, she saw the visitor was Claire Williams. Katie stopped at the bottom of the steps, and her face turned red as she covered her mouth with her hand.

"Oh, my gosh, Mrs. Williams, I apologize. I forgot about our lunch date today at Scott's. Please forgive me." Her eyes filled with tears.

Claire walked down to the bottom step and put her arm around Katie. "Sweetie, please don't worry about it, once we heard about your grandfather's death, I dismissed our plans altogether," Claire took two of the bags from Katie's arm, "we'll have lunch another time."

Katie felt a sense of relief as she prided herself on being dependable. As Katie took her bags up to her room, Claire cleaned up their teacups and straightened up the front porch area where she and Nora had spent the afternoon. Claire gathered the bag which she used to transport their food, and as she prepared to leave, Nora and Katie walked with her to the front door. Claire reached for a hand from each of them and said, "I want both of you to know I am just a phone call away if either of you needs me." The remark could have sounded empty or patronizing. But when Claire stood in the front door of the farmhouse, there were tears in her eyes as she spoke, and both women knew she spoke with sincerity.

When Claire left, Nora went back into the kitchen, and Katie stopped by the parlor and removed the stack of papers from the basket. She went into the kitchen and dropped the mail on the table while Nora sat down and laid her head on the back of the sofa.

Once Katie had opened the sympathy cards, she arranged them for Nora to read; she noticed a large parcel from the Williams real estate firm. She tore into the envelope and realized it was a contract which was dated the day before her grandfather's death. As Katie continued to go through the mail, she sorted the items in the order of importance. Then, she opened her grandparents' bank statement and paused when she saw the balance in the account was over $60,000.

She looked up from the statement and asked, "Nana, has anyone made a large deposit into the bank account, perhaps from the sale of equipment or livestock?"

Her grandmother was resting because her eyes were closed, and she held a pillow to her tummy.

Katie spoke louder. "Nana, did you hear me?"

Nora opened her eyes and with a puzzled look, said, "What are you talking about, sweetheart?"

"I haven't reconciled the bank account in several months, but it appears a large deposit was made into your account, and I was wondering where the funds came from. The night before Papa passed, he told me we needed to discuss a few items of business. And, I put him off since I was planning to be here over the weekend. Perhaps he had expected to discuss the deposit with me then."

"I remember Tom mentioning that he needed to discuss a business matter with you."

"But, he didn't tell you what it was about?"

"No." Nora shook her head.

"Here is an option for the land purchase from the real estate firm. It's dated the day before Papa's death. We've discussed the possibility of an option on the land in the past, but I'm surprised the investors continue to show interest... I read an article in the local paper several months ago that suggested they had purchased enough property to complete the last stage of the industrial park."

Nora got up from the sofa and walked over to the kitchen table and picked up the contract that included an option. "This contract is from The Williams Real Estate Firm." She turned back to the sofa as she handed the document over to her granddaughter.

"Yes."

"The other one was from The Abington Industrial Park Group."

Katie turned in her chair to face her grandmother and said, "What are you talking about, Nana? We hadn't received an offer before this one unless Papa didn't tell me." She paused, "Perhaps he was trying to tell me about it the night before he died."

When Katie finished sorting the papers, she also caught up on some paperwork for the farm. After several hours, Katie finished the bank reconciliation, and then she organized the documents to file. When Katie returned to the kitchen, Nora was snoring softly, and the pillow was still pressed to her abdomen area. Instead of waking her, she found a soft blanket on the top shelf of the hall closet and gently wrapped it around her grandmother for warmth. As she did, she noticed her grandmother's skin was Jaundiced, which she had seen earlier but had not mentioned while Claire was with them.

While Katie tidied up the kitchen area, she thought about Teddy, and she wondered if he had contacted her grandfather recently. Her eyes filled with tears as she pondered if he had experienced a premonition about his death.

She went up to her bedroom to change into her pajamas, and she remembered the envelope from Teddy. The address was handwritten, and she wondered why there were two contracts. It saddened her to think that her grandparents had once again considered selling the family farm.

Katie wiped her eyes as she grabbed a pillow from her bed along with a blanket and headed back downstairs to sleep in the overstuffed chair near her grandmother.

The bright red embers, remnants of the fire which she had built earlier in the evening, were hot and aglow in the stone fireplace. She sat down on the hearth and stared at the flickering fire as she considered whether she should call Teddy to ask him for an explanation about the contract or wait for him to contact her. Of course, she hoped he could tell her about his last conversation with her grandfather.

Before Katie settled into her makeshift bed, she added more wood to the fire since she was confident that sleep would be difficult.

CHAPTER TWENTY-SIX

A s Teddy reviewed his financial options, he focused on the extensive list of collateral Drew had pledged to secure the bank loan. There had always been little nuances about Drew that irritated Teddy, such as the time they caught him cheating on the golf course by misrepresenting strokes on his scorecard. Also, there were times when they were at dinner with their wives when Drew would have forgotten his wallet as the time approached to settle the dinner bill. The guys enjoyed a long history together, and Teddy had often overlooked the unethical manner in which Drew conducted himself.

Although Drew's profession was law, his narcissistic behavior justified his motivation to flirt with breaking the rules. Teddy had noticed that Drew appeared to enjoy a euphoric drug-induced, high, as he pushed the limits of the law to the extreme edge. However, the behavior he exhibited regarding the bank loan was bordering on a criminal type behavior. Drew was a legitimate partner in the law firm, but his misuse of collateral could have landed himself in prison if he had worked for anyone other than his father.

Teddy needed someone with whom he could discuss the situation. So, he reached for the phone and called his grandfather Simpson's younger brother, Frederick. He was the only person other than his father, who understood the dynamics of the family finances.

* * * * * * * *

Teddy's Great-Uncle Frederick Simpson owned a small law firm in Savannah, Georgia, that catered to successful corporate types. The City of Savannah, with the bordering towns of Tybee Island and Hilton Head Island, S.C., became a local gold mine for his uncle's established tax attorney practice.

Frederick was an eccentric type who married late in life to a lovely artist. Mary explained to Frederick during the early stages of their relationship that she could not bear children. A romantic at heart, Frederick wanted a family, and he found the news disappointing, but he was so smitten with her he could not endure living without his Mary. They married in a small country church on the coast of Georgia, spent their honeymoon in Savannah, and had remained there for forty-five years.

His uncle answered the phone on the second ring, and Teddy immediately recognized his deep voice. They spent a few moments catching up on Theodore's medical progress. Then Frederick asked about Claire, whom he and Mary loved as their own. Teddy skirted around the industrial park inquiries until they had exhausted discussions about the family. Then as soon as the conversation settled down, Teddy explained the reason for his call.

Teddy described the current situation with which he found himself involved, and he was grateful that Frederick listened without interruption. Teddy told his uncle he considered him a brilliant businessman, and he trusted his interpretations of tax law better than anyone else in his circle.

As the two men bounced ideas back and forth, Frederick asked, "Son, could you come down to Savannah for a few days so we can sit down, face to face, and examine the legal and financial options?"

"Yeah, that sounds like a wise move, and I look forward to visiting with you and Aunt Mary."

"Mary will be so pleased. I've been wondering how to entice you to come to Savannah for a visit. I'm not sure if Claire has told you, but Mary is growing weaker with each passing day. I hate to end on a negative note, but you know when she passes, I won't be far behind." Teddy ran his fingers through his hair as he considered the seriousness of the situation, which could send a family friend to prison if not handled with delicate care.

When he hung up the phone, Teddy decided he should contact Drew's banker. He needed more time to pay off the law firm's loan. He dialed the phone number to the bank, and the call went straight through to his office. "Mr. Johnson, this is Teddy Williams with the Williams Real Estate Company."

After exchanging pleasantries, Teddy said, "Drew Byrd and I met with you last week to discuss the loan his firm has with your bank, so I thought I should call and provide you with an update on our situation."

Mr. Johnson was cordial and encouraged Teddy to continue.

"As you may have heard, my father is in an assisted-living facility because of declining health. In the interim, my goal is to complete the industrial park project. However, now I am unclear of my authority to transact business at this level, which would allow me to borrow money on behalf of my dad's company. The good news is my great-uncle is a tax attorney in Savannah, and he has handled the legal matters for my family for several decades. I contacted him this morning and agreed to meet with him on Thursday at his office. During that meeting, I hope to gain a better understanding of how to resolve the loan. Therefore, my question to you is, can you allow me a few more days?"

Teddy could tell from Mr. Johnson's tone of voice that he was glad he had called and agreed to allow more time. Teddy also thought from talking with Drew, that Mr. Johnson's position at the bank was possibly compromised, as a result of making the loan to Drew.

When Nora awoke on the sofa, she allowed herself to enjoy the tranquil moments of the new day. She thought about her conversation with Katie the previous night. She had wanted to tell her granddaughter about the visit from Drew Byrd, but she hadn't had the energy to discuss anything more about their finances. The intensity of the pain had returned to her body, and all she wanted was to be still and pray that the piercing pain would soon subside.

There were so many things to handle. Nora wondered if it was too soon following Tom's death to begin. However, Drew's visit to discuss the fate of the farm had affected her emotional state and was foremost on her mind.

Nora had not moved from the sofa when Katie came back into the kitchen. She knew Katie was ready to discuss the options regarding the farm, so Nora got up from the couch and left the room. She returned to the kitchen with an envelope in her hand and placed it on the table. The short walk to get the document had exhausted her as she took slow, deliberate steps towards the kitchen sink. Nora poured a glass of water from the faucet and swallowed her morning meds, and then she turned and faced the table while Katie stared at the document. When Katie finally picked it up, she turned to the last page, which bore the signature of the individuals representing the two parties. Someone had attached a photocopy of the earnest money check to the document. Fifty thousand dollars to hold the land until Tom and Nora's deaths, at which time the family would decide the final fate of the farm. The large sum of money showed the investors' level of interest in the property.

Nora winced as she leaned into her left side while she prepared the coffee. Katie was quiet as she read over the document, but she looked up when she heard her grandmother's moan and saw her grab her waist.

When the coffee finished making, Nora poured two mugs of coffee, walked over to the table, and sat down opposite her granddaughter. "Mary Katherine, would you mind throwing a few logs on the fire, please? We have a few matters to discuss, and a nice fire will knock the chill off while we're talking."

"Good idea." Katie immediately busied herself with the job of building a fire, and the heat soon permeated the kitchen area. "Is it safe to assume the large balance in the checking account is from the $50,000 earnest money deposit, right?"

"Yes." The comforting sound of the crackling wood burning in the stone fireplace, and the smell of freshly brewed coffee, allowed Nora to relax as she explained the contract from Drew.

When Nora finished telling her about Drew's visit, the pain was better, "Honey, I have some other news I need to tell you."

Katie asked, "Something other than the contract?"

"Yes. I have been to Emory Hospital for extensive testing, and they've confirmed that I have late stage pancreatic cancer."

And with a gasp Katie said, "What?"

"The night before Tom died when you came by to stay because of the bad weather, if you remember, I cried when you came in the door. Well, that was because the doctor had confirmed the diagnosis of cancer that day."

"Did Papa know?"

"No, honey. He did not."

"But, when I asked him about the tears, he told me you had been going with a friend to Emory for testing. Was that what you told him?"

Nora nodded and said, "Yes, honey. I wanted to spare him the worry of waiting for the test results. I planned to share the news with both of you and Sammy on Saturday."

Katie looked up at the ceiling to hide her tears. She got up and knelt beside her grandmother's chair and laid her head in her lap and cried.

Nora stroked Katie's hair and said, "It's okay to cry, honey. It's not healthy hold your tears in, you need to get it out."

"I'm trying to be strong for you, Nana."

"I know you are, and I love you for it," then she choked up. "I wanted to tell you after the funeral on Sunday while the family was together. But I couldn't do it. This has been such a difficult week for all of us, and I was afraid I wouldn't be able to discuss the diagnosis without breaking down. Keeping the news quiet has been hard. I've been waiting to share the news with you, but now that I've spoken the words, I'm at peace."

* * * * * * * *

Following their talk, Katie showered and prepared to go into town on the pretense she had a few personal errands that required her immediate attention. She dressed casually, grabbing a comfortable pair of jeans from her closet. While thumbing through the folded tops on the closet shelf, she chose a white turtleneck sweater and reached for her favorite blue blazer. When she looked in the mirror, she knew the perfect shoes to complete her outfit; she slipped her feet into the ballerina style Tieks and marveled at the comfort of the shoes. The classic signature outfit would allow her entrance into any professional office. Combing through her hair, she thought of the one person with whom she needed to speak, and she felt a sense of enthusiasm for the first time since her grandfather's death.

As Katie walked out the backdoor of the warm farmhouse, the crisp autumn air was a refreshing welcome. But, tears filled her eyes as she looked out over the beautiful pasture of the farm her grandfather had spent his life nurturing. Katie wiped her tears from her face and thought, *the separate offers for the property is the challenge. I need to stay focused.* It had been tough maintaining a sense of composure the past few days, and she was eager to get away for a few hours to sort through her feelings. Perhaps more importantly, to meet with the last person outside the family to speak with her grandfather before his death.

As she pulled into traffic, Katie touched the list of questions on the passenger's seat. Then she glanced in the mirror, removed her tinted lip-gloss from her pocket, and patted her lips. Katie was ready to learn the extent of Teddy's involvement with the industrial park. At the corner of Maple and Pearl Nix Parkway, the light turned red. While she waited for the light to change, she spotted Teddy's vehicle in the parking lot at the real estate office, and she prayed that he was an honorable man.

Katie turned into the parking lot and found an available space. She grabbed the list of questions along with her purse and got out of the car. Because of habit, or perhaps nervousness, she glanced at her reflection in the car window and noticed a hint of sadness on her face. Katie put a smile on her face and walked toward the entrance of the building.

As soon as she opened the solid mahogany door, she felt a shift in the atmosphere as she stood and examined the interior. The grandiose building represented success on such a large scale that it impressed Katie. She felt a sudden tinge of intimidation by her surroundings, as she recalled a remark made by her grandmother on the day of her first meeting with Teddy at the farm. It was something about the Williams being high rollers and very sophisticated. She now understood the reason for the remark. Katie took a deep cleansing breath as she noticed the elaborate high ceiling of the enormous lobby. It reeked of old money. Then it occurred to her that Teddy was a man born into prominence, and his pedigree had allowed him the comfort of no pretense.

As Katie entered the large suite which housed the real estate office, an attractive, middle-aged receptionist greeted her. She introduced herself and told the receptionist that she was there to see Teddy Williams. The receptionist suggested she take a seat as she went into the next room to examine his schedule. When Katie walked over to take a seat, her shoes mired down into the plush carpet, the floor covering was a luxury on a grand scale.

Within a few minutes, the receptionist returned to the reception area, walked over to Katie, and said, "Dear, if you will follow me, I will show you to Mr. Williams' office." Katie suppressed a smile as she witnessed the formality the receptionist displayed while directing clients to the private office. As they entered, the receptionist continued her performance by introducing Katie, and as Teddy rose from his seat to shake her hand, he dismissed the receptionist with a nod.

Then he walked over to the chair opposite his father's desk and offered Katie the other seat as he inquired about her visit on such a chilly Wednesday morning.

Katie looked around the office and said, "Do you mind if I walk around your office for a moment?" She thought *you can tell a great deal about a person and their values by the contents of their office.*"

"Of course. You're welcome to look around, but please remember this is my father's office, which I am using until the industrial park is completed. Therefore, you will find little history regarding my life in these surroundings."

"Oh, I beg to differ, Mr. Williams. Look at this picture of you." She picked up the frame from the desk. "These are your roots. Whether you recognize this grand office building as important or not, it is your family's legacy."

Teddy squirmed in his chair, and she thought *perhaps his modesty caused his discomfort,* but she was interested in the pictures and awards placed throughout the office.

Katie continued to look around and said, "Are these your siblings?"

"Yes. That's my younger brother and sister, they died in a car accident when they were in their teens. Perhaps, that is more information than you care to know about my family."

She looked over at him and smiled, realizing he understood the pain she was going through. The death of her grandfather granted her entrance into an elite society, and only those members understood the pain which comes from losing someone dear. They understand the pain never ends, it just gets more comfortable to carry.

When Katie completed her inspection, she found her way back to the chair next to where he was sitting. With a raised brow, she turned her head sideways and said, "Do you know what would be nice?"

"What's that, Katie?"

"Would it be too much trouble to ask your receptionist for a cup of coffee?" Katie said with a grin, trying to maintain a happy demeanor.

Teddy jumped up from his seat and rubbed his hands together, "I have a better idea. There is a Starbucks around the corner, only a brisk walk from here. Are you up to walking a few minutes for a cup of coffee and a breakfast sandwich? I woke early this morning and didn't eat breakfast; I could use a quick snack."

Katie showed a slight sign of animation, and Teddy asked, "What is that expression? What do you find so exciting about walking around the block for a cup of coffee?"

Leaning into him as they approached the door, she asked, "Will you have to check out with the formidable office security guard?"

* * * * * * * *

Teddy paused and looked into her eyes, and then he saw it. There was pain in her eyes, and the forced smile showed she was trying hard to keep it together. Then, Teddy considered that Katie O'Neill had found her way to him twice during the past week. The first time being the night before her grandfather's death. A faint grin appeared on his face as he flung open the door and walked into the reception area with the confidence of a man who had recognized her need to seek him out.

Their discussion on the way to the restaurant was light. Teddy expressed his sympathy regarding the death of her grandfather and explained how the eulogy she delivered at the memorial service provided him with insight into her childhood.

Once inside the restaurant, Teddy placed their order while Katie secured a table. The two settled in to enjoy their breakfast sandwich and coffee. Because there were few people in there to overhear their conversation, Katie shared the events of the past two days with Teddy. She also confided the relief she felt in knowing her grandmother had not spent the day alone. Embarrassed for having missed the luncheon at Scott's the previous day, Katie explained how Claire had made her feel at ease. She chatted about the last evening and how she and her grandmother had awakened to a lengthy discussion about a $50,000 check. To further pique Teddy's interest, she mentioned Drew Byrd had come to the farm the previous day and had parked behind the house as if to claim ownership.

Teddy realized that Katie was staring at him, but his eyes were glazed and knew she noticed that he hadn't been paying much attention until now. His head jerked, and he blinked several times when she mentioned that her grandmother had noticed a blond-headed woman in the front seat of Drew's car. She continued to tell him about their conversation. For reasons she did not explain, her grandmother did not invite the woman into her home. She mentioned the envelope she found from his office while reviewing the mail. She told him it confused her to see two options for her grandparents' property.

Perhaps Teddy should have listened more carefully regarding the events of the previous days, but he thought it was a lot of nervous chatter, until Katie shared the contents of the option signed by Drew and her grandmother.

"I can't wrap my head around my grandmother signing a contract and accepting earnest money for the farm without discussing it with my grandfather. It makes little sense that my grandfather didn't sign it himself."

The mention of the earnest money check caused Teddy to realize this conversation involved much more critical information than he had imagined. When Teddy finished his breakfast sandwich and coffee, his stomach churned. He watched Katie, who had been through the most complicated week of her adult life, as she explained the information which caused much trepidation. The final bit of news was that her grandmother had undergone extensive testing at Emory, and the results of the medical tests revealed pancreatic cancer.

Katie placed her face in her hands and sobbed as she told him that her grandfather wasn't aware of the diagnosis before his death.

Teddy tried to process the information surrounding the option Drew had prepared for Mrs. Hawkins and could only imagine where he had gotten the money to pay her.

When Katie began to cry, Teddy recognized the needed for a diversion as much for himself as for her. The urge to wrap his arms around her was too tempting, so he suggested they leave the coffee shop before the lunch crowd gathered. He thought the only decent thing to do was to get her away from the public's eye and perhaps take her for a drive so she could work through her grief. They walked back to the office, and when they got to his car, Teddy tossed his keys to Katie and then went inside to rearrange his afternoon schedule with his assistant.

When he returned to the car, she asked, "Where are we going?"

While fastening the seatbelt, he glanced at Katie and noticed the mascara smudges that escaped her eyelashes during their discussion at the restaurant was gone, and her lips were shiny. The few moments Teddy had spent with the receptionist had allowed Katie to recover from her breakdown.

Teddy said, "I thought you needed to get away for a while to process all that's happened during the past week. There is a quaint little vineyard about 35 miles north of town. It is a quiet venue with a magnificent view of the Blue Ridge Mountains, where we can spend a few hours together while tasting some decent wine choices."

He could tell that his intentions touched Katie, but she seemed angst. And, then he knew. She had come to his office, not for a social visit, but because she needed someone to talk to about the contract.

Teddy noticed her silence, and said, "Is this not a good time for visiting a vineyard?"

"It's fine," she fidgeted.

Teddy was careful to allow Katie to lead the conversation. He was eager to find out about the alleged option signed by Drew. As they approached the county line, Teddy noticed the manila envelope positioned on the console, and he asked, "Katie, is that your envelope?"

"Yes," she replied.

* * * * * * *

The time passed quickly on the drive to the winery, and the mountain scenery on the bright autumn day was worth every minute of the ride. Katie looked over at Teddy and thought this was the one component in her life that was missing. Recently, she had felt an enormous void in her life, not only because of the death of her grandfather but mainly because there was no one in her life with whom to share her sorrow. As she enjoyed the picturesque scenery, she remembered the day her friend, Tyler, and she had discussed sitting around as a happily married couple. The comfort she experienced with Teddy fit the description of a married couple; it required no words.

She placed her hand on the envelope and looked at Teddy. "I brought copies of the two options with me. I was hoping you could explain what is going on regarding the industrial park project." Katie realized her vulnerability with her involvement regarding her grandparents' property. As much as she liked the Byrd family, she feared that Drew had used his charisma to manipulate her grandmother. As Teddy walked around and opened her car door, under her breath, she said, "What do I have to lose?"

"What's that?"

She smiled and said, "I was talking to myself."

It embarrassed Katie that Teddy had heard her comment. She thought, *A lot has happened in the past week, I could have been recalling a memory with my grandfather.* Her mood improved when she noticed that Teddy had not read too much into her reply.

Once inside the winery, Katie sipped a bottle of water while Teddy studied the menu from the board above the bar. Teddy began with a tasting of spumante champagne and asked Katie's opinion about his selection.

Her eyes danced with excitement. "I like it! You are my kind of guy."

Teddy shrugged his shoulders and turned to the waiter and with a raised eyebrow and with a sly grin, said, "She likes it."

While opening the bottle, the sommelier explained the history of the wine. "The Champagne wine region is in the historical province of Champagne in the northeastern region of France. However, spumante is a sparkling white wine from the Piedmont region of Italy. They call it Asti or Asti spumante, and they make spumante from the Moscato Bianco grape, which is much sweeter than used in the Champagne from the country of France." As the sommelier finished the delivery of the historical information, Teddy finished the tasting and looked at Katie.

When he sat down at the table, Teddy saw the manila envelope. "So," he said, "would you like for me to review the contents of that envelope?"

"Yes, please." She carefully laid the two options on the table. Teddy spotted the document he had prepared the previous Wednesday morning, and said, "I prepared this option as agreed between Drew and me, so I know the contents of this document." He picked up the other option and said, "However, I wasn't aware of this one until today."

"I believe you, Teddy. I'm confused by these documents, aside from the fact that my grandmother agreed to transact business without my grandfather's knowledge. I'm so disappointed that Drew would try to cheat my family. This document is written in such a way that the fifty-thousand dollars would buy him the land. Drew Byrd of all people, the son of the well-respected Andrew Byrd, one of the most decent and faith-filled gentlemen whom I have ever had the privilege of meeting. How could he go against you like this, and why would he approach my grandmother of all people? I am so angry with him on so many levels. I realize he is an attorney but doesn't this border line on criminal?"

"Katie, do you mind me asking how you know the Byrd family so well?"

She hesitated and measured her response with caution, "Well, let's just say I have a professional relationship with them."

"Okay, that's a good answer. Have the Byrd's represented either you or your family members in previous legal matters?"

"Oh, no. I'm not aware of an incident when my grandfather used their firm for any serious legal matters. Although, I understand Mr. Byrd served as a counselor for the county while my grandfather was on the commission board. Perhaps he contacted him to answer a random question as businessmen often do. Apparently, my grandfather contacted a local attorney to make the revisions to his will, but I don't know the name of the firm he used. Why do you ask, Teddy?"

The waiter appeared with their champagne and Teddy raised his glass and said, "Katie, how do you feel about a toast?"

"I love them. What should we toast?"

Teddy said, "Let's toast to the future... our future, and a bright one. But, let's be clear, there are certain areas of our lives that require closure before we can advance to the next stage of this relationship. You have been through a terrible week, losing your grandfather, and now finding out about your grandmother's cancer."

Katie raised her glass, and she tilted her head and said, "And, we've also got to figure out why Drew only approached my grandmother."

"That's true. We'll figure that one out together."

She smiled, "Here's to a brighter future."

The hours passed as they discussed Drew's interest in the industrial park project. Teddy explained to Katie the recent development to relieve Drew of the debt to the bank, without divulging specific information regarding Drew's involvement of the law firm.

* * * * * * * *

Katie's involvement with the audit, which she had not discussed with Teddy, allowed her to read between the lines. She now realized the loan Drew had taken out to fund his portion of the project was being paid by his father's law firm. The day before her grandfather's death, Katie had reviewed the ledger of bank payments. She couldn't believe Drew had intentionally miss-classified the entries, but she filed the information away for a later time.

She mentioned the discussion with her grandmother about the woman who came with Drew to the farm the previous day. Katie asked Teddy if his mother would have recognized the woman in the front seat of Drew's car as his wife, Colleen.

"Well, yes. Mom knows Colleen well, she would have recognized her. In fact, she would have spoken to her. You know my mom is the social butterfly."

It was late afternoon, when Katie looked outside the window and noticed the crisp daylight was turning to dusk.

"Can we call your mother, Teddy, and ask if she recognized the woman in Drew's car yesterday?"

"We can beat that. Let's stop by the house on our way back to town. It'll allow me to change out of my work clothes. These new shoes are killing my feet."

Neither Teddy nor Katie had noticed how quickly the time had flown by; however, they each left the winery with the information they had set out to gather. As they reached the end of the short drive to the main highway, the heater warmed the car quickly. Katie rested her head on the back of the seat and dozed off.

The envelope in Katie's lap held the evidence that Drew had undermined Teddy by preparing the first option. But, Katie and Teddy were eager to learn the identity of the woman who sat in the car, while Drew visited with Nora, which provided the missing piece of the puzzle.

They arrived at the Williams' house a few moments after Claire had returned from her daily visit to The Summerhouse. She explained she was a little later than usual since she had stopped by the pharmacy to pick up a prescription for Theo. Claire had made a pot of coffee and was setting out the chicken salad and tomato slices when the two came into the house. Delighting in seeing Katie again, she winked at her son as he brushed her cheek with a kiss.

She set the table for three and began her nervous chatter regarding the patients at the assisted living facility where her husband lived. As the three completed their light meal, Teddy asked his mother a few questions about Drew's visit to the Hawkin's farm the previous day. Claire became quiet and Katie noticed she was not sure how to proceed with the conversation.

Teddy looked at his mom and said, "Mom, do you know the identity of the blonde woman at the farm yesterday?"

Claire nodded and said, "Yes, son. It was Nancy Leigh."

Teddy's mouth dropped open as he stared at her.

Katie recognized the change in Teddy's disposition, "Who, may I ask, is Nancy Leigh?"

Claire cleared the dinner dishes and excused herself as she needed to deliver the medication she had picked up from the pharmacy on her way home. She grabbed the pharmacy bag along with her car keys and pocketbook and left the house.

Once the sound of her car was out of range, Katie turned to Teddy and said, "I realize this is none of my business, but who is Nancy Leigh?"

Teddy went over to the counter, poured himself another cup of coffee, and said, "Actually, Katie, it is your business. Do you remember the toast I made this afternoon about needing to tie up loose ends before taking our relationship to a deeper level? Well, Nancy Leigh is the loose end. She is my soon-to-be ex-wife. We are living separate lives and have been for some time now. However, we have not settled our divorce. Although we purchased no assets during our six-year marriage, she is certain I have hidden wealth she should receive in the divorce settlement."

"I'm so sorry, Teddy. I realize the news of her involvement with Drew is harrowing. Had I known I would have never involved your mother."

Teddy sat back down and said, "I found Nancy Leigh in a passionate embrace with the tennis pro at the club on the same day we met at your grandparents' farm."

Katie touched his arm, "Teddy, I am so sorry."

"I'll be honest with you, meeting you earlier in the day helped to reduce the blow to my ego. But, please understand her involvement with Drew, if there is indeed an involvement, means nothing to me. I feel no emotion at all, other than disappointment because of the pain she has caused my family. Her presence with Drew yesterday shows her involvement somehow in the first option, which evidently proves they are working together to steal assets from my family. I've heard rumors that Drew is looking for property to build a storage business.

It's apparent, he and Nancy Leigh were working together all along. The real irony of this situation is that we agreed to let Drew handle the divorce to save time and money."

Katie reached for his hands, "Drew and Nancy Leigh may have teamed up against you, but now you've got me and mark my words, we will win this fight." There was a determination in Katie's voice as she looked into Teddy's eyes. He lifted her hands to his lips.

CHAPTER TWENTY-EIGHT

On Thursday morning, November 20, Teddy headed to Savannah during the pre-dawn hours in hopes of getting through Atlanta before the rush hour traffic began. Still his focus was on the discoveries of the previous few days. The sight of Katie as she entered his office the previous week should have suggested an omen, or at least be cause for alarm. Although he could tell she had been crying, he did not entertain a motive for her visit. The hours he had spent with her had been pleasant, but the end of the day was bittersweet.

The discovery that his estranged wife and former best friend had connected to undermine him for financial gain was mind boggling. Considering Nancy Leigh's motives to prolong the divorce proceedings, he realized Drew was perhaps the mastermind of providing legal counsel for their divorce.

Merging onto I-75South, which was more of a highway divide than an exit, one could easily miss it if driving in the wrong lane. He reached for his coffee in the drink holder, and as he swallowed the warm liquid, he prayed that the caffeine would keep him focused throughout the morning.

With cruise control engaged, Teddy considered Drew's motives for wanting to prolong their divorce proceedings. Drew had asked such personal financial questions as he explained his need to be 'fair and just' to both parties. In hindsight, it appeared he was more interested in the discovery of the Williams' family wealth. Looking back over the years, Teddy recalled many times when Drew had made inappropriate comments about his family's wealth.

Now, he realized he had misinterpreted the remarks as friendly banter. Drew had allowed his envy and jealousy to emerge within the confines of social settings, knowing that Teddy's impeccable breeding would prevent him from retaliating in public.

When he approached the city of Macon's exit, he pulled off to stretch his legs and take a quick break. While enjoying his coffee and breakfast sandwich, his thoughts returned to the conversation between him and his father on the Saturday afternoon after his meeting at the Hawkins's farm.

Remorse engulfed him. He would never hurt his dad, but there were feelings of apprehension as Teddy remembered the scene in the Hawkins' kitchen when Katie spoke about the family legacy.

Once again, he wondered if his dad's heart attack and subsequent stroke were due to his inability to close the sale of the property. If so, why had he not been more transparent with Teddy before scheduling the meeting, which included Katie? Unlike Teddy, patience had never been one of his father's virtues, and a constant state of anxiety could explain his current state of health.

When he left the restaurant and continued his trip, the signs on the interstate marking I-16 on the outskirts of Macon were in clear sight. His decision to leave home before dawn had been a good one. The traffic on the interstate was light, and he looked forward to seeing his Uncle Frederick and Aunt Mary again. He couldn't remember the last time he had visited Savannah. Before Theodore's health issues began, his uncle and aunt had traveled to Abington to visit several times each year to be with family. They enjoyed long weekends on the lake, dining at the club, playing golf and tennis, and were regular guests at holiday and family events.

Teddy remembered Frederick had often encouraged him to seek advice from his own father. It concerned Frederick that Teddy's relationship with his grandfather prevented him from getting closer to Theo. He remembered one such discussion about his dad being a powerful businessman from whom he could learn a great deal. Being an attorney and handling the financial dealings for three generations allowed Frederick access to information regarding the success of the family business. Teddy and Claire enjoyed a charmed life, but neither of them knew the actual level of financial success enjoyed by Theodore Williams.

When Teddy arrived in Savannah, he observed the beauty of the old southern town. The sunlight peeking through Spanish moss hanging from the low limbs of the enormous trees provided a natural canvas for the exquisite architecture found in the century-old buildings. He traveled toward East River Street in search of The Cotton Exchange Tavern, the restaurant where his uncle had suggested they meet for lunch. The business district was booming with activity as the locals navigated the city on foot and enjoyed the brisk autumn weather. As he looked out over the river, he noticed a sky that one could only describe as robin egg blue. Teddy parked his car and looked around to gain his bearings when he saw an older gentleman standing outside the restaurant leaning on a cane for support. Recognizing his uncle, Teddy hurried across the street, and as soon as he greeted him, he remembered how much he had missed him.

They arrived at the restaurant at 11:30. The waiter asked about Mary as he directed the men to their table. Many of the staff greeted his uncle, and Teddy could only surmise that this was the restaurant most frequented by his uncle and aunt. As they settled into their table, they discussed the signature dishes, as Teddy spotted the Reuben sandwich and then closed the menu. All he needed was a glass of sweet tea with a slice of lemon, and he would be ready for a long afternoon with his uncle. Frederick decided on a bowl of chowder and a cup of hot tea.

They discussed the events leading up to Teddy's phone call earlier in the week, and he hoped they would circle around to discuss his pending divorce case. Other than the limited information he had shared with Katie and his mother, Uncle Frederick, was the only other person he could trust. Teddy realized the damage to the family relationship between Drew and his father, Andrew. He explained the bank loan Drew had secured with the assets of the law firm without his father's knowledge. Teddy enlightened Uncle Frederick on how he had used money from the industrial park's account to cover the overdraft the previous week. He mentioned that he had initially thought assuming the loan with the bank would be a breeze until he discovered the level of collateral necessary to cover a loan of that size. As an interim CEO, he had little negotiating power regarding financial matters other than signing on the bank accounts. Teddy explained to his uncle that his father had never given him or his mother any latitude regarding the family finances.

When the waiter brought their food, Teddy dove into his meal and savored each bite of the tender meat of the Reuben sandwich. As Teddy finished his meal, he noted that his uncle had not eaten his soup, and he wondered if there was a lingering health issue.

"This meal was delicious." Teddy wiped his mouth with his napkin as his uncle motioned for the waiter to remove their dishes.

"Teddy, you mentioned earlier in our conversation that your father had never given you or Claire much latitude regarding the family business. Perhaps it's time we discuss the trust funds we established during the early years of your grandfather's practice. And, the mass of real estate, insurance policies, stocks, and bonds he acquired over the life of his career." He reached in his briefcase and removed a manila envelope containing a document which detailed the 10,000 shares of various stocks and he placed the report in front of Teddy and waited for him to study the information.

"As you can see, the cumulative value of the stock as of today is a decent size portfolio for a man of your age. However, Claire has control of the stock until you are ready to begin your medical practice. Your grandparents also left an insurance policy to your mother to cover the capital gains tax she will incur since the stocks remain in her name."

"Uncle Frederick, who has control of this account?"

"Your father and I have managed the stocks for Claire." Frederick had spent his career shielding the family's income from excessive taxation.

"Where does he keep these documents," Teddy asked as he looked up from the envelope. "In a safe deposit box?"

"Perhaps. I'm not sure... Obviously, the family was cautious to protect the value of the various stocks to fund your medical practice."

"I appreciate all you've done to ensure the money is available," said Teddy.

Frederic replied, "No problem. I've meant to call and discuss with you the phone call I received from Nancy Leigh earlier in the year. Please understand the phone call and visit happened during the time we learned of Mary's terminal diagnosis by her medical team. Mary's doctor had suggested bringing in Hospice to help with her daily care. All I can say is we were numb, and during those first few weeks, we found it difficult to breathe," he paused. "The call from Nancy Leigh involved her demand for information regarding your inheritance from your grandparents' since you are the surviving grandchild."

"Why would she contact you about my inheritance? It's not like we ever discussed an inheritance."

"I don't know the answer to that question. But, when I received the unexpected call from Nancy Leigh, she said she was in the Savannah area and asked if she could drop by for a quick visit. She was close by when she called, because she arrived at my office a few moments later, and her charming personality was on display as she controlled the conversation. Evidently, her attorney had prepared a list of questions that required answers, and she had memorized the questions as best she could. I knew of the delayed proceedings surrounding your divorce, and I have regretted that I did not offer my services. She was in a desperate search for family assets, which she might claim in the divorce."

"As usual, her visit was ill-timed."

"I agree. When Theo and I met with Nancy Leigh before the wedding for her to sign the prenuptial, in her haste, she only skimmed over the first page. I doubted she could have interpreted the document because we used percentages instead of actual values."

"Yes, I remember there were percentages involved and her percentage was less than one half of a percentage of any funds which passed to me during our marriage."

"Your grandfather's estate was substantial. I had suggested establishing a revocable trust when his medical practice became successful in protecting much of his liquid estate. But the value of his assets had surpassed the limit of the trust at the time of his death. We executed the will according to his instructions. Although all assets passed to your grandmother, precautions to limit taxation for Claire and her children were secured through an irrevocable life insurance trust. I realize this is a lot of information, but it's important."

"It is a lot of information to digest. I'm sure I remember most of it from previous conversations down through the years," said Teddy.

"Nancy Leigh told me she had forgotten about the prenuptial agreement until I produced a copy for her to review. I asked a few questions to determine her level of understanding. After a few awkward moments, the switch flipped and Nancy Leigh's charm was replaced with words I hadn't heard since my military days. It dawned on her you would not receive the inheritance until your parents were deceased."

"I'm sure that was a surprise."

The last response she made was "Well, I guess we'll just have to think of another angle. As soon as the remark rolled from her lips, she caught herself. The faux pas that should have remained unspoken had caused her pause, and then her charming personality and mannerisms returned. It was clearly like a switch going on and off."

"I remember how she could turn on that charm."

"And, then with a deliberate swing to her step, extenuating her tight skirt, she sashayed out of the law office with her head held high."

Remembering the scene, Frederick laughed and said, "A casual observer might conclude she had been born into an aristocratic family."

Teddy said, "It seems she was filled with drama. I'm sorry you had to sit through that uncomfortable meeting."

"I've witnessed this behavior many times, and I am always surprised by the actions of the pathetic individuals who lay claim to the assets they played no part in earning. Son, I wish you had been a fly on the wall as Nancy Leigh reviewed the prenuptial agreement she had signed before your marriage. Considering her manipulative nature and her desire to get her way, the look on her face was priceless."

Teddy looked at his uncle with furrowed brows and shook his head.

"Nevertheless, I was unprepared for the foul and unbecoming language, which followed Nancy Leigh's discovery. Please forgive me for saying this, but Nancy Leigh's parents did not raise her to share a life with someone of your prominence. Teddy, she demeaned herself the day she came here and delivered a well-rehearsed performance to intimidate me into providing a list of assets to include in your divorce settlement."

Teddy could feel the anger swell up inside his body as he tried to understand why Nancy Leigh would stoop to such drastic measures. He considered how he had ever allowed himself to get into this predicament. And, as much as he hated to admit it, his uncle confirmed his theory that Nancy Leigh had been scheming on getting his family's assets.

Frederick cut his eyes at Teddy and realized he had upset him. "There is one more thing I need to share with you regarding the comments Nancy Leigh made after figuring out you had not yet received your inheritance. Then, perhaps we should move on to another subject."

"Should I even ask what she said?"

"She said, 'Well, well, well. I guess this divorce settlement will just have to wait until both of Teddy's parents are dead."

"Uncle Frederick, it sounds like the light bulb finally came on."

"She was only stating the obvious. But Teddy, it was the delivery of the remark that caused the hairs on my neck to rise. It was as if she wasn't above speeding the deaths along."

"Surely not," said Teddy.

Frederick raised his eyebrows and continued, "Then," she asked, "how much longer do we expect Mr. Williams to live? I'm sure it's expensive for someone to receive twenty-four-hour care in one of those places. I thought her line of questioning was complete. And, then out of the blue, she said, 'so, how about your estate? Will Teddy inherit your money when you and your wife pass'?"

"You're joking."

"No, I am not joking. Her assertiveness shocked me," Frederick then lowered his voice when he continued, and replied, "Young lady, that line of questioning is inappropriate."

He looked around the restaurant and then said, "Can you imagine her asking such a personal question? During her visit, she opened her pocketbook in her lap and dug around for something, perhaps a pen, when I noticed she was carrying a small handgun."

"I didn't know she owned a gun. Uncle Frederick, I don't even own a gun." Teddy's gaze settled on the centerpiece.

"When you decided to meet with me today, I took the liberty to contact a colleague, Dan Ellis, who specializes in detective work. My previous meeting with Nancy Leigh and the behavior she exhibited caused me concern for your mother's safety. You should know that Dan is a professional and my friend, and he has assigned three shifts of private detectives to protect your mother while you are away. The first shift began at 12:01a.m. this morning and will continue until further notice."

Frederick reached inside his briefcase and pulled out a file with Nancy Leigh's name on the tab. He opened the file which contained the evidence and laid it on the table. "When assets are remaining at the end of one's life, some of the most decent people you know will allow greed to dictate their actions. When I first contacted Dan, we discussed Nancy Leigh's visit and the remarks she made about Theo and Claire. And, Dan's team has been trailing Nancy Leigh since the day following her visit to Savannah. This is my gut feeling, but I saw the icy determination in that girl's eyes, which exposed a look of a cold-blooded killer. It's my opinion she's capable of deadly intent. The report you are holding confirms my worst fears regarding your wife and proves she purchased the gun over 10 years ago. You will find an interesting article involving Nancy Leigh the summer before her freshman year in college. They never proved the accusation, but you will find the story interesting. Please take the file with you and read it as soon as possible. Once you have digested the information, please know I will provide any help necessary to protect you and your parents, going forward."

Teddy said, "Thanks, I'll look through it tonight."

"Now, we must discuss the financial arrangements of the real estate business. Theo established a limited liability company using your mother's initials, so tracking assets in her legal name would prove futile. After the accident, he amended the corporation to include your name. I'm not sure Theodore ever mentioned the business structure he prepared for you and Claire. However, the corporation lists you as the secretary/treasurer, which allows you to transact business without the claim of ownership."

Frederick reached for another envelope and said, "This document is a copy of a revised corporate resolution for Theo's business. Please understand, this is a complicated situation. However, we have intended to shield your inheritance until your grandparents and parents are deceased. Otherwise, these family assets could become part of a divorce settlement between you and Nancy Leigh."

"Are you saying my parents restructured their estate after my marriage to prevent Nancy Leigh from getting their money?"

"Yes, son. They were doubtful the marriage between you and Nancy Leigh would last, and we structured the prenuptial agreement to include the minimum amount allowed by law," said Frederick.

Teddy picked up his spoon and toyed with it for several minutes. "Uncle Frederick, do you think Drew had been privy to information because of his father's friendship with my dad? Perhaps it was Drew that tipped her off about the inheritance."

"Son, I don't know, but that's a thought."

"In fact, they could get certain information regarding the LLC through the state's website, correct?"

Frederick considered Teddy's question. "Technically, yes, the information is available on the website you mentioned; however, one would need the name of the LLC. I don't believe Theodore would have divulged the name of the corporation to anyone outside the family circle except to his accountant responsible for filing the annual tax return."

Teddy's eyebrows bunched up as he looked at his uncle. "Do you mind me asking the name of the corporation?"

"Not at all, son. The LLC is in the name of TRE, LLC." Teddy's facial muscles went slack when he gazed at his uncle. Frederick said, "Theodore, Robert, Elizabeth, the initials of the first names of his three children. Isn't the name unique? Who would ever think to find assets for the Williams Real Estate Company in that name?"

As he considered the origin of the name, Teddy smiled, and it pleased him to know his father had considered his family at the time he established the corporation.

"What will happen to the corporation when we finish the industrial park, and we either sell the real estate company or close it down?"

It surprised Frederick that his nephew was considering closing his father's business. He pondered his answer. "Well, Teddy, are you aware that someone approached your father about selling his business? If I remember correctly, it was a few weeks before his stroke."

"Mom mentioned something about it, but she knew none of the specifics."

"The guy has kept in contact with me. In fact, his most recent call was last week. I've meant to tell you about the call, but it was vital for you to fulfill the promise you made to Theo, and I didn't want the negotiation of the sale to interfere. But, perhaps this is a decision to consider soon. You would be remiss to allow an interested buyer to move on to his next venture without as much as an open discussion."

"Yes. And, even though my father never mentioned mom's role in the corporation, we will involve her with the negotiations, right?"

"That is correct. But, there was never any reason for her involvement in the business. Theo knew I would take care of Claire. And, I will relinquish my holdings to you once your divorce settles, or, upon my death." He passed another manila envelope over to Teddy and said, "Keep this in a safe place. If anything happens to me, you will be the head of this family, with Claire's help, of course."

Teddy reviewed the stocks and realized the five-million-dollar value far exceeded the amount needed to fund a medical practice.

"Also, before we leave to go over to the house to visit with Mary, please understand she is not aware of the intimidating tactics used by Nancy Leigh on her last visit. Once you see her, you will understand the reason I didn't tell her about the threatening remarks."

CHAPTER TWENTY-NINE

Whenen Teddy walked into the Hyatt Regency, darkness had descended upon the historic southern city. The Four-Star Bay Street hotel in downtown Savannah, near Reynolds Square, was a favorite of Teddy's. Once again, the long day had exhausted him, just like the days of the past two weeks. Each day had been a discovery of new information which enhanced the developing saga involving Nancy Leigh and Drew. As he deposited his overnight bag in his room, he considered his options, either change clothes or go for a quick run or head to the bar and review the contents of the detective's file, which contained the name of his wife. He decided on the latter.

As he walked through the lobby towards the lounge, he saw Katie standing at the front desk. He moved in that direction. Katie and the steward were completing her paperwork when she sensed someone standing next to her, she turned and said, "Teddy, my goodness, where did you come from?"

Teddy said, "Hello, beautiful, this must be my lucky day. I came to Savannah to meet with my uncle for lunch, and when I left their house, it was getting late, so I'm staying here for the night."

In a dramatic gesture of raising her hands and increasing her voice an octave, she said, "I have been on the road for seven hours and got caught in traffic south of Atlanta at the worst time, so I am starving. Have you had dinner yet?"

"Let me guess? Bottlenecked at the I-75/I-85 junction, right?" Asked Teddy.

Katie shook her head and rolled her eyes. "Correct. Hey, would you like to join me for dinner?"

"Well, I can't let you eat alone," he said as he winked at the young steward hanging on Katie's every word. The steward smiled as he turned to gather the door card for her room.

"Get checked into your room and meet me in the lounge when you are ready. Take your time. I need a few minutes to review this file." As Teddy turned to leave, he placed his arm around her lower back and brushed her cheek with a light kiss.

The Moss and Oak Room, which overlooked the Savannah River, showcased the lights from the city and provided a picturesque setting in the lounge. The locals often gathered after work to entertain friends or clients as they enjoyed the scenic views. Teddy entered the bar and considered the ambiance of the charming room. He scoped out a perfect table for he and Katie to enjoy while viewing the scenery surrounding the historic river which had served as a natural border separating the states of Georgia and South Carolina. As he sat down at the table, Teddy was careful to leave the chair with the best view of the river vacant. He smiled as he considered how fate had once again brought them together.

The information he learned from his Uncle Frederick had scared the hell out of him, and as he drove away from their home, he considered turning north and heading back to Abington. He was too tired to drive the six-hour trip back home, and a strong urge had convinced him to stay the night, so he turned south towards the familiar Hyatt Regency.

He found it difficult to concentrate on the open file and wondered if Katie's job had brought her to Savannah. Teddy had spent an entire day with her the previous week, and she had not mentioned going out of town. But, neither had he. In fact, his mother and the banker, Tom Jordan were the only two people other than Uncle Frederick, who knew he would be in Savannah.

Katie appeared at his table in a perky mood. Teddy stood to greet her and offered her the seat with the best view of the waterways. "You look lovely tonight, Katie." He noticed that she had changed her clothes, and her lips were shiny.

"Well, thank you, Mr. Williams. Girls love flattery." As she sat down, she looked out over the beautiful river, and her face radiated a natural healthy beauty.

"Why don't we order a drink while you scan the menu? What would you like?"

Katie picked up her menu and said, "A glass of chardonnay will be fine. It will only take a minute to decide on dinner."

"Take your time, I'm in no hurry," he said.

Once she decided on her dinner order, she looked around the lounge, and with a playful smile, she asked, "How did you secure the best table in the room? Teddy, did you beat someone up?"

He shook his head, looked down at his hands, and said, "Only the best for my Katie." He intentionally used the same endearment that Katie's father had used for her when she was a little girl. But, her reaction startled him. The look on her face told him she wanted him to kiss her right here, right now. He raised his eyebrows and said, "Watch the way you look at me, pretty lady."

Katie sipped her water and looked away.

Teddy changed the subject. "What brings you to Savannah?"

"I'm here for a continuing education class."

"Where is the class held?"

"Over at the Marriott. But, on the day I enrolled in the class, I didn't book a room, and when I called back, the Marriott was full, so I booked two nights here instead. It appeared at the time to be an inconvenience, but when I arrived and found you wandering aimlessly," her head moved back and forth, and she rolled her eyes, "around the lobby, I guess it was a blessing instead."

"I'm sure I looked lost. My mind was a million miles away." Teddy chuckled.

Katie looked at the view overlooking the town. Her eyes grew big as she said, "I love this city."

"Yeah, me, too."

"Oh, I almost forgot to tell you. You won't believe who I ran into this morning while getting coffee?"

"Who?"

"Your mom. And, she graciously agreed to stay at the farm with my grandmother while I'm in Savannah. I was so concerned about her being alone, and then your mom volunteered to stay with her. It was such a random act of kindness, and one I will always remember... Are you staying the weekend?" she asked.

"I planned to return home tomorrow, but if you are extra nice, I may wait until Saturday to leave with you. Have you made any plans for dinner while you are here?"

"No. But on Friday night, they always schedule a cocktail party followed by a seafood buffet. The evening provides a great opportunity to network with colleagues in various financial circles, but I'm under no obligation to attend."

"If you're not required to attend, there's a great restaurant over on Hilton Head Island, which is about 45 minutes from here. Perhaps, we could drive over to the island tomorrow afternoon and have dinner."

"Sounds fun."

"Alexander's is a popular restaurant in the Palmetto Dunes Resort, and it's operating under new management. I've meant to go over for a long weekend and check it out."

"That sounds nice."

"When I was a kid, my family vacationed on the island every summer, and Alexander's was my dad's favorite restaurant. My parents would bring us kids in from a day at the beach and scrub the sand from our fingers and toes," Teddy chuckled, "then they dressed us in matching clothes. My brother and I wore shirts that matched our sister's sundress."

"Oh, how cute! I'm sure the three of you were adorable."

"I don't know about the adorable part, but it was at Alexander's that our parents taught us table etiquette. We learned to use cloth napkins as opposed to paper towels, and the place setting included more than a fork or spoon. You can imagine how boring it was for three little kids. But, it became a family ritual, and as we grew up, we looked forward to our night at Alexander's."

"That is a sweet memory," replied Katie.

"Have you ever been to Hilton Head Island?"

"No, I've never been, but I understand it's a w-o-n-d-e-r-f-u-l place for couples," Katie said with passion. "Several of my friends have been to Hilton Head for a honeymoon or to celebrate an anniversary, and they l-o-v-e-d it."

Teddy played with her a bit as he grinned, "I love Hilton Head Island myself." He raised his eyebrows and winked, "I agree with your friends, it could provide an intimate venue to celebrate a wedding. I could stay and honeymoon for a month or two on the island."

"Oops, Teddy, I didn't mean to imply anything like that; I only meant that although I have never been, my friends consider the island a lovely oasis of romance, and unlike the beaches farther down the coast which are often swarming with kids with the sole desire to party all night."

Teddy reached across the table and placed his hand on her fingers, "I knew what you meant, Katie." He gave her a little wink and continued to touch her fingers ever so lightly. He looked around the room and decided the atmosphere in the lounge overlooking the Savannah River was more romantic than anything he could have planned. The setting was seductive, with the linen tablecloths, the subtle lighting, and the exquisite food.

Teddy looked at his watch and realized if he planned to call his mother, he should call soon, or else she would be in bed. "Katie, if you don't mind, I need to go to the lobby and place a call to check on my mother before it gets much later. I'm not getting a reception on my phone in here. It could be because of all the metal in the building. When I finish making the call, perhaps we can take a walk down on River Street. What do you say?"

"Why don't we go up to your room and place the call in private?"

Teddy knew going to his room was a bad idea. He longed to sweep her up in his arms, but, he couldn't trust himself to be alone with her in a hotel room either.

"The hotel lobby phone is closer, right?" She folded her napkin and picked up her purse.

Teddy followed her into the lobby and asked the concierge if he could use the lobby phone to make a personal call. They sat in the club chairs in an alcove off the lobby, which provided just enough privacy to communicate without being disturbed. Katie's disappointment when he dismissed the suggestion to make the call from his room was evident.

* * * * * * * *

The dinner had been perfect, and Katie didn't want the evening to end, but perhaps she had misinterpreted the intent of the romantic setting. She wondered why he wouldn't let her get too close to him. She scrolled through her phone and pretended not to listen as Teddy spoke to his mother in a concerned tone as he asked her about her day, and she detected a surprise in the information Claire was sharing.

Her cell phone rang, and Katie waved her hand to get Teddy's attention, "I'm going outside to take this call."

Teddy winked and mouthed okay, and continued his conversation without mentioning that they were together, careful to hide any sign of his true feelings.

Katie was standing outside the lobby door, watching Teddy as he hung up the phone. But, instead of getting up from his chair, he started checking his phone for messages, which allowed a few more moments to finish her call. Her face was flushed when she came into the lobby, and she took a deep, cleansing breath while she walked over to the place where Teddy was sitting.

He looked up and said, "Shall we go on a romantic stroll down River Street?"

"Sure," she said.

"Are you okay?"

"Of course, I'm fine."

"Did it bother you that I interrupted our evening to check on my mom?"

"Of course not, Teddy, it's adorable that you checked on your mother. One can tell a lot about a man by how he treats his mother."

Katie thought, *did it bother you that I took a call from the guy who asked me to marry him less than a month ago?*

Teddy cocked his head. "So you think I'm adorable, huh? Seriously, no one has ever referred to me as adorable."

Katie placed her arm through his as they exited the hotel and said, "I very much doubt that, Teddy. Perhaps no one ever told you, but I'm pretty sure most females have found you to be adorable."

As they continued toward River Street, he asked, "Who called you on your cell? Was it your grandmother, or one of your many male admirers?"

"Oh, I guess I should explain. It was a guy who works in my building," careful not to mention that she had been seeing him. "He delivered some files to the farm tonight and he just wanted to let me know that my grandmother was in a good mood."

"No need for an explanation. That was a nice gesture. He obviously knew you would be concerned about your grandmother." He flashed a charming grin, "I'm relieved Mom was at the farm so she could check him out for me. Probably a good idea I didn't mention your name while talking to her, huh?" Teddy said in a playful tone as he nudged her with his arm.

The comment surprised Katie. "What does it matter if she knows I am with you tonight? Your mother likes me, Teddy."

Teddy patted her arm and ignored her defensive response. They remained quiet as they walked with locked arms down to the street, which ran next to the Savannah River. The landscape surrounding the beautiful evening was spectacular, with the display of a million stars shining against the backdrop of the black sky. Teddy stopped next to the river, leaned back against a railing, and took Katie's hands in his own as he pulled her close to his chest and looked into her eyes. Without uttering a word, ever so subtle, he kissed her lips. Katie leaned into him, and he could sense the desire in her body.

He continued to hold her hands at his chest and said, "I need to explain something to you, okay?"

Katie nodded in agreement, although he could tell she was on the verge of tear.

"I find myself in uncharted waters. It's difficult to have romantic feelings for someone without the freedom to express the depth of my love. But please keep in mind, I am a married man. Although my marriage ended two years ago, I am still legally attached to her."

Katie was silent as she looked at a boat moving up the river. Teddy noticed there were white lights strung from the open deck, and the people on the boat were laughing and enjoying the beautiful autumn evening. They were savoring every moment as if they knew the upcoming weather would impede their ability to enjoy the opened air party deck during the months ahead.

He placed his hand under her chin and turned her face towards him. "When I first saw you on the day we met at your grandparents' farm, we connected. There was strong chemistry between us, and I believe you felt it, too. The feelings I have for you are unlike anything I have ever experienced. Please listen when I tell you I care too much to involve you in an adulterous fling or a one-night stand." An endearing smile appeared on his face and he said, "I'm afraid if I did, your grandfather might strike me impotent."

She smiled at the thought of her grandfather.

"Do you have any idea how beautiful you are when you smile?"

"Only when I smile?"

"No, you are a beautiful woman, but a different beauty emerges when you smile. I want to make you so happy that your smile never leaves your face."

He continued with a more somber tone. "You know, this is taking a lot of discipline on my part. If my divorce was final, there is no way in hell we would stand outside in this frigid weather next to the Savannah River."

Tears streamed down Katie's face, and Teddy was once again facing a situation he had never encountered with any other woman. He said, "What is it, Katie? Did I say something to upset you?"

She responded, "No, no, I'm fine. In fact, I'm very much relieved. I just want to be with you. I have dreamt of that occasion, since the first time we met. Ironically, fate keeps bringing us together. But you are right, you are still married, and that too is disturbing, because I didn't know that fact until the other night."

It troubled Teddy to learn of Katie's misery, and he hugged her close. "Okay, I should call my uncle in the morning and schedule another meeting. I will explain to him our situation, and perhaps he can offer a suggestion to speed up the divorce proceeding. He should have been the one to represent me in this divorce instead of Drew, but I can't dwell on that now. However, going forward, if he will represent me then perhaps he can negotiate a settlement that will make everyone happy."

Katie reached up to stroke his face. She mouthed, "Thank you."

"If it will help matters, I'll go home tomorrow after meeting with my uncle to allow you time with your colleagues' tomorrow evening. I apologize, Katie. I've been insensitive to your feelings." He reached in his pocket to retrieve a handkerchief and dried the tears from her face.

"My grandfather also carried a handkerchief in his pocket that he used to dry my tears, which was often."

"Your grandfather was a classy guy."

"Teddy, please don't leave tomorrow," a sparkle came to her eyes. "I want to go over to Hilton Head with you, and I promise to be on my best behavior."

It relieved Teddy to know she wanted him to stay in Savannah through Saturday, and after he stuffed his handkerchief back into his pocket, he reached for her face and kissed her with a passion that left no doubt about the feelings he had for her.

CHAPTER THIRTY

Nancy Leigh woke up, and as she lay in bed, she became frustrated with Drew's performance as their attorney. He had taken way too long to settle the divorce that she had wanted for a long time. She turned over in bed and looked at her lover, Brad Carlisle, deciding he was the perfect person to execute her plan. She thought, *it's time to end this charade of a marriage*. She realized, after six years of marriage, there should be more tenderness in her heart toward her in-laws, but she didn't feel any. It was clear that neither of them had ever approved of her as Teddy's wife. They were always respectful, but Teddy never noticed the facade. Teddy and his dad did not share a strong bond. Therefore, any exchange between father and son regarding the latter's choice of women was ignored by Teddy. As a mother, Mrs. Williams would have tried to love anyone for whom her precious son cared.

Drew's failure to find any assets to use in the divorce settlement further compounded Nancy Leigh's anger. All the wasted years, she had compromised her happiness in hopes of winning a considerable divorce settlement to gain financial freedom for a lifestyle she had never known was now in jeopardy. But now, she questioned the information Drew had mentioned when he presented his plan to cheat Teddy out of half of his inheritance.

Well, right here and now, that changes, she thought. *Brad is a smart guy, and he can help solve this problem with Teddy's parents in a way that no one will ever suspect.* Smiling as she picked up her toothbrush, she wondered why she hadn't thought of the plan earlier. When Nancy Leigh finished rinsing her mouth, she peeped around the corner and noticed Brad was still sleeping. She felt a powerful urge to wake him, but she knew better than to wake him up from a sound sleep.

She found it difficult to string two sentences together before her morning coffee. So, Nancy Leigh went into the kitchen and made a pot of coffee, and as she stood on the cold linoleum floor, listening to the soothing drip of the liquid, she searched for a notepad and pen to document her plan. Rubbing the pen between her forefinger and thumb, she stopped and looked at the coffeepot, but wasn't seeing the object on which her eyes rested. Since her father-in-law was in an assisted-living facility, she decided they could execute the plan without difficulty. She was unaware if he would be on life-support. If so, that would be an easy target. But, she thought, *he could be awake, or perhaps be in a comatose state.* If it were the latter, one could walk right into the facility at dusk, carrying the items she needed in a large pocketbook, and no one would know the difference. If anyone asked for identification, she could pretend to be his niece from Savannah, Georgia. She thought it was a smart idea since Mrs. Williams' uncle and aunt lived in the Savannah area, a fact she knew about because she had visited his law office earlier in the summer.

She made a note to research a chemical that she could use if necessary. Then she stared at the paper and stopped referring to Mr. Williams as her father-in-law, because using that form of intimacy just added unnecessary complications to the situation. Nancy Leigh could not allow emotions or personal feelings to cloud her judgment. She needed to devise a plan, convince Brad to assist her, and execute the plan at their earliest opportunity. *I'll show Drew Byrd who he is dealing with,* she thought. *We will just keep his percentage of the money since he ain't done what he promised.*

Carrying two cups of coffee into the bedroom, she saw that Brad was awake and staring at the ceiling. A slow smile formed on his lips as he lifted his head from the pillow when he saw the steamy cup of coffee. He took a deep breath and inhaled the aroma as he reached for the cup and lifted himself to an upright position. "There's nothing like the smell of freshly brewed coffee in the morning. What are you doing up so early, Nancy Leigh?"

She climbed onto the bed to face him, and she almost mentioned her plan but decided it wasn't sound enough to appear workable. She knew she would need to spoon-feed Brad bits of information throughout the day until she became confident he was on board. The clock on the bedside table flashed 7:30 a.m., and there was plenty of time to prepare for the evening visit to the facility.

She smiled as she asked, "Did you sleep well?"

As he answered, her thoughts were back on her plans, and she only heard the chatter of his voice. But, her eyes never left his toned body.

Later, Nancy Leigh finished her shower and was careful in choosing an outfit for the day, realizing that she would not be changing clothes again until her return home later in the evening. She selected a pair of black jeans and a blue denim shirt, and layered a black camisole underneath. She secured her hair with a black headband that removed her bangs from her face and then gathered and tied the length of her hair with a rubber band. Nancy Leigh grabbed a pair of Nike running shoes from her closet because if things got crazy, her plan might involve a little running. For her final act, she popped in a pair of green contact lenses and used a dark brown pencil to enhance the color and shape of her eyebrows, which created a subtle change in her appearance.

With the deed complete, and being out of harm's way, she planned to remove the headbands, freeing her long, blonde hair. Nancy Leigh also planned to ditch the oversized denim shirt and layer a pink cardigan sweater over the black camisole. She found a pair of white sunshades in her dresser, which would provide a different visual if anyone tried to identify her.

While Brad was in the shower, Nancy Leigh did a quick search on the internet about poisons one could ingest or inhale. She found that chloroform could be a dangerous chemical that irritates the eyes, respiratory system, and skin. The website had explained it could cause immediate damage to an already compromised respiratory system, and the body could absorb the chemicals through contact with the skin or from inhalation or ingestion. It explained the solution had been responsible for 'sudden sniffer's death,' which is a fatal cardiac arrhythmia some people suffer upon exposure. The chemicals required to produce the chloroform poisoning were active ingredients found in household bleach and isopropyl alcohol, neither of which would cause reasonable suspicion if purchased at the local market.

Since Nancy Leigh and Teddy had split up the weekend that Mr. Williams suffered the heart attack and stroke, she had not seen him in over two years. All Drew ever said regarding his condition was that it would have been better for everyone involved if he had died at the time he suffered the stroke, which had left him dependent on others for care. She found it hard to envision her strong and powerful father-in-law in a vegetative state. Nancy Leigh admitted his death would require less planning than her mother-in-law. Her thoughts raced forward to the time when Claire would be the object of her vengeance, and she realized that she would be a far more significant challenge because of her mobility.

When Brad left for work, Nancy Leigh busied herself by locating the household bleach, rubbing alcohol, some fresh rags along with two pairs of rubber gloves and breathing masks. Confident that the chemicals chosen would be enough, she ran a few errands. Exercising caution as she drove up the driveway to The Summerhouse facility with the intent to scope the surroundings to prepare their entrance and exit properly. As she circled the building, she recognized Claire Williams' car parked next to the shade tree, it was the same vehicle parked outside the Hawkins' farm on the day she and Drew went for a visit. Nancy Leigh was quick to turn her head in case Claire was in the vehicle. Drew had told her that Mr. Williams' suite was in the back, and the entrance to his room was accessible through the side door. Claire always parked her car near the side entrance to avoid having to walk through the entire facility. However, Nancy Leigh's concern was they may lock the side door before she and Brad visited later in the day.

Satisfied with her plan, she left the facility and made her way down to the town square. She went into the coffee shop to order an espresso, and she chose a small table on the sidewalk to enjoy her drink. She decided to take lunch to Brad. After finishing her coffee, Nancy Leigh picked up sandwiches from the local delicatessen and headed to the tennis court around 11:45. Brad was not expecting her, and she noticed her visit rattled him because his face drained of color, and his eyes twitched when she walked through the door. But as soon as she produced his favorite turkey sandwich on rye his mood lightened, and he walked out the back door and turned and motioned for her to follow. They sat on the back porch overlooking the tennis courts, and although it was a chilly November day, the sun provided enough warmth to allow them to enjoy their lunch while Nancy Leigh explained her decision to remove Drew from their plan.

Brad rolled his eyes at her while he chewed his food. "Are you serious? You've spent six years of your life married to this guy waiting to get a cut from his inheritance, and now you are so impatient you're willing to kill his parents. What has happened to you, Nancy Leigh? You don't love him! Wouldn't it be easier to sign the divorce papers and just get a job?" He wiped his mouth with his napkin after he took another bite of his sandwich. "And, what about Drew? You've decided to just cut him out of the deal. Remember, Nancy Leigh, Drew approached us with the plan to get his friend's money. I'm not so sure you can cut him out of the deal at this point."

"Well, don't get so worked up, Brad. It ain't fair to split the money with Drew since he hasn't even settled the divorce. We can do this without his help."

"I swear, Nancy Leigh, I think you're losing your freaking mind. A ten-year-old could find the holes in this plan." He shot her a cold penetrating look. "I refuse to let you drag me into this. I have a career to consider. If you need a hitman to take care of Mr. Williams, you might want to reconsider your decision to cut Drew out of the deal. Think about it, Nancy Leigh, Drew's an attorney, and you need him more than he needs you."

"Okay, okay. I'm not asking you to commit a crime, Brad. I just need you to drive me out to the home so I can scope it out. You can do that for me, can't you?"

Brad was sure Nancy Leigh would never follow through with this plan, but he wanted to finish his lunch in peace.

"Yes, I can drive you, but I will not carry a gun in my car."

Nancy Leigh reached over and planted a slow seductive kiss on his lips, "You love me, don't you?"

"Yes, and falling in love with you, apparently was a big mistake."

CHAPTER THIRTY-ONE

H arry, a detective, hired by Uncle Frederick, the family attorney from Savannah, drove a black Lexus with dark-tinted windows through the afternoon traffic and stayed several car lengths behind his target.

The three detectives assigned to Claire's case each worked an eight-hour detail, which began at 12:01a.m. Robby, the third detail was late; they scheduled him to arrive ten minutes earlier at The Summerhouse. But, now that 'Magnolia,' the name the detectives had assigned to Claire Williams because of the two large magnolia trees which shaded the front of her two-story brick home, was about to turn into her street, the shift change would be delayed.

The office had no information regarding the delay and asked Harry if he would stay on duty awhile longer. Harry didn't mind, and he noticed that he had already worked thirty minutes overtime. He watched Magnolia walk from the detached garage to the back entrance of her home.

As a single man, the only living creature depending upon him was his Labrador retriever, and Sam was happy to greet him, regardless of how late he got home. As Harry rode through the neighborhood, he parked on the far side of the property, close enough to watch the driveway, but far enough away to keep a watch on the backyard. He parked the car and congratulated himself as he glanced around at the three-dimensional view of the property. Then he reached for his thermos and poured the last of his coffee to enjoy while waiting for the backup to arrive. He lifted the thermos cup to his lips as a car came up the street and stopped in front of Magnolia's home.

Although the sun was setting, there was enough light to make out a male driver wearing a dark toboggan cap and a female passenger with blonde hair, secured with a black headband, and pulled back in a ponytail. Not quite an image of the socioeconomic level of persons living in this upper-class neighborhood he noted to himself. After a few seconds, the car resumed regular speed and proceeded to the end of the cul-de-sac. On the return trip, the car slowed to a stop at the edge of the property. Harry pulled out his binoculars and documented the license plate number, and as an extra precaution, began to video the back and side of the vehicle as best he could from his angle. As he finished the last of his coffee, the radio alerted him that the detail was in route, and they agreed to meet at the gas station across the street from the subdivision entrance 15 minutes later.

Harry focused on the car as the passengers watched for movement within Magnolia's home. The upstairs window was lit, and he could see movement inside the house. However, after a few minutes, the window darkened. Harry waited precisely 14 minutes before he left his post to meet the third shift detail, and as he prepared to leave his assignment, the car pulled off and left the subdivision.

As a peace offering for being late, Robby brought Harry a club sandwich, a bag of chips, and a homemade cookie for dinner. Robby explained that his wife had taken their youngest child to the doctor because he had run a fever throughout the previous night, and he couldn't leave his other child home alone. The two guys talked for a few minutes as Harry shared the video of the car that stopped at the corner of the property, and he provided an update regarding the day's events.

When Robby assumed his post, he noticed a few rooms in the Williams' house were dimly lit. As darkness covered the sky, he couldn't see Magnolia's car in the garage. However, the suspicious vehicle which Harry mentioned leaving the subdivision had not returned. Robby radioed the office to report his arrival and relayed the recent activity regarding the suspicious car. Ordinarily, the third shift of the day was quiet with little movement, especially with an older individual involved. However, this shift did not have the promise of a slow evening since the compact car with the shady-looking passengers lurking around the property earlier in the evening created somewhat of an ominous sign.

CHAPTER THIRTY-TWO

On the drive home from visiting with her husband, Claire made mental notes of the items needed for the next two nights at the Hawkins' farm. Eager to gather her belongings and arrive at the farm before nightfall, she hurried up the steps of her two-story home to retrieve her overnight bag, which she had packed and left on her bed early in the day. Claire went into the bathroom, applied lipstick, ran a brush through her short blond hair, and on her way out of the bedroom grabbed her overnight bag. As she walked through the kitchen area, she spotted her keys and purse, and since both hands were full, she left a few lights burning in the downstairs area. As she headed for the back door, she turned to engage the door lock and was ready to go. The sunset was descending upon the yard, but she could comfortably see the garage as she approached her car and unlocked the trunk. As she headed down the driveway, she noticed an older car rounding the corner of their property. She waited for the vehicle to pass before pulling onto the street; she saw the person on the passenger side of the vehicle and noticed the woman bore a striking resemblance to her daughter-in-law.

The Thursday afternoon traffic was heavy. People rushed around after work, picking up their kids, and preparing to meet friends for dinner. However, the gods governing the synchronization of the traffic lights showed favor as Claire traveled through the downtown area, approaching the end of the city limits in record time. She was eager to arrive at Nora's house so they would have a longer evening to enjoy.

Pulling into the long driveway at the farm, Claire exhaled with relief that she found the house with no problem. The only other time she had been at the farm was during the daytime, but things looked much different at night. The porch light came on as she turned off the ignition of her car. Nora appeared on the front porch and waved casually to her as she acknowledged her friend. Within seconds, Claire had retrieved her overnight bag from the trunk and was walking toward the front steps of the farmhouse, as Nora watched with a broad smile on her face.

"Claire, you are a sight for sore eyes. Please come into this house and tell me all about your day," said Nora.

Her teary eyes sparkled as she held the Kleenex to her nose, and Claire was glad that she had planned to come early in the evening. If Claire had not agreed to meet her friend for coffee before visiting Theo and had not run into Katie, she would have never known Nora would be alone in her house while Katie was in Savannah.

Nora's son Sammy lived on the farm, but he had not come around the first day she visited. Perhaps she would get to meet him tonight, but if not, the two ladies could enjoy an evening of girl talk. Claire had brought the ingredients to prepare her special marinara sauce and planned to make several meals of lasagna for Nora to freeze and pull out over the next couple of months.

Claire found immediate calm upon entering the guest room. The colors, which included walls painted a pale gray with accents of varying shades of blue, was soothing to the eye. There was a thick white down comforter that looked so inviting. And a duvet of bold navy blue and grey stripes which lay across the foot of the bed, with coordinating pillows scattered along the headboard. As she placed her overnight bag on the floor in the small closet, she saw the quart Mason jar filled with fall-colored flowers sitting on the marble-top dresser along with an assortment of recent magazines. The thoughtful gesture caused her to pause. Nora had suffered through an extraordinarily challenging week with the visit to Emory and the sudden death of her husband, but she had made every attempt to create a welcoming ambiance for Claire.

Realizing she had admired the guest room longer than was necessary, she quickly applied fresh lipstick and went downstairs to visit with her friend. As Claire walked into the kitchen, Nora dried the tears from the corners of her eyes. Claire sat on the hearth directly across from Nora, grabbed her hands, and said, "Please, tell me what you have done with yourself today?"

Nora couldn't hide her distress as fresh tears formed in her eyes and rolled down her face. Claire identified with her reaction; although she had not buried her husband, the heart attack and the stroke had changed her life. She had spent many lonely days in that big house, with no one aware of the sadness she had endured.

Claire looked around the kitchen and decided they needed a strong cup of tea. She asked Nora if she could put on the kettle before they shared the events of the day.

Nora said, "I think a cup of tea is a good idea. You know the kettle is always on the stove, and I store the tea in the cabinet above. Please, help yourself. You will also find a plate of sandwiches in the refrigerator. Mary Katherine brought me a pint of homemade chicken salad from a local grocer downtown, along with a fresh loaf of sourdough bread. When the tea is ready, we can enjoy a sandwich and a cup of fruit, if you like."

"Ooh, that sounds delicious. I've eaten only a tiny bit today."

Nora tucked her Kleenex in her sleeve and said, "I've not been too hungry as of late, but those little sandwiches are the perfect amount of food to satisfy my current appetite."

While the tea steeped, Claire removed the small platter of sandwiches from the refrigerator and noticed the plastic container filled with chicken salad. She held up the container and laughed, "I know exactly where Katie purchased this chicken salad. In fact, my dear father grew up in the town of Flowery Branch, Georgia, where the original owner of this grocery store lived. I'll never forget going into that store as a young girl. My father would buy me a coke to drink while he visited with his friend. The owner stored the cokes in a deep red chest he filled each morning with crushed ice. When the bottle opened, the liquid was so cold that ice had formed inside. It was the best drink of my life."

Claire removed the plate of sandwiches from the refrigerator along with the bowl of assorted fruit chunks, she put her hand on her left hip as she said, "Now those were the days, Nora, you know what I mean? We didn't have a care in the world. The highlight of my day was when I drank that frozen coke. But, the nicest treat was being with my dear father and his friend as they reminisced about growing up in Flowery Branch. Isn't it interesting what the mind conjures up when one sees something that reminds us of old times?"

As Claire handed Nora her tea, she could tell that her mood was better. A bright smile had replaced the tears that covered her face when she arrived.

When they sat down at the kitchen table to eat their supper, they heard a car coming up the graveled driveway. Claire said, "Sounds like you have a visitor tonight."

"Well, I've had a good bit of company this week. But, I'm not expecting anyone tonight."

They heard a knock from the front door, and Nora walked into the foyer and turned on the porch light. She opened the door and said, "Well, hello, Tyler, how are you?"

Tyler was standing on the porch, holding a briefcase in one hand and a white orchid plant in the other. "Hi, Mrs. Hawkins. Is Katie here?"

"No, Tyler, she isn't home. But, please come in. You've got a load there." Nora showed him into the kitchen.

Claire got up and reached for the orchid plant, and said, "Hi there. I'm Claire Williams. What a beautiful plant you have there."

"It's nice to meet you, Mrs. Williams. Katie loves orchids, so I thought this might brighten her day. I ran into her boss this morning, and he asked me to bring some work files for her to review while she is up here. Will she be back later tonight?"

Nora said, "No, she's gone to a conference and won't be back until later this weekend. But, I'll let her know that you came by."

"Okay, please do. When you talk to Katie, please ask her to call me. I've not heard from her since the funeral."

When Tyler left, Claire said, "He's a nice young man. Is he a friend of Katie's?"

"Yes. They've been seeing each other for over a year."

Claire thought, *that's a long time.* As she ate her sandwich, she thought about the previous Thursday night when Katie and Teddy came by after spending the afternoon together. And, then, she thought about the night at The Exchange, and she remembered the look in Katie's eyes when she looked at Teddy, and she thought she couldn't possibly love Tyler.

Nora touched her hand and said, "Are you okay, Claire? You look troubled."

"No, no. I'm fine. Tell me what you did today."

Nora mentioned her doctor's appointment earlier in the day. Claire asked, "Was your family aware that you were going back to Emory for a follow-up appointment?"

Nora smiled as she shook her head. "Claire, as you well know, there are things that mothers must do themselves, and this was one of those things. The boys are busy with their families and careers, and Mary Katherine almost canceled her trip to Savannah when she found out about my cancer. And, I just couldn't bring myself to tell her I had a follow-up appointment today."

Claire said, "It's for the best, Nora. There was no reason for her to miss the meeting. And, lucky for me, I ran into Katie this morning. It pleased her when I offered to stay with you."

"I sensed the reason for the follow-up was negative because the nurse who called yesterday to confirm the appointment mentioned that the doctor wanted me to know I should bring as many family members as I wanted with me to the appointment."

"Oh, honey," Claire said, "If I had only known. I could have driven you to that appointment."

"That's sweet of you, Claire. But, the trip to Emory is an easy drive from here, and I've now made the trip several times by myself. The appointment to confirm the accuracy of my local doctor's diagnosis was the day before Tom died. I hate to admit this, but I told him I was going with a friend to Emory for some tests. I couldn't bring myself to tell him that my doctor had found cancer until I was certain. So I went back to Emory to check and double-check the test results. My local primary care doctor was correct, and Emory confirmed pancreatic cancer."

Nora gazed into the fire. "Today, however, my doctor delivered news I was not expecting. By his prediction, I only have a few months to live. This may seem unusual to you, Claire, but I have declined treatments to extend my life. I am choosing to enjoy as many days I have left in this life without taking chemotherapy that will cause me to feel worse than I already do." Nora dabbed the Kleenex to her eyes. "My time is almost up, and my biggest regret is that neither Tom nor I will be here to witness Mary Katherine walk down the aisle on her wedding day. Life has cheated her on every front. I promised myself on the ride back home today, I'll just have to trust God has a prince in mind for her. Someone who will love and cherish her, and who will take care of her as we have done since her parents died."

After supper, the ladies sat in front of the fire and discussed living in different areas of the county. Claire enjoyed a life of privilege in an upper-class neighborhood in town, while Nora enjoyed a simpler lifestyle in the country on a large horse farm. Both women had married well, and although the circumstances of their lives differed, they had endured the pain of losing their husbands and burying children. The parallels in their lives were uncanny.

As Claire lay awake in the early morning hours, listening to the chirping of the last crickets of the season, her thoughts returned to Nora and her wish for her granddaughter. Nora was very fond of Tyler and Claire knew that she was thinking of him when she mentioned Katie's prince. But, Claire thought otherwise. Teddy had also experienced unfortunate situations in his life, especially regarding his relationship with Theo and his marriage to Nancy Leigh. Claire was sure that her son was in love with Nora's granddaughter, however, she wasn't ready to share the news with Nora just yet.

CHAPTER THIRTY-THREE

(Friday, November 21, 2014)

Teddy waited until mid-morning to call his uncle to ask if he could join him for lunch. During the call, he explained his decision to stay in Savannah for an extra day and mentioned several items he needed to discuss regarding the family business and his pending divorce. The pitch of his uncle's voice showed he was pleased Teddy had stayed in town, and suggested meeting at Vic's On The River at eleven-thirty before the lunch crowd showed up.

When Teddy shook his uncle's hand and hugged him, he noticed the frailty of his frame. It was during situations like these that Teddy longed to confide in his grandfather. Frederick was a viable substitute and was the closest thing he had to a father figure. Besides, he was the only person privy to his family's financial structure.

"I can see from the way you walked in the door you are a man on a mission. What's up?"

Teddy explained to his uncle the situation that had developed between him and Katie.

"I will not lecture you against entering a romantic relationship while the divorce proceedings remain pending. But, I want you to move on with your life, and it's time this divorce gets settled. We both know your marriage to Nancy Leigh is irreconcilable. Perhaps I can put the squeeze on Drew, and get this thing settled so you and Katie can get on with your life."

"Okay, that is probably for the best, but as I told you before, because of the limited amount of assets we own, we thought it would be smarter to use the same attorney."

"I understand, son." Frederick looked over the restaurant and settled his gaze on Teddy.

"Since Mary's diagnosis, we have been getting our affairs in order. We updated our wills a few months back. However, after discussing the situation regarding Drew and the law firm, Mary and I have agreed to buy his part of the investment. Also, now that we know of your blooming romance with Katie, we could move twenty-five thousand dollars into an investment vehicle at a bank in your area and allow the funds to become the hidden treasure Nancy Leigh needs to sign the papers. I'm doubtful, she will disappear without recompense for the time she spent as your wife."

"That's true. Nancy Leigh and Drew seem to think there's a pot of gold lying around someplace."

"To be honest, Teddy, splitting the money is a small sum to pay to get rid of her. Hell, give her the entire twenty-five thousand dollars if you think she'll settle. It's a drop in the bucket considering the problems she could cause our family. I'm certain your father would agree."

"I don't know what to say. That is very generous of you guys."

When the food arrived at their table, Teddy devoured his food while Frederick continued to discuss an adequate settlement for Nancy Leigh.

"Are you serious about buying Drew's part of the industrial park? We have enough money in the real estate account to pay back Drew's investment, but I've been hesitating to use the money." Teddy could tell his uncle was working out a plan in his mind, and the excitement which appeared in his eyes was encouraging.

"I've just had a brilliant idea, why don't I make a quick trip to Abington to meet with Drew and his father?"

"No, no, Uncle Frederick, we should not involve Drew's father in this problem. I gave Drew my word I would relieve the law firm of the debt and repay the interest they incurred."

Uncle Frederick nodded his head in agreement. "Of course, we will honor your agreement. By all means, let's pay off the loan at the bank and relieve the firm of that financial obligation. I was thinking about a discussion regarding your desire to retain my services to handle your divorce settlement. If I can schedule to meet with Drew while his father is present, I'm certain I can let Drew know during the meeting the industrial park project is on the tip of my tongue. Any action on his part to resist my legal representation of you would cause a full-blown disclosure."

"I don't know. As frustrated as I am with Drew, using intimidating tactics just isn't in my nature."

"Listen, Teddy, Drew may have gone to law school, but, as your father stated so eloquently, he didn't graduate at the top of the class. Let's consider that scenario for a few minutes."

"That sounds just like Dad... because Drew never impressed him."

"Yes, and I share his sentiment. But, my presence, along with his father's, should cause Drew considerable anxiety. Obviously, my first move in this chess game is to make your intentions known regarding your change in legal representation in the divorce. Let's not dismiss the idea that the little charade Nancy Leigh pulled in the golf shop on the day of the fall golf tournament could very well have been a plan to persuade you to file for divorce."

Teddy nodded as he shot his uncle a look of dismay.

"Let's be clear, matrimonial law is a staggering 28-billion-dollar industry. Divorce happens in all socioeconomic levels. Although, the rate of divorce is lower among college-educated adults and individuals raised in affluent families. People who grow tired of their spouses and are after a monetary settlement seldom consider the high cost involved."

Teddy listened to his uncle as he considered his advanced age and the ingenious way in which his mind operated to outsmart the opponent.

As they were leaving the restaurant, Teddy listened as Frederick explained the plan to meet with Drew and his father within the next few days. Frederick looked ten years younger as Teddy watched his uncle walk away with a renewed task of helping his brother's grandson through a difficult situation. Teddy was uncertain of the outcome, but he was confident that placing his trust in his uncle was the right decision.

* * * * * * * *

Teddy pulled into the parking lot at the Hyatt Regency with thirty minutes to spare, smiling as he noticed Katie's car was already there. He had allowed just enough time for a quick shower before meeting Katie in the hotel lobby at 3:30 p.m., as agreed to the previous evening when he kissed her goodnight outside her hotel room. He jumped out of the car and rushed into the hotel without speaking to anyone.

Thirty minutes later, Teddy sat in the alcove where he held a magazine and pretended to be reading while he watched the elevator door. When it opened, and Katie stepped into the hotel lobby, she scanned the area. Teddy stood up and walked toward her. She was wearing a pair of white linen slacks with a blue and white striped t-shirt and a navy-blue blazer; her sunshades were resting on top of her head. His eyes looked her over and smiled with approval, and she rolled her eyes as she reached up and kissed him on his lips.

"I could get used to you in a hurry." He kissed the tip of her nose and reached for her hand. "Are you ready to go on our first official date?"

"Oh, my goodness. You didn't mention that last night, you just said we were having dinner at a lovely restaurant in Palmetto Dunes Resort. You never mentioned this was a date."

Teddy laughed as he enjoyed the drama she displayed and then said, "And, I might add, I plan to hold your hand the entire evening. I don't care what your grandfather might think of me."

Katie looked at him with adoration and said, "I believe my grandfather would approve of you."

As they exited the plush hotel lobby, Teddy put his shoulders back as he noticed heads turn to watch as he and Katie walked hand in hand. He knew she was oblivious to the attention placed upon them by the people in the lobby.

CHAPTER THIRTY-FOUR

W hen Claire and Nora finished their breakfast, they lingered at the table while they enjoyed another cup of coffee. Then, Claire cleaned up the dishes and started preparing her famous marinara sauce, which she planned to leave simmering on the stove under Nora's watchful eye while she went to check on Theo.

"You seem in much better spirits this morning. If you feel like it, you can grate the cheese and cook the lasagna noodles while I'm gone, and when I get back, we will be ready to assemble the lasagna," said Claire.

"I'm looking forward to staying busy while you are away."

As Claire and Nora hung out in the kitchen and prepared the sauce, Claire noticed the window above the garage. "Does anyone live above the garage? I noticed a light in that window last night."

"Yes," said Nora. "Sammy lives there. Several years after the accident, he started talking about renting an apartment in town." Nora laughed at the memory. "How did he put it? Oh, yeah, he told us he needed more independence. Then, he came up with the idea to convert the attic into an efficiency apartment."

"That works out well, doesn't it?"

"Yes, it's good for Sammy. He showers and sleeps over there. Tom put in an efficiency kitchen, but he takes most of his meals with us at the house. He usually walks over the farm and checks on the livestock first thing each day, but sometime during the morning he comes into the house for a cup of coffee and a bowl of fruit or cereal."

Claire stood at the kitchen sink, looking up at the window. "Perhaps, he gets lonely after spending evenings up there by himself."

"He seems to enjoy his solitude, Sammy's not a big talker. Each morning after breakfast, he heads out to feed the horses and other livestock, one of the many jobs Tom had assigned to him because of his love for animals and his special gift as a horse trainer." Nora got up and said, "Let's go out to the porch, we can finish our coffee out there."

Claire turned to look at Nora and smiled. "I need to go check on Theo, but I'll join you for a few moments."

When they settled on the porch, Claire said, "I didn't realize Sammy was a horse trainer. How old was he when you discovered that talent?"

"It was obvious from a young age. Sammy was perhaps ten years old when we noticed horses responded well to him," said Nora. "Tom used to say if humans communicated with each other the way horses communicate with Sammy, we would have far fewer problems."

Claire laughed, "Was there any concern about the size of the horses, perhaps hurting Sammy?"

Nora looked out at the pasture and smiled. "No. The concussion he suffered from the accident caused bad headaches and impaired his vision, and caused him to move slower than before the accident. A few years later, during Sammy's annual visit, Tom and I mentioned his love of horses. Once the doctors understood how well he interacted with animals, they thought it would be therapeutic if he once again tried his hand at horse training. In fact, one of his doctor's children had recently been diagnosed with a mild case of autism, and he asked if he could bring his child to the farm to visit with Sammy. The specialist had told him his son might benefit from having a horse, and he wanted to see firsthand how Sammy interacted with the animals."

"How did that work out?"

"The little fellow and Sammy bonded almost immediately. For a long time, we wouldn't leave Sammy and Jake alone. It was the funniest thing, Sammy would talk to Jake about life on the farm and about horses in general, and then after a few visits, Jake asked to go for a ride. So, Sammy told him the horse would need to warm up to him, much like warming up to a friend. But, once Jake and the horse became friends, he taught him to ride."

"Goodness, Nora. It was like Sammy had studied Hippology, and he was teaching Jake about the study of horses."

Nora laughed and continued, "You're absolutely right. He just had all this information about horses, and although we knew he could train them, we didn't realize his level of knowledge was so extensive. And, he had never discussed any of this with us. Anyway, one day before Jake showed up, Sammy went down to the barn and brought three of the mare's out into the smaller pasture. When Jake arrived, he let him pick out the mare he wanted to ride. You wouldn't believe the look on Jake's face when Sammy told him he could take his pick."

"Jake must have felt like he was in a candy store that day."

"Yes, that's true. But, that's not the end of the story. Sammy didn't realize Tom had bought another mare that morning at the sale, and when he brought the mare home, he had left her in the same pasture to acclimate. Of course, when Jake saw that horse, he decided that was the one he wanted. So, Jake watched Sammy train the mare and Jake picked a name. After a few weeks, Jake was ready to ride, and when he sat on that horse the first time, his whole personality changed. It was such a transformation! He had the confidence of a king."

"Did Jake's condition improve while he was enjoying his time with Sammy?"

"Oh, yes. When Jake first came here, he talked very little. But, within one month, Jake was talking and interacting with the farmhands. Sammy has always worn cowboy boots and jeans. After a few sessions, we saw Jake walking down to the barn. When Sammy came out to meet him, they had dressed in identical jeans, plaid shirts, and western boots. Jake was also wearing a cowboy hat like Sammy's, too. It was the sweetest sight I'd ever seen. That day, his father, the doctor, brought along his spelling words, and he asked Sammy if he would call out the words to Jake while they rode around the pasture.

And, by the end of their session, Jake could spell each of the words correctly. Apparently, children with autism require kinetic learning techniques, which come from movement. They find it difficult to sit still and learn, but the movement helps with their ability to process information."

"Good for Sammy and Jake. That's such a beautiful story."

"Who would have known, right? After the sessions with Jake ended, we gave Sammy the title of a horse trainer, and this year, two of his horses have taken part in organized races."

Claire wanted to sit and talk with Nora longer, but she knew she needed to leave so she could get back from visiting Theo. "Well, I guess I should get going. But, I can't wait to get back and hear more about Sammy and his prized horses. Do you need me to pick up anything from town?"

"No, I have everything I need. But, thanks for the offer."

As Claire drove down the driveway, she looked in her rearview mirror and noticed Sammy walking around to the front of the house to talk to Nora, who was sitting in the swing finishing a cup of coffee. Disappointed, she had missed the opportunity to speak to him, she made a mental note to invite him to join them for supper later in the day. As she pulled onto the main road, Claire headed for home for a quick shower before going over to see Theo. As she approached her house, she noticed a black vehicle rounding the curve at the corner of her property. The car came to an abrupt stop. As she turned into the driveway, she noticed the passenger of the car was looking at her house.

She parked in the garage and sat there wondering why the vehicle was parked in front of her house. Then she walked cautiously to the back of the house and let herself in through the back door. Claire grabbed the cordless phone and sat down at the breakfast table and dialed Frederick's number. She hesitated to interfere, but it was time Teddy got on with his life.

Frederick had told her about his visit with Teddy, at lunch the previous day. The discussion about liquidating an investment held by her and Theo, if needed, to pay off Nancy Leigh and settle the divorce required more time than Claire had intended. When she hung up with her uncle, she called The Summerhouse to check on Theo's condition. There had been no change. However, there had been an issue the previous evening as a young man entered through the back door and had been rambling through the facility when one of the maintenance guys noticed him and escorted him out of the building. Claire dismissed the event and explained that she would be away for the next couple of days, and she would see them on Saturday afternoon.

Once the calls were completed, she went upstairs to shower and change. As she adjusted the blinds on the windows, she noticed the black car had returned and had stopped a few hundred yards from her property. Then, it dawned on Claire that someone in the neighborhood was being watched.

When Claire finished dressing, she found a loaf-size pound cake in her freezer along with a quart of frozen strawberries, and she placed the items in a thermal-lined container to transport to the farm. She thought Sammy would enjoy having a slice of cake and strawberries following their Italian meal, then she gathered the other belongings and left the house. As Claire backed the car out, she thought she caught a glimpse of someone standing to the side of the garage. She stopped the car and looked around, realizing it could perhaps be just a shadow. However, because of the vehicle she had spotted earlier on the street, she reached for her cell phone and called the security service and reported the incident. Then she left for the farm.

Luckily for Claire, the midday traffic was light, and she was pulling back into the driveway of the farm before the clock struck noon. Sammy and Nora were sitting on the front porch when she arrived. She walked up the steps and introduced herself to Sammy and invited him to join her and Nora for their evening meal. To tempt him further, she showed him the pound cake with fresh strawberries she had brought for dessert. Sammy's face lit up, and he licked his lips as he looked at the homemade cake. Claire could see that her plan had worked.

After agreeing to join them for dinner, he explained that a horse was preparing to give birth, and he was keeping a close eye on her condition. Then, he headed back to the stable.

While walking into the kitchen, Nora asked, "Claire, how did you know that pound cake and fresh strawberries were Sammy's favorite dessert?"

"Remember, I raised two boys of my own," Claire said with a knowing smile.

"Of course, you did Claire." She said, as she reached and squeezed her hand, "I wasn't expecting you to return so soon, but I'm so glad you're back. How did you find Theo?"

"Well, to be honest, I didn't visit with Theo today. I went home and called my Uncle Frederick and that conversation lasted longer than I had planned. Then I called the facility, and they reported that there was no change in Theo's condition. I finished my errands and came back down here to spend the afternoon with you." She continued, "I have spent every day with Theo since he suffered the stroke. My visits with you the past couple weeks have been my only respite from my worries about Theo. Perhaps, it is because you are such a gracious hostess, but I couldn't wait to get back down to this farm and make our lasagna."

"Well, I can't tell you how glad I am that you are here. I've already forgotten about the excruciating pain in my stomach before you arrived. There is something about you that just takes my mind off my worries."

They spent the afternoon preparing four medium pans of lasagna, three to freeze and one to cook for dinner. With the dishes washed and the pots and pans all dried and put away, Claire suggested they should sit down and enjoy a cup of tea while their dinner baked in the oven.

"It takes between 45 minutes to an hour for a pan of thick lasagna to finish baking. We deserve a rest following the afternoon of hard work. I didn't intend for you to stand on your feet for so long."

"Earlier today, I was experiencing some of the worst pain in my body, but the activity this afternoon kept my mind off of my pain. And although the pain remains, it isn't as piercing as it was this morning."

"Well, I have just the thing to help with that pain," Claire said. "I brought a nice bottle of rose' wine for us to enjoy with dinner, and once we finish our tea, I suggest we enjoy a cocktail while the lasagna finishes cooking."

While Claire set the table and removed the salad from the refrigerator, Nora sipped her wine and was resting her eyes when Sammy came in through the kitchen door. His hair was still wet from the shower, and he had changed into a blue oxford shirt and a pair of jeans. Claire noticed he was a nice-looking man when he got cleaned up. She fussed over Sammy and offered him a glass of rose' to enjoy while the lasagna finished baking.

Sammy laughed and said, "Don't reckon I remember seeing anyone drink wine in my mama's house before."

Claire stopped and looked at Nora and said, "Nora, should we put the wine away?"

Nora laughed and said, "Heavens, no, this is just what I need for a good night's rest." Directing her attention to Sammy, she said, "I believe both of us are old enough to enjoy a glass of wine with our guest, don't you, Sammy?"

Sammy responded, "Yes, ma'am, I believe we are old enough." They lingered in the kitchen, and as Sammy sipped the wine, he relaxed and began to talk about his afternoon in the stable with the mare waiting to give birth.

"I called the vet and told him we might need him pretty soon. If you hear a truck coming up the driveway during the middle of the night, you'll know who it is." Sammy explained how some mares drop or stream milk for several days before foaling. The vital first milk contains antibodies and a laxative for the newborn foal, and if the horse loses a significant quantity of milk, then someone should collect the colostrum and freeze it for later. He further explained that a mare showing spontaneous milk flow required a careful eye.

It thrilled Claire to learn that the mare could give birth during her visit to the farm. "Sammy, have you already chosen a name for the foal?"

"Not yet. We usually wait until the foal is born to choose a name."

The entire birthing experience fascinated Claire, and her excitement was contagious as Sammy told her that sometimes something happens during or after the birthing process that helps him decide on a name.

"This will be the first birth since my dad passed, and I'm a little nervous about the delivery without dad's help."

"Now, Sammy, you stop worrying. You'll be fine. You know as much about the delivery process as anyone," said Nora.

The conversation continued during dinner as Sammy explained his role as a horse trainer. When they finished their dinner, Sammy asked his mother if they could eat their dessert in front of the fire.

Soon after they finished their dessert, Nora began to yawn and was showing signs of getting ready for bed when Sammy took his dishes over to the sink. "Thanks for supper and that cake and strawberries really hit the spot. But I need to get back to the barn."

"Do you plan on sleeping out there tonight, son?"

"Not sure, Mama, I'll see how she's doing. But I left a light on just in case."

Nora and Claire continued to sit in front of the fire while Sammy let himself out. "Let's just sit here awhile longer, I may have few evenings like this to enjoy. And, if you don't mind, I think I'll pour myself another glass of wine?" She went over to the counter and poured the last of the wine, and as she walked back to the fireplace, they heard steps on the back porch. Sammy had just enough time to get to the barn and was out of earshot when a loud knock on the kitchen door startled her and Claire.

CHAPTER THIRTY-FIVE

THe detective agency reported the prior shift detail to Harry as being uneventful, and he was ready for his day to begin when he drove through the neighborhood. Two hours into the shift, Harry decided to cruise through the subdivision to check for suspicious activity when Magnolia's car entered the neighborhood and slowed down to make the turn into the driveway. Robby had not mentioned that Magnolia had left the premises during his shift. He brought his detective car to an abrupt stop. After Magnolia pulled into the garage, Harry resumed a slow speed and parked in the same spot as before... He radioed the office and reported that Magnolia had returned home from what looked like an overnight visit. She removed a small bag from the trunk, and she appeared to be wearing the same clothing she had worn the previous day. One thing Harry knew with certainty was women in this high-class neighborhood didn't wear the same outfit two days in a row.

The dispatcher at the office went ballistic when he heard that Magnolia had spent the night away from home, since there was no documentation from the third shift reporting her departure. After twenty minutes of rambling conversation, Harry told him that the car he had seen the previous afternoon had returned. A blonde headed woman had exited the vehicle and was lurking around the back of the garage. The driver of the car wore the same dark toboggan cap as on the previous afternoon. The dispatcher reported that he had radioed for backup, and to expect an unmarked white van in the subdivision within a few minutes. When Harry disconnected with dispatch, he started videoing the car and got a side shot of the woman as she moved from the front of the house to the garage.

"Dispatch, this is Harry. Please direct the backup to the cul-de-sac, he can go through the woods to the back of the house where he might have a better angle of the garage and the blonde. If Magnolia follows her daily routine, she will leave soon to go to The Summerhouse. I'm watching for her exit." As he finished the report, he grabbed his radio and left his vehicle and hid behind a patch of trees shielded by hydrangea bushes. Using his binoculars, he noticed she had moved around the garage to the backyard. Her hands skimmed the rough red brick while the movement of her feet resembled that of a graceful ballerina. Then she skirted quickly back to safety behind the garage.

The white van entered the subdivision and made its way to the end of the cul-de-sac. As anxiety mounted inside Harry, he went back to his vehicle and reached for his thermos and poured his first cup of coffee. Perhaps a morning coffee break was ill-timed, but lately, his nerves had shown signs of wear. He thought the caffeine might help calm him as he watched his backup sprint through the woods with the grace and speed of a deer.

While watching the movement around the house, Harry almost missed Magnolia as she left. "Magnolia has just left the subdivision." Harry relayed to dispatch. When the car moved from sight, the man in the toboggan cap appeared in the backyard and was tiptoeing around the patio. Suddenly, he produced what looked like a Glock and fired the gun into the wooded area behind the house. Harry gasped at the unfolding events happening in front of him as he watched the toboggan-clad man turn, run to the side of the house, and disappear into the woods. Harry heard three more shots, at which point he had lost visual contact with the woman and wasn't sure where she had gone.

In a state of panic, Harry was trying to radio the office to call for additional backup when he heard another shot. The sound was so deafening, and it startled him so badly that he dropped his coffee all over his lap. As he looked up, his last thought on this earth was, 'Where did all that blood come from?' Then, he fell forward into a sea of blackness.

CHAPTER THIRTY-SIX

A s Frederick left Vic's On The River, the restaurant where he and Teddy had met for lunch, he drove out to the house to check on his wife. Mary's cousin from Cumming, Georgia, had come down for a few days, and Frederick needed to ask her to stay with Mary while he made a quick trip to Abington.

When he got to the house, Lynn was already there, and she had settled into an overstuffed chair and was chatting with Mary when Frederick found his way into the master bedroom. Frederick greeted Lynn with enthusiasm. "If I were twenty years younger, I'd run off with you right now."

"Freddy, you are a hopeless flirt," she said as she winked at Mary.

"You can't blame an old man for trying, can ya?"

The compliment seemed to please Lynn, and then she turned to her cousin and said, "Mary, what did you do to capture the heart of your prince charming? My only regret is that you found him before me."

While the charade was being played out, Frederick went to where his wife was resting and gently kissed her cheek. Mary was smiling as she drifted off to sleep. Then, he turned to Lynn and asked, "would you come into the kitchen?" He whispered, "I have something to ask you, and I don't want to disturb Mary."

Lynn followed him into the kitchen, and he explained, "I have some unfinished business regarding my niece and great-nephew that needs my immediate attention. Would you be okay with me traveling to Abington for a few days while you are visiting with Mary?"

Lynn responded, "Yes. That will be fine. Are the Hospice ladies here around-the-clock now?"

"Yes, they have been here for a few weeks as I mentioned to you the last time we spoke."

The phone rang as Frederick wrote a list of phone numbers for Lynn to refer to during his absence. He grabbed the receiver from the wall unit, grateful that the telephone cord was long enough to navigate around the kitchen while he took the call. Frederick stopped compiling the list and listened to the information being told to him by the caller. As soon as he replaced the phone to the wall unit, another call came in. Frederick's face turned pale as he shouted, "Hell, no! That woman must be an imposter." Frustrated, Frederick placed the back of his arm over his eyes. "Has anyone spoken to Claire?"

When the call ended, he dropped the phone from his ear and rushed into one of the extra bedrooms where he had moved his clothes to free up space for the Hospice supplies in their master suite. He crammed a few items into an overnight bag, grabbed his medications from the adjoining bathroom, and headed to the master bedroom. He explained to Mary that he must travel to Abington to help Claire with some of Theodore's business. He did not tell her that Theo had passed away, he just didn't want to upset her before leaving. Mary, exhausted from the earlier visit with Lynn, was drifting off to sleep as her husband kissed her cheek and patted her bony, bluish hand that lay upon the pristine white sheets.

He stopped at the kitchen door and noticed the phone still hanging from the wall. As he replaced the receiver to the cradle, he turned to Lynn and said, "I promise to explain everything to you when I return on Monday. Please understand, this trip is necessary; otherwise, I would never leave my Mary at this stage in her illness."

Lynn hugged her cousin's husband, "Don't you worry about a thing. I promise to take good care of Mary. Take as long as you need, Freddy. We'll be fine."

Frederick kissed her forehead and left the house.

As he headed toward the interstate, he reached for his cell phone as he recounted the conversations in his head. Teddy's phone went straight to voice mail, but he couldn't tell Claire about the death of her husband over the phone. Dan had explained the events of the previous evening involving the attempted assault made by a man at the assisted-living facility where Theodore Williams received care. But, the information which scared him most was losing two of the detectives on Claire's assignment detail earlier in the day.

The administrator of The Summerhouse called to make him aware of Theodore William's passing. She had implied that he had died of natural causes, and explained his only visitor of the day had identified herself as Theodore's niece from Savannah. Although the description of the woman was not consistent with how Nancy Leigh typically dressed, a particular expression she relayed to him, left no doubt that the blonde-headed woman whose hair was in a ponytail was Nancy Leigh.

The five-hour trip to Abington was uneventful. When Frederick pulled into his niece's neighborhood, the investigative team had stretched the yellow crime-scene tape around the property, and it extended into the wooded area behind the house. Someone had installed battery-operated spotlights to aid the authorities in combing the woods behind the Williams' home in a search for clues to build their case. The deputy sitting in the drive exchanged a few comments before Frederick asked if anyone had talked to Claire.

Frederick pulled out a key and said, "Officer, if you don't mind, I'd like to look around."

"Sorry. They've given me strict orders that no one is to go inside. Because this is being investigated as a crime scene."

Realizing their need to follow protocol, Frederick decided he should drive over to The Summerhouse, hoping they had found Claire during the time he had driven to Abington. As he drove up the winding driveway to the facility, he noticed a lack of presence by local law enforcement. There was only one police car in the parking, and unlike the scene at Claire's home, there were no signs of an ongoing investigation.

268 · RENEE PROPES

CHAPTER THIRTY-SEVEN

....

Nancy Leigh displayed her charming personality as she introduced herself to the receptionist as Theodore Williams' niece from Savannah, Georgia.

She had contacted a guy from her college days skilled at altering drivers' licenses, and had hired him to make a duplicate to include an address in Savannah. When she received it back, she noticed that it looked authentic. As she produced it for the receptionist, she was careful to hold the permit in a way to obstruct her picture from sight except for the part that revealed her blonde hair.

As she found her way to Theodore's room, she breathed a sigh of relief. When she entered the room, Nancy Leigh was unprepared for what she saw. As she stared at the remnants of the strong, vibrant man whom she once knew as her father-in-law. The once-handsome, tanned face lacked any resemblance to her husband's father. Concerned she had perhaps walked into the wrong room, because she entered through the front entrance rather than the side door as Brad had done. She stepped outside the room long enough to observe the name inserted on the metal plate nailed to the wall next to the door. Satisfied the plate was inscribed with the name Theodore Williams, she returned to the room and began to look for identifying items, which would further confirm she was in the correct place. As she canvassed the room, she spotted a Holy Bible sitting on a small table next to a leather recliner. The Bible inscribed with the name of Claire Williams, was further confirmation that she was in the right room. As she opened the pages of the Bible, she saw a piece of a paper someone had cut from a magazine that read, "There is a common thread that binds us together because we are all children of the Most High God."

Aware that she had wasted more than a few minutes, she hurriedly secured the mask to her face, placed the rubber gloves on each hand, and busied herself with the chemicals which she had carefully wrapped.

Nancy Leigh paused again when she looked at the unfamiliar face of the man lying in bed. With the words written in her mother-in-law's Bible still resonating in her head, it occurred to her she was committing the murder of an innocent individual who had already experienced much pain and suffering. Guilt swept over her, but she quietly rationalized her actions by remembering the life of poverty where she grew up. She thought, *Nancy Leigh, you are wasting valuable time. Let's get this done so we can get the money.* So, she saturated the towel with the toxic cocktail, and then placed it under his nose while removing the oxygen tube.

Theodore thrashed about violently as if his lungs were engulfed with flames. After he finally succumbed, Nancy Leigh replaced the containers of the toxic chemicals, and in her haste, she dropped a zip lock bag on the floor next to her large pocketbook. Nancy Leigh had intended to replace the oxygen tube to the patient's nose, but in a hurry to leave the room, she forgot. A third mistake was her rash decision to exit the facility through the back door instead of the front entrance, where she had signed her name on the visitors' sheet. When she exited the building and fled towards the corner of the facility, she hoped Brad was watching the sides of the building.

Her heart was pounding, and she could barely breathe, but when she turned the corner, Brad's car was no longer in the parking lot. Nancy Leigh stopped and looked around, realizing a staff member could have been watching her from the large picture window. She turned and went to the side of the building and headed toward the driveway as the car appeared. Brad leaned over the seat to open the passenger door and slowed as Nancy Leigh jumped into the car. She struggled to close the heavy door of the moving vehicle as they circled around and sped down the driveway into the nearby traffic without being noticed.

"Where in the hell have you been? I almost had a heart attack when I couldn't find your car."

"Calm down, missy. You were in there much longer than I expected, so I went down to the convenience store to get a snack." He pitched her a can. "Here I got you a Coke, too. How is Mr. Williams?"

"Are you kidding me, you left me here to suffocate my father-in-law, while you went for a snack?" Nancy Leigh opened the Coke and took a swallow.

"Yes, I was hungry. And, stop talking to me with that condescending tone. I drove you over here, didn't I?"

Brad removed the toboggan cap and slammed on the brakes to avoid running a yellow traffic light. "What did you say about your father-in-law?"

"I said you left me here to suffocate my father-in-law. What did you think I said?"

Brad looked at each of the mirrors on the car as if someone might have followed them. "I can't believe you killed him. What were you thinking?"

"Well, well, well. Look at you, Mister. You killed two people today, and now you are getting all righteous because of what I did?"

"Nancy Leigh, I saved your life! One guy was tracking your movements from the woods, and the other one was watching from the wooded lot beside the house. Had I not moved when I did, you would be dead."

CHAPTER THIRTY-EIGHT

Once he presented proper identification, the receptionist identified him as one of Theodore Williams' next of kin. She buzzed the administrator to advise her of Frederick Simpson's arrival. As he sat waiting in the conference room sipping a Diet Coke, he made a mental list of questions that needed answering. The first of many included the date and time of the staff's last contact with his niece.

The administrator, Suzanne, entered the room along with a local uniformed policeman and one other employee whom she introduced as her administrative assistant.

Frederick asked. "When was the last time a member of your staff spoke with my niece, Claire Williams?" The administrative assistant paused, asked to be excused, and quickly exited the room. She returned with a log of daily phone calls, and reported that Mrs. Williams had called at 10:54 a.m. to say that she would not be coming today, as she was visiting with her friend, Nora Hawkins. She said she planned to return, and would visit Mr. Williams on Saturday afternoon. Frederick looked at his watch and calculated she would have called the facility following the conversation they completed earlier in the day. He also realized the administrative assistant should not have revealed the whereabouts of his niece. Under different circumstances, Frederick would have pointed out the apparent liability involved in disclosing the location of a family member; however, in this situation, he was thankful for the information. He then pondered the unfamiliar name of Nora Hawkins.

"Have you tried to contact my niece by phone? She has a cell phone, but she's prone to leaving it in her car."

"Yes, we have called her home and her cell. And, we have also tried to get in touch with her son, Teddy. But, we did not leave a message. It's our policy to never leave a phone message regarding the news of a patient's passing." Suzanne said.

Then, she asked Mr. Simpson if he was familiar with the relationship between Mrs. Williams and Mrs. Hawkins, to which Frederick answered, "No." She explained about the death of the prominent landowner Tom Hawkins earlier in the month and told that Claire had developed a close bond with the deceased's granddaughter and his widow. She said Claire's husband had shown an interest in purchasing the Hawkins' property. The dialogue involving the established relationship between his niece, Claire, and the Hawkins family showed the closeness of the relationship between Claire and the administrator. Naturally, Claire had made friends with several members of the staff as she had spent many hours visiting her husband. Claire previously mentioned Suzanne in their conversation earlier that day as she described a lovely luncheon they had enjoyed the previous day on the back terrace. Frederick could not remember Claire mentioning Nora Hawkins during their frequent conversations.

Frederick turned to the uniformed policeman and asked, "Are you familiar with the location of the Hawkins' property?"

The officer shot a quick glance at the administrator for permission to answer the question. She nodded. Then he removed a notepad and pencil from his shirt pocket and wrote the address of the Hawkins farm and handed it to Frederick. As Frederick reached for the paper, he noticed the beautiful star-filled sky outside the window, and he realized that Claire's plan to spend the night away from home was a good omen. He felt relief that she was in a safe place.

When he looked over at the administrator, Frederick thought *if ever there were grounds for a legal suit, the events of this day had warranted one.*

Then, Suzanne did something he least expected. "Would you care for a turkey sandwich or a salad? I didn't eat lunch today, and I'm developing a headache."

Because of Frederick's southern upbringing, he was gracious and accepted the food. Her generous sign of hospitality caused their relationship to soften, and the tone of the meeting improved.

When they finished their meal, Frederick said, "Thank you for the delicious sandwich. Would you allow the policeman to direct me to Theodore's room? While I'm here, I could prevent Claire from enduring the pain of having to clean out Theo's room."

"That is very thoughtful of you. Since you're listed as the next of kin, we can allow you to clean out his room," said Suzanne.

Then she turned to the policeman. "Please provide Mr. Simpson with anything he may need to prepare the items for removal."

While walking to Theo's room, the policeman explained to Frederick that the owner of the property had transformed the building from a high-end spa to an assisted-living facility. As the men continued their discussion, Frederick began clearing out the room.

The policeman sat in the leather recliner, leaned back and said, "Bet you hadn't heard about the excitement they had here last night?"

"No, what excitement was that?"

"A crazy man walked through the side door and started peeping into rooms on this hallway. Fortunately, a custodian saw him and led him out the back door. It caused quite a stir."

Frederick looked over at the policeman and said, "Does that sort of thing happen often?"

"No. Don't think it's ever happened before. It was a fluke. Probably someone high on meth."

As the conversation stalled, he picked up the Holy Bible, which lay on a small table next to the chair. "Listen to this." He opened the book and found the following words printed on the inside page: "*Faith makes all things possible, Hope makes all things bright, and Love makes all things easy.* As a native Abingtonian, I knew of Theodore

Williams' success in real estate. And, I've also followed his decline since arriving at The Summerhouse." He smiled as he re-read the words found in the Bible.

"I'm sure my niece has reflected on that mantra many times since Theo became ill."

Frederick continued to look through the room in search of personal items belonging to either Claire or Theo. Almost done, he slid the bed to reach Theo's bedroom slippers, which he noticed lying underneath the bed. When he did, he saw a large Ziploc storage bag stuffed with a kitchen towel. When Frederick opened the bag, strong fumes escaped. He realized the bag might contain evidence that suggested Theo had not died of natural causes. Frederick motioned for the policeman to join him on the opposite side of the room next to the bed. He lifted the bag by the extreme corner to eliminate additional fingerprints, and he raised an eyebrow, as he handed it off to the officer.

CHAPTER THIRTY-NINE

Nora's first thought was, *please don't let that be Drew Byrd*! But she remained quiet as she looked over at Claire, who was sitting on the hearth, warming her back against the fire.

"Who would come around at this time of night, Nora? Wouldn't the vet go straight to the barn?" asked Claire.

Nora shook her head as she was careful to not appear anxious. She then peeked out of the kitchen window to see if there were any vehicles parked in the backyard.

"Sammy might come back up to the house to share the news of the mare's delivery. If so, he would knock on the door, knowing it might startle us if he barged through the door as he normally does."

Nora walked over to the kitchen door and said, "Sammy, is that you?"

"No, ma'am, my car broke down on the highway, and I need to call for help. Would you mind if I use your phone?"

Nora turned to look at Claire, but Claire was already behind her at the door.

Claire whispered, "Where is your phone, Nora?" She pointed to the phone hanging on the wall in the next room. Claire responded, "Well, I see no reason we shouldn't let him use the phone. Open the door and let's talk to him a few minutes. He could give us the number, and we can make the call for him."

They opened the door, and Nora said, "Young man, do you not have a cell phone?"

The guy standing on the back porch was nondescript in appearance, except for a black toboggan cap, which he had pulled

277

down to cover his forehead. Shuffling his feet and showing a slight irritation unmistakable in his voice, "Ma'am, my phone is dead, and I don't have my charger. I just need to make a quick call for help, and I will be on my way."

Claire stepped up to the screen door and said, "Son, you look familiar to me, do I know you? My name is Claire Williams, my husband is Theodore Williams."

They noticed the young man seemed to be growing more agitated by the second and as his irritation increased. He jerked the screen door with such force the latch fell to the porch, and he barged into the kitchen. Then he revealed the gun which he had previously concealed. He barked orders about where he wanted them to sit as he walked wildly around the kitchen in search of the phone, which he found in the adjoining room. He walked over to the phone, pulled the cord from the receiver, and then knocked the phone off the wall.

Nora yelled, "Why did you do that, don't you need to call for help?"

Realizing the seriousness of the situation, Claire grabbed her friend's hand and whispered, "Let's be quiet, and follow his instructions."

The young man continued to walk through the house until he found the duct tape in a nearby drawer, which he used to tie each woman's hands together. As he busied himself, Nora dropped her wineglass on the floor, and the glass broke, leaving a large piece near her feet, which she quickly pushed under the sofa. When he finished wrapping their hands, he pulled off two long pieces of tape and wrapped a bit around Nora's head to secure her mouth. Anger rose in Claire, unlike anything she had ever felt, and she devised a plan to remove herself and Nora from this dangerous situation. As he inched his way between the two women to complete wrapping Nora's head, Claire carefully leaned down and picked up the most significant piece of broken glass and placed it under the cushion next to her. He turned toward Claire and tore another piece of tape, and then he began to tape Claire's mouth shut in the same fashion. He stood up, stepped back, and looked at the women as they sat on the sofa with their hands and mouths taped. With a sarcastic tone, he said, "Well, now, you ladies sit there and chat among yourselves while I go about my business, okay?"

He went from room to room as he opened drawers and closet doors in an apparent search for something, or perhaps, nothing. The stranger was vandalizing the beautiful home in the outburst of his anger. As Nora watched the madman destroy the order in her home, the pain which had diminished earlier in the evening returned with intensity. Tears welled up in her eyes as she noticed the clock on the stove was now showing 10:15 p.m. The time-release pain medication was due at nine o'clock, and she had forgotten to take her medicine at the appointed time.

Now, the pain was almost unbearable. Nora's thoughts turned to the conversation she had with the doctor concerning her pain. *The immediate goal is to manage the pain before it reaches a critical level. The only medication that is available to eliminate the severe pain you will eventually experience are heavy narcotics. When the pain reaches an unmanageable level, the mind and body will separate from each other, and the comatose state at the end will help with the transition process.* Nora suddenly wished he had already prescribed a few of the narcotic drugs. Because maybe it would help her to survive her current situation.

* * * * * * *

As Claire sat motionless on the sofa, she thought about the irony of the situation. She had only wanted to relieve Katie of worry about her grandmother while she went to Savannah for a class that she had scheduled months earlier. What was the chance of something like this happening to them? As she saw the terror in Nora's eyes while the intruder continued to search throughout the house, there was an unexpected knock from the kitchen door. She hoped Nora might recognize the voice of the person standing outside. The man with the dark toboggan cap stomped towards the kitchen, and with an agitated tone, he ordered the two women to follow him into the other room. While he walked toward the front of the house, he realized the women couldn't raise themselves from the sofa because of their taped hands. So, he returned to the sofa and forcibly lifted each woman. He then pointed them toward the front of the house, and pushed them into the darkened parlor toward the loveseat. Then, he went back to the kitchen to open the door.

"Who is it?"

The ladies strained to hear him ask for the identification of the person standing on the back porch. Finally, he opened the door, and someone walked into the kitchen.

"What took you so long? I've been standing out here in the dark, and it's creepy as hell out here."

Claire thought she recognized the female voice of the second person, but their voices lowered to a whisper, and neither Nora nor Claire could understand the discussion between the intruders.

Following a few moments of whispers, the woman raised her voice and said, "Why did you take them to the parlor? Did you recognize her?" To which the man must have replied in the affirmative, because the woman's voice raised several octaves, "Then you should have killed her. Now she has a visual of you and can identify you in a lineup."

The man shuffled around the kitchen in anger and laid the gun down on the kitchen table with a loud force.

"Listen, bitch, I told you I would have no part in killing them. I can't believe I have let you manipulate me this far. Let me tell you how this is going down. I will wait until you finish your business here, and when you're done, you will find me waiting in the car. I refuse to do your dirty work. You should have involved your attorney friend if you wanted to carry out this ridiculously constructed plan." The man stomped out the back door, and they could hear his footsteps as he exited the porch in search of the alleged car.

The ladies sat in a profound state of fear. Unfortunately, they did not know the identity of the person with whom they dealt. At least before they had seen the young man, and although they knew he had an agenda, his demeanor at no time showed that he would cause them harm. As was evident in the manner with which he assisted each of them from the kitchen into the parlor. He had moved around the house with a purpose in his pursuit of rummaging through drawers and closets, but he had left them alone other than when he taped their hands and mouths shut and moved them into the parlor. But, because of the mean-spirited tone of the previous exchange, it heightened their senses, and they feared for their lives as they sat in the darkened room.

Claire tried to use her mind to recall happier days with her husband and children. Then, she thought of Sammy. He was somewhere on the property waiting for a mare to give birth and was unaware of what was happening inside the house. As she continued her wait, she prayed that maybe someone would show up and rescue them.

They heard footsteps coming in their direction. Someone turned on a small lamp in the foyer to provide just enough light to make out images in the room. The small-framed woman had dressed in dark colors and wore a baseball cap with white NY embroidered on the front. Otherwise, they could tell very little about her appearance. She carried a gun as she walked toward the front of the house and never even glanced toward them. She set the gun down on the marble-top sideboard in the foyer. A wingback chair was just inside the room, and she slid the chair to the entrance as if to stand guard throughout the night. Claire looked over at Nora and noticed that her body was shaking. When Nora turned to face her, there was terror in her eyes. Neither knew what to expect next, but it was clear the woman with the animated voice waited with expectation. And, the wait began.

CHAPTER FORTY

Frederick stood outside Theo's room while the policeman went to find Suzanne. Confident the discovery of the Ziploc bag would warrant an investigation, he wondered if the coroner had already released the body to the funeral home or was waiting for contact from the next of kin. Removing the body and allowing access to the room had destroyed much of the evidence in the case. He stuck his head in the door and looked around the unoccupied room. He noticed the cordless telephone on the small table next to the chair, and he stepped back into the room and picked up the receiver and got a dial tone. As he walked back into the hallway, he pressed the number to Teddy's business cell, but no one answered. Then he dialed Claire's cell number. Frederick hoped that Claire had not left the phone in her car.

The phone rang. One, two, three, four, five rings, and Frederick was about to disconnect when he noticed the phone had stopped ringing but didn't cut off. There was a movement, but no static on the other end of the line. No one spoke. Frederick said, "Claire, Claire, are you there? Can you hear me? This is Frederick. Are you okay, Claire? Please answer me! Please, Claire, I need to speak with you at once, as you may be in immediate danger!"

The policeman and Suzanne appeared at Theo's door and heard Frederick's phone conversation. Suzanne, whose concern showed on her face, turned to Frederick with a puzzled look, and he knew she had been unsuccessful in contacting Claire. He was unfazed by their presence and continued to speak into the phone, hoping Claire could hear his voice.

Frederick explained to the policeman about the call to Claire's cell when the policeman motioned for the phone. The officer grabbed it and walked out into the parking lot and yelled into the phone. Suzanne interrupted and questioned Frederick about the discovery of the Ziploc bag. But, Frederick ignored her as he watched the officer storming around outside for a while longer, then he walked back in the room and began to explain the events that led to his finding.

After they combed the room for further evidence, Suzanne suggested they contact the Poison Control Center to determine the identity of the chemicals on the towels.

Realizing she was out of her realm of responsibility, Frederick cleared his throat and said, "With all due respect, Suzanne, Officer Anderson has already contacted the authorities, and when they arrive, they will handle the contents of the bag according to protocol. As he and I discussed a few moments ago, additional tampering could compromise the evidence."

Suzanne paused, and then nodded in agreement. When she turned to leave the room, she said, "Let's go up to my office and make the call."

Frederick understood Suzanne wanting to leave the room, but he waved her off and said, "Perhaps someone should wait at the door to prevent access from anyone who might compromise this investigation."

As she turned and left the room, she said, "I should contact the owner immediately."

Heading for her office, she mumbled, "This may not end well."

CHAPTER FORTY-ONE

A fter leaving his parents' house, where he dropped off his father following an afternoon of golf, Drew stopped by the office to make a call to Nancy Leigh. He had avoided calling her from his cell phone because he didn't want the calls traced to a number that Colleen might see on the monthly statement. They had discussed making another visit to the Hawkins' farm to persuade Mrs. Hawkins to sell the property. He wasn't sure if Nancy Leigh would be home so early in the afternoon, but he wanted to contact her before going home. More importantly, he needed to check the mail. When the office closed at noon, the mailman had not been by, and Drew was anxious to see if they had received any checks. As he pulled into the firm's driveway, the parking lot was empty. Relieved to have the place to himself, he went straight to his office. It had become their practice to close the office on Friday afternoons during the summer months as a reward for the long hours the employees worked during the week. At the end of the previous summer, Drew had suggested to his dad they continue the practice through the fall and winter months.

Drew entered his office and looked around and walked over to his desk and dropped the mail, and then he locked the door behind him. He sat down at his desk and dialed Nancy Leigh's phone number. She was expecting his call at five p.m., but she answered the call immediately.

They discussed their upcoming meeting with Nora Hawkins. Drew said, "Let's plan on meeting at the farm around 11:00 p.m."

"Don't you think it's a little late? We'll scare the poor lady to death if we show up at that time."

"No, I think the element of surprise at such a late hour might work to our advantage. I've promised to take Colleen over to the club for the prime rib buffet. We'll be back in plenty of time for me to make it to the farm by then."

His plan allowed enough time to enjoy their night out before heading out for an unexpected trip to the store, which would be his excuse for leaving the house at 10:30 p.m. on a Friday night. Colleen would be so tired following a meal of rich food she would fall asleep as soon as her head hit the pillow, and wouldn't wake until sometime late Saturday morning.

With the meeting scheduled with Nancy Leigh confirmed, Drew sorted through the items of mail on his desk. He noticed an envelope addressed in muscular, bold letters, and he immediately recognized the penmanship of one of his recent clients. It was a thank you note along with a check for the remaining fees for his services.

Drew had kept him from serving time in prison because of a tip he had received from an anonymous caller regarding the whereabouts of his client on the night of the alleged murder. His client had maintained his innocence throughout the month-long trial.

During the weeks leading up to the trial, Drew recalled several discussions with his client about the fear he experienced waiting for the trial to begin. On the night before the start of the trial, Drew had sat across the table as he watched his client's body literally stiffen from the paralyzing thoughts of going to prison.

When Drew finished reading the note, he folded it and placed it back into the envelope and filed it away, and he put the check in the stack with the others.

Drew secured the office building, and on the way to the bank, he thought about the first meeting with Nancy Leigh and Brad at The Nighthawk's Bar in Athens. He remembered his surprise at the ease with which they executed their plan. Nancy Leigh broke off the relationship with Brad after two years, just as Drew had predicted. But, they had hooked up the year of Nancy Leigh and Teddy's sixth anniversary. When Nancy Leigh was ready to cash in and get her money, she had told Drew that she needed to keep Brad close to help carry out the plan.

However, the careful execution of the kiss on the afternoon of the fall golf tournament almost did not happen. Drew had forgotten to tell Nancy Leigh that Teddy had a meeting on Saturday afternoon and wouldn't be playing in the competition. She hung around the pro shop all day, waiting for someone to spot Teddy, but, thanks to the last-minute decision to leave his father's office early, the kiss went off without a hitch. The threesome had spent years scheming against Teddy's family. But the hours following the kiss, as Nancy Leigh and Brad waited for the phone call from Drew confirming that Teddy was ready to file for divorce, was the longest period of the entire plan.

CHAPTER FORTY-TWO

It concerned Nancy Leigh that Brad had not yet returned to the house. He was quick-tempered and often grew angry with her, but his anger was usually short-lived. She noticed the time was 10:30 p.m. She had only agreed to meet Drew at this late hour because of his insistence, but now she was thankful for the delay. She needed to leave the house and go speak with Brad before he showed up.

She had not told Brad about the conversation between her and Drew earlier in the day. He thought Nancy Leigh had cut Drew out of the deal, and he wasn't expecting him to be at the farm.

Nancy Leigh got up from her chair and tiptoed to the kitchen where she found the back door standing wide open. She couldn't remember leaving the door opened, so, she stepped out onto the porch and looked around the yard. There was a detached garage a couple hundred yards from the house. She noticed a dim light shining from the window of the second story. On the day she had been at the farm with Drew, she had not seen the window above the garage. Unfamiliar with the living arrangements of the Hawkins' family, she wasn't sure if anyone lived above the garage.

She went around to the front of the house and scaled the steps to the porch. When she tiptoed over to the parlor window, the lamppost light from the yard allowed her to see the outline of the two ladies sitting on the loveseat. But, the darkened room prevented her from seeing their faces. She wondered what might go through their minds as they sat alone in the parlor, and then she heard a noise that sounded like a door slamming shut from the back of the house. . . Hopefully, Brad had recovered from the fit of anger and had come back up to the house to apologize. Nancy Leigh rushed down the steps and went back around the house the same way she came. When she entered the back door, she looked around and did a double take. She had expected to find Brad standing in the kitchen waiting for her. Nancy Leigh looked in the adjoining room and discovered a door at the far side. With curiosity, she opened the door and found steps leading up to a landing. To her right, there was another door, but it had no lock, and it opened easily. There was the graveled driveway, and she wondered who used this entrance. Then, she went into the foyer and peeped into the parlor, but no Brad. She looked up the stairs from the hall, and stopping mid-stride decided against going up for fear whoever stayed above the garage might detect the light from her flashlight. A sick feeling appeared in her stomach, and she considered leaving the house once again, and run down to the deserted road to check on Brad. She thought as soon as she would find her way to the car, Drew would probably show up, and the scheme to get both men there would be ruined. Returning to the kitchen, she opened the fridge and found a Diet Coke, and she went back to her seat in the darkened foyer with the only light coming from the illumination of her watch and a flashlight in her hand. She checked her watch, and she waited.

She prayed Brad had fallen asleep in the car and would remain asleep until the meeting was over, or perhaps get pissed off, and go back home. Her original plan was for Brad to act as her hitman, but he had forced her hand and refused to leave the car at the assisted-living facility. Once again, Brad had turned the tables on Nancy Leigh, and if he didn't come back up to the house soon, she would have to kill her mother-in-law after resolving the option with Mrs. Hawkins. Her initial, well-calculated plan of manipulation had not worked out as she had intended. And, now she had to deal with Drew, too. Nancy Leigh jumped as the grandfather's clock positioned behind her in the foyer struck eleven o'clock. Her acute senses had increased since arriving earlier in the evening, and the silence magnified every sound on the farm. She was sure that she had heard a door slam when she was on the front porch. But now she pondered the dilemma of two women tied up in the parlor, while Brad, her collaborator in the plan, was nowhere to be found. Drew, the person responsible for her involvement in this absurd situation, would be ill-prepared for what he would find waiting in the parlor.

Nancy Leigh heard a car from a distance, and she let out a sigh of relief. She waited for Drew to find his way up to the house. Ten minutes passed, and Nancy Leigh's anxiety had increased. She suspected that something was amiss as she walked into the kitchen and looked out the picture window into the darkness. Nancy Leigh detected movement, perhaps a large dog or farm animal, positioned on the ground behind the giant oak tree. Startled by the unexpected knock at the front door, she turned and made her way into the foyer.

When Nancy Leigh opened the door, holding the gun in her hand, Drew stood on the porch. He stepped back and said, "What the hell is that?"

Oblivious to the gun she had carried around since Brad left the house earlier, she looked down and said, "Oh, this is a gun."

"Well, yes, I can see that, Nancy Leigh, but what are you doing with a gun, and where is Mrs. Hawkins?"

Nancy Leigh unlatched the screen door and motioned for Drew to come into the house. She walked towards the kitchen, where she stopped and pointed into the parlor. Drew turned towards the room and saw Mrs. Hawkins and his mother's best friend, Clara Williams, sitting on the sofa. There was a sensation of things moving too quickly to process when he felt a loosening of his bladder. Drew looked at Nancy Leigh and said, "What the hell is going on, Nancy Leigh?" She turned, rushed into the kitchen, and waited for Drew to join her as the kitchen door closed.

CHAPTER FORTY-THREE

D rew and Nancy Leigh were arguing in the kitchen while Nora and Claire listened from the parlor. Drew was in a full state of panic as he considered the consequences of having the sheriff's department called to the farm. It filled him with fear thinking about how best to leave the property now that they had seen him entering the house.

While visiting one of his clients at the local jail during a pre-trial meeting, he had told Drew the worse thing about fear was the hypothetical situations the mind would conjure up in the middle of the night. It was akin to waking from a night of deep sleep to find someone with a gun held to their head. And, several of his clients had wished for those scenarios to happen, so the pain would end. Unable to stop the constant mind games, the sensation was deafening.

He had often laughed at their descriptions as he relayed the stories to his buddies at The Club, and they would agree these men whose reports of fear was horrid, were cowards. But he had just experienced a different level of anxiety, and he wasn't laughing now.

What was I thinking? He thought. Then, as he sat on the sofa, he re-traced the timeline of his involvement with Nancy Leigh, all the way back to the first meeting with her and Brad Carlisle at the Nighthawks' Bar. Disgusted with himself, he ran his hand through his hair, a nervous habit he'd developed while in law school. He shuddered as he thought how devastated his family would be when they discovered his involvement with Nancy Leigh. Until recently, he had merely been the originator of the plan, and on two occasions, he had stepped outside the box when he contacted Mrs. Hawkins about an option for her property.

A trickle of sweat went down his back as he thought about why he had prepared the option in the first place. Drew's mouth went dry at the thoughts of spending time in prison for the little escapade thought up by Nancy Leigh. They had only meant to scare Mrs. Hawkins into signing over the property to them. But, after their call ended earlier in the day, Nancy Leigh must have lost her sense of reality, all because he hadn't settled her divorce. He had only included Nancy Leigh in the option because he needed to use her money from the divorce settlement to buy the farm.

As he sat on the sofa in a depressed state, his hand slipped between the cushions. He felt a sharp object and pulled out a large piece of jagged glass. His mind raced, and he thought, *this is the perfect instrument to use to end my life.* Then, he thought about how his father had trusted him and had made him a partner in his firm. As a criminal lawyer, he represented people like Nancy Leigh. He took their money, but he didn't get in bed with them. They were so close to removing the law firm from the bank loan, thanks to Teddy's generosity and the bank's extension of time. Disgusted with himself, Drew looked at the sharp object and threw it across the room. As he continued to think about his family, his eyes had filled with tears and his body had begun to shake uncontrollably.

CHAPTER FORTY-FOUR

W hen the homicide investigation was completed, Frederick turned to the policeman and asked, "Mr. Anderson, are you officially off duty now?"

"Yes. My shift ended at 10 p.m. Why do you ask, sir?"

Frederick looked at his watch and realized the time had passed quickly while the room inspection was underway. "Well, I see it is now approaching 2 a.m., and I would very much appreciate you going with me over to my niece's house. We should inspect the inside of her home before going to her friend's house first thing in the morning. I need to make a few calls, but I would be remiss if I didn't inspect the contents of her home before notifying her of the two deaths that occurred in her backyard, and then delivering the news of her husband's death."

"Sir, I understand. But, we must check in with the police chief for permission to enter the home of a crime scene. One must follow protocol regarding these types of situations, and I'm sure you understand the need to leave the scene untouched, until the investigation is complete. If you will excuse me, I'll call the station before we head out."

Frederick leaned against the back of his car while Officer Anderson sat in the patrol car and spoke to his chief. The starlit night was beautiful, and the air was nippy. However, after breathing the faint smells of urine masked by industrial-strength cleaning solutions in the confined space for several hours, the crisp air was refreshing. He thought about his niece and the circumstances of which she was unaware.

Unsure of what they might find inside Claire's house once they arrived, Frederick offered a prayer for her safety and guidance for himself and Officer Anderson as they navigated through the next hours in search of his niece.

Although his beloved wife, Mary, was a woman of deep faith, he had never been one to subscribe to her religious theology. However, on this chilly Saturday morning, less than a week before the traditional Thanksgiving holiday, he found himself in a place of indecision and considered why people could become dependent upon a direction from a higher deity. As he turned toward the patrol car, he saw Officer Anderson with the phone to his ear. He opened his car door, slid into the driver's seat, and continued to pray for comfort for his wife as she often lay awake during the early morning hours as pain wrenched her cancer-ridden body. Her death was imminent, and he also prayed to her God that He would see fit to let her live until he could return to her side and hold her frail body as she passed from this life into the heavenly paradise she often referred to throughout their marriage. When Frederick finished his prayer, it filled him with peace. It was like the peace one feels on a Sunday morning following a restful sleep, savoring the luxury of staying in bed awhile longer, while the world outside remained quiet and undisturbed. He experienced a warmth that he had never known, and Frederick knew one way or the other, his Mary, and he would be fine.

Deep in thought, it startled Frederick when the officer tapped on the roof of his vehicle and motioned for him to lower the window. Frederick wiped the tears from his face as the officer cited permission from the police chief to accompany him to his niece's home for an internal inspection. The dispatcher had recommended sending along a backup unit for assistance, which Frederick thought was unnecessary, but he did not voice his opinion for fear his voice would break.

As instructed, Frederick followed the officer through the sleeping city as they found their way to the quiet street on which Claire and Theodore had built their beautiful home and raised their family. The temporary lights proved useful as Theodore, and Officer Anderson walked around to the back of the house and unlocked the door. Once inside, they found a few lamps lit, as if Claire were planning to return during the pre-dawn hours. As the men inspected the house, it reassured Frederick to see the house was tidy and undisturbed. They saw a neat stack of mail on the breakfast table, which showed that Claire had checked the mailbox recently. Confident, the bottom floor was secure; they proceeded up the stairs to the second level, and once again found the contents of the home to be in order.

From the upstairs landing, Frederick noticed the backup patrol car had arrived, and he mentioned to Officer Anderson the car was sitting in the driveway. "Yes," replied the officer, "the backup unit radioed me a few minutes ago to let me know they were on the premises. Do you see any reason for them to come inside?" Frederick shook his head, continued down the stairway, and headed for the kitchen to make a pot of coffee while he gathered his thoughts. Officer Anderson responded to the backup unit, then walked over to the breakfast table and pulled out a chair, and asked, "May I sit?"

Frederick responded, "Of course, son. I apologize for my lack of manners this morning. Please make yourself at home, the coffee will finish brewing soon, and perhaps we should prepare a game plan for how we approach my niece with an explanation surrounding the events involving her home and the death of her husband."

Officer Anderson said, "Of course. Yesterday, I worked my regular shift for the police force. An hour or so before the end of the shift, they dispatched me to the assisted-living facility when the nurse found Mr. Williams unresponsive. And, as you know, I remained at the facility throughout the evening until the investigative team completed their inspection. I just need a quick catnap. Do you mind if I stretch out on the sofa in the family room for a few moments?"

"Not at all. I'm going into the study and try to get some sleep myself." Once the coffee brewed, Frederick poured himself a cup and went into Theodore's study, where he found a lightweight blanket on the back of the leather sofa. As he drank his coffee, he reflected on the many times he and Theodore had sat in the study to discuss the family finances. Frederick was fond of Theodore, and although he and Mary often referred to Claire as their daughter, they felt the same level of affection for Theo.

He refused to call Claire about her husband's death; he intended to be with her when she heard the news. Theo would have done the same for him if the roles were reversed. When he drained the last of his coffee, he lay down on the large sofa, pulled up the blanket, and drifted off to sleep. By 3 a.m., both men were fast asleep.

CHAPTER FORTY-FIVE

(Saturday, November 23, 2014)

T he lobby of the Hyatt Regency in historic downtown Savannah was quiet on this Saturday morning in November before the demanding Thanksgiving week. Teddy awakened before daybreak, unable to sleep as the memories of the previous evening with Katie were still fresh on his mind. He took a leisurely shower, but when he sat on the bed to put on his shoes, it reminded him he had not called his mother as was his practice when he was out of town. Realizing the predawn hour, Teddy waited to place the call thinking that his mom and Mrs. Hawkins might have stayed up chatting late into the night and would sleep late. He gathered a copy of the morning paper he found outside his room, made his way to the elevator, and waited for the door to open to carry him to the lobby in search of a cup of coffee. As the elevator descended to the lobby floor, Teddy considered his few options for Thanksgiving. He wondered if it would disappoint his mother if he decided against attending Thanksgiving dinner at the Byrds' house this year. He made a mental note to discuss Katie's plans later when they met for a light breakfast before leaving for home.

Inside the restaurant, they displayed the continental breakfast in classic Hyatt style. Teddy slipped the newspaper under his arm while he poured his coffee, and then he found a table in the corner. He was engaged in an article regarding the current infrastructure within the city limits of Savannah when Katie appeared in the restaurant at the agreed-upon time. Detecting a movement within his peripheral vision,

Teddy saw Katie and rose from his seat to greet her, but noticed she had a look of concern on her face. "Good morning, sunshine."

Katie responded with a sweet smile, "Did you call your mother yesterday, Teddy?"

Embarrassed, Teddy shook his head "no," as he reached over and kissed her cheek. "No, I didn't. You probably won't believe it, but I had a smoking hot date last night. In all honesty, the thoughts of calling my mother did not even enter my mind until this morning, and I realized it was a bit early to call her on a Saturday." Shaking his head, he continued, "I know, I'm a bad, bad boy."

Katie was once again captivated by his charm. She reached across the table to touch his arm and said, "You are not a bad, bad boy, Teddy Williams."

Teddy noticed the look of concern had returned to her face and asked, "Are you okay? Were you able to contact your grandmother?"

She shook her head and said, "No, the weirdest thing happened when I called the number; there was a fast-busy signal. So, I contacted the local telephone company, and they could not find anything wrong with the line. However, they confirmed a fast-busy signal when they also dialed. The operator suggested that someone might have left the phone off the receiver, which would cause a fast-busy signal. That doesn't sound like my grandmother. Especially with your mom visiting, surely one of them would notice the phone being off the receiver. Sammy is in and out of the house several times each day, and he would have noticed the phone being out of service, too. I called his apartment over the garage and got the same signal. In fact, now more than ever, he is in daily contact with the veterinarian awaiting the delivery of his mare."

"Does Sammy have a cell phone?"

"Yes, he does. And, I called his number, but the reception in the barn area is questionable, so, he didn't answer either time." She scoped out the restaurant to find the coffee bar and excused herself for a moment to get a cup.

When Katie returned to the table, Teddy said, "When we go back up to our rooms to retrieve our luggage, I'll make a call to Mom's cell phone. I'm sure we'll learn that a storm swept through the area last evening and knocked out the power or some other random occurrence, which will put both of our minds at ease regarding the elders of our families."

Katie raised her eyebrows and said, "I'm not so sure your mother would appreciate being referred to as a family elder. She doesn't fit the description of an elder at this stage of her life."

Teddy laughed and continued, "So true. I misspoke, and perhaps we should keep that comment between us. What do you say?"

"I believe I mentioned to you that Mom and I have accepted an invitation to Thanksgiving dinner with the Byrds this year. However, because of the events involving Drew and Nancy Leigh, I'm considering changing my plans. Have you and your grandmother made plans for Thanksgiving yet?"

Katie added more cream to her coffee and said, "Yes. Grandmother plans to spend the holiday weekend with Stephen's family in Atlanta," she paused, and then she scrunched her face.

Teddy waited for her to continue.

"Believe it or not, Mr. and Mrs. Byrd also invited me to spend Thanksgiving with them this year."

Teddy folded the morning paper, and placed it to the left of his plate. He put his hand around his coffee cup, and said, "Perhaps, we have discussed this before, but how well acquainted are you with the Byrd family?"

Katie touched her napkin to her lips as she measured her response. "I have gotten to know the Byrd family through business connections."

Teddy looked at his watch and said, "Well, fair enough. We should go up to my room and make that call. We need to pack our cars and get on the road." He reached over and touched her fingertips. Producing that boyish smile, he said, "Now, can I trust you to be alone with me in my hotel room while we place a call to my mom? Or should I ask the concierge to accompany us?"

Katie's head went back, and she rolled her eyes as she jerked her hand away, and said, "I hate to be the one to break this news to you, Teddy Williams, but you really aren't that special."

Teddy dropped his head. "Now that is where you are wrong," he said as he stood up and walked over to her side of the table. He offered his hand, and as soon as their hands joined, he winked and raised her hands to his lips.

Katie said, "Quit, Teddy, you will not make this easy, will you?"

He shook his head, and with a deep voice, he said, "No way. I'm gonna make you love me."

Remembering a popular song from another decade, she asked, "That was a song, right?"

Teddy nodded and winked. Then Katie mumbled, "I already do," as she headed for the elevator. She was standing inside, holding the door open when Teddy finally appeared in the lobby. As soon as the door shut, he reached over and kissed her. At first, it was a playful kiss, and then he found her hand and began kissing the tips of her fingers. The kisses were very sensual, and he enjoyed watching her melt beneath his embrace. When the elevator reached their floor, they rushed to his room. As soon as the door closed, he gathered Katie in his arms and kissed her with the same passion he showed in the elevator. A desire arose in her, and in him, and then they fell onto the bed and clung to each other until they heard the key enter the door lock and a loud knock.

"Housekeeping, coming in."

They jumped up, and Teddy grabbed his cell phone and dialed his mother's number. As he waited for the connection, he thought it was a good thing the cleaning staff showed up when it did, or else the chances of them leaving the hotel room were not very good.

When he heard the fast-busy signal, he looked over at Katie, but his face showed disappointment. She left his room to retrieve her luggage and was back in a few short moments when she said, "Let's go, sweetheart, we need to get home and find out what's going on. Let me warn you, if you insist on following me up the interstate, please keep up." Then Katie reached over, brushed his lips with a casual kiss, and turned and walked out of the room, holding the door for his exit.

Once out in the parking lot, Teddy lifted her luggage and placed it in the trunk and was about to leave when he put his arms around Katie and said, "So, you already love me, huh?"

"Yes, Teddy, I love you. Let's be clear, my biological clock is ticking along at a rapid speed."

"And what exactly does that mean?" He asked with a smile.

She wiggled out from beneath his hold, but as she walked away, she turned her head back and said, "You're a medical doctor, figure it out!"

CHAPTER FORTY-SIX

Colleen Byrd covered her head with the comforter. She must have been dreaming because she thought she had heard a bell.

Drew, being a light sleeper, got up early on Saturday mornings to make his standing tee time with "The Tour Group."

As she turned over in the big comfortable bed, the doorbell sounded again. Either, Drew had already left for the golf course, or he could not answer the door. She jumped up, grabbed her sweatshirt, found her house shoes under the bed, and headed for the stairs before the sound of the bell woke her girls. Rubbing the sleep from her eyes as she went down the stairs, she saw her father-in-law through the beveled glass, which encased each side of the front door. Panic rose in her chest as she considered the worst. She realized Drew had not kissed her goodbye before leaving for the golf course, and she couldn't remember him coming to bed the night before.

Colleen turned to glance around the downstairs area as she unlocked the front door and noticed the house was exactly as she had left it the previous night. Andrew, unsuccessful in trying to deliver a smile to his cherished daughter-in-law, appeared shaken. Colleen said, "Are you okay? You look as if you have been up all night."

"Sweetheart, I need to speak with Drew. Has he already left for the golf course, or did he run out to pick up breakfast for you and the kids?"

"I can only assume he left early for the golf course because he's not here. He knows better than to wake me up on Saturday morning." Fear swept through her body as she remembered the comforter on his side of the bed was much too neat for him to have slept next to her. He was such a restless sleeper and created a mess each night with the covers.

Andrew saw the change in her demeanor and reached out to steady her when he said, "Let's sit down."

Colleen watched as her father-in-law quietly and methodically brewed a cup of coffee in the Keurig machine. As he moved skillfully around the kitchen, Colleen suspected the reason for his visit was to deliver bad news. She cleared her throat, but her voice cracked anyway, "Has anything happened to Drew or Daisy?"

"No, sweetheart, please don't jump to conclusions." He smiled as he wiped the kitchen counter. "Daisy is at home, making calls. And, if I know my son, he is over at the club eating one of those delicious, calorie-filled breakfast sandwiches he loves, although he would never admit it." He paused for a moment to allow that news to register.

Carrying two cups of coffee, he walked over to the antique trunk in front of the large, sectional sofa, and set down a cocktail napkin, placing the coffee cups on the table. Andrew then looked around the room, chose a chair across from the sofa. "Daisy and I received some unexpected news during the night, and I was hoping I could catch Drew before he left this morning."

Colleen took a sip of the hot liquid, laid her head on the back of the sofa, closed her eyes, and waited.

Andrew paused for Colleen to enjoy a few sips of her coffee before he explained.

"We received a call early this morning from Frederick Simpson. Frederick is Claire's uncle and the trusted family tax attorney who lives in Savannah. He handles the Simpson and Williams families' financial matters." Careful not to move too fast in his explanation, for fear Colleen may not yet be engaged in the line of discussion, he allowed her time to process the information as she continued to sip her coffee.

"Frederick explained that Nancy Leigh had visited him in Savannah at the start of the summer, and because of that meeting, he had reason to believe Claire was being targeted for harm. He hired a detective detail for Claire while Teddy visited him in Savannah to review a few financial matters related to the real estate firm."

Colleen perked up and said, "I'm surprised Nancy Leigh would travel to Savannah to visit Teddy's uncle. But, considering how distraught she has been about the divorce settlement, I guess nothing is out of the realm of possibility."

"Indeed. Frederick received a call yesterday afternoon when he got home. His friend, who owns the detective company, told him about a problem that had occurred earlier in the morning at Claire's. While they were watching her house, someone murdered two security employees. Although Claire had been home earlier, she had already left her house before the incident occurred. You know Claire. Her focus was on her visit with Theo, so perhaps she was not aware of any abnormal activity in her neighborhood."

"Oh, my goodness, that's awful! That gives me chill bumps. Can you imagine how creepy that would be?"

"Claire was lucky."

Colleen raised her finger and said, "I need a comfort break. Can you give me a moment to run upstairs?"

Andrew smiled at her modesty and nodded his head in agreement. "Would you like a second cup of coffee?"

She yelled from the foot of the stairs, "Yes, sir! That would be great," She ran up the steps, aware of the need for extra minutes to make a call. When Colleen passed the girls' bedroom, she opened the door and found both of her daughters asleep. Then, she closed their bedroom door and went straight to the master suite and checked Drew's side of the bed. She felt the tucked sheets in the mattress, and she could tell he had not been home. The chair where he usually threw his clothes before going to bed was empty. Colleen's eyes filled with tears as she grabbed her cordless phone and went into the bathroom to dial Drew's cell phone. But the call went straight to voicemail. She called Teddy's cell phone, and it too, went straight to voicemail. Then, she made a call to Donna Gilbert at the club. However, Donna wasn't due in to work for another hour. She wiped her eyes and went back downstairs.

Andrew had prepared the second cup of coffee and sat across from the sofa when Colleen returned. As she entered the room, he asked, "Are my grandchildren sleeping-in this morning?"

"Yes, I checked in on the girls, and they are sleeping like little princesses. Jacob, however, went up to Asheville with his friend Ryan and his family. We talked to him last evening, and they were having a blast in downtown Asheville with plans to play golf today."

"Ryan comes from a fine family. It's good that Jacob has strong friendships as he enters this new phase of his life."

Colleen smiled and responded, "Well, his ability to maintain healthy friendships with guys and girls seems to be his strong point."

As Colleen got comfortable, Andrew waited before he continued. "When the call from the detective's office ended, Frederick received a second call from the assisted-living facility. Suzanne, the administrator, had been unsuccessful in contacting Claire or Teddy, and since Frederick was the third person listed in the file to contact when an emergency occurred, she contacted him to report that my friend Theodore was unresponsive and had passed away a few moments before the afternoon shift change."

Colleen shook her head, "My heart goes out to Teddy. Not too many children would put their father's dreams above their own. Somehow, people like him always land on their feet, and life just has a way of making up for the sacrifices they make for others. Now that's what the experts would call karma." She took another sip from her coffee and continued, "I'm assuming the authorities have notified Claire and Teddy of Mr. William's passing?" Relieved, the purpose of this visit did not involve Drew, she suspected Teddy had contacted Drew once he heard the news of his father's passing.

"No. Daisy and I thought perhaps Drew would know where Teddy was staying in Savannah and when he would return. I called Drew's cell phone several times this morning, and he didn't answer."

"What time did you start calling him?"

"Around six o'clock. Although Frederick had lunch with Teddy yesterday, he was very vague about his plans for the rest of the day, and Frederick wasn't sure when he planned to return to town."

"Well, how about Claire, if she left the house before the shooting occurred and she wasn't at the assisted-living facility, does anyone know where she went?"

Andrew responded, "Yes, Claire and the administrator at the facility have developed a close friendship. Claire had told her the previous day that she planned to spend the day with a friend and would stay the night, planning to check on Theo later in the afternoon. Frederick was planning to go to the friend's home sometime this morning to break the news to Claire. I'm certain Claire will try to contact Daisy and me after she returns home. The authorities have agreed to postpone a press release of Theo's death until they notify Claire and Teddy. However, in a town of this size, who knows how that will work out. It would be difficult to keep news of someone's passing secret from the other residents at a small facility. Someone would be apt to talk, don't you think?"

Colleen hesitated before responding because she couldn't remember Drew coming to bed during the night, and her eyes and cheeks grew hot. "Well, yes, that would be difficult. It is human nature to discuss things like that. You know those people live together and often become like family members. Are we sure Claire is okay? I mean, did someone confirm that she left the property before they fired the shots? It makes little sense that Claire would go off for a day and spend the night with a friend. That doesn't sound like the behavior of a woman her age."

"I agree, Colleen, it sounds suspect. Frederick promised to call me as soon as he saw Claire. He just couldn't bring himself to deliver the news of her husband's death by phone." Andrew stood up, walked toward the front door, and said, "I apologize for interrupting your Saturday morning slumber, but I could not leave you unaware of the night's circumstances after such unexpected news. So, sweetheart, I need to go over to the golf course and talk to Drew before they tee off this morning. It is always helpful to have a bright, young mind around at a time like this, don't you think?" He hugged his daughter-in-law at the front door and said, "If you hear from Drew, please ask him to call Daisy or me at his earliest convenience, okay?"

As her father-in-law pulled away, the phone rang, and she rushed to the kitchen in search of the cordless phone.

"Good morning! Thank you for returning my call. Drew must have left his cell phone in the car or either in his golf bag. I was hoping you could ask him to call me before he heads out to the golf course."

A pause.

"Donna, please don't tell me he's eating one of those bulldog breakfast platters before going out to play golf this morning."

As Donna began to talk, Colleen's face turned white as she began to rub her chest and pressed down on her breastbone.

CHAPTER FORTY-SEVEN

A t six a.m., like clockwork, perhaps from the many years of waking at the same time each morning, Frederick stirred from a sound sleep. As he looked around the study, his thoughts turned to Mary and realized he had not checked in with her and Lynn since leaving Savannah. He walked over to the large mahogany desk and sat down in Theodore's chair. The aroma of cigar smoke and bourbon, a scent that was uniquely Theo, engulfed him. He then reached for the desk phone and dialed the familiar number. As expected, Lynn answered with her typical happy voice, at the sound of which one could visualize the perpetual smile on her face. While discussing Mary's sleep patterns, Frederick knew that Mary would typically sleep until close to noon, at which time he promised Lynn that he would call back and speak to his wife.

When he finished his call, he looked at the clock and decided he and the policeman should go out for a quick breakfast and arrive at the Hawkins farm around 8:30. As he left the quiet study, he heard loud snoring from the family room. Although. he had intended to wake Officer Anderson to drive him in the police car to the farm, when he saw the deep state of sleep the officer was enjoying, he placed the empty coffee cup in the kitchen sink, tiptoed through the kitchen, and locked the back door behind him without leaving a note of explanation for the officer.

Once he turned his car around in the small area between the officer's vehicle and the garage, he headed out of the driveway. He remembered a restaurant around the corner, where he and Theo had eaten, that served a buffet of hearty breakfast items, and he drove toward the restaurant as he considered the size of the homemade biscuits. His stomach was growling, and he craved a cup of strong coffee.

As he went through the buffet line, he noticed a table of men he heard discussing the activities of the holiday week, and another group discussing their upcoming tee time at the local club as they enjoyed eating their breakfast and drinking coffee. Frederick found a seat at the end of a nearby table, and remembered he had left the address to the Hawkins farm on the desk in Theo's study. He waited for the discussion to pause from the table next to him, then he asked, "Excuse me, gentlemen, would any of you know the address to Tom Hawkins' farm?"

A silence fell over the table as everyone turned to look suspiciously at Frederick. The oldest of the gentlemen wiped his mouth with his napkin and said, "Sir, may I ask the nature of your interest?"

Frederick responded, "Yes, sir. I'm Frederick Simpson, Claire William's uncle from Savannah."

The older gentlemen then got up from his seat, walked over to Frederick, and extended his hand. "I thought you looked familiar. I remember meeting you and your wife when Claire's mama died. Didn't you stay with Claire and Theo for a few days during that time?"

Frederick stood, shook his hand, and said, "Well, sir, you have a razor-sharp memory as I had forgotten all about that visit. But, to answer your question, yes we stayed with Claire and Theodore for a few days during and following my sister-in-law's funeral."

Satisfied with Frederick's connection to the Williams family, the men turned their chairs around and discussed the recent death of Tom Hawkins. They also explained that his son Sammy, who had suffered a head injury on the farm several decades earlier, had been the one who had found his father in the pasture during the early morning hours. After spending thirty minutes discussing the family connection around the table, a few of the guys offered to go with Frederick to the Hawkins farm. Frederick declined, as the news he needed to deliver to his niece should come from either him or Teddy. Although he appreciated their kind offers, he could not allow Theo's death announcement to hit the newsreel until he notified Claire and Teddy. When they finished the last of their coffee, the group of gentlemen left the restaurant together and followed Frederick through the parking lot as they discussed the best route to the farm.

When Frederick entered his car, he pulled a small notepad from his shirt pocket and documented the directions. Being an attorney required notes, and although many of his colleagues had embraced iPad devices and laptop computers, he was from the era of handwritten notes and letters. As he completed the task, he started his car and began the twenty-five-minute drive to the rural area of town. He was thankful that he had waited for the sun to rise and until he had eaten a hearty breakfast before leaving for the farm. The closer he drove to the rural area, the more confusing the directions became, until he came upon a large farm surrounded by brown fencing. In a flat area, an entrance sign displayed a prominent announcement of the Hawkins Farm. Frederick rolled past the entrance drive and looked around to take in the property's size. He thought *it's no wonder Theo found this farm attractive. If the partnership hadn't used the land for the industrial park, they could use the property for hunting.*

He pulled into what he thought was a deserted side road and turned his car around. Heading back up to the farm entrance, he noticed a suspicious-looking vehicle that appeared occupied, sitting about 200 yards down the road. Seeing the deserted road was next to the Hawkins' farm, for the first time since leaving Claire's house before daybreak, Frederick began to second-guess his decision to make the trip to the farm without Officer Anderson.

When he reached the entrance to the property, the cell phone he kept for emergency situations rang. The sound of the telephone startled Frederick. The only people who had access to his private cell line were Mary, Claire, Teddy, and now Lynn. Frederick stopped his car and reached over to his briefcase on the passenger seat, digging through the contents until he retrieved the phone. He answered by the fourth ring, expecting Teddy to be on the other end of the line. Instead, the sound of Lynn's cheery voice sounded loud and clear. She explained that Mary had awakened a few minutes earlier, and had expressed disappointment that she had missed his morning call. She asked Lynn to call him back. Frederick was eager to speak to his wife, although the call was ill-timed, but how were Lynn or Mary to know he was about to tell Claire about the events of the previous day? Mary was on the phone now and spoke in a weak voice, "Hi Freddy. It disappointed me to miss your call earlier. I just wanted to hear your voice again."

Frederick visualized his wife sitting up in their large, four-poster bed as she held the phone with her frail hand, and he responded. "Well, I must be one lucky fellow to receive a call from my favorite lady."

Mary gave her best effort at a light laugh and said. "You have always called me your favorite girl. Have I suddenly grown old to you now?"

Frederick smiled. "No, sweet girl, you are as beautiful today as you were the day I first laid eyes on you." His response seemed to satisfy Mary, and he could tell from the sound of her labored breath that she was growing tired.

"Well, know how much I love you, and please join me soon." Knowing the call was about to end, he proceeded up the graveled drive. Frederick then told her he would be home as soon as he could, before the end of the weekend, as he stopped the car in the area outside the farmhouse. As the call disconnected, he heard a loud noise.

CHAPTER FORTY-EIGHT

Nancy Leigh had fallen asleep in Mr. Hawkins' large recliner during the early morning hours. An unexpected sound from outside the house awakened her. She saw Drew lying on the sofa crying, and his body was shaking uncontrollably. Besides having two ladies tied up in the parlor, there was now a middle-aged man on the sofa clearly amid a nervous breakdown. Nancy Leigh became enraged, and she jumped up from the chair. She went over to the kitchen sink, filled a pan with cold water, and poured the liquid over Drew's head. As she backed up to escape the arm that swung in her direction, she heard a shot from outside the kitchen door. She dropped the empty pan on the floor when hearing the car horn sound, and reached for the gun from the seat of the recliner. Within seconds, Nancy Leigh bolted out the back door and went barreling down the steps behind the house with the revolver in hand. She stopped and lowered the gun when she saw the driver of the car was Teddy's Uncle Frederick.

Then, seeing a movement to her right, she turned, and there stood Brad at the edge of the yard with an intense look of hatred on his face. He was still holding the gun in the firing position while pointing it at Frederick's car. He looked straight at Nancy Leigh with an intense, fevered stare. Without hesitation and misunderstanding that Brad was in shock as he stood in a frozen stance, Nancy Leigh aimed her gun at Brad and fired. He fell to the ground as blood poured from the hole that was once the top of his head.

Stepping back a few steps as if needing time to process the situation, she suddenly came to her senses when she realized she had just killed Brad in cold blood. Screaming hysterically, she said, "Oh my god! What have I just done?" Then, she turned and ran back towards the house to get Drew. As she climbed the steps onto the porch, the screen door had separated from its hinges and was swinging back and forth. Shaking her head with denial, Nancy Leigh stood in the middle of the empty kitchen wondering what had happened to Drew.

CHAPTER FORTY-NINE

Officer Anderson awakened to the sounds of dogs barking in the distance, and when he opened his eyes, the sun was already up. When he checked his watch, it surprised him that he had slept for almost six hours. He sat up on the sofa and listened for sounds of movement in the house, but there were only the sounds of the barking dogs. Then, he walked over to the kitchen and checked the coffeepot. There was a half pot of coffee remaining, but it was cool to the touch.

He stumbled upon an extensive study as he walked towards the back of the house looking for Mr. Simpson. A lightweight blanket lay bunched up at the end of the leather sofa. Otherwise, the study was tidy. Officer Anderson looked around on the desk for a note explaining Mr. Simpson's absence. And, he found the paper on which he had written the address of the Hawkins farm. Walking back through the kitchen, he looked on every surface, including the breakfast table and the top of the refrigerator, but there were no messages. He stepped outside the backdoor and saw that Mr. Simpson's car was gone. When Officer Anderson reached his patrol car, he called dispatch and asked if they had heard from him or anyone from the Hawkins' farm. The sergeant came on the radio, asked a few questions, and then directed Officer Anderson to the farm, advising him that someone had just called 911 and reported an intruder at the location. It wasn't in the sergeant's nature to overreact, so he tended to err on the side of caution. The sergeant reasoned to Officer Anderson that Frederick Simpson had cooperated with the police throughout the previous day and had respected their authority. He had also proven to be a rational individual, but his disappearance this morning was confusing. However, considering three people connected with the Williams family had already died, the sergeant wasn't taking any chances regarding the welfare of his officers or Mr. Simpson. And, he had already dispatched a backup unit to meet him there.

Officer Anderson backed out of the driveway, and at the main road, he turned left and headed toward the farm. The traffic was light for a Saturday morning, and he sped through several traffic lights. Once he reached the end of the city limits, he turned on his flashing lights and stepped on the accelerator. True to his sergeant's word, the backup unit was waiting for him on the side of the road. He nodded to the officers and pointed towards the entrance to the farm, and they pulled in behind his vehicle and followed him up the driveway. When they reached the grassy area at the house, Officer Anderson noticed Mr. Simpson's car in the drive with the horn blasting.

"Damn, him! I can't believe he came down here by himself. What was he thinking?"

An officer in the backup unit jumped out from the passenger side, drew his gun, and approached the car. "There's an elderly man slumped over the steering wheel." Then he walked around to the driver's side and saw the shattered window. There was blood dripping from the dashboard and the front window. He reached through the window and felt the body for a pulse.

"He's dead. There's no way he could have survived."

Officer Anderson radioed dispatch, "Hey Sarge, Simpson's vehicle was at the farm when we arrived, and he's been shot. He's dead, but we're going to need an ambulance." Then he saw the officers scoping out the area behind him. He turned to look toward the wooded area, when he saw what appeared to be a body down at the edge of the yard. The top of the victim's head was missing as the body lay in a pool of blood and brain matter. He motioned to the officer closest to the area, and he took off to where the victim was lying. The other officer followed his lead and moved around the side of the house.

Officer Anderson reached for his radio again, "Hey, Sarge, we need a second ambulance... this place looks like a war zone." The sergeant freaked out in the background as he barked orders and fired questions into the receiver. Stopping to answer questions cause a delay, and he feared the worst was inside the house. Any unnecessary time wasted answering questions at this critical moment could cause further deaths, and he was not about to take a chance of that happening. The three officers stood at the side of the house, away from any windows, to plan their attack. Officer Anderson took charge and assigned each officer a door to cover. With only one officer wearing a radio, and he had instructed him to keep it muted until it was needed to report an incident from inside the house. The other two officers would charge into the house together, if possible.

The officers went to their assigned posts. One of the officers took the front door, while Officer Anderson and the remaining backup officer covered the back of the house. The back door was open when Officer Anderson approached, and he extended his arms in front of his body with his gun pointed straight ahead as he entered the kitchen. When he stepped over the threshold, a hysterical scream came from someone in the front room.

"I'll kill both of you, get your money, leave the country and no one will find me!" She was screaming between sobs in such a manner that Officer Anderson was satisfied the woman was on some hallucinogenic drug.

Then, an unarmed man peeked at him from midway up the stairs, and he realized the man was perhaps the person who had made the 911 call to report the intruder. He put his hand to his ear and mouthed, "Did you call for help?" The man hesitated, but they communicated through eye contact and mouth movements. Finally, he nodded, and the officer knew that trust had been established between them. He motioned for him to go back upstairs, and the guy retreated slowly from where he came when Officer Anderson turned the corner to the foyer.

"Hands in the air!"

Upon seeing the police officer, Nancy Leigh froze, and she lowered her arms to her side. The officer stepped towards her, and she raised her hand to stop him.

In a soft voice, he said, "Drop the gun, ma'am."

"Don't come any closer!"

"I promise, I'll stand right here, but you need to put the gun down and tell me what's going on here."

"Well, I just wanted half of his inheritance." Nancy Leigh sobbed. That's all I wanted was half. They have so much, and I've never had anything. Drew promised me, if I would just live with him for four or five years, then I could get half of his money."

"Okay, I hear what you're saying, but whose money were you after?"

Exasperated, she pointed her gun in the direction of the sofa.

"Please, ma'am. Let's put the gun down on the table, and you can tell me all about it, okay?"

"This wasn't supposed to end like this! I struggled when I suffocated Mr. Williams, because he looked pitiful lying in that bed, and he didn't even look like himself. But I can't kill her. I just can't kill Teddy's mama, too."

"You know what, you don't have to kill her. You don't have to do anything. Let's just place the gun on the table. I really need you to do that."

For the first time, she turned and looked at the officer in the eye. There was something real about the way she held his gaze, "You're a good man, aren't you?"

"I try to be a good person. But you know some days we do better than others."

She turned slightly, as if she were going to place the gun on the table. Nancy Leigh looked back at Claire and said, "Mrs. Williams, your son is a good man, too. And so was your husband. I'm sorry for what I've done." She began to laugh hysterically, as she lifted her arm and fired the high-powered gun into her mouth. And, just like that, she had snapped, and it was over. Officer Anderson was within a few feet of her when her body fell back onto the marble-topped sideboard and landed on the floor in a pool of blood as stifled screams came from the parlor.

The officer walked over to the stairs and said to the man in a low voice, "Is there anyone else here?"

Sammy ambled down the stairs and mumbled, "No." Then he went over to where Nora and Claire were sitting. He dropped to his knees, wrapped his arms around his mother's waist, and placed his head in her lap as he began to sob.

The backup officer walked through the foyer to unlock the front door and let the other officer into the house. They soon began to remove the tape from their hands and mouths, as Officer Anderson spoke to the women in a reverent voice. There was a wandering gaze among the people in the room that didn't settle as everyone avoided looking at the body.

There was Sammy, who had shown tremendous courage sneaking up the back stairs of the house, used his cell phone, and placed the 911 call to the authorities. And, although his sixty-odd years in age was visible, he sobbed like a young child kneeling next to his mother.

As soon as they removed the tape from Claire's head and hands, she reached over to Sammy and hugged him. "Thank you, Sammy. You saved your mother's life, and mine, too."

Officer Anderson saw Nora staring at the victim's body and watched as Claire steadied herself and walked closer to the body lying on the floor in the foyer. "You're Mrs. Williams, right?"

"Yes, officer. My name is Claire Williams."

"Ma'am, do you know the victim?"

Claire looked from the officer to Nora and said, "Yes, sir, her name is Nancy Leigh Williams."

Nora said, "Claire, are you sure?"

Claire began to scream, "Yes, I'm absolutely certain, and she killed my Theo!"

Sammy and Nora grabbed Claire and held her while her body shook from the sobs until the officer escorted them to his patrol car.

As they pulled away from the house, a third ambulance was turning in the driveway. Nora turned and said, "Why are there three ambulances here?"

The officer stopped the car, turned in his seat, and told them about the shooting in the yard that started the chain of events. And, as gently as he could, he told Claire that her Uncle Frederick Simpson was one of the victims.

CHAPTER FIFTY

Traveling up I-985, Teddy noticed Katie's signal light was blinking. It looked like she was pulling off at the Flowery Branch exit. *Perhaps she needs gas*, he thought. He turned on his signal light and followed as she exited and pulled into a convenience store parking lot.

Teddy jumped out and said, "Do you need gas?"

"No, I just need to take this call. It'll just take me a moment."

He walked into the store and bought two bottles of water, and went out to where Katie was standing beside her car.

"Yes, Tyler. Thank you for calling me. Are they alright?"

Teddy watched as concern appeared on her face.

"Of course. I'm about fifteen minutes away. I'll be there shortly."

Katie shut off her phone, "There has been an accident. Grandmother is at the hospital, and your mom and Sammy are there, too."

Teddy said, "Let's leave your car at my office, and we'll ride over together. Parking at the hospital is minimal."

Once they got to the hospital, Teddy said, "I'm going to drop you off at the front door, and I'll park the car and come in right behind you, okay?"

Katie had said very little on the way to the hospital, but Teddy knew her grandmother's condition must be bad for her friend to have contacted her.

He rode around the parking area for close to ten minutes before he found a place to park. He jumped from the car and sprinted to the emergency room entrance, and when he stepped inside the door, a gray-headed man was standing inside.

"Hi Teddy, I'm Sammy Hawkins."

Teddy was startled by Sammy's appearance. He had heard about Sammy from his father and Katie, but he had never met him.

"It's nice to finally meet you, Sammy. I've heard a lot about you." Teddy shook his hand.

"How is Nora?"

"She's resting right now. The doctor said she was dehydrated and needed fluids."

Teddy knew that was common for people of her age, and began to relax a bit about her condition.

"Your mom is all done and waiting for you down this way." Sammy pointed to a hallway. "This is it, go on in."

Teddy opened the door and saw his mother sitting in a small room by herself. He quietly walked toward her, but the closer he got, the more he sensed something was terribly wrong. When she turned to face him, a beautiful smile appeared on her bruised face, and although he had never seen her hair other than neatly coiffed, it was in total disarray. He froze when he saw her hands, which were bruised and swollen.

"Mama, what happened to you, are you okay?"

"Yes, son. I'm fine. We're just grateful to be alive." She reached for Sammy's hand and said, "Sammy, here, saved my life this morning, and he also saved Nora's."

Teddy turned to Sammy.

"Well, I'm going to leave you two alone," Sammy said. "I'm going back to check on mama."

"Thanks, Sammy. Thanks for all you did," said Teddy.

When Sammy left the room, Claire patted the seat beside her and said, "Come, sit next to me son, I have a lot to tell you."

Claire took her time and began her story on Thursday morning when she ran into Katie at the coffee shop...

When she finished, they sat in silence. Teddy knew he should say something comforting to his mom, but he was trying to process the information. There was an overpowering guilt, and he could not understand how he had lived with Nancy Leigh without noticing her sickness. He went back over his mother's account of the past three days, and he counted five murders and one suicide. Greed was responsible for the deaths of five innocent people and had Sammy not shown such courage, he would have lost his mom, too.

Claire looked at her watch and said, "Teddy, we've been in here for almost two hours, and I need to go to the ladies' room. Will you walk with me, son?"

"Yes, of course. Afterward, we should check on Nora. Katie probably thinks I've deserted her."

"Well, I'm sure she's fine, now that Tyler's here."

* * * * * * *

Teddy knocked on the door of Nora's hospital room, and Sammy opened the door. Nora burst into tears when she saw them, and Claire immediately went to her bedside and began to calm her.

Katie was sitting on a small loveseat while Sammy, Stephen, and Roger all stood around the room. Sammy took the lead and introduced Teddy to his brothers, and then he said, "Well, y'all just missed Katie's fiancé, Tyler. He left about five minutes ago to get his car. He's going to take Katie back over to your office before it gets dark."

Teddy was suddenly dizzy, and he realized he had not eaten since breakfast. He looked over at Katie, and she said, "He's not my fiancé."

Sammy responded, "He told us that he asked you to marry him. I guess he is your fiancé."

Katie got up and walked over to her grandmother's bed, "Nana, I'm going to leave for a few minutes to get my car. But, I'll be back to stay the night with you."

"Okay, sweetie, please thank Tyler for me. I don't know what we would have done without him today."

Katie smiled, "I'll be sure to tell him. I'll be back soon."

She looked at Teddy and lightly touched his arm and said in a low voice, "Will you walk me out?"

Teddy hesitated, he looked down at her hand, and without looking directly at Katie, he said, "I should wait for mom."

* * * * * * *

The morning before Thanksgiving Day, Teddy awakened to the sound of rain pelting against his bedroom window. He had slept little over the past four-nights, his pillowcase was damp, and his eyes were red and moist. His father would never experience the joy of retirement life, or just sitting in his study with a good novel. He would never again enjoy the solitude of going out on Lake Lanier in his fishing boat during the early morning hours, or the fun of playing a round of golf with his buddies. A refreshed sadness swept over Teddy as he continued to mourn the many events that his father would miss. The emotional pressure built within his chest as he remembered the other times his heart experienced the same level of pain. The first was the day his siblings died in a car accident. The second which was mainly a matter of pride, was the day he saw Nancy Leigh kissing Brad in the Pro Shop, which was also the last day he spoke with his father, and the only time in his life he had stood up to him. The irony of events occurring on the same day was evident, yet so much had transpired since then. In the blink of an eye, life had changed for Theo, the same as it had for Teddy. During the two years, he'd taken over his father's real estate firm and completed the industrial park project, which had been his father's dream. The divorce from Nancy Leigh was of no consequence now as she had killed herself with the gun intended to take his mother's life. The guy whom he had called his best friend was last seen at the Hawkins' farm the weekend they held his mother and Mrs. Hawkins hostage.

During his tenure at the real estate office and in his spare time, Teddy had established a corporation, applied for a business license, and found a facility to house his pediatric practice. Perhaps the most significant change was when he had met Katie O'Neill, his soul mate, the woman whose memory motivated him while he navigated through the changes of the past two years. Their chance meeting pointed to the rainbow he could see in the distant future, so close he could almost reach out and touch. But the news that she was engaged to another guy had caused his blood to boil.

Yes, much had changed for everyone connected to the Williams family, and the man Teddy had grown to respect while incapacitated, was gone. The grief was more than even Teddy could manage.

Teddy got up, slipped on a pair of sweats, and walked down the stairs to the kitchen. Claire was sitting at the breakfast table, drinking her morning coffee, and making notes on a legal pad when Teddy opened the cabinet door in search of a cup.

"Good morning, love. Did you rest well?"

"As well as expected. Did the meds Dr. Jackson prescribed help you fall asleep?"

"Oh, I slept a few hours. But, I've been up since daybreak following the weather forecast. They're calling for rain for this afternoon." Pointing to the note pad, "here are some notes for the funeral and the reception to follow. Because of the rain, perhaps we should suggest to Dr. Moore to keep the service short and simple. Are you in agreement, love?"

As Teddy poured himself a cup of coffee and sat down at the kitchen table, he pondered his response as he looked over at his mother. It pained him to see the marks still visible on her beautiful face from the duct tape applied during the previous hostage weekend. He could not get his head around the fact that Nancy Leigh had hurt him by planning to kill his parents. He looked away and shifted his thoughts to his grandmother.

"A simple funeral is fine with me, Mom. Grandma Simpson used to say we preach our funerals each day as we live."

"She said that often, didn't she?"

"Even amid my grief, I realize how fortunate I am to come from a long line of good people. Uncle Frederick and I ate lunch on Thursday and Friday. And, we spent several hours discussing the family finances, my unsettled divorce, and Katie. He was an old man who knew the love of his life was about to leave this world. And what did he do? He left his wife with her cousin and came up here to settle my divorce so I could marry another woman. His very last act on this earth was an effort to bring me happiness. I venture to say that few people have one friend or family member who would use their last act in such an unselfish way." He fought back the tears and said, "I am so humbled."

"I still can't believe that Mary passed away as soon as she hung up the phone, at almost the same moment, Frederick was shot. So, he fulfilled his purpose, and yet he was able to escort Mary into the pearly gates." She reached for a fresh Kleenex and wiped her eyes.

"Mom, are you okay?" Teddy asked as he got up from the breakfast table to refill their coffee cups.

"Yes, love, I'm okay. The feelings we're dealing with are very real. However, time has a way of easing the pain. Each day it gets a little easier until you realize that you have turned the corner and that you will survive. I remember that memory when my own mama died. I remember thinking, Claire, you have made it through one of the most difficult times of your life." She took her coffee cup from him, paused, and closed her eyes as if freezing the exact moment in time. Then she continued, "But, I felt as if I had reached the end of a dark and lonely road, and in the end I realized my mother's love had given me wings, and I had found peace."

"Dad's death should be a relief because of his quality of life. Perhaps, if he had just gone to sleep and died peacefully, I could deal with it. But, when I consider the agony and pain he suffered from exposure to those chemicals, and that my wife held a rag to his face, the burden of responsibility for his death is overwhelming. And, then, coupled with the fact that her lover killed Uncle Frederick. I just can't understand it." He put his head down on the breakfast table. Teddy heard Claire going out the back door. He watched as she walked to the end of the driveway to retrieve the morning paper.

When she came back into the house, Teddy sat straight in the chair, and his face was damp. "Son, I realize you're hurting. I speak from experience when I tell you that one day, the pain you are now feeling will subside." She reached and touched his hair. "It maybe six months, one year, or perhaps a short time from now, but the pain will no longer be that stark, hollowing pain. There will be many lovely reminders of your father as you go through life, and those reminders will seem random and may occur at the oddest of times. It may be an article about property development you read in a magazine, and you will think, *Dad would enjoy reading this article.* Or, you may notice a fishing boat drifting in the early morning fog lingering over Lake Lanier as you pass over the bridge, or perhaps the smell of the pungent fragrance of that familiar pipe tobacco." Claire reached over and placed her bruised hand on his arm. "When a smile appears on your lips before the tears form in your eyes, you will know you have survived. I have buried my parents and two of my children, and I know this to be true. As hard as this seems, you will survive this."

Teddy wiped his face with the sleeve of his sweatshirt. "But, how can I ever forgive Nancy Leigh for what she did to Dad and what she put you through? My God, she almost killed both of you. What kind of person could conjure up such a grotesque plan and follow through with it?"

"We should have picked up on Nancy Leigh's problems long ago, and maybe we knew she wasn't like us. But, what she did during the last two days of her life resulted from misplaced anger and an unresolved disappointment from an unhappy childhood. Honey, I'm not sure if any of us understood her well enough to know the depth of her mental and emotional pain."

Claire added cream to her cup and stirred her coffee. "I never shared this with you, but one of the last conversations your father and I had on the Sunday afternoon before his heart attack was about your future."

Startled, Teddy wondered if his father had told her about their conversation in his office, "Please, Mom, tell me about it."

"When we returned from lunch that day, your father mentioned the golf tournament you missed because you met with Mr. and Mrs. Hawkins at their farm. I asked him why an urgent meeting on Saturday afternoon? He explained that during one of his visits to the farm, he noticed a picture of a beautiful young woman on the mantel in their kitchen. He asked her identity, and Nora told him about their only granddaughter. While she was explaining the attributes of their accomplished granddaughter, your father recognized some same attributes in you. He had an epiphany that the two of you should be together. He also thought by suggesting a meeting between you and Katie that she would be more open to discussing the contract, as opposed to having to meet with an old man. Those were his words, not mine."

Claire squeezed Teddy's hand and said, "Son, your father was so proud of you." She paused for Teddy to consider those words. "It may not have seemed like it, because he always held you to a higher standard. It was sometimes hard to reach the level he set for you. But, I got to hand it to him, he recognized your special gifts at a young age, and he wanted to help you reach your full potential."

"This is true."

"When he got home on Saturday night, I believe I told you he ambled in the house, and his color was off. However, there was something in his demeanor that had changed. It was like Theo left home that morning as the man I had always known, but returned that night a different person."

Teddy said, "When you say his demeanor changed, how do you mean?"

"He was just different. Perhaps kinder, more considerate, he displayed a sweeter spirit." Claire paused. "The next day, we spoke at length about his dream to complete the industrial park. As you know, your father seldom shared his real estate vision with me. But, as we sat on the sofa in the family room, the last day we were together in this house, we shared a closeness that we had not enjoyed since the early years of our marriage. After your brother and sister died, our marriage almost crumbled. Our problems were so much bigger than either of us. He blamed me for the accident, and I blamed him, we were barely keeping it together. Unfortunately, we never resolved the core problem. But every day, I continued to pray that God would restore our marriage."

A soft smile appeared on her face, "But, that afternoon, it occurred to me that Theo had changed. And, the few sweet hours we shared that day was God's gift to me for staying in a difficult marriage." Claire wiped the fresh tears from her face and said, "I remember your father chuckling to himself. Then he explained that when you left his office that Saturday afternoon, he had realized that the reason he had pursued the Hawkins' property was to find the perfect wife for you."

Teddy laughed and said, "I can't imagine my stoic dad playing the role of Cupid." He paused, "Dad never cared for Nancy Leigh, did he?"

Claire weighed her words with care and said, "Son, we only wanted the best for you and for Nancy Leigh."

"I'm ashamed to admit this, but marrying Nancy Leigh wasn't one of my finer decisions, and it definitely wasn't a noble one."

Teddy ran his hands through his hair and leaned back as he balanced his chair on two legs and stared up at the ceiling.

"Mom, I'm having a hard time reconciling that she murdered dad. How will I ever be able to forgive her for what she has done to our family?"

Without hesitation, Claire reached over, pulled his chair back down, and put her hand on the side of his face, "But, you must forgive her, son. And, remember, I'm struggling, too. I've lost my husband and my favorite uncle and aunt, and I'm also trying to find the grace to forgive her. But we will never have peace until we do. We cannot change that Theo died a tragic death. Think about it, your father is in heaven, and now his legacy lives through you."

CHAPTER FIFTY-ONE

Katie knew Tyler had been staying in Abington with Colleen and her family since Drew's disappearance. He had been leaving daily messages on her voice mail, providing updates regarding his sister, Colleen. Unfortunately, the sparse information submitted to the family since the hostage situation was troubling. Because of the closeness of the two families, he told her that Colleen felt she should attend the funeral of the father of her husband's best friend. But, Tyler was worried about her because she was an emotional mess. Sleep would not come, regardless of the medication the doctor had prescribed; Tyler had found her ambling through the house at all hours of the night. And, one night he found her standing in the middle of their closet with Drew's sports jacket over her head, breathing in his scent. She could not get her head around Drew's involvement with Nancy Leigh, or his disappearance.

When they drove up at the graveside service, Katie noticed the tenderness Tyler showed to his sister while helping her to get out of the car. It was a cold, damp day, and they had sat in the car until the last moment before the minister began.

As they stood listening to the message, Katie saw Tyler and Colleen from a distance. Mr. and Mrs. Byrd and another couple, who Katie assumed were Tyler's parents, were all hovering around Colleen. Katie saw Tyler slip away, and he headed in her direction.

She had not spoken to him since he dropped her off at the real estate office on Saturday afternoon, but she had listened to his messages on her phone. Nora had spent Saturday night in the hospital, and Stephen and Roger had encouraged Katie to take Nora to her apartment on Sunday until they could get someone in to clean up the house and the surrounding property.

Nora and Claire had talked each day by phone, but Teddy had still not reached out to Katie since learning of Tyler's proposal. She had texted him a couple of times, to no avail.

When Tyler reached her side, he said, "Hi, lady, where have you been? I've been trying to contact you."

Katie smiled as he spoke to her grandmother and shook her Uncle Sammy's hand. Then she said, "A lot has happened to me since we last spoke, Tyler. We've been staying at my apartment until they get the house cleaned up. It sounds like those beautiful hardwoods in the foyer were ruined. How have you been?"

"Well, I've been waiting for my answer."

"I apologize, Tyler, but I think we both know the answer to that question," Katie said, as she glanced at Mrs. Williams and Teddy.

He looked at her with surprise in his eyes, and suddenly, he knew that Teddy Williams was the man who had captured her heart.

* * * * * * *

Following the graveside service, Teddy stood looking at his father's casket, waiting for internment. He spotted Katie, Mrs. Hawkins, and Sammy as they stood away from the crowd. Teddy turned to his mother and told her that he needed to step away for a moment. He noticed she watched as he walked toward Katie O'Neill, and as soon as Nora saw Teddy coming in their direction, she walked over to stand with Claire. Teddy paused and watched as Nora placed her bruised arm around his mom's waist as they stood in silence. Sammy was standing next to an oak tree, and he heard Claire say, "Oh, Sammy came, too," and she choked up as she motioned for him to join them. Before he walked on over to Katie, Teddy watched as the two of them stood holding on to each other, and to Sammy. It appeared that neither woman could find words to speak, but he knew none were necessary.

When Teddy found his way to Katie, he reached for her hands and said in an octave scarcely above a whisper, "Hey, you." Without thought, he lowered his head and kissed the tip of her nose. He placed his arm around her waist and drew her close. Then, he recognized Tyler Brock standing next to her. He extended his hand and thanked Tyler for bringing Colleen to the funeral.

Teddy then introduced Katie to Tyler, to which Katie said, "We know each other, Teddy."

"Excuse me, baby. I didn't know you two had met," Teddy turned his attention back to Tyler and thanked him again for coming to the funeral.

"No problem." He pointed to Katie and said, "Katie and I have been dating for almost two years."

"So, you are the Tyler that called us on Saturday about Nora and mom being at the hospital."

Tyler looked at his feet, "Well, actually, Nora called me and asked me to call Katie. But yes, I am the one who made the call."

"Well, this may not be the most opportune time to ask this question, but are you two engaged?" Teddy looked at Tyler with a stone, cold look. Then, he looked at Katie as he raised his eyebrows.

Katie said, "No, we are not engaged."

And, without another word, Tyler walked away.

The heavy clouds parted as the sun warmed the damp autumn air. Katie and Teddy walked away from the other mourners.

"Dr. Moore did a great job. He summed up life rather simply, didn't he, Teddy? A man's legacy lies not only in his personal accomplishments, but perhaps more importantly, in that of his children. People will now look at you and remember the fine qualities of your father, because a son gets his identity from his dad. I wish someone had explained that analogy to me when I was a little girl.

That is the most comforting thought I've ever heard, and it puts everything into perspective for me."

"He's awesome, isn't he? I'm glad to hear Dr. Moore's words were helpful to you. I'm ashamed to admit it, but I've been struggling, Katie. It almost killed me when my mom told me what Nancy Leigh had done. Innocent people died because of her deadly intentions. But, when Sammy announced that you had a fiancé, as I stood in your grandmother's hospital room, I felt like the air had gone out of my lungs. I can't sleep, I can't eat, and for the first time in my life, I find that I'm in a funk."

Katie smiled at him, and her eyes were bright with fresh tears as she placed both arms around his waist, "And, you haven't been returning my text messages, either."

"No, no, I haven't."

She pulled him close to her, "You know, Teddy, it seems those loose ends you've been talking about are all tied up."

He looked at Katie and smiled, "Well, yes, they are. But," he looked around at the mourners, "has anyone else here asked you to get married since we spoke on Saturday? I really need to know."

"No, sweetheart. You're my guy, and I love you more than I have ever loved anyone else in my life. Perhaps now we have a future that is much brighter than either of us have imagined." She noticed the confidence and strength return in his demeanor.

"I hope you can find forgiveness in your heart to put the pain and heartache of the recent months behind you."

He cupped her face in his hands, "I already have, baby. Amid all this turmoil, I have found peace."

Katie shot him a suspicious look and asked, "How did you manage to do it, Teddy? You've been through so much, you've lost your wife and your father in the past week. Your best friend has disappeared. Uncle Frederick and Aunt Mary literally died within moments of each other, and that's a lot to process."

Teddy smiled and said, "You may not believe this, Katie, but my dad helped me find peace."

Katie said, "How so?"

"Mom told me this morning that the last conversation she had with my dad was about my future. He saw your picture on the mantel in your grandparent's house during one of his visits to the farm, and my dad decided we should be together."

As they walked a few more yards in silence, Teddy told Katie, "I was so pissed off at my dad for scheduling the meeting with you and your grandparents on the day of the fall golf tournament. But, he just wanted us to meet. I realize now, meeting you was like his parting gift to me. Think about it. Even in death, my dad's focus was on my future. His death makes it possible for us to be together." Teddy turned to her, placed the back of his hand on her soft cheek, and said, "Katie, my dad chose you for my wife. He chose you. And, when you said you were not engaged to Tyler, I knew that I would be okay. That's the thing about memorial services; by design, they help us heal."

He watched as she fought back the tears when she spoke, "That is beautiful. However, that doesn't explain how you could sort through all the pain Nancy Leigh inflicted on your family." She reached in her purse for a fresh Kleenex, wiped her nose, and said, "I haven't slept much thinking about what is best for me, and for you. How could you possibly have found peace so soon?"

With all the charm he could muster, Teddy flashed that beautiful, boyish smile and said, "It's called grace, my love. IT'S ALL ABOUT GRACE!"

Acknowledgments

There are many people without whom the writing of this book would have been impossible. Many of them have gone on to their heavenly home. First, my parents, Ruffin and Lois Ladd, whose influence in my life is reinforced with each new day. As I look back on my childhood in (then) a small southern town, I realize their selflessness and generosity of spirits molded me into the person I have become. I give credit to my parents for their practice of extending grace to every person with whom they came in contact.

A special thanks to my brothers, affectionately referred to throughout my life as "the boys," Barry Ladd, Maxey Ladd, and Bobby Joe Peck. They have always challenged and protected me. Thanks, guys, you are the best brothers a gal could ask for!

I am grateful to have married into the strong southern family of the late Ben Hill Propes, Jr. and Hazel Brown Propes, whose many comical and endearing stories involving their families sparked a desire within me to write this book. Although my book is purely fictional, occasionally I drew from the events of their childhood tales. Their love, influence, and spirits are now an integral part of my life story. Thanks to both of you, and to Dr. Steve and Kittie (Propes) Ross for the warm welcome into your tribe!

Never one to underestimate the power of a kind word, I am thankful to Mrs. Nell Wagner (deceased), my English Lit teacher in high school, who encouraged me to pursue and develop the skill of creating an interesting story. Thank you, Mrs. Wagner, for planting that seed!

Thanks to retired educator Shirley Shockley (deceased), who offered words of encouragement throughout the early phase of the manuscript, and whose notes (which I read regularly) prompted me to keep writing. Also, thanks to Elaine Fitzpatrick for reading the original twelve chapters of the book. Elaine offered support and suggestions, which proved invaluable to the completion of the book.

Fortunately, perfect timing allowed my introduction to a wonderful and talented lady, Elizabeth Jones Waidelich, who earlier in her career edited proofs for a book company in Tennessee. Liz quickly became a dear friend. She graciously went through the original draft and provided guidance. Thank you, Liz, for your many thoughtful suggestions.

A heartfelt thanks to Lynda Anderson and Mitchelle Johnson for the hours they spent reading the unedited drafts. Also, thanks to Terri Crumley and Paige Pinson for their encouragement and support throughout this journey. Thank you for the roles the four of you play in my life! I cannot imagine my life without you all in it!

Thanks to Stan Anderson for the expertise he provided as a published author.

I am grateful to a retired nurse practitioner and a member of the Northeast Georgia Writers Group, Julianna Ramsey, who offered helpful insight regarding the areas involving health care issues.

A special thanks to a friend and member of my church family, Chris Parks, for her introduction to Ronda Rich, a local author. When I contacted Ronda, she was amid writing yet another book. Still, she graciously stopped to answer questions from a novice writer! A mark of a true southern lady, Ronda extends kindness and professionalism to anyone in need.

Grace Wynter, The Writer's Station, who provide an honest and instructive edit. Thank you, Grace, for your friendship.

And, a word of thanks to Southern Author Dr. William Rawlings, who took the time to read the manuscript while researching his eleventh book and for providing the blurb included on the jacket.

Also, thanks to Trisha Covin, Rosemary O'Keefe, Dr. Deborah Jones-Smith, and Annette Hinton for the generosity they extended in reading through the manuscript prior to submission. You ladies are the best! Thanks for the time and energy you gave to this project. I cannot thank you enough.

Many thanks to Dr. Sidney Washington for providing the final proof! How did I get so lucky to become friends with your sweet wife, LuAnn?

Thanks to Rosemary O'Keefe and William H. Venema for your contribution to the naming of this book.

A special thank you to my publishers, Kim and Martha Megahee, of The Kimmer Group, for guiding me through this arduous process. You guys rock!

I would be remiss if I did not thank the numerous people throughout my life who have lifted me up every day. For the many friends, cousins, sisters-in-law (Sandra Leach Ladd and Sue Poole Ladd), nephews, nieces, and business associates of all ages that provide influence, both large and small. Thank you for the roles you play in my life! I love living life and learning from each of you.

A special thanks to my husband, Hardy, my love and dearest friend. He has walked with me throughout this journey, lending support, encouragement, and providing the gentle first edits. He, along with our son, Zach, daughter-in-law, Katie, and our loving dogs, Lucy and Ollie, complete our family circle and make me blessed beyond measure. Many things in this life cause me immense joy, but nothing brings a smile to my lips or a swell of pride in my heart as being known as Hardy's wife and Zach's mother. I would have never dreamt as a young girl that I would grow up to enjoy such a charmed life. Thank you for making it possible. I love you all to the moon and back!

Above all, to my sweet friend, Jesus, without whom my life would have no meaning!

ABOUT THE AUTHOR

From an early age, Renee Propes felt destined to become a writer. Perhaps, the most important legacy she received, was her mother's love for the written word, which became Renee's inspiration to write.

She was thirty-five years old when she started her first novel. Upon retirement from a career in accounting, she edited the original twelve chapters, and with a determined perseverance, completed *duplicity, A Story of Deadly Intent.*

https://authorreneepropes.com